MIDNIGHT BEAUTIES

MEGAN SHEPHERD

HOUGHTON MIFFLIN HARCOURT
BOSTON   NEW YORK

hmhbooks.com

The text was set in Adobe Garamond Pro.

Library of Congress Cataloging-in-Publication Data
Names: Shepherd, Megan, author.
Title: Midnight beauties / by Megan Shepherd.
Description: Boston ; New York : Houghton Mifflin Harcourt, [2019] |
Summary: Seventeen-year-old Anouk is forced into a sinister deal with
Crown Prince Rennar in order to help her friends, who are trapped in
their animal forms, and save Paris from the Coven at Oxford.
Identifiers: LCCN 2018060799 (print) | LCCN 2019000534 (ebook) |
ISBN 9781328811912 (E-book) | ISBN 9781328811905 (hardcover) |
ISBN 9780358173045 (Int'l ed)
Subjects: | CYAC: Magic—Fiction. | Witches—Fiction. |
Princes—Fiction. | Betrayal—Fiction. | Paris (France)—Fiction. |
France—Fiction. | London (England)—Fiction. | England—Fiction.
Classification: LCC PZ7.S54374 (ebook) | LCC PZ7.S54374 Mid 2019
(print) | DDC [Fic]—dc23
LC record available at https://lccn.loc.gov/2018060799

Printed in the United States of America
DOC 10 9 8 7 6 5 4 3 2 1
4500766601

For the beauties and the beasties — and those yet to find their place

PART I

Chapter 1

T HERE WAS BLOOD EVERYWHERE, even in her
hair.

Anouk tripped through fallen leaves in gold-studded
Goblin boots two sizes too small, the laces undone, the novelty
tread leaving bloodstained prints in the smeared shape of hearts. Her
leather shorts were ripped. Her velvet jacket was punctured once in
the sleeve and twice near her ribs. Blood oozed down her side.

The birds were right behind her.

One crow swept down from a lamppost in a flurry of black wings,
going for her ear. Its beak sliced her cheek. She swatted at it, but its
talons snagged in her hair or, rather, in the blue wig she wore. The
wig slid forward over her eyes, blinding her. She pulled it off and
threw it—tangled crow and all—into a sewer grate and raced ahead.

Toward 18 Rue des Amants.

The former residence of a witch, the townhouse was now hers. Her
home. Her haven. Or, since Prince Rennar had set his winged spies on
her, more like her prison. Her hair had become a sweaty mess beneath
the wig, clinging to her neck and face. Another crow launched itself
at her back. Talons ripped at her clothes. She grabbed the railing to
the stairs. *Just a few more steps.* The Goblins were inside, faces pressed
against the townhouse windows, motioning for her to hurry.

A crow landed on her shoulder, its talons piercing through the velvet jacket. Pain exploded in her arm. She faltered on the steps. She would have used a spell against it, except that her bag of ingredients was the first thing the crows had gone for, knowing that without it, she was no more powerful than the Pretty tourists strolling down the street, magically oblivious to Anouk's distress.

Gasping, she grabbed the crow by its wing and yanked with all her strength.

"Let *go!*"

She hurled the crow against the steps and, before it could take wing again, yanked open the townhouse's front door, threw herself inside, and slammed it closed behind her.

She collapsed against the door, breathing hard.

The townhouse was protected with a spell so ancient that it hadn't been broken at Mada Vittora's death, unlike most of her other enchantments. It was the only thing keeping Rennar and his crows out, which unfortunately meant that to be safe, Anouk had to stay *in*. Over the past six weeks, she and Viggo and the two dozen Goblins who had survived the siege of Montélimar might as well have been prisoners. The first time she'd tried to leave was two days after the siege; she'd needed baguettes to feed the hungry Goblins. The crows had been waiting in the trees. They attacked her as soon as she crossed the first step. She'd barely made it back inside in one piece.

The second time she'd tried to leave, she waited until night fell, when it was foggy and hard to see more than three feet on either side. That time she made it ten steps before they spotted her. They would have dug in their talons and dragged her all the way to Castle Ides if

Viggo hadn't hurled an empty gin bottle at them and pulled Anouk back inside.

The third time, she'd brought knives. Many, many knives, hidden in pockets and strapped to her belt. But the crows were fast enough to dodge them, their own talons just as sharp.

Today, she'd thought she stood a chance, that the Goblin disguise—the blue wig, the punk boots, and the velvet jacket—would be enough to conceal her identity from the birds. They were merely Rennar's pawns, after all, just dull-witted spies.

But they'd still known.

She'd made it only five steps.

The sound of a *tap-tap-tap* came from the foyer. She opened her eyes. Viggo stood in the hallway. He leaned heavily on a cane. His face was pale. It was a wonder he'd survived at all after losing six pints of blood, but he was tougher than his black eyeliner and slouchy hat made him look. He'd nearly recovered in the six weeks since the siege.

"I take it the disguise didn't fool them," he said.

She slid him a frigid glare.

Blood rolled down her fishnet tights, over her studded boots, and onto the floor. Her tawny hair was knotted. A few blue strands from the ripped wig still clung to the buttons of her jacket. The wounds in her side throbbed. She straightened and took a lurching step forward. Her legs gave out and she started to collapse, but Viggo dropped his cane and grabbed her around the waist.

"Help me to the kitchen," she said, grimacing.

Together they hobbled through the townhouse's grand hallways. They passed the library and the salon, which were littered with signs of her guests—spilled tea, threadbare hats. Goblins peered at her through doorways, their stomachs audibly growling, their faces full of false smiles as they tried to hide their disappointment that she'd failed once again. She narrowly avoided tripping over a butterfly net as Viggo helped her into the kitchen, where she'd spent so many early mornings baking bread and so many late nights scrubbing dishes. She grabbed a dish towel, turned on the hot water, and plunged her hands into the sink. Steam rose around her. She scrubbed the blood and feathers from her arms, revealing fresh wounds and old wounds —now crude scars—from her previous attempts to leave the townhouse.

"Shall I bandage those for you?" Viggo asked, pulling out a roll of gauze from a drawer.

"No, I'll take care of it myself. Just hand me that mint."

He held out the potted mint plant and she crushed a few leaves between her fingers, then swallowed them whole. She ripped off a strand of fake blue hair that was caught in her buttons, laid it over the wound on her left arm, and whispered, *"Attash betit truk."*

Warm magic prickled over her skin in a way that was half pleasant, half unbearably itchy. The sides of the cut started to pull together as the strand of blue hair plunged in and out of her skin, stitching the wound closed. *Attash betit truk* was a spell for fixing loose buttons, not mending flesh, but true healing spells required stronger magic than Anouk was capable of. When she finished, the wound was ugly but it had stopped bleeding. She peeled off her shirt and performed the same spell with the puncture wound on her shoulder. Viggo hobbled upstairs and came back with one of Mada Vittora's robes. It was made of charmeuse silk and worth a small fortune. But what use did a dead witch have for couture?

Anouk pulled on the robe.

She boiled water for a cup of tea to settle her nerves. Not that it would help. Her hands kept shaking. Her stomach growled. She caught her reflection in the curved copper kettle. Goodness, she looked a fright. December had painted full Goblin makeup on her: glittering gold eyeliner, pale pink hearts on her cheeks, black lipstick. Now the blush was smeared and there was glitter everywhere. She scrubbed her face in the sink, then pulled her tangled hair into a ponytail, and she felt a little more like herself.

Viggo stood awkwardly at her side. "We'll try again tomorrow. It's supposed to storm. If it rains hard enough, maybe the birds won't come."

"Rain's never kept them away before." She leaned on the counter and closed her eyes. It had been six weeks of trying to divide every last morsel of stale bread twenty-five ways. Six weeks of living with Goblins who blared The Clash at full volume at first light of dawn. Six weeks of hunger. Six weeks of crows.

Six weeks of a dog by her side instead of Beau.

There had been five of them—five beasties. An owl, a dog, a cat, a mouse, and a wolf, all of whom had been enchanted into people with their own quirks: Anouk, Beau, Cricket, Luc, and Hunter Black. Now only Anouk remained human. The others were cursed to live in their animal forms, and all of them except for Beau were imprisoned in Castle Ides.

She'd tried everything to help them. After the siege of Montélimar, she decided to go to the academy in the Black Forest of Bavaria known as the Cottage where a girl could train in magic and, if she worked hard, possibly transform herself into a witch. She'd be powerful enough to turn Beau and Cricket and Luc and Hunter Black—assuming he was even still alive—human again. Even Prince Rennar would have no choice but to bow before her.

She'd studied maps of Bavaria. She'd learned a smattering of German. She'd squirreled away valuables to trade for money to buy passage. But her weeks of preparation meant nothing if she couldn't get past the front steps.

She sank onto a wooden stool and buried her head in her hands. A cloud of dust rose around her. The kitchen, like everything else, was a disaster. Crumbs everywhere, pantry shelves bare, dirty dishes stacked in moldering piles, blue eye shadow streaked on the stove. (She hadn't bothered to ask about that one.) She felt like the only adult in a houseful of children, never mind that she'd been human for only one year and the Goblins had lived centuries. It was no longer her job to clean, and yet she often found herself with a rag in her hand, brushing crumbs into the wastebasket. Frustrating as the Goblins could be, they had no other place to go. They'd been lucky to make it back to the townhouse at all. Not everyone had. The memory of Tenpenny transformed into stone, then exploded into dust, flashed darkly in her mind.

She heard a clicking on the tile, and then a wet snout pushed into her knee. She blinked at the big brown eyes studying her. The dog had tracked in mud and left dirty paw prints all over the kitchen floor. She sighed as she scratched him behind his ears. "You know,

Little Beau, when you were a boy, you were much tidier. Well, not really, but let's pretend."

When Beau was human, his eyes had been blue. There was nothing of the dog to make her think of her friend, except perhaps the way he cocked his head as though he were trying to figure out her thoughts. What would he see now tumbling around in her brain?

The dog licked her nose.

She sighed and looked at Viggo. "We can't go on like this, Viggo. Look at Beau! And Cricket and Luc and . . . and Hunter Black. They're depending on me." Viggo's face paled at the mention of Hunter Black. Last they had seen of him, he'd been in wolf form, bleeding out and left for dead. Anouk looked toward the bare pantry. "Not to mention we're going to starve if we stay here."

Viggo gazed into the pantry wistfully. "I tried ordering a pizza. It never came. Rennar must have even gotten to the delivery boys."

An odd-sounding thump suddenly came from the front door, startling Anouk. It was heavier than the usual crisp tap of the knocker. Little Beau growled and ran out of the kitchen, barking.

December, the closest thing the Goblins had to a leader since Tenpenny had died, called from the foyer, "Um, Anouk? You might want to see this."

Viggo shifted his cane to his other hand. "Are we expecting visitors?"

"Of course not." Anouk wiped at a smear of blood on the robe's sash. "Everyone we know is either captured or dead."

The dog barked louder. Viggo and Anouk exchanged a look, then Anouk pushed up from the stool and cautiously entered the foyer. A dozen Goblins were at the front window, faces pressed to the glass. The house seemed suddenly very quiet, and Anouk realized that whatever was happening outside was serious enough that the Goblins had shut off the music. And they never turned off The Clash.

December turned away from the window and bit her blue-tinted lips in worry. Anouk's pulse raced. She swallowed her own trepidation and approached the door. The cane stopped thumping as Viggo reached the foyer and joined her.

Anouk pressed her eye to the peephole.

Behind her, Viggo said, "I'm guessing it isn't the pizza."

Chapter 2

VIGGO WAS RIGHT. It wasn't pizza.

It was exactly the person who, in the weeks since the siege of Montélimar, Anouk had most feared seeing. The crown prince of the Shadow Royals stood mere steps from the front door, a breath beyond the point where the protection spell prevented him from crossing. He was dressed in black trousers and a gray shirt and he had his hands shoved in his pockets against the November chill. His cheeks were chapped. His eyes shimmered. Even without his crown, he turned the head of every Pretty who passed on the street.

"It's Rennar," she said.

A sharp blade of anger started to slice through her but faltered when she squinted through the peephole again and, with a frown, peered closer at his clothes.

"He's wearing only one shoe."

Viggo made a sound somewhere between a laugh and a growl. "Well, his toes can freeze, for all I care. He can't come past the front steps. We can wait him out."

Anouk didn't answer. She admired Viggo's spirit, but *could* they wait any longer? Four walls and an ancient spell couldn't protect them from starvation. Anouk looked at the wound on her arm, stitched together with magic and blue strands of a wig. Sooner or later, the crows would win.

"Anouk, open the door!" Rennar's voice was hoarse. "We need to talk."

Another thump rattled the door, and when Anouk squinted through the peephole, she saw Rennar was now completely shoeless.

"That's one way to knock," she muttered.

She scanned the nearby trees and rooftops for the familiar black shadow of his crows, but he appeared to be alone. She inspected him again, the peephole distorting his proportions. He wasn't just hunched against the autumn wind; he was tensed, as though bracing for some unseen danger. His blue-gray eyes were unfocused; his gaze darted around nervously. What she'd thought at first was an arrogant expression she now recognized, incredibly, as fear.

What did *he* have to fear?

Despite a warning voice in her head, she reached for the doorknob, but Viggo shoved her hand aside, blocked the door with his body, and asked, "Have you lost your mind?"

"We can't stay here forever, Viggo. Cricket. Hunter Black. Luc. Beau." She counted the names off on her fingers. "They're depending on me. I can't help them if I'm trapped in here. Rennar commands the crows. He's our only way out."

Viggo held up four stiff fingers of his own. "Cricket, Hunter Black, Luc, and Beau currently have tails. In case you've forgotten, their primary concern at the moment is sniffing each other's backsides."

She caught the warning look on his face, but she nudged him aside with her elbow and, before her own nerves could get the better of her, threw open the door.

12

Prince Rennar's face lit up when he heard the scrape of hinges. For a second, the fogginess in his expression dissipated and he turned his piercing eyes on her. He was wearing the same scarf he'd worn the first time they'd met, the gray-blue wool one that matched his eyes. He took a step forward on bare feet. He limped only slightly. He'd learned to hide the fact that at the siege of the château, his right leg had been turned to stone. His foot still looked like a foot, but one the milky-white color of marble. "Anouk—"

"This house is protected with old spells," she warned, cutting him off. "Neither you nor your magic can enter without an invitation. I gave you my answer in Montélimar. You changed my friends to animals and caged them. If you want a princess, you'd best look elsewhere. And your *mauvais* crows can go straight to hell. Call them off, wherever they're hiding." She scanned the rooftops.

"I'm alone."

"They attack me every time I leave." She folded her arms in an attempt to hide the scars. "At your order, I presume."

A month and a half had passed since the siege, October to late November. The cold was creeping into the streets and robbing the city of life. The last time she'd seen Prince Rennar, he'd asked her to be his princess. What did he see as he looked at her now? Still a princess? Or just a messy-haired girl, barefoot and barefaced, with stains on her robe and clumsy blue stitches in her arm?

At least he was barefoot too.

And there was that look in his eyes. That fog.

His brows pinched together as his gaze fell to the wound on her arm, repaired so hastily with the wrong kind of spell, and his lips parted. "You're hurt . . ." He took a step forward.

13

"Stay back!"

He stopped. "Your arms. Your neck. I didn't realize the crows would hurt you." She gave a harsh laugh, but he shook his head. "I didn't. I promise." He was distracted by something and caught off guard by her wounds. "I hadn't thought . . . for us it's so simple to heal ourselves. Blood and wounds are nothing. To get a Goblin's attention, I'd just as soon pluck out one of his eyes as call his name —and he'd only shrug and put it back in. I hadn't thought that my crows would *really* hurt you."

If only she had her Faustine jacket. If only she could hide her scars with the quilted red silk and the mythical creature's embroidered feathers and claws.

"Let me fix your scars. I can help."

She jerked back. "Like you helped my friends?"

"Your friends are safe with me."

"Even Hunter Black?"

Prince Rennar reached into his trouser pocket and pulled out a small, round mother-of-pearl-backed mirror that bristled with enchantment. "See for yourself."

She scoffed. "You're *fou* if you think I'll reach through the protection spell."

He gave an arrogant sigh but set down the mirror and took a few steps back. Her heart pounded. It could still be a trap. But if Hunter Black was alive . . .

She took a quick step forward, grabbed the mirror, and darted back. Her breathing was rapid. Rennar hadn't moved. Cautiously, she looked into the mirror. It didn't reflect her face. Instead, she saw three cages within its round silver frame. One held a mouse; one held a cat; and in the last one, there was a wolf with careful stitches across its throat, stitches that could only have been made by a hand highly skilled at magical healing. The hand of a prince.

Her heart leaped.

Hunter Black was alive.

She was so fixated on the animals in the mirror that she didn't notice Rennar had stepped closer until he said, "Things have changed, Anouk."

Her heart shot to her throat. Her fingers curled around the mirror. She narrowed her eyes at his feet, which were just inches from the protection spell. *Wary* didn't begin to describe how she felt. And yet there was a tremble in his voice. A haunted cast to his eyes. His face was perfect, of course. The skin smooth and taut. But she had lived in the house of a witch long enough that she could see beyond perfection. His skin had an odd sheen to it. It looked too fresh, too new. She'd seen that sheen on Mada Vittora every time the witch had healed herself after battles with other witches. Mada Vittora had remade torn skin, reformed broken bones, and replaced missing fingers, but she couldn't hide that sheen. Judging from the extensive repair work Rennar had done on himself, he must have been shredded nearly to the bone.

She glanced back at the front window. Viggo and the Goblins had mashed their faces against the glass to get a better view. She turned around and stepped down the front steps slowly, chin held high, until she and Rennar were one step apart on either side of the protection spell.

"What happened to you?" she asked.

He looked surprised that she could see beyond his magic. He brushed at a glossy patch of skin that began beneath one ear and ran

15

down the side of his neck. The skin was smoother than the rest of him, as though that patch had taken effort to repair. "London. London happened."

She blinked in surprise. "London?"

It might as well have been another world.

"While you and I were distracting each other in Montélimar, the Royals in London went silent. First Prince Maxim, then Lady Imogen, now everyone within the Court of Isles. I went to investigate. They've all vanished." He touched his throat again, flinching at some dark memory.

She made a show of raising a careless shoulder. "My problems are here, in Paris. My problem is with *you*. Why should I care about the Court of Isles?"

"Because as much as you hate me, as cruel as we've been to each other, even as much as you worry for the fate of your friends, all of that pales in the light of what I've just seen."

That tremble returned to his voice. It was caused by more than fear. Beneath his perfect hair and perfect face, he was traumatized.

She narrowed her eyes. "You have two minutes before I slam this door."

"They closed the city," he said in a rush. "The Coven of Oxford. The same witches who evicted your Goblin friends. They put up border spells to prevent any living magical thing from passing into or out of London."

"You seem to have made it out in one piece."

He barked a laugh before the look in his eyes turned nasty. "Two pieces, as a matter of fact. They cast the spell as I was crossing into the elevator portal. Have you ever seen a person cut down the middle? I can't say I've quite experienced such pain. It wasn't easy to put myself back together again." He touched that odd sheen running down his neck again.

She stared at him in disbelief. "They cut you in *half?*"

He dismissed that with a flick of his fingers. "The important thing is, most of me ended up on the right side of the elevator, back in Paris. But the things I saw, Anouk. Surely you've noticed the increase in technology over the past few weeks. The city is crawling with it. Every Pretty in Paris has his head bowed over some new device and another one beeping in his pocket."

Anouk looked back at their Goblin audience fogging up the window. Little Beau had joined them, his wet nose against the glass. For weeks she'd been sitting at that window, watching for a break in the crows. She'd heard the usual dinging of bicycle bells and scuffing of shoes through autumn leaves, but more and more often, she'd also heard the chatter of mobile-phone conversations. Podcasts. Teenagers tapping away on tablets. The whir of the drones that photographers used to capture the city from above.

"I suppose so, yes. Mobile phones, that kind of thing?"

"Oh, far more than that. The witches have unleashed technologies that the Haute agreed should remain undiscovered. Advanced cloning. Macro-robotics. Time relativity. That's just to name a few. Magic and technology do not mix well, as I'm sure you know. The Coven witches knew this too. They anticipated that a sharp spike in technology would throw the magic in London into chaos and that they could use the distraction to steal power from the Court of Isles. But they haven't been able to reel back in the chaos they unleashed. Playing with relativity has splintered pockets of the city into time loops. Cloned toads are raining from the sky. Advanced optics caused a glitch that created two moons. All the coal waste from the robotics industry is making black rainbows."

She could only stare at him. Black rainbows? Double moons?

"I watched British Pretties step into a time loop and never come out again," he added quietly, his eyes flashing. "Entire families choked by black smoke. Schoolchildren driven mad by the two moons. I'm not the only one torn apart by what the witches are doing; I'm just the only one able to put myself back together again."

Anouk thought of a fairy tale that Luc had told her, "White to Red." Once, in a kingdom by salt-encrusted cliffs called the White Coast, there was a string of prosperous cities that traded with one another in a spirit of innovation and equity. A handsome king ruled the northernmost city, Kosu. One day a sea witch emerged from the waves and fell in love with him, but when he told her his heart belonged to another, the witch cursed his city with a plague. The rulers of the other cities on the White Coast, fearing her wrath, did nothing to help, and everyone in Kosu fell ill and died. But then the illness spread to all of the cities. One by one they fell, and for centuries the kingdom was known as the Red Coast. Hundreds of years later, children's rhymes still held warnings:

Cities falling one by one
White to Red
White to Red
A coughing girl, a bleeding son
Love the witch or you'll be dead.

That was why Rennar had come to her door. London had fallen, and they didn't have the luxury of watching the tragedy from a distance. Tragedy, like evil, had a way of spreading.

"Do you understand?" Rennar asked.

"We've scrambled for our lives," she said softly. "Now we have to scramble for our world."

He nodded gravely. "I can't defeat the Coven of Oxford on my own. Neither can you." An almost regretful look wavered in his eyes. "Wearing the crown means making difficult decisions. Knowing when to hold on to power and when to give it up. I'm tired, Anouk. Tired of these silent wars over magic. Tired of feuds with witches and the other Courts. It's time for all that to end. For too long, power has been in the wrong hands. We want the same thing now, you and I. It will be a scramble for both of us."

She blinked in surprise. Tired of ruling?

She'd never much wondered what life was like for someone like him, someone with all the world's power at his fingertips. He might have been alive for centuries, but now he was only a young man alone on her doorstep without any shoes on, asking for help, admitting that his power was unearned, that it belonged in the hands of the Goblins, the beasties, even the Pretties.

She leaned against the railing, wondering whether or not to believe him. She could think of worse things than a prince needing her help. To be honest, she would enjoy watching him beg.

Chapter 3

ANOUK TILTED HER CHIN HIGH. "Do you mean that? That power should change hands and you'll do what you must to make that happen?"

"I swear it," Rennar said.

She raised an eyebrow. She wasn't foolish enough to believe that a Royal would willingly give up power, but she would play along if it freed her from the townhouse. "I can't help you like this. Trapped here, starving to death."

"Shall I summon you a feast?"

She leveled a hard glare at him. "You need me because I can wield magic with no consequences. But look at me. Look at the scars. I used a mending spell for buttons to sew up this wound. That's the best I can do." She didn't try to hide her arm this time. "Did you never wonder why I kept trying to leave? Why I kept fighting your crows?" Her eyes flashed. "I was going to the Cottage."

"The Schwarzwald?" he scoffed. "That's an awful idea."

"It's a place where Pretty girls go to become witches."

"It's a place where Pretty girls go to die. No, it's impossible. I won't allow it."

Her pulse raced. She didn't dare look at him for fear that his piercing gaze would see straight into her heart, see that, yes, she'd heard the stories, she knew the risks, and she was just as afraid as she should be.

"I need strong magic, Rennar. Witch magic. Without it, I can't turn back Beau and Cricket and Luc and Hunter Black, and I can't fight the Coven of Oxford."

He scowled. "You've never been to the Cottage. I have. Royals from all the near realms travel there every wintertide to witness girls die in the Coal Baths."

"I know about the Coal Baths."

"You may have heard of them, but no stories match the reality. The ceremony lasts three days. There's a feast the night before for the girls who are about to risk their lives, and then in the morning, we light the blue flames and observe as the acolytes enter, one by one. The odds are bleak. Most years, only one out of ten girls survives. Some years, none at all. The rest burn so completely that even their bones vanish. And do you know what we do while this is happening? We drink wine. We eat chocolate *Bethmännchen*. Because we've seen so many girls die, Anouk, it means nothing to us. The only time we care is when one survives, because then we can use her. Every realm wants the loyalty of a fresh witch."

Anouk traced the stitching on her arm. It might have been rough, but it had done the job. "My chances are as good as anyone's. Better. I can already do some tricks and whispers."

He hesitated, then shook his head. "Magic won't save you from the Coals. That isn't how they work. Perhaps if you had years to study there, or even months. But wintertide is in six weeks. It's impossible."

"They said it was impossible for a beastie to cast spells. They said

21

it was impossible to stand up to Mada Zola at Montélimar." She raised an eyebrow. "Maybe you need to reconsider your use of that word."

He stepped as close to her as the protection spell allowed. "Come with me, Anouk. I'll train you myself." He held out his hand. The same one that had imprisoned her friends.

Her own hands curled at her sides. "No. It's my turn to make *you* a deal. Give me my friends back. Call off your crows. Grant me safe passage to the Cottage. I'll undergo the Baths and I'll survive. Then, when I am a witch, I'll help you with London."

Slowly, he paced, barefoot, his marble foot scuffing against the stone step. "I am fond of deals," he said at last, "but I'll counter yours with my own. There are three beasties you care about in my possession, so I will make you three bargains. If Viggo and your Goblin guests come with me as collateral, I'll free Luc and turn him human. If you become a witch and swear loyalty to my realm, I'll free Hunter Black and turn him human. If you agree to become my princess, I'll free Cricket."

"And turn her human."

"By then, you'll be a witch. You'll be powerful enough to turn her back yourself."

Anouk narrowed her eyes, trying to find a trap in his words. "Why do you care if I'm your princess? We don't need to be married to work together."

His eyes flashed. "Royal weddings happen rarely. When one does, not only must all Courts send a delegation to attend, but they also are bound to grant the new couple a Nochte Pax—think of it as a wedding gift. If we're going to achieve our goal, we'll need the help of the other Royals. They won't be able to refuse our Nochte Pax request."

"A political arrangement, then." She hesitated. "Nothing more?"

A heavy moment of silence hung between them.

Then his lips quirked in a half grin. "Let's just say nothing more would be required, but everything is up for negotiation."

"If you think you'd get as much as a kiss from me, you're wrong. But a strictly political union—if it will force the Royals to help us—maybe." She glanced at the front window, where the dog still had his nose against the glass. "And you wouldn't try to stop me from turning Beau back if I become a witch?"

He grumbled in annoyance. "If you must."

She hesitated. On the other side of the window, Viggo was shaking his head and mouthing something that looked like *No, you idiot, whatever he's offering, say no.* But Viggo didn't know that the Coven of Oxford had cut off London and were aiming for Paris next. Viggo hadn't peered into the darkest corners of her heart, didn't know how much she wanted—*needed*—witch magic.

Rennar looked at her intensely. "Well?"

She said quietly, "Okay."

"Okay?" A glimpse of pleasant surprise crossed his face, but then that arrogant mask slipped back over it. He jerked his chin toward the mirror. "Keep that, then."

"So you can spy on me?"

"Yes, exactly, and don't act surprised. I need to know that you're holding up your end of the bargain. I can see you through this mirror. I'll know when you've made it to the Cottage. In return, you'll be able to see that I am holding up my end. And if you get into trouble, you can use it to summon me."

"Beg you for help? I'd sooner an elevator cut me in half."

He flinched. "Don't be foolish, Anouk. Take help when it's offered. You think I'm your enemy, but I'm not." He leaned as close as the protection spell would allow him. "Be careful. There is dark magic out there."

Without another word, he strode down Rue des Amants, limping slightly. Anouk waited for him to disappear around the corner and then stuffed the mirror deep into her robe pocket, where the only thing he could spy on was lint.

"There's dark magic," she whispered after him, "everywhere."

Viggo was waiting for her in the foyer, hands on his hips, scowl on his face. "You shouldn't have said three words to him," he scolded. "Not unless it was *Va te faire foutre.*"

"That's four words."

"Whatever."

She dismissed his concern with a wave. Now that the deal had been made, a nervous energy was stirring in her chest. "He's calling off the crows."

Viggo raised a cautious eyebrow. "What does that mean?"

"It means I have a bag to pack."

Before she could witness the dawning look of alarm on Viggo's face, she ran for the stairs, Little Beau following at her heels. She took the steps two at a time. Little Beau sensed her excitement and barked as he ran after her. There was the dull thud of Viggo's cane far behind. What did she know about the Black Forest? Only what she'd been able to glean from the maps in the library and from Luc's fairy tales: Castles hidden in glens. Trees as tall as city buildings.

Wolves and stags and bears. Mad princes who drowned in lakes. None of Mada Vittora's books described an ancient academy deep in the woods, a place where it always snowed, where girls wanted magic bad enough to die for it.

"Anouk, stop, for God's sake!" Viggo called from the stairs. "Slow down—I'm impaired!"

She went to the library and pulled out the heavy stacks of maps. She laid them on the floor and traced the routes with her fingers, the trek from Paris to a remote corner of Germany that would involve trains and taxis and miles on foot. Little Beau wagged his tail, fluttering the maps, and some loose pages fell out. She caught one, a drawing that Luc had made of charcoal trees and swirling snow. It was a scene from one of his fairy tales, "The Frozen Labyrinth," about a Goblin girl who had ignored her family's warnings and trekked into the Black Forest after hearing rumors of a castle filled with candy.

"*Goblins know better than to go to the Black Forest,*" Luc had said. "*There's dark magic there. Ancient creatures who keep to themselves.*"

"*What kind of creatures?*" Anouk asked.

"*Creatures who like the cold, who especially like girls who wander into their woods. They can help travelers find their way, but they'll want something in return. There's a reason few girls ever make it to the Cottage. Whatever you do,*" Luc warned, "*don't let them kiss you.*"

Anouk made a face. "*Why, what happens?*"

"*Nothing good.*"

At the memory, Anouk bit her lip. If only Luc had finished the story, she might have some clue as to what she was getting herself into.

Huffing with effort, Viggo at last reached the library. "You can't trust Rennar," he protested, dabbing sweat off his brow with his shirtsleeve.

"We don't have a choice."

"And what am I supposed to do, stay here and babysit a houseful of Goblins?"

Her excitement dimmed. "Oh . . . right. Ah, I actually promised that you and the Goblins would stay at Castle Ides."

"You bargained us away as *hostages?*"

"You've seen the Castle Ides kitchens! You'll feast on suckling pig and petits fours every day! That's hardly torture."

She expected Viggo to sputter about how Rennar was the enemy, to stomp around in a fit of melodrama, but instead his face grew disturbingly calm. "There's something I haven't told you about the Schwarzwald."

She raised an eyebrow. "Have you been there?"

"Yes, once, with Mada Vittora when I was a boy." He shuddered at the memory. "The Cottage is a bleak place filled with desperate girls. Girls freeze to death just trying to find it. The ones who make it don't have a much greater chance of survival. You've heard of the Coal Baths? They're a mystical bed of coals so hot that most girls don't even burn when they try to cross it—they just vanish. Only their screams remain. The year we went to observe the trials, all of the initiates burned. Not a single one got to the other side of the bed of coals. I had nightmares for months."

Little Beau, at her feet, rested his chin on her knee. She set her hands on the dog's head to keep them from shaking. "I'm no stranger to nightmares. Besides, I won't be alone. I'll take Little Beau with me."

Viggo scoffed. "A dog won't save you from the dangers in Bavaria."

"I think you're underestimating dogs."

Outside, the last of the autumn leaves blew against the windows. Winter would be here soon. She stood up and peered out the window. A group of young Pretties stood at the corner, heads bowed over devices that cast an eerie electric glow over their faces. Drones whirred above them. Rennar was right; technology was spreading faster. If they didn't do something to curb it, would magic disappear before she'd even had a chance to master it? With no magic, would the whole Haute vanish? And the beasties?

Cities falling one by one
White to Red
White to Red . . .

A cold nose pressed against her and she felt her tension melt away. She turned from the window and knelt down so she could gaze into Little Beau's face. "Beau, are you in there?" she whispered.

Little Beau cocked his head and looked as though he might miraculously answer, but then he only scratched an itch on his side with his back leg.

Anouk sighed.

Viggo folded his arms testily across his chest. "If you and that dog have finished your heart-to-heart, do you mind sharing your decision?"

She hesitated.

"Tell me you aren't going to go through with a deal with that *imbécile*, Anouk."

"Um . . ."

"Tell me you aren't *complètement fou*."

"Well . . ."

He groaned toward the ceiling and muttered a curse that would have made even a witch blush. "You're going to get yourself killed and leave me alone with the Goblins."

That evening Anouk took a step back to examine the supplies she'd gathered on the bed. The maps. A hooded fur coat. A knife from the kitchen. Some hard cheese and sausage the Goblins hadn't yet discovered. Most of it went into the pockets of her Faustine jacket. Once she was a witch, she would enchant the pockets to serve as her oubliette —her magic bag—but for now, they were simply pockets, and they bulged with the bulk of everything.

"You are going to say goodbye, aren't you?" Viggo asked from behind her.

She turned. "To the Goblins? No, they say that goodbyes are bad luck. To you?" She smiled. "Of course."

Viggo returned a half smile. Although they had lived in the same house and considered the same woman a mother, they'd never been friends. In a million years, she'd never imagined that she'd find a new sort of family with Viggo, and yet here they were. Her heart tightened. "You'll look out for them?" she said, nodding toward the Goblins' rock music coming from downstairs. "They'll need someone at Castle Ides to keep them safe."

"I should think I can babysit some Goblins. At least until you return." He paused. "You *are* coming back."

"I'm coming back," she promised.

She wrapped her arms around him. His knit hat scratched her skin, but she didn't mind. Viggo would always be like that hat of his —a little irritating, a little silly, but also a little endearing.

He gave her a curt but warm hug in return. "Watch out for the other girls at the Cottage. It isn't a tra-la-la kind of place. Are you certain you can find it?"

She dug around in her pocket and eventually produced a small piece of carved antler with a broken tip. "I have this. It's a piece of a clock that's imbued with magic. Duke Karolinge gave this portion of it to Mada Vittora, who kept it hidden in a dresser drawer. I found it once while putting away her laundry. It's made of antler from elk in the Black Forest, and the rest of the clock is still there, in the Cottage. If Beau is any good at being a dog, he'll be able to track its scent back to the rest of the clock—to the Cottage."

She slipped the piece of antler in her jacket pocket, next to Rennar's mirror, which brushed against her fingers like ice.

"Good luck, Dust Bunny," Viggo said.

"Stay alive, okay?" she answered. "And try not to do anything stupid."

"Me? Never."

They went downstairs. She opened the door. Little Beau followed at her heels, silent and loyal, as, for the first time in weeks, they both stepped beyond the protection spell and into the city.

Chapter 4

WHEN IT CAME TO TRAINS, the magic was the easy part for Anouk—with a few whispers, she was able to cloak Little Beau in a shroud of shadows that let her get around the strict "no dogs" policy. Figuring out timetables and ticket booths wasn't nearly as simple. By the time she'd found the right train and plunked down on a second-class seat across from two German tourists, she was frazzled.

The tourists were hunched over a guidebook with a castle on the cover. If they noticed the perpetual shadow at her side, they didn't comment on it. The train carried them across countries that the Pretties called France and Germany (the Royals just called them "ours"). Fields bled into mountains with their heads in the clouds, and then the world turned dark as the stars came out. The rumbling of the train took the edge off Anouk's worries, even as she knew the calm would never last. She got off at a small station outside of Baiersbronn and was immediately glad she'd worn one of Mada Vittora's fur coats over her jacket. It was past midnight and the promise of snow hung in the air. Wind bit at her cheeks as she turned down an alley and whispered into the shadows: *"Egrex et forma veritum."*

Little Beau shook off the shadows cloaking him as if he were flicking off water. Anouk consulted her map. The chances of getting a ride by hitchhiking were slim so late at night, so they set out along the road on foot. Trees grew taller and houses became more spaced out, and soon there were no more homes or even roads, only forest.

Her feet ached by the time they reached the entrance marked on her map. Dawn was just breaking, and sunlight illuminated a well-trod path with a sign telling her she'd reached the Schwarzwald, the Black Forest.

But there were two Black Forests.

There was the one written about in guidebooks like the one the tourists had on the train, the Black Forest with quaint woodland trails and mountain lodges and squirrels and grouse — that one was a pleasant illusion created for the Pretties.

The real Black Forest had no well-marked paths. It was a place of perpetual snow and eternal winter, where trees grew tall enough to block out the sun and where monstrously huge wolves and boar stalked smaller creatures in the murky dark.

Anouk took out the broken piece of antler and knelt down.

"Take us there, Beau," she whispered.

Little Beau sniffed it thoroughly, then lifted his nose and bounded toward the untamed forest.

"Little Beau, wait!"

He'd taken off over tree roots and brambles. She scrambled to follow. There was nothing to indicate this was a path. No markings. No signs. The ground was damp with autumn leaves. Little Beau tracked the scent in short bursts — pausing to sniff the air, bounding in a new direction, then doubling back and herding Anouk forward when she was too slow. After an hour of the two of them trudging through thick forest, the topography grew steeper. The temperature dropped as they entered a valley. The ground here was dusted with a light snow. More flakes floated amid the trees, growing heavier and thicker the farther they walked. Her boots started to sink into snowdrifts. When she turned around to check her footprints, they were already hidden by fresh snow.

The tips of the trees glistened like knife blades. Everything appeared in shades of white and green. The pine boughs were thick with ice. Except for the falling snow, it was perfectly still.

Too still.

She slipped on mittens and pulled up her hood. She couldn't shake the feeling that somewhere, someone was watching her.

"Luc told stories about these woods," she said into the eerie quiet for the comfort of hearing her own voice. "Magic is concentrated here, which leads to strange things."

The snow was so thick now that she couldn't see more than ten feet on either side of her. The wind picked up, sending the snow flying diagonally into her face. The sky was only a smear of white. Little Beau tried to curl up in the lee of a stump, but she tugged on the scruff of his neck. "Come on," she told him. "We have to keep moving."

She offered him a sniff of the antler again and was relieved when he got back up and put his nose to the ground. She tromped behind him. Even though she had on mittens, her fingers were going numb. She'd prepared for snow, but not for a blizzard. What would happen if the storm got worse before they found the Cottage? How long could they go without stopping to make a fire? She trailed behind Little Beau on a path of dizzying switchbacks that made her feel as though they were hiking in circles. She could swear they'd passed by the same trees several times, but if their footsteps had ever been there, new snow had already hidden them.

As evening fell, the forest plunged into an even deeper cold, and she collapsed against a rocky outcropping that provided a windbreak from the storm. Her feet were rapidly turning numb. If she didn't start a fire and warm them, she wouldn't make it another mile. With frozen fingers, she hunted through the snow for branches and formed a small pile of kindling, but even with dry matches, she couldn't get a spark going. The wood was too wet. She dug through her pockets and found a scarf and a fresh pair of socks, but they weren't enough to keep her warm. She needed magic. With a swallow of powdered herbs, she cast a whisper to conjure an enchanted spark that would burn through damp wood. She added more wood onto the pile, whispering softly, and the fire grew. Her shoulders sagged in relief.

The snowdrifts around them began to melt. Water trickled down, forming a puddle in a bowl-shaped indentation in the rockface. She cupped the water in her hands and drank deep.

The dog, though, kept his distance from the flames.

"What's wrong? Aren't you thirsty?"

She turned back to the snowdrift and let out a cry. The snow had melted away and now lifeless eyes looked back at her. Pale blue eyes, pale blond hair, skin the same sickeningly white color as the snow itself.

A corpse.

Anouk pressed a bare hand to her mouth. It was a girl. Younger than Anouk. Melting snow clumped in the girl's hair. She'd been dead for, what, weeks? Months? A sickening bubble rose in Anouk's throat.

A few broken twigs lay at the girl's feet. She must have tried to make a fire too. Anouk started to notice other oddly shaped snowdrifts scattered on the ground throughout the woods. How many of them hid bodies? Was this a forest or a graveyard?

A branch snapped under Anouk's foot and she cringed, picturing a snapped femur beneath the snow. It was getting darker. Night was falling and there was no sign of the Cottage, no paths, no signposts, no traces of lights anywhere. The Cottage could be a stone's throw away and she might not see it. With the wind changing directions so erratically, Little Beau would never keep hold of the scent.

She felt something at her back, a shadow. She jumped up, twisted to look at the clearing, and scanned the trees. She found nothing. But the hair on the back of her neck was prickling.

Cautiously, she turned back to the fire.

She let out a cry.

A boy had appeared on the other side of the clearing. Anouk's heart began beating as violently as the storm. There were no tracks in the snow around him. He'd appeared supernaturally, as though blown in with the snow.

The boy cocked his head and said in a voice that clinked like ice, "I'm cold. Can I share your warmth, lovely?"

Chapter 5

ANOUK DIDN'T DARE RESPOND to the stranger.

His skin was smooth enough to give him the look of a child, but there was craftiness in his gaze that seemed ancient. His long white hair was pulled back at the nape of his neck, but a few jagged pieces hung sharp and straight in the front, like icicles. His skin was so pale it was nearly blue, but his eyes gleamed with a black so complete that it bled beyond his irises.

Whoever he was, he wasn't human.

Little Beau growled. He should have picked up the boy's scent long ago—unless, like the snow, the boy *had* no scent.

"Stay back." Anouk plunged her hand in her jacket pocket, searching for her knife.

He cocked his head at her curiously. "It's been a long time since I've felt fire." Despite his insistence that he was cold, he kept a wary distance from the flames. "You aren't like most girls who wander into these woods. They come seeking magic, but you already have a glimmer of it."

"How do you know that?"

"It's impossible to light a fire in the Black Forest. The wood is too wet. The wind is too fierce."

With a shiver, Anouk thought of the frozen girl and her paltry collection of twigs. She asked, "What kind of magic handler are you?"

"Snow Children don't handle magic," he chided. "We *are* magic. Whenever there's snowfall, we are there." The reflection of flames danced in his eyes. "You want to be an acolyte at the Cottage."

She nodded. Her left hand, thrust into her pocket, curled around the hilt of the paring knife.

"I can take you." A curl formed at the corners of lips. "It isn't far if you know the way." The winds shifted, throwing stinging snow into Anouk's face. "If you don't, it might as well be in another world. You'll never find it, even with magic."

A log popped in the fire. Heavy flakes caught in her eyelashes. Little Beau pressed protectively against her leg. She eyed the boy warily. He was doubtlessly one of the creatures from Luc's fairy tale, something outside of the four orders of the Haute.

"I don't need magic to find the Cottage. My dog is leading me there." She showed him the piece of carved antler. "This is part of a clock that belongs to Duke Karolinge. Little Beau can track its scent to the Cottage."

The boy regarded her pityingly. "Poor lovely. The dog is tracking a scent, yes, but not the one you think. He's following a herd of elk. You're going in circles, trailing the elk as they forage. It isn't the dog's fault. He can't tell the difference between the scent of a carved antler on a clock and the real thing."

Anouk knew in her heart he must be right. They'd been walking for hours in circles. The storm showed no signs of dying. The cold had seeped into her bones. Her teeth were chattering. Little Beau had a coat of fur, but it was soaked with melting snow, and the pads of his paws were exposed. He was shivering violently. Even with the fire, they'd be lucky to survive the night.

She swallowed and asked against her better judgment, "What do you want in exchange for showing us the way?"

His eyes gleamed. "From a lovely girl like you? I'll settle for a kiss."

She shook her head firmly. "Not that."

"So wary of a kiss?"

"I've been warned against kisses from your kind."

He feigned indifference. "Well, then, it'll be a shame to have another girl freeze in these woods. It's already so full of the dead. And the dog won't last much longer than you." He tsked. "Pity. I'm fond of dogs. And there's nothing more tragic than a dead dog who easily could have been saved, don't you think?"

The wind changed direction again. Snow swirled in heavier flakes, some as big as her palm. She could barely see across the clearing. The boy started to fade into the storm until she couldn't tell which pieces of him were flesh and which were snow.

"Wait!" she called.

She was afraid the wind had stolen her voice, but the boy slowly reappeared on the far side of the fire. He still looked as insubstantial as a snowdrift, ready to blow away.

She blurted out, "What's your name?"

"Jak."

"Let me make you a different deal, Jak. Not a kiss. Something else."

He lifted a snow-white eyebrow. "What do you have to offer?"

She thrust her hands into her coat pockets. What *did* she have to offer? What would a Snow Child want beside a kiss? Her fingers fumbled through the various objects she had stashed away, both mundane and magical things, jars of herbs and the hard cheese and—

Her thumb grazed something round. Rennar's mirror. He had said she could summon him if she was in danger, but she wasn't that desperate, was she?

She continued to rummage in her pockets. It was peculiar how the boy avoided coming close to the fire. And then it hit her: A boy made of snow would fear heat. He'd melt just like the flakes that fell in the embers.

"Wait a minute. You say you want to be warm, but you mean a different kind of warmth than the kind that comes from mittens and campfires. It's a riddle, isn't it?"

"Warmth without heat. You understand."

She wrapped her hand around a flask in her pocket that she's swiped from Mada Vittora's bar cart. "I think I have what you need."

It was a risk, she knew. A Snow Child might not consider gin to be as warm as a kiss, but this wasn't just any gin. This was the Mada's 1892 Plymouth English Gin. So potent that Viggo—normally more than capable of holding his liquor—had taken a single sip and gagged for days. Anouk had packed the flask as an afterthought, thinking the gin would make a good antiseptic for cuts.

She drew the flask from her pocket and waggled it temptingly. "If it's warmth without heat you're after, this will do the job."

Jak took the flask from her with both caution and curiosity, uncorked it, held it to his nose, and recoiled. But he must have sensed something he liked, because he dared a sip. In the next second, he sputtered gin into the snow.

Anouk grinned. "Good, right?"

He coughed harder until it turned it a barking kind of laugh. "Different kind of warmth indeed." He straightened and admired the flask with dancing eyes. "Very well, lovely. A deal is a deal. I'll take you to the Cottage. I *am* curious what Duke Karolinge will make of you, whatever you are."

He gave her back the flask, then extended his hand. She shook it. His skin was cold, as she'd imagined it would be, but soft as a child's.

"Sooner or later," he added before releasing her hand, "I'm going to get that kiss."

She pulled her hand back sharply.

She kicked out the fire while he stood at a safe distance. Without the flames, the forest was once more plunged in the deep blues and blacks of night. She could barely make out Jak's silhouette, just the streak of his long white hair, which she followed through the forest. It was impossible to tell how much time passed in a place where every direction looked the same—trees and snow, snow and trees —but eventually she spotted the glow of a light ahead. That one light became several as they trekked out of the forest and stomped their boots on a rocky path lit by flickering gas lamps that ran along the edge of a cliff.

Anouk filled her lungs with fresh air, relieved to be out of the thickest part of the woods.

"Mind your step," Jak warned. "It's a long way down."

The path led to rocky stairs hewn straight into the mountain. Jak climbed them in small, quick movements, as graceful as the wind. His feet barely touched the ground. She and Little Beau huffed after him, trying hard not to look down, where the valley plunged dizzyingly far. The muscles of her legs burned. When Jak finally stopped at a switchback lit by a gas lantern, she collapsed against the stairs.

"We're almost there. Look." Jak pointed along the mountain ridge. Through the storm, Anouk could just make out a looming structure in the distance. A massive stone bridge spanned a gorge to reach it. Only a few lights blazed in the lonely windows.

"That's the Cottage? I was picturing something small and cozy."

"Don't let the name fool you. It was a grand abbey once, founded by Pretty monks in the fifteenth century. They came here for the isolation." He brushed back the white hair falling in his eyes. "They froze to death, of course. They didn't know they had wandered into the wrong Black Forest. The abbey lay empty for many years. For the past few centuries, Duke Karolinge has used it as his academy."

"Couldn't he have found someplace less dreary?"

"The Duke prefers solitude. He doesn't much care for his fellow Royals—they come only once a year to observe the Coal Baths. He'd rather be alone with his books. Most headmasters must be forced to take the post, but not the Duke. He volunteered."

She massaged her calves, hoping to revive them. Had Mada Vittora come here? And Mada Zola? She couldn't imagine either witch ever deigning to toil in such a miserable place.

Jak pointed to the bridge ahead. "This is where I leave you, lovely. For now."

"For now?"

"I go where the snow goes. You'll see more of me."

The blizzard picked up and snow swirled around him. In the darkness she wasn't able to tell where the storm began and where he ended, and by the time the wind settled, he was gone, leaving Anouk alone on the switchback with Little Beau.

The cold was savage. The dog looked up at her and gave a soft whine.

"I know. I'm almost frozen too."

They made their way along the narrow steps toward the bridge. With no trees for windbreaks, the storm bit at her cheeks and lips, threatening to blow her off the mountain. Her boot slipped and she only just caught herself on the post of a gas lamp. Snow had collected an inch deep in Little Beau's fur, making him look more like a polar bear than a dog.

The Cottage loomed as they approached. Gas lamps lit the way to the front door, though the lights were mostly obscured by the storm. Shivering, Anouk hurried across the bridge. She squinted up through the swirling snow at two enormous iron doors. A knocker in the shape of a falcon's head peered back at her. With one last look at Little Beau, she drew in a deep breath and knocked.

Chapter 6

NO ONE ANSWERED.

Anouk hugged herself against the wind. She tugged off her mitten so she could get a better grip on the knocker and pounded again. Her fingers felt like they belonged to a stranger. The skin around her nails was swollen and had a black sheen. *Frostbite*, she thought. She plunged her hand into her pocket and felt with numb fingers for dried cayenne, the best life-essence for warming spells. Her teeth wouldn't stop chattering. At her side, Little Beau was so buried under snow that he was nearly indistinguishable from a snowdrift.

She couldn't find any cayenne. She dragged out instead a wilted stem of mint and a jar of seeds. The wrong kind of life-essence for a warming spell. Frustrated, she chucked them into the snow.

"Let us in!" She pounded on the door. "You have to let us in!"

She paced up and down the front stairs. She leaned over the bridge railing, looking for another entrance, but the ravine plunged on both sides. The only way to reach the abbey was from the bridge. Somehow, she and Little Beau had to get inside. If she froze to death, where would the rest of the beasties be? Trapped forever in animal form. She forced her stiff fingers to hunt through her pockets until she found Rennar's mirror, and she pulled it out, breathed on it, and cleaned it with her sleeve. In the faint light reflecting off the snow, she could just make out three cages. The cat. The wolf. The mouse. Rennar, that *salaud*! Why hadn't he changed Luc from a mouse as he'd promised? Surely Viggo and the Goblins had moved into their captive luxury at Castle Ides by now.

She shivered, and the mirror slipped from her hand into the snow, landing next to the jar of seeds. Anouk considered her situation. Her options were bleak. She'd sooner kiss a Snow Child than summon Rennar for help. There was no other way into the Cottage except the front door. There was a stained-glass window above it, but it had to be fifteen feet up.

She squinted into the door lock. Cricket had taught her a lock-picking spell, but it was finicky. Without knowing if the door was deadbolted, chain-locked, or barricaded, she might end up casting the wrong spell and seal her own mouth shut instead. Little Beau shook off his pelt of snow and went to the door, whining. He looked plaintively back at Anouk.

"I know. I know."

She squinted up into the snow. The front of the abbey was made of massive stone bricks worn smooth from wind and rain. She tried to climb them, but her frostbitten fingers slipped right off. Still, that window was her only option.

She dropped to her knees, shoved the mirror back in her pocket, and grabbed the jar holding the seeds. They were flat and brown, each as big as her thumb. Mada Vittora used these seeds when she wanted to summon a vine strong enough to string up a Goblin by the ankles.

Clutching the jar, she crawled to the base of the abbey and dug through the snow until she hit frozen soil. She chipped away at it until her fingernails were torn and bloody and she had a hole just large enough for one of the seeds. She buried it beneath the ground. She placed another on her tongue along with the wilted mint and a few strands of hair from her own scalp. The sweet taste of mint took her back to summertime, to warmth and Luc's garden, and she swallowed the life-essence with a handful of snow and whispered: *"Jermis-s-s . . ."*

Her teeth chattered so violently that she couldn't get the whisper out. She cupped her hands over her lips, puffed warm air into them.

"Jermis!"

A spark of magic flared to life in her throat, spreading a ripple of warmth through her lips. The soil beneath her hands trembled and parted. A sprout rose so fast that Anouk had to jerk back to avoid being smacked in the face by a leaf. The vine rose two feet, then four, then six, and kept going. It was as thick around as her wrist and forked into alternate branches every foot or so, branches that found weaknesses in the grout and fastened themselves on. Anouk grabbed the hairy vine and tugged it as hard as she could to test its strength. It could have been hammered in with nails. It climbed all the way to the roof and might have kept going—she couldn't see that far with the snowstorm.

She shrugged off her fur coat and twisted the sleeves into a makeshift sling that she slid around her shoulder. Beneath it she wore the Faustine jacket over a few layers of sweaters. Snow caught in the beautiful colored threads. "Come on, Little Beau. You'll have to climb on my back."

It wasn't easy to get a hundred-pound dog on her back. After some shuffling, she hoisted his wet paws onto her shoulders and secured him there in the sling. His panting was strained. He was shivering uncontrollably.

She began to climb.

It was slow going, but she made it up inch by inch. Before, the only ladder she'd climbed had been the one that led from Mada Vittora's attic to the rooftop. How long ago had she and Beau climbed to the roof and marveled at the beauty of Paris? The glittering lights of Paris were far away now.

Don't look down, she told herself. The vine rose straight up the abbey face; if she slipped and the wind caught her, she might fall beyond the bridge into the ravine.

Little Beau hunkered down against her back, not moving a muscle, as though he knew how precariously he was tied to her. His nose was tucked into the fold of her jacket collar. How high up were they now? Ten feet? Warm, flickering light came from the other side of the window. She pictured herself and Beau curled up by a hearth, drinking hot tea. It gave her the strength to climb the rest of the way, and, muscles burning, she hauled them both onto the wide window ledge. She paused to catch her breath. Little Beau whined softly. From somewhere, she caught a whiff of fresh bread, and her stomach ached.

She twisted the window latch, but it didn't give. Frozen shut. *"Zut alors!"*

She gritted her teeth and shoved again. Something squeaked. Then groaned. Without warning, the latch gave way and the window swung inward. Before she knew it, she was falling forward. *No!* She tried to grab the vine, but it slipped out of her grasp. With Beau still strapped to her back, she plunged down into the abbey. A fifteen-foot fall. She glimpsed church-style lanterns hanging from the ceiling. A cavernous room. A fire roaring in an enormous fireplace at the far end. And then—

"Ow!" She smacked into the floor hard enough to rattle her bones. Little Beau scrambled, his limbs tangled in the makeshift fur-coat sling. His paw collided with her head. She clamped a hand over her temple. Every one of her muscles screamed. If she hadn't broken anything, it would be a miracle.

She cursed and rubbed her backside.

Little Beau managed to get himself onto all fours. She hoped he hadn't broken anything either.

Slowly, she became aware of their company.

They'd fallen into what appeared to be a great hall, though, judging by the stained-glass window and high ceilings, it could once have been the nave of a church. There were no pews or altars or pulpits now. There was only the massive fire roaring at the far end and two long wooden tables flanking it.

A few girls sat at either table, each curled over a bowl of something steaming, a glass of water, and a small hunk of bread. All their eyes were on her. The girls seemed just as surprised to see Anouk falling through their window as Anouk was to see them.

"I've . . . come to . . . study under . . . Duke Karolinge." Her teeth were chattering so hard, she wasn't sure they could understand her. "I'm sorry about . . . the window. The . . . door was locked."

A girl who looked to be around twenty years old, with black skin and hair cropped close to her scalp, stood from the bench. Like all of the girls, she was wearing a plain gray muslin dress with a white smock apron and a rope belt.

"That's because we locked it." She had a British accent. Her tone was blunt but not without kindness. "We didn't let you in for a reason. The Duke isn't taking new acolytes."

Well, *merde.*

Anouk's muscles gave out. She fell back to the floor and stared at the ceiling. She'd come all this way. Her friends were depending on her. "He'll make an exception for me."

One of the other girls snorted. "Not likely."

Anouk took a deep breath.

Then she sat up and prepared to do whatever it took to remain within those four walls.

Chapter 7

ANOUK PUSHED UP to her feet, wincing as her joints popped, and attempted to disentangle herself from the makeshift sling she'd fashioned out of Mada Vittora's fur coat. Her pants were torn. Her hair was undone and snarled. Her legs were soaked in snow up to her knees. The only thing about her that seemed in one piece was the Faustine jacket. She made an attempt to brush snow and dirt off herself, but as usual, it was useless.

Now that her eyes had adjusted, she saw that behind the grand fireplace were three sets of curving staircases, two that led to an upper level and one that plunged downward into darkness. The stone floor was slick as ice, polished smooth from centuries of footsteps, and there were uneven marks where she assumed pews had once stood.

There were five girls in all. The tall black girl with the British accent, who looked like the oldest. At her table there was a girl with a storm cloud of black hair down to her waist and eyebrows in desperate need of tweezing, and a pretty girl with glasses who peered at Anouk curiously. At the other table were two girls who looked to be at least five years apart in age, but, judging by their stocky frames and their identical shade of red hair pulled back into the same severe bun, they must have been sisters.

Anouk gazed at the fire longingly. What she wouldn't give to strip out of her soaked clothes, kick off her frozen boots, wrap herself in a blanket, and warm herself and Little Beau by the flames.

The girl with the storm cloud of black hair stood, circled Anouk with a suspicious scowl, and then peered up at the stained-glass window. The other girls didn't move.

The older of the sisters grinned and said in a German accent, "You'd better turn around and leave, whoever you are."

The younger sister frowned at the puddle of melting ice beneath Anouk's feet. "You'll have a better chance with the cold things out there than the warm things in here."

The dark-haired girl loomed close to Anouk, like a shadow come to life. She reeked of sweat and onions. She narrowed her eyes and grunted.

Anouk moved a few feet away from the girl. "We'll freeze if we go back out there."

"Heida is right—you'd better leave," the British girl said regretfully. "I don't know what you've heard about this place, but it isn't some school for magic. It's a graveyard for the soon-to-be departed."

The storm-cloud girl dropped to her hands and knees and began inspecting Anouk's fur coat, which was crumpled on the floor. She ran the strands between her fingers. Little Beau let out a low growl, and the girl bared her teeth and growled back. She picked up a piece of vine and sniffed the leaf.

"Magic!" She pointed an accusing finger at Anouk.

All the girls became quiet. Their eyes went from Anouk to the piece of vine and back.

"Jermis," the girl with glasses said quietly, and hearing a spell on a Pretty's lips jolted Anouk for a second. Pretties, like these girls,

couldn't cast magic, but that didn't mean they didn't know the word-ing of spells. "She used the *jermis* spell. Growing." She sniffed the air. "With mint as the life-essence."

"Witch!" the storm-cloud girl cried, then she jabbed an accusing finger at Little Beau. "Witch's demon!"

The British girl rolled her eyes at the other girl's ramblings. She cocked her head toward Anouk. "Can you really cast whispers?"

Anouk felt skewered by five sharp sets of eyes. These were Pretty girls who had clawed their way here through that forest of death, only to face even more danger.

Anouk hesitated, then said, "Let me to talk to the Duke. I'll make my case. He'll accept me."

"Will I?"

All eyes turned to the top of the stairs. A hulk of a man stood on the upper level, dressed in a full-length red cloak more suited to a knight from one of Luc's fairy tales than the headmaster of an academy. His hair was graying at the temples, though everything else about him spoke of immense strength. He had deep-set eyes and wore wire-rimmed spectacles. Around his neck hung a gold chain that held a vial of powder. The cloak did little to disguise his massive stature; two thousand years ago he might have been a gladiator. What struck Anouk most was his unkempt shadow of a beard. It was rare to see anything less than coiffed perfection among the Royals.

"Who has come knocking in the thick of a storm," he asked, observing Anouk, "with a mongrel on her heels and a whisper on her lips? Not a Pretty acolyte, surely. This is a place for those who seek magic, not those who already have it."

Anouk hugged her jacket around herself as if it were battle armor.

"I know a few tricks and whispers, but I need more. I need to become a witch."

There were bags under his eyes—he looked as though he'd been up late squinting at a book by poor light—and yet now a spark lit up his gaze. He made a point of checking the time on a massive clock at the front of the hall, set into a full rack of elk antlers that had been intricately carved with depictions of forests. One of the antler tips was broken off. Anouk felt for the broken piece in her pocket, wondering if the Duke knew she possessed it.

"She made a vine grow in the snow," the younger redhead said.

The Duke circled Anouk slowly, his cloak dragging on the floor. "You aren't a witch, though you can do magic," he mused. "You aren't a Pretty, though you seem of their world." He brushed back her hair. "No pointed ears. Not a Goblin."

Anouk's gaze shifted toward Little Beau, and the Duke followed her eyes and then raised an eyebrow.

"Ah. Interesting." He adjusted his wire-rimmed glasses. "I thought the last of your kind had been killed centuries ago. I can't fathom how you ended up on my doorstep, beastie, but this isn't the place for you."

She lifted her chin. "I deserve a chance as much as anyone else."

He stroked his unshaven chin in consideration. "So you've come in search of stronger magic than you possess. I wonder what you've been told of this place."

Anouk told the Duke what she'd gleaned from overheard conversations in the townhouse: that for centuries it had been the place Pretty girls went to become witches. She'd assumed it involved learning spells and making potions, dangerous tests and having to prove one's mettle. "You evaluate them and determine who is worthy," she finished. "There's a ceremony, the Coal Baths. All the Royals come to light the flames and bear witness."

The older redhead snorted. "She doesn't know anything." She turned back to the table and bit off a hefty piece of her hunk of bread, apparently finding her supper more interesting than Anouk.

"My dear," the Duke said to Anouk, "you've been misinformed. I do not decide anyone's fate. It is the Coals and the Coals alone that determine whether to burn a girl or birth a witch. I am merely a guide on the journey. It is up to each girl to find her own path to magic — her missing crux."

"Crux?" Anouk was tired and cold and wet, and the last thing she wanted was more riddles. She rubbed her bleary eyes. "I don't know what that is. But whatever it takes, I'll do it."

He dismissed her weariness with a *tsk*. "I'm afraid it's too late for that. The Coal Baths are in less than six weeks. Most of these girls have been here for the better part of a year. The last acolyte to come arrived two months ago. Now, with the Baths so close? No. I cannot."

"I'm not leaving," Anouk said.

"I'm turning you away for your own good. No one finds her crux so soon before the ceremony. Most never find it. Come wintertide, the Coals will burn your flesh from your soul."

"I can . . . I can help you," Anouk offered desperately. She considered the cobwebs underneath the long tables. "I can clean."

"We already have Heida and Lise to clean." The Duke motioned to the pair of sisters and began to walk toward the door, clearly ready to throw her back into the cold.

She thought fast. The Cottage was a bleak place, the kind of place where good meals were probably in short supply. The chunks of bread the girls were eating looked rough as sandpaper. Those bowls of soup didn't seem likely to win any culinary prizes either. "I can cook too."

The Duke stopped. The girls at both tables sat up straighter. The girl with glasses looked with distaste at her bowl of soup.

"French cuisine, if you like," Anouk added quickly. "Or German. I don't mind slaughtering the animals if I have to. If you have chickens, I could make a cassoulet."

Duke Karolinge and the girls exchanged a long look. Someone's stomach growled. Anouk felt an inward flush of success. Nothing won over doubters like the promise of a good meal. She felt the uncanny sensation of being watched and found the storm-cloud girl, still on all fours, staring at her with pointed intensity. Anouk touched her own cheeks and forehead, wondering if she had dirt on her face. She did. But even after she wiped it off, the girl still stared.

"Can you bake . . . strudel?" the Duke inquired, raising one woolly eyebrow. Before she could answer, a dark shadow swooped through the open window and soared across the grand hall on wide-stretched wings. Anouk gasped and ducked.

What was it? A crow? *An owl?*

The bird circled and flew toward them, then landed gracefully on the Duke's left shoulder. Anouk straightened, her heart still pounding. A falcon. Smaller than she'd thought at first, with a beautiful array of feathers ranging from tan to gray. It wore a bell around its neck.

"Ah, Saint. You've returned."

The Duke stroked the bird's chest with one finger and studied Anouk for a long time. He no longer seemed concerned about strudel.

"Girls die here," he said at last. "You will most likely die here if you choose to stay and undergo the Coal Baths. Many girls think they want magic, only to falter before the Baths' blue flames. They return to the Pretty World and to lesser ambitions."

"I've never faltered."

He grunted. "These acolytes are no strangers to sacrifice. They've left behind what they love most. Their families. Their futures. The comforts of the Pretty World. Are you also willing to make a sacrifice?"

She didn't blink. "Yes."

What hadn't she already sacrificed? She'd lost the closest thing she had to a mother. She'd left the only home she'd ever known. The people she considered her family were now locked in cages.

He nodded in slow approval. "Then I'll have to take it. It isn't fair, I'm afraid, for one acolyte to have greater abilities than the others."

"I don't understand. Take what?"

His thick fingers twisted around his falcon's bell, and it rang with a strangely pitched sound that struck fear in her heart. "Your magic."

Chapter 8

A SACRIFICE.

Before Anouk could speak, Duke Karolinge twisted his thick wrist with a flourish and something sharp tugged in her throat. She fell to her knees. It felt as though he'd cast hooks into the space between her vocal cords and was now teasing something out, like separating magic from flesh. She clutched at her neck. A coughing fit seized her so painfully that she worried she'd tear the lining of her esophagus. She gagged. It suddenly felt like she'd swallowed a swarm of gnats. She thrust her fingers deep into her mouth and groaned at a sudden sharp sting. She leaned over and coughed until the stinging swarm rose up her throat and into her mouth. She spat it out. It was a chaotic ball of green lights that floated on the air like dandelion fluff straight to the Duke.

He caged his fingers around the ball of energy—her magic— and whispered it between the metal leaves of the golden bell around his falcon's neck. "Now you may stay, if that is still your intention."

Anouk pressed her hands to her throat. Her tongue felt raw, as though she'd vomited up salt and thorns. "Wait . . . *Armur ver . . .*"

She stopped abruptly. Something had changed. Ever since the first time she'd cast a spell, she'd felt a warming sparkly fizz with each word of the Selentium Vox, like sips of champagne. But now the fizzy warmth was gone. Her throat felt frigid, like it held a clutch of coals doused with ice water. There was no magic behind her words anymore.

"Wait," she said again. "I need my magic." The taste in her mouth was dry and ashen. Repulsed, she wiped her lips frantically on her sleeve. "Give it back. You have no idea what I went through to get that magic. It's a part of me. You can't just take it!" She stood but then tottered and fell; she felt like she'd just stepped from a long boat trip back onto solid land.

"And yet I did." The Duke calmly turned to the table of girls. "Esme, thaw out our new acolyte, bandage her frostbite, and then give her a bed—the corner room upstairs with the other new girl."

Esme, the British girl who'd first addressed her, hitched up her muslin dress and climbed over the bench, muttering a curse as she fought with the stiff fabric as though she were more used to tulle skirts and silk blouses.

"And Lise," the Duke said to the smaller redhead, "take the dog below and lock him in the cellar."

"No!" Anouk shoved herself to her feet. Her cry echoed throughout the great hall. The sound crashed back on her, ringing in her ears. If only she had her magic, she'd cast a whisper to stop this. "No," she repeated fiercely. Her hands were balled at her sides, but she forced herself to take a deep breath. "I can do without magic," she said, though the thought pained her. "I can try, if I have no other choice. But I can't do without that dog."

Her voice broke. She forced her chin high and gave him an icy stare.

No one would say that his face softened, exactly. Like all the

Royals, he'd been alive for centuries, had seen kingdoms rise and fall, had seen greater tragedies than a girl separated from her dog. But he took off his glasses, rubbed them on his shirt, put them back on, and considered her afresh.

"The Cottage," he said, "is no place for loose creatures. The forest that surrounds us is ancient and filled with capricious spirits. There are things beyond that door that wouldn't hesitate to make a meal of your dog, should he wander down the wrong hall. We lost three goats last week. The only thing we found were their livers."

Anouk thought of Jak and his sharp teeth. Would he eat a live goat? A dog?

At her uncertain silence, the Duke signaled again to Lise, who untied the rope belt knotted around her waist and started toward Little Beau. Anouk panicked. Was Beau's freedom worth begging for? She had sworn that she'd never trust any Royal. Not Rennar, not the Parisian Court counts and countesses, and not a self-exiled duke either.

"Wait."

Anouk's head whipped around. Esme had spoken. She was starting to untie her own rope belt. "If the dog doesn't get salve on those paws, he'll lose them to frostbite just like she'll lose her fingers. I'll take them both to the infirmary and then she and I will put the dog in the cellar."

Anouk felt a rush of gratitude. If Beau had to be locked away, at least it wouldn't be by a stranger, and she'd have a few more minutes with him.

The Duke shrugged. "As you wish."

Esme finished untying her rope belt and started to fasten it around Little Beau's neck, but Anouk shook her head. "He doesn't need a leash. He'll follow me."

"Even to a locked stall?"

Anouk flinched, thinking of Cricket and Hunter Black and Luc locked up in Rennar's cages. "He'll follow me anywhere."

Esme shrugged and motioned for Anouk to follow her down a corridor that led off the back of the great hall. The other girls were silent, but Anouk felt energy brimming just under the surface—she knew as soon as she left the room, they'd talk about her and Little Beau. The storm-cloud girl, who had moved from all fours to sitting cross-legged on the floor, twirled the remnants of the vine between her fingers.

Anouk shivered. She was so distracted that she didn't see the three other girls who had popped up from the lower staircase until she practically ran into one of them. The girl giggled. The three of them wore matching dresses and the same expressions of curiosity. The one Anouk had nearly trampled looked about twelve years old and had long blond hair pulled back into a braid. The other two were older; one had a shaggy bob, the other a mop of brown curls and red cheeks. Their aprons were streaked with potato peels.

"Hey! Scamper back to the kitchen, you three. You can meet the new girl tomorrow," Esme said.

But their eyes were on Little Beau, not Anouk, and the three of them were already making silly little noises to entice him over so they could scratch his head. Esme shooed them away and then opened a door to a glass-enclosed breezeway. The cloistered arches were encased in glass, which kept out the wind, though Anouk still had to hug herself for warmth. Beyond the glass, the storm howled.

"Forgive them," Esme said. "It's been a long time since any of us have seen a dog. The goats don't make good pets, and we aren't allowed to touch the Duke's falcons—especially Saint, the one back there."

Anouk's boots echoed eerily in the hallway. "Is he very cruel?"

Esme gave her a surprised look. "The Duke?"

Anouk thrust her hand deep into her pants pocket and clasped Rennar's mirror. "I've known more than my fair share of Royals," Anouk explained darkly. "They're as cruel as they are beautiful."

Countess Quine. Lord and Lady Metham. Any of them would have betrayed Anouk at the drop of a hat. And that was just the Parisian Court. She'd heard rumors of the other Courts: The Crimson Court, with its three ruling sisters. The Court of the Wood, run by the imposing Baron Winter. The Court of Isles, the Barren Court . . . She'd meet some of them soon enough, she imagined. Representatives from each Court would, according to tradition, journey to the Cottage at wintertide to witness the Coal Baths. She'd have more than Rennar to deal with.

"I wouldn't call the Duke beautiful." Esme snorted before adding offhandedly, "I wouldn't call him cruel either." They reached a door at the end of the cloistered hallway, and Esme paused, her hand on the iron knob. "He's reserved. Cold, even. He doesn't get close to any of us. Can you blame him? He advises girls for the better part of a year, gets to know their dreams, and then watches almost all of them die. Every year for hundreds of years, he's done this. Considering that, I'd say he's agreeable enough."

Anouk stared at Esme in disbelief. Had he twisted their minds to think he was a simple academic? That he had their best interests at heart? That he wouldn't sell their souls for a good bottle of Pinot Noir? Or maybe even a *bad* one?

"By the way," Esme said, "that's a great jacket. It's a shame you'll have to take it off. If you haven't noticed, we all wear the same thing. This awful frock. The Duke says uniforms help us focus."

Anouk continued to stare at her. "It's just . . . you can't possibly *trust* him." She touched her throat. "You saw how he took my magic. And before that, he was going to throw me back out into the storm."

Esme stroked her chin. "I see how that might look cruel, but I promise, turning you away would have been a kindness." Her face grew very serious. "Do you know what my first thought was when you came crashing through the window? Just another body for the fires. There are nine of us—ten, now that you're here. We were ten before. There are always ten, every year, without any planning or anything; that's just part of the Coals' magic. But one girl left over the summer. She was frightened by the spirits in the woods. The Snow Children—I'm guessing you came across one of them? Most girls do, for better or worse. We were hoping she'd count as one of the ten and that another girl wouldn't come to take her place. But here you are."

Anouk hesitated. "That girl with the black hair . . ."

"Frederika." Esme let out a puff of air as if to say that Anouk didn't know the half of it. "Frederika's wild. I don't mean she's a handful, I mean *actually* wild. She grew up in the Black Forest in a valley not far from here, raised by pagan Pretties. She's mostly harmless, but the rest of us keep out of her way." She eyed Anouk. "Hey, are you okay?"

Anouk noticed she was reeling slightly. She straightened and touched her cold lips. "I didn't realize how warm my magic kept me, like a little fire always kindled in my chest. Without it, I feel so bare. Hungry. Cold."

"Well, get used to it. I've been cold and hungry for nine months. The sisters back there, the redheads? Heida and Lise, from Munich. They're the only ones who have been here longer than me. Marta— she's the pretty one with glasses—arrived a week after me. The trio who popped up from the kitchen were Karla, Sam, and Jolie. They're all from Ireland. Then there's Lala, who arrived about two months ago. She'll be your roommate. She keeps to herself, but she's cool. Each of us learned about the Haute in our own way."

"What was yours?"

"I made friends with a Goblin. I thought she was just a chick with weird clothes at the time. My father was a diamond trader. We met Skye while he and I were looking for a new supplier. She told me everything: Witches. Goblins. This place. Said if I was ever in trouble to come here and not to kiss any boys in the woods. I thought she was crazy." Esme pressed her lips together tightly. "But two days later, we found Skye in our car. Throat slit. Soon after that, whoever killed her killed my parents too. I barely got away."

"Did you think you'd be safe here?"

"Oh, no. Anyone who comes here looking for safety is making a terrible mistake."

Chapter 9

ESME CONTINUED THE TOUR and took Anouk to a room that might once have been a chapel, judging by the shape of the boarded-up windows. It was now filled with medical supplies. The infirmary wasn't much to speak of, just a dreary stone chamber packed with dusty wooden drawers that smelled of salves and ointments. Several pairs of crutches were propped up in one corner. Two giant woven baskets were bursting with bandages, clean in one, bloodstained in the other.

"Boots off," Esme ordered, taking down a jar of salve from the shelves. As soon as Anouk had removed her boots, Esme frowned. "You're missing your little toes."

"It's a long story."

Esme applied the cream to Anouk's fingers and the blackened tips of Anouk's toes, then put some on the sensitive pads of Little Beau's paws. There must have been magic in the salve, because moments after Esme applied it, Anouk's fingers began to come to life again. It was cold in the infirmary and hardly comforting, but at least the lantern was warm.

She cleared her throat. "The Duke said something about finding a . . . crux?"

Esme looked up from where she was dabbing the salve carefully around Little Beau's claws. "All the girls come here thinking they're going to learn spells and potion-making. That's part of it, of course. There's a library filled with books on the Selentium Vox and the history and politics of the Haute, and there are storerooms filled with samples of every kind of life-essence imaginable. But this is, above all, a place for searching. The Duke will explain it to you."

"I'd rather hear it from you."

Esme sat back on her heels. "Do you know that every witch has a preferred kind of life-essence? A certain type of flower, or butterfly, or herb?"

Anouk's mind flooded with the cloying smell of Mada Vittora's roses. "I do."

"Here, we call that her *crux*. It isn't just that, say, the Rébeval Witch of Lucerne liked the smell of peonies so she favored them for her spells. For her, peonies held a unique power. Decades ago, she came to the Cottage as a Pretty and spent months searching for her crux before she found it. Cruxes are a symbol of each witch's unique connection to magic."

Anouk hadn't heard them described as *cruxes* before, but she knew what Esme was talking about. For Mada Vittora, it had been roses. For Mada Zola, fresh-cut lavender. Though witches could and did use all types of life-essences, there was one living element that each witch seemed preternaturally drawn to; it could be goose down, dragonfly wings, allium bulbs, or any of a nearly infinite number of possibilities. That life-essence would be included, even in a tiny portion, in almost all of the witch's potions to give it a personal touch of power.

"Where are we supposed to find our cruxes?"

"Well, that's the question, isn't it? That's the purpose of the Cottage. To figure out what your crux is. A lot of girls spend hours in the Duke's storerooms, sniffing and tasting every flower and herb and living thing, hoping that they'll suddenly just *know* what the right crux is, but that's a misguided approach. Cruxes don't work that way. In order to discover one's crux, one has to delve deep into magic —into spells, history of magic, politics, physical casting. Some girls discover their cruxes through study. Like Marta. She spent months in the library studying the Selentium Vox, and then one day, we found her passed out on the floor in a puddle of spilled tea. When she woke, she chattered on about bees, bees, how honeybees were the secret to everything. She must have learned thousands of words in the Selentium Vox, but it wasn't until she learned the word for 'bee' that something clicked for her." Esme swatted at an invisible bee with a shiver as though glad that wasn't her crux, and then she continued. "Not all of the girls are certain of their cruxes yet. But they'd better decide soon. Time is short—I don't have to tell you that. Karla thinks hers is marigold. She came across a drawing of a marigold in an old manuscript and dreamed about a field of them that night. Sam can't decide between thorns and anise pods—she's been taking long runs every morning, barefoot in the snow, hoping that the exertion will give her clarity. Jolie—ah, that's an interesting story. She discovered her crux by accident. A literal accident. She spent months studying, meditating, doing physical casting exercises in the courtyard, and she still didn't have a clue. But then she fell from the bridge and plunged into the ravine. She nearly died. We brought her here, to the infirmary, and when she woke up, she said she'd had a vision of butterfly wings. Frederika won't say what hers is. Either she doesn't know or it's something embarrassing. Heida suspects Frederika's crux is poppy seeds. You know, opium. Crazy drawn to crazy. And the sisters! Heida and Lise have a theory that their crux is *each other*. That for each girl, it's a lock of her sister's hair. They think their power lies in their sisterhood."

"Have you found your crux?"

Esme didn't answer right away. Anouk got the sense she'd asked a taboo question, but then Esme tipped her chin up and said, "Maybe. I've spent months in prayer—no books or barefoot jogging for me. Laugh if you want. I know prayer is out of fashion in the Pretty World. I'm the only girl here who prays. But in my prayers, I see something white, like stone, but living." She paused, her eyes glistening. "I think mine is bone. I'm not quite sure. I need to pray on it more."

"What if you think it's bone but it isn't?"

Esme gave a sardonic grunt. "If I'm right, I'll clutch my crux and walk through the Coal Baths in one piece. If I'm wrong, I'll burn." Esme put away the salve, closing the drawer a little too force-fully. "Obviously most girls are wrong, despite how they rave about visions and signs and dreams. The ones like the Rébeval Witch, who thought hers was peonies and was right, are the exception. There are ten of us here now. We'll be lucky if even one of us is still alive after wintertide."

Anouk had been stroking Little Beau's head but now her fingers curled in the scruff of his neck.

Esme opened a cupboard full of muslin dresses and undergarments. "No girls come here on a lark. All of us want something. Revenge. Strength. Ambition. Becoming a witch is the only way we'll get it."

She handed Anouk a stack of dresses. Little Beau pressed his nose into them. Anouk could smell the mustiness. Lye. Wool. Dust. So different from the delicate smells of Paris.

"Sorry again you'll have to lose the jacket. Put it somewhere safe. Hope you live to wear it again."

Esme continued the tour, showing her the laundry rooms and the kitchen, a confectionery and canning room, and the floor that housed the Duke's offices and his personal library. By the time Anouk had been shown the endless chambers of storerooms where every type of life-essence was cataloged, the courtyard where they could exercise, and a few dreary rooms for studying ancient texts, Anouk was yawning.

"One more stop, I'm afraid." Esme's gaze fell on the dog.

Anouk's stomach twisted as she and Little Beau followed Esme back through the great hall, where the pair of sisters were now scrubbing the floor on their hands and knees, and down a set of curving stairs to the cellars. Anouk could tell from the smell, even before seeing it, that it had been converted into stables for the goats and chickens. Esme opened a dusty stall door with a metal bolt. "Marta's in charge of the animals. She'll feed your dog and bring him water, and you can visit him when you have free time, but I'm afraid that won't be often. The Duke keeps us busy with our chores. If you have goodbyes to say, say them now."

Anouk sank to her knees and ran her hands through Little Beau's fur. She pressed her forehead against his. When Beau had been a boy, he'd hated to be alone. He was always hunting out someone to talk to, even if it was just a Goblin or the Pretties who delivered packages. As a dog, he'd barely left her side.

"I'm so sorry," she said. "You have to stay here. It isn't safe otherwise."

His big dark eyes swallowed her. He plunged his nose into her side, hungry for her familiar scent. On a whim, she set aside the stack of muslin dresses and shrugged out of the Faustine jacket. She straightened her bulky sweater underneath, pulled the collar high around her neck to keep out the chill, and gently tucked the jacket into the corner of the stall.

"Here. For you. A little piece of me so that you aren't all alone." Anouk leaned forward and planted a kiss on the dog's head. He tried to follow her when she left, but she closed the stall door. He whined softly. "I'll visit you whenever I can, Beau. I'll bring you treats." She turned away with tears in her eyes. Suddenly she felt so trapped. Cold all the way to her bones. Her fingers skimmed over the bare place at her throat.

She'd lost her magic.

She'd lost her friends.

She was separated from Beau.

Little Beau started scratching at the door and she pressed a hand to her heart and hurried to the steps. Esme followed silently. When Anouk stopped at the top of the stairs, leaning against the wall and breathing hard, Esme touched her shoulder.

"I'll take you to your room. It's late. You can get some rest."

"Just tell me which one it is."

"Last on the left. The corner one."

Anouk wanted to thank her for showing a glimmer of kindness in such a dreary place, but it was all she could do to race up the stairs to the dormitory floor. She ran past open doors. They were small monastic cells, built as a solitary room for each of the original monks, though now two beds had been squeezed into each room.

Her chest felt tight. She kept thinking of Beau trapped below, all alone. And of girls dead in the woods, and girls dead in fires. She was tired of living in a world where girls were so expendable.

On the verge of panic, she threw herself into the last room on the left and slammed the door behind her. The cell was empty and identical to the others except that since it was on a corner, it had two high, tiny windows instead of just one. There were two wooden beds with a trunk at the foot of each one, and it was so cramped that Anouk could barely turn around. There was little to tell her about her roommate other than a pink sock peeking out from the sheets and a vase of dried lavender on the nightstand.

She leaned back against the door, wondering if she'd made the biggest mistake of her life. Why had she ever dared to dream of stepping beyond thresholds? What had that gotten her? Maybe she should return to Paris. Listen to Duke Karolinge and throw herself out. How could she possibly find her crux when it had taken the other girls months and they were still filled with doubt?

In six weeks Rennar would arrive in an expensive car with servants at his bidding and clothes cut for a god. He'd take one look at her and know that she'd lost her magic. Would he still want her as his princess then? Would he claim that their deal was invalid since she'd lost the one thing he cared about?

She dug through her pants pocket until she found Rennar's mirror. She cleaned it with her sleeve. Her vision was blurry from tears, which she wiped away angrily.

The mirror showed the three cages.

A white cat.

A bandaged wolf.

A small gray mouse.

No!

Anouk was so mad, she wanted to hurl the mirror across the room. He hadn't changed Luc back! That was their deal, wasn't it? What was Rennar waiting for? Was this all a game to him? Was it a trick?

She opened the door, planning to throw the blasted mirror down the length of the hall, but then froze. Someone was there, a girl who ducked and shrieked in surprise at Anouk's raised arm. The girl had strawberry hair pulled back into a messy bun and angular features.

Anouk gaped. *"Petra?"*

Chapter 10

ANOUK GLANCED BRIEFLY at the lavender on the nightstand. "Petra, *you're* the other new girl?"

Petra straightened, still shaken from the sight of Anouk ready to smash a mirror in her face. "I wouldn't say *new*. I've been here two months. That's two months of gruel. Two months of this hideous dress. It's been an eternity."

"They said my roommate's name was Lala!"

Petra snorted. "That's just a nickname that Esme gave me. I sing in the bathhouse. *La-la-la.*" She shoved past Anouk and into the room, then whirled around. "What are *you* doing here? I can't believe the Duke let you stay."

"I offered to cook."

"Ah! All men put their stomachs over their heads."

Anouk sank onto one of the beds, glancing at Petra's hands on her hips. "And he let you stay? Did he ask you about your past? Does he know?"

"That I'm transgender? Yes, he knows. They all do. My first night, one of the girls said it wasn't right for me to be here, that only women can undergo the Baths, not men. I said that I didn't see what the problem was." She pulled her hair out of her bun and gave her strawberry-blond locks a flip. "The Duke agreed. He said they'd never had a transgender acolyte but that I was as welcome as any other girl."

"Do you think it will make a difference?"

Petra shook her head. "I know who I am." She put her hair back up in a bun and sat on the bed opposite Anouk. She lowered her voice. "*You're* the one I'm worried about. It was foolish for you to come with only weeks before the Coal Baths."

Anouk let out a sigh. It must have been past midnight. Her limbs were so heavy. Without her magic, she felt like she was still wandering in the woods, lost and frozen.

"I didn't have a choice." She explained about the growing plagues in London and the unlikely bargain she'd stuck with Prince Rennar, her trip to Bavaria and the awful moment when Duke Karolinge had drawn the magic out of her. She pressed a hand to her throat, wincing at how frigid her skin felt. Then she glanced at the door and lowered her voice. "What happened to Cricket and Luc and Hunter Black? You said you'd watch out for them, but Rennar has them caged in Castle Ides."

Petra ran a hand slowly over her face. "I tried to help them, I promise. But it wasn't that simple. After you fled the château with the Goblins, Rennar rounded up your friends and caged them. It wasn't like I could walk up to him and demand that he free them. He'd just murdered my mother."

"Is that why you're here? You want to become a witch so you can get revenge against the Royals?"

Petra snorted. "Give me more credit. I have loftier aims than revenge." Her eyes sparked as she leaned forward and said conspiratorially, "I have to know what magic feels like. I know that you understand. You had magic, even if it's gone now. Look at you — you look sick without it, like someone's ripped your heart out. That's because no one can live her life on the edge of a magical world and not want to be a part of it. No one can walk away from tricks and whispers, from Goblins and spells. I want it all, Anouk. Everything Mada Zola had and more."

Anouk's fingers fluttered over the base of her throat as she remembered the warm champagne fizz that was gone now. "Can the Duke be trusted?"

Petra gave a wavering head tilt. "I don't know about *trust*. Most of the girls here have only heard rumors about the Haute. They've never met a witch, let alone a Royal, so they have their Pretty little heads in the clouds. When I first arrived, the Duke invited me to his study and kept me up all night droning on about the long history of girls burned alive, trying to frighten me off. I told him what he could do with his scare tactics. Ever since then, he hasn't offered to advise me again."

"And this crux business — have you found yours?"

Petra's lips quirked in a movement that could have been a smile or a grimace. "I'm working on it." She leaned back. "When I first got here, I tried studying with Marta, learning the Selentium Vox, memorizing spells, understanding the history of magic. Marta says study takes her to a place where her soul feels whole, like her eyes are open for the first time, and that with those open eyes, she was able to see her potential cruxes in the subjects she studies, and that's how she discovered hers." Petra puffed a lock of hair out of her face. "But all I saw were dull old textbooks filled with dull old history lessons." She glanced at the window. "The Duke encouraged me to look for it in physical ways. Exercise in the courtyard, he said. Spar with Frederika, he said. Ha! I can tell you one thing—I know myself well enough to realize that I'm not going to discover my crux by sweating in the snow." She leaned forward with a smirk, a strawberry lock falling in her eyes, highlighting that fire that blazed there. "Mada Zola studied here six hundred years ago. She didn't find her crux through any of the usual ways either. She was the first Pretty to find a crux through a creative path. Every morning that she was here, she climbed down the ravine and gathered clay from the riverbed, then began sculpting it. She let her mind go blank and allowed her hands to take control. For months she shaped nothing but meaningless lumps, and the other acolytes laughed at her. But the night before the Baths, after the Eve Feast had concluded, she stayed up late and her hands worked the clay into an etching of flowers. Lavender. She found dried lavender in the Duke's storerooms and carried it into the flames with her. She was the only acolyte who didn't burn. Guess who was laughing then." She pushed back more loose strands of hair that had escaped her messy bun.

"So your plan is to experiment with mud?"

Petra's grin vanished. "*No.* But Mada Zola was my mother, even if not biologically. I know I'll discover my crux while doing something creative too. So while the other girls stay up all night with their noses in books or praying until their knees have bruises, I've been doing artwork . . . of a sort." She hitched up the hem of her dress, exposing her calf and thigh.

Anouk's eyes went wide.

Tattoos ran up Petra's leg all the way from her ankle to her thigh. They weren't like any tattoos Anouk had ever seen. Goblins adored tattoos, but theirs tended to be colorful and bizarre, things like squid tentacles holding teaspoons, and they changed them with a whisper every few weeks anyway. Petra's tattoos were abstract, bands of indigo and black, some thin as a strand of hair and some as thick as Anouk's thumb, with concentric circles at the curve of her calf.

"They're beautiful," she breathed, mesmerized. "Did you ink them into your skin yourself?"

Petra lowered her dress hem. Something prideful flashed in her eyes. "They aren't done with ink," she said. "It's an ash I made myself. After a few weeks here, I started dreaming of the battle at Montélimar. The flames destroying the lavender fields. I realized that was a sign: something charred and transformed. I etched these tattoos with a sharpened chicken bone and all kinds of burned life-essence, but the answer was so obvious. Mada Zola's crux was lavender. Mine is lavender ash—well, I think. I need a few more weeks to finish the tattoo I have in mind, see if a new dream comes to me."

A bird cawed overhead and Anouk tipped her head up and studied the ceiling.

"It's the falconry mews," Petra explained. "They're directly above our bedroom, in the abbey tower. It's where the Duke keeps his birds and maintains communication with the Royals. It's forbidden to the acolytes, except for Marta, who's in charge of cleaning all the animal cages."

Anouk's hand drifted to her neck. "Does he keep it locked?"

Petra narrowed her eyes. "What are you scheming?"

Anouk leaned forward. "When he took my magic, he enchanted

it into a ball of light that he trapped in a bell around Saint's neck. You said yourself that it's crazy to come here with only six weeks before the Baths. But it wouldn't be crazy if I had my magic. Then I could whisper a spell in the library that would show me my crux."

Petra didn't look convinced. "Saint doesn't live in the mews with the other falcons. He has a stand in the Duke's chambers. They're never apart, not even when the Duke is sleeping." She tapped her chin. "*If* he sleeps. He's always up roaming the halls with a book in his hand, even in the early hours of the morning."

Anouk fiddled with her sweater sleeves, thinking.

Petra nudged Anouk's knee with her toe. "Where's that gorgeous jacket of yours? The Faustine."

"I left it with Beau down in the cellar so he'd at least have a familiar scent. Would it really be so dangerous for him to be loose? The Duke assured me he'd be eaten."

"Hmm. Maybe; these woods are mysterious. Mada Zola told me she thought she'd met her own double there, but it turned out to be some kind of mirror creature. And there are boys and girls made of snow—"

Anouk raised her eyebrows. "I met Jak."

"You're lucky. Jak is the most tenderhearted of them." She reached out and squeezed Anouk's foot. "The Duke put me in charge of his filing—it's a nightmare of paperwork—but I have more free time than the others. I'll go down and visit Beau when I can." She yawned. "*Dieu*, it must be one in the morning. You'd better sleep if you have to be up at dawn to make breakfast. Actually, thank God you're here. It's been gruel for weeks."

Anouk gave her a smile, not sure how to convey how glad she was that Petra was here. She peeled off the sweater and her layers of warm clothes, folded them, put them in the trunk at the foot of her bed, and changed into the loose cotton shift that Esme had included in the stack of clean clothes. She closed the trunk. Her heart ached for her old room, the townhouse full of books, the closets full of beautiful clothes. She was about to climb into bed, but marks on the lid of the trunk caught her eye. Girls' names. There must have been hundreds, most of them so faded they were illegible. She grazed her fingers over the carvings.

"All the girls who have been here before us," Petra explained quietly, lying down in her own bed and pulling a blanket up to her chin. "Most—if not all—of them dead now."

A chill ruffled the hem of Anouk's nightgown. Viggo had warned her about the Cottage. She pictured him at Castle Ides, playing checkers with Goblins while drinking brandy, and something pulled taut in her chest.

She considered opening the trunk again and taking out her mirror. Checking one more time to see whether Luc was still a mouse or if Rennar had kept his promise. But in such a small room, it would be impossible to hide the mirror from Petra. And though she trusted Petra, she didn't trust the Cottage. Who knew what spy holes might be in the walls of their room, what girls or falcons might be listening outside the door? She couldn't risk the Duke thinking that that she still had the use of magic. She sat on the trunk, frowning.

"Anouk," Petra said in a serious tone, "how are you going to find your crux with just a few weeks left?"

Anouk drew in a deep breath. Beau, Cricket, Luc, Hunter Black —they needed her to succeed. It wasn't just her own fate on the line.

She glanced out the window, saw the moon high overhead. "Esme showed me the library. Is it open all night?"

If there were a million possible ways for a girl to discover her crux, then she'd better get started. She could try prayer, like Esme. Or touch all the samples of life-essences in the storerooms. Or jog through the snow barefoot, like Sam. But spells had always held a special place in her heart, as had the Selentium Vox. She might as well begin there.

Petra made a face. "You aren't seriously going to stay up all night."

"Tonight and every night. As long as it takes." She slid her feet into the coarse wool slippers she'd found by her bed, lit a candle, and headed for the library.

Chapter 11

FOR DAYS, ANOUK'S WORLD was filled with books. She spent every minute between her kitchen shifts in the library, bent over a dusty volume. She memorized hundreds of new phrases in the Selentium Vox. She learned the eleven words that meant "night," the four words that meant "day." She found a yellowing old volume on a top shelf that had been handwritten by one of the original Royals, an ancient baron of the Lunar Court, the pages so old they barely stayed intact in her hands. She memorized spells for withering trees, tricks for flooding a riverbed, whispers for mending a broken heart. Marta kept her company, though she was such an unobtrusive soul that Anouk often forgot she was there. Marta liked to study while wrapped up in a blanket on the floor, stacks of books around her, eating from a jar of pickled black walnuts. Anouk had glanced at Marta's books—they were mostly political theory of the Haute and histories of the ancient Royals. When Marta read, it was like the world stood still; the only sounds were pages turning and walnuts being nibbled.

Anouk rubbed her eyes. She'd been at the Cottage for a week and didn't have a clue what her crux might be. No lightning had struck her when she'd read references to sunflowers. She'd gotten no flashes of insight when she learned the Selentium Vox words for "fox fur."

She slammed her most recent book shut—a genealogy of previous witches and their cruxes—and opened a new one at random. Her candle flickered over a page streaked with dust. Her eyes snagged on one phrase.

Gray rainbows

She was suddenly aware of how quiet the library was. She frowned and scooted the book closer. It had been handwritten by the Pretty monks who lived here centuries ago. *Gray rainbows*. It was eerily similar to the plagues in London that Rennar had told her about. *Black rainbows,* he had said. Could it be a coincidence? She held her candle closer and kept reading.

> *. . . besieged by the curse, overtaken by the plagues. The triple moons and gray rainbows. Rainstorms of worms. Dublin . . . to Prague. A madness over the population . . . they call it . . . the Noirceur . . .*

"The Noirceur," she whispered to herself. The book was badly damaged, though the words were legible. She scanned the next few pages, which told of plagues that were similar to what was happening in London. Gray rainbows in the past, black rainbows now. Triple moons before, double moons now. Rainstorms of worms then, falling toads now. How could history written about centuries ago in a random book be repeating itself?

She ripped out the pages and put them in her pocket before rifling through the rest of the book for similar references.

. . . worms falling from the sky . . .

. . . the Noirceur, the Darktime . . .

She ripped out those pages too. She skimmed through the rest of the book until her candle burned out, and the next night, she moved onto another book written by the same monk. She spent long nights poring over the books, hoping for another passage that might explain the odd references.

One night a week later, Marta stuck her head around the shelves, startling Anouk. Marta grinned. "I'm going to get some of the leftover bread from supper. Do you want anything?"

Anouk hesitated, and then, before she could stop herself, she took out one of the pages that she'd been collecting throughout the week. She smoothed it out and tapped a word.

"Marta, have you ever come across references to something called the Noirceur?"

Marta blinked, thinking. "Not that I recall."

"Or plagues? Strange phenomena like creatures raining down from the sky, multiple moons, that sort of thing?"

Marta cocked her head. "There are some accounts like that,

legends about the early Royals. About the Snowfire Court, what is now part of the Hammer Court, far north in Siberia and Scandinavia. And there are a few ballads about the mystical King Svatyr and Queen Mid Ruath and how they banished a dark evil while dressed in fabulous bearskin cloaks and wearing glittering powder on their lips. Sometimes that 'evil' is referred to as plagues. The accounts of King Svatyr and Queen Mid Ruath aren't in any of these books, though. I saw them in the Duke's personal library while I was feeding Saint. I used to browse through the books until he caught me. Since then he doesn't let me feed Saint unless he's there."

Anouk ran her finger over the page, thinking.

"Don't take this the wrong way," Marta said hesitantly, adjusting her glasses. She motioned to the stack of books by Anouk's side. "But I don't think you're going to find your crux through study. You've been at it for almost two weeks. If you're on the right path, you don't fall asleep with your face in a book." She motioned to a drool stain on Anouk's collar. Anouk wiped it away guiltily. Marta grinned. "You need to find something that makes your soul sing. That fills you with joy like you've never known. Only that feeling can guide you to your crux."

Anouk looked around at the dreary library, at the desiccated books and the cold stone floors, so different from Mada Vittora's cozy library with its overstuffed chairs. If spending hours hidden away in here brought Marta such ecstatic joy, maybe Anouk *was* on the wrong path.

Marta leaned forward, pushing her glasses up. "You have something in you, Anouk. A fire. It was clear the night you arrived." She touched her own chest. "You want magic as bad as I do."

Anouk raised an eyebrow. "How did you learn about the Haute?"

Marta let out a puff of air and said dreamily, "I was in my first year at university. I was studying in a café for end-of-term exams. The café closed for the night, and I left to find a place where I could continue reading. I wandered the city and came across a drunk guy by the river. I was afraid he'd try to drown himself. He saw me calling to him and laughed. He said, 'Can't you see, pretty girl, that I'm walking on the water? Of course you can't. Your eyes are closed. Here, my pretty. See.' He raised the glamour and I saw him for what he was —a Royal. A minor count of the Minaret Court. That night, we sat on the riverbank and drank his wine and he told me about millennia of magic, of powerful spells, of passionate Royal affairs. I forgot about my exams. What did I care about school anymore after learning about the Haute? Screw the exams. Screw my degree. I wanted magic."

"Didn't he glamour you once the sun rose?" Anouk asked.

Marta grinned and shook her head. "He passed out. I'm not sure he ever remembered our conversation. Or me." Her face grew serious, and she rested a hand on Anouk's arm. "Do yourself a favor and stop torturing yourself with these texts. Try prayer, maybe?"

Anouk wrinkled her nose.

The antler clock in the great hall chimed three o'clock in the morning, the sound echoing through the entire abbey and reaching them in the library.

"Chores." Marta sighed.

Anouk perked up. "Could we swap?"

"Me make breakfast? I can't even boil water."

"Just for today."

Anouk didn't say anything about Little Beau, but she didn't have to. Marta seemed to understand. She reached into her pocket and set a piece of biscuit on the desk. "Just for today. Here. Give your dog this. I saved it from yesterday's breakfast. We all like him, you know."

Anouk briefly debated telling Marta that Little Beau was actually a boy with shaggy hair and a love of fast cars, but then she took the biscuit and closed her books. It wasn't until she was halfway down the cellar stairs that it hit her: as soon as winter fell, just a few short weeks away, she or Marta or, most likely, both of them would be dead, as would Esme and Petra and all the other girls.

Her thoughts were dark as she descended the stairs.

"Sang vivik."

Anouk shrieked and pressed a hand to her chest. She wasn't alone. Frederika was lurking on the landing. Her hair was its usual wild black storm cloud. Her eyebrows shadowed her eyes into dark pools.

"Frederika!" Anouk swallowed. "What did you say?"

In the two weeks Anouk had been at the Cottage, Frederika hadn't spoken a single word to her. She rarely spoke to anyone except Sam, who did the laundry, and then only to tell her that she'd torn another one of her dresses while exercising in the courtyard. Still, Anouk had felt Frederika's glistening eyes fixed on her at every meal.

"Sang vivik," Frederika repeated.

Anouk's eyebrows rose. She glanced toward the top of the stairs, wondering if anyone else was within earshot. "Is that in the Selentium Vox? Something about blood? I don't know that usage of *vivik*."

"A witch took two of your toes. Esme says."

Anouk glanced over her shoulder in the direction of the kitchen. It was after three o'clock in the morning. Karla and Lise should be there, up early to start making the daily bread, but they were both notoriously deep sleepers, and they knew that Anouk, the head chef, wouldn't scold them too severely. No sounds came from the kitchen.

"That's right." Anouk's toes curled in her shoes.

Frederika lifted two fingers to her mouth and started gently gnawing on them, all the while staring at Anouk.

"Are you all right?" Anouk took a step down the stairs, away from her. Maybe Frederika was nervous about the delivery the previous day—just after breakfast, two enchanted Pretties had shown up leading a string of mules loaded down with firewood, having just barely survived the precarious mountain path. They carried in load after load until half the courtyard was filled with stacks of wood. It had shaken Anouk when she realized that preparations were already beginning for the Coal Baths. Tomorrow, Duke Karolinge would begin the grueling, four-week-long process of whispering the wood into coals that would form the basis of the trials. Then, the Coals would need the magic of the Royal Courts to convert them into blue flame. Rennar would be there. She'd confront him about why he hadn't turned Luc back yet. She'd force a promise out of him—one sealed in magic this time.

Suddenly, Frederika pulled her fingers out of her mouth and dropped to the floor. She started doing pushups on the landing, counting out the numbers in German.

Anouk took another step away from her, then made her way down to the cellar as quickly as she could. When she got there, she closed herself up in the stall with Little Beau and swept him into a hug.

"Beau," she breathed into his fur. "This place is getting to me. What's my crux? I haven't had any insight. Nothing's called to me. If

I learned anything from the Goblins, it's that I'm not drawn to rats or cockroaches. I know it isn't roses, like Mada Vittora's crux. I like thyme, but that's only because it reminds me of Luc." She groaned. "This would be easy if I had my magic."

Little Beau went to the stall corner, took her Faustine jacket in his mouth, and dragged it over to her. He nudged it into her lap and ran his bandaged paw over the winged creature on the back. He whined softly.

Anouk reached out and scratched his head. She pulled the jacket up over the both of them, and they lay in the straw and slept a dreamless sleep.

Chapter 12

LATE NOVEMBER BLED into December, and every morning when Anouk passed through the glass-enclosed hallway outside of the courtyard on her way to prepare breakfast, she saw Duke Karolinge whispering to the coals. At the break of dawn, he would swallow a powder of rosemary and pine bark that he ground himself and then whisper into the piles of firewood. They sparked and smoked. Day after day Anouk watched the wood transform from fresh-cut logs into chunks of blackened charcoal, reducing more and more until they were each the size of her fist. More mules arrived, carrying supplies for the coming Royals and the Eve Feast: Crates of fine wine. Silk linens for the guest rooms on the upper floors. Truffles and lavender soap and argan oil, until the Cottage's normally sparse pantry was bursting with exotic treats.

She did her best to find time to visit Little Beau. She kept her distance from Frederika, who'd taken to stalking behind her around the abbey like a shadow. She checked Rennar's mirror obsessively, growing more worried as each day passed and Luc remained a mouse. It occurred to her that maybe the plagues in London were part of the reason why Rennar hadn't held up his side of their bargain. What if he'd managed to get into the city on his own? What if he'd already faced the Coven of Oxford without her? She found herself worried for his safety, and that made her worry for her *own* sanity.

She spent long hours trying to discover her crux. Each morning she rose before dawn and ran laps around the courtyard until her muscles ached. She forced herself to stand barefoot in the snow, then hold her hands an inch from the scalding stove. She memorized and practiced ritual patterns of movement that spell-casters used. She locked herself in the Duke's storerooms, even though Esme told her it was folly, and examined every herb she could find, from dried rosemary to Spanish thyme, sniffing each one, tasting them all, studying the effects they had on her to see if any one of them gave her some special spark. Then she tried the dried flowers that he stored in glass jars, laceleaf and gardenia, lotus and calla lilies. By the third week, she was desperate enough to move on to poisons. She read about each one in the stained old guidebook before carefully placing a drop of it on her tongue, but this only sent her to the infirmary with stomach cramps, where Esme made her a soothing drink of warm goat milk and honey and gave her two contraband pills (smuggled from a Pretty pharmacy in Berlin) for the pain.

"You're going to kill yourself, going on like this," Esme said, handing her the warm milk. "If you have a death wish, the Baths will take care of that for you."

Anouk gulped down the glass of milk and wiped her mouth with the back of her hand. "I have to find my crux. The Baths are in two weeks. Some Pretties came this morning on the mountain path with a delivery of fresh pears — the Royals are practically on their way."

She thought of Prince Rennar and felt a stab of pain again. What if he'd given up on her? She bent over and threw up. Esme grabbed the bucket just in time.

"You need to speak with the Duke," Esme said.

"I don't trust him."

Esme hesitated. "Yesterday the Duke asked me—pointedly—to carry a load of bandages down to Sam in the laundry room. A bunch of bloody towels spilled out—Frederika cuts herself a lot while exercising. The bloodstain on one of them formed a ring around a perfect circle of white fabric." There was a glint in her eye. "I felt like I'd hit my head. The circle of white. I just knew, Anouk. And somehow the Duke had known too. That's why he asked me to run the errand. I was wrong: My crux isn't bone. It's pearl."

Anouk raised her eyebrows. All the other girls had decided on their cruxes. Frederika hadn't outright stated that hers was poppy seeds, as Heida had insisted, but she claimed that she knew what it was. Esme had been the only one other than Anouk who hadn't yet chosen.

Esme rested a hand on Anouk's shoulder. "You still don't know what you're going to carry into the flames. The Duke could help you."

Anouk wiped her mouth. "You can't trust Royals." She hesitated. "There's a prince . . ."

Esme's eyebrows arched. "Mmm, I like princes. Go on."

Anouk looked away, toying with the damp cloth she'd used to wipe her face. "He's not just any prince. Prince Rennar of the Parisian Court. Head of all the Haute. He conspired with a witch to trap my friends and me. They're in cages now. He won't free them until I do as he wants."

"What a complete bastard. Is this prince coming for the Eve Feast?"

Anouk nodded.

"He'll be there to watch you walk the Coals?"

"Yes."

Esme leaned forward. "Then you'd better walk into those Coals as the strongest beastie in the world and walk out of them even stronger—the most powerful witch any Royal, even your prince, has ever seen."

Anouk smiled, but only briefly. "You shouldn't hope for that, Esme. The odds are poor. One out of ten. If I survive, or Marta, or Petra, or any of the girls, your own chance of survival is so much less."

"That's not how odds work."

"That's how *these* odds work. Almost every year, only one girl lives. Sometimes not even that. I can count on one hand the number of times in centuries when two have survived."

"I choose to believe that odds are meant to be defied." She rested a hand on Anouk's shoulder. "I'll let you in on a secret. Tonight, after the Duke retires to his chambers, some of us are going to walk the coals."

Anouk frowned. "You can't. The Coal Baths aren't like striking a match and sparking a fire. The Royals have to light them themselves with a whisper. They aren't here yet."

"Not *those* Coals," Esme said. Then she grinned mischievously. "Meet us at midnight in the courtyard. Bring Petra too. You'll see."

"I can't believe you talked me into this."

Petra stood in the falling snow with her blanket wrapped around her and hooded over her head. The moon was hidden by the storm clouds. Anouk hugged her own blanket around her shoulders, letting the snow land on her bare hair. The courtyard was quiet. The beds of coals that Duke Karolinge had carefully been preparing lay untouched. For a few humiliating moments Anouk wondered if Esme had been playing a joke on her—get the new girl to stand outside in the snow in the middle of the night.

But then the clock struck midnight, and she heard footsteps on the cobblestones.

"Esme?" she asked.

"Shh!" Four girls, hidden by makeshift cloaks, scurried into the courtyard. Anouk could barely make out the glint of Esme's dark skin. "We can't let the Duke hear us. The punishment for meddling with the preparations for the Coal Baths is expulsion."

Petra gave Esme a long, doubting look. "Why exactly are we meddling?"

Before Esme could answer, two more girls appeared at the far end of the cloister and tiptoed across the courtyard to join them. Anouk recognized Jolie's braid and Karla's skipping walk.

"Is this everyone?" Esme whispered to them.

"Sam's too scared to come." Jolie rolled her eyes, but she looked anxious too.

Karla gave a guilty smile. "I didn't tell Frederika about it. She's so strange! I was afraid she'd do something crazy and the Duke would find out."

Esme nodded. "Let's begin, then. You've all seen the Duke preparing the coals, right? They won't be ready until the day before the Baths, when the Royals arrive. There's nothing magical about them at the moment. They're just charcoal bricks." She grinned. "We're going to light them for a firewalk."

"Um, why?" Petra asked.

Esme gave her a sly look. "A firewalk is tradition. I found instructions carved under my bed by the previous girls who came here. Every year, acolytes walk the coals early as a sort of blessing. They say that the scariest part of the Coal Baths is taking the first step into the flames. But the eight of us will have already taken that step. Well, a practice step. For luck."

Petra rolled her eyes. It was snowing harder now and she didn't seem amused. She turned to Anouk and muttered, "There's a reason I never applied to university. I'm not a fan of hazings."

"We need all the luck we can get," Anouk countered.

Petra grumbled, but she didn't leave.

Esme produced a book of matches from her pocket. "Karla and Jolie, take some matches and light the coals from that end. Anouk and Petra, take the other end. Marta and Heida, we'll light the coals in the middle."

The girls set to work. Anouk held a flame to the nearest blackened chunk of wood, and Petra crouched by the bed of coals and poked them with a hemlock branch to stir the embers. Karla did the same, stirring the coals until they sizzled, then she tossed the hemlock branch on top and dusted off her hands.

"The real coals in the Coal Baths won't be like these," Esme explained. "They're sparked by a Royal whisper, not a match. It's possible for us to walk across these hot coals and not burn our feet, even without magic. The first thing you have to do is kick off your slippers and plunge your bare feet into the snow. Then walk quickly, but don't run. The lighter your steps, the less likely you'll disturb the coals and snag one between your toes. Saying a prayer first wouldn't hurt." She kicked off her own slippers and gave the other girls a hard look. "No screaming. No crying. Wake the Duke and we're all out."

Anouk swallowed.

"You first, Anouk," Esme said. "In the real Baths, we go in order of height. But I'm making the rules here, and it's last to arrive, first to firewalk."

Anouk didn't move. All of them stared at the live coals. No one else seemed inclined to step forward either. Heat rolled off the coals in waves. Anouk followed the wavering bands of air upward, past the falconry mews. She nearly jumped when she saw a face framed in the window. Frederika. A chill spread over her. She nudged the others and nodded toward the window. "We have an audience."

Heida shrugged it off. "Frederika won't tell the Duke. Even if she did, he'd just think she was crazy."

But Anouk couldn't shake off Frederika's presence so easily. Just that morning, Frederika had been in the kitchen before dawn when Anouk, still half asleep, arrived to start cooking their porridge. Frederika was holding a paring knife. For a second, they had only stared at each other, Anouk suddenly fully awake, an awful tension between them, and then Jolie and Karla had come in, yawning and tying their aprons, and Frederika plunged the knife into an apple, chopped off a hunk, and chewed it slowly.

Anouk reluctantly toed off her slippers. She knew that rubbing her feet in the snow would numb them and also create a layer of water that would insulate her soles from the heat. There was nothing enchanted about walking over hot coals. This was a poor substitute for magic and only made her miss the real thing fiercely.

She lifted her foot, felt a wave of heat, and winced. Even if it wasn't magic, it was still dangerous. But if she couldn't walk across plain coals, how would she walk across enchanted ones?

Heida taunted, *"Sizzle, sizzle, little worm, how I want to watch you squirm."*

"Knock it off." Petra gave Heida a shove, but Heida just snorted.

"Oh, come on! If you don't like to think about burning alive then you shouldn't have come. Admit it. We all know the odds we face. There are ten of us. We'll be lucky if one of us survives. We have two weeks left to breathe. To eat. To dream. Then . . . *sizzle, sizzle, little worm.*"

"Shh." Petra's scold was quick. "What are you, a poet now? Don't say that. More than one of us could make it. There could be two survivors." She glanced at Anouk. "It's happened before."

"Yes, *once* in the last fifty trials," Lise put in.

Esme rested a hand on Anouk's shoulder. "You're the only one who hasn't decided on her crux, Anouk. Some witches say that it was during the firewalk that it came to them, like a flash of lightning. This could be your chance."

It could be her only chance.

Anouk tossed aside her blanket and stepped onto the coals. They hissed as they burned off the wet snow that had been giving her feet a small bit of protection. Heat radiated upward around her. She clenched her jaw and took another step. Miraculously, she didn't burn. The coals felt rough beneath her feet, hot but not scalding. She walked with quick, light steps. The other girls cheered her on in hushed whispers. She grinned. It really wasn't that difficult. Then the sound of barking, close and fierce, ripped apart her concentration.

She stopped.

Little Beau was loose in the courtyard. He was by the gardening shed, with his head tilted up toward the falling snow. He was howling, howling, howling. Anouk saw it in a flash. It didn't seem real. Like a vision. She looked up in the direction he was howling, squinting into the falling snow. A bird was flying overhead. Its shape was just a dark shadow, and for a second Anouk thought it was one of Rennar's crows, but then she heard the faintest tinkling sound. A bell. It was Saint.

It all happened in a split second. But that was a split second longer than it was wise to stand on burning coals. Pain suddenly shot through her feet, and the vision—if it was a vision—disappeared. All she saw was red. She threw a hand over her mouth, stifling a scream, and sprinted the last yard. She plunged her feet into a snowbank, fell back, and stared up at the sky, breathing hard.

The other girls surrounded her.

"Are you okay?"

"Why'd you stop?"

"How did Little Beau get free?"

She sat up abruptly. So it wasn't a vision. Little Beau ran up and licked her cheek. She grabbed him by the scruff of his neck to make sure he was real. Despite her burned feet and the cold snow seeping into the rest of her, she suddenly grinned.

"Oh Lord, she's lost her mind," Karla lamented.

"No," Anouk said, grinning wider. "Little Beau just showed me my crux."

Chapter 13

❧

ESME BANDAGED ANOUK'S FEET. Petra helped her hobble up to bed. But even with their ministrations, it was ten days before Anouk could walk again. They told the Duke she'd fallen ill after eating poison sumac while trying to find her crux, and he hadn't questioned it. Petra kept her informed as the preparations intensified. Every morning, a near-constant string of enchanted Pretties arrived with mules laden down with supplies: Boxes of dried rose petals that they were ordered to sprinkle around the entire abbey. A hundred silver place settings, enough for everyone in all of the eight Courts, and a hundred crystal wine goblets. Crates of Anjou pears, Majorcan oysters, cured Spanish ham, champagne bottles packed in straw. The pantry was overflowing with fresh ingredients from all corners of the globe. The dessert pantry—usually used to store potatoes—now actually contained chocolate and marzipan and Madagascar vanilla.

Once Esme declared Anouk healed, she peeled off her bandages and carefully tested out the tender soles of her feet.

"Not a moment too soon," Petra observed coolly. "The Royals will be here in three days and it wouldn't look good to have you hobbling around." She leaned forward. "Come on, tell us. What's this crux that you discovered in a fit of burning feet? You'd better dig around the storerooms and get a sample."

"It isn't in the storerooms."

"Everything's in the storerooms. The Duke has fossils of ancient creatures I didn't think actually existed. There are seeds from some bizarre fruit tree that went extinct centuries ago. Thank God my crux isn't anything rare. Could you imagine if your connection to magic was something that existed only on, like, one random island?"

Anouk slid on her shoes, wincing slightly, then belted her dress with a rope. "Is the Duke in his study?"

Esme raised an eyebrow. "I thought you didn't trust any Royals."

"I don't."

She gave the two of them a wry smile and then gingerly made her way through the dormitory hallways and down to the private wing that housed the Duke's chambers. Through a window outside his study, she caught a glimpse of the courtyard. The coals were now almost as fine as sand; they glittered beneath the sun. The ground had been freshly swept, and chairs—more like thrones—were arranged in front of the coals. Frederika was out there now, dragging freshly cut hemlock branches into a pile, and Lise was shoveling snow.

Anouk took a deep breath and knocked on the Duke's door.

There was a pause, and then: "Come in, beastie. I've been waiting."

Anouk had never seen the Duke's private study. The only ones allowed inside were Marta, to feed Saint, and Heida and Lise, to clean. Anouk blinked, surprised by the sudden opulence. Glittering gold goblets, velvet drapes, and the books! Row after row of books, each bound in rich leather, lovingly cared for, books that looked far more valuable than the ones in the library that she and Marta had thumbed through.

Her gaze settled on Saint, perched on a stand at the end of the bookshelves, the golden bell around his neck.

The Duke was seated at his desk, writing something. He stood when she entered. "You're surprised by what you see." He motioned to the glitz. "It is not my choice. I prefer a simpler atmosphere. It is strange for a Shadow Royal not to care about pretty things, I know, but they are merely artifacts entrusted to my care. If I could, I'd ship all of them back to Castle Ides." He paused. "Except the books. Those could stay. Tell me, are you feeling better? Poison sumac, was it?"

His gaze was firmly planted on her feet in a knowing way. She cleared her throat and eyed Saint. "Yes . . . poison sumac. But I came to ask for help. The ceremony is in three days and I'm still not certain what my crux is."

"I know why you're here." He studied her for a long time, so long that she started to shift uncomfortably, and then he sighed and rubbed the bridge of his nose. "Sooner or later every acolyte comes for help."

Had Petra come? Had Esme come? Had Mada Vittora once sat here on this hard wooden bench with doubt and fear in her heart?

"I remember your mistress when she was your age."

Anouk's eyes snapped to him. "You were in charge of the Cottage then?"

"No, it was run by a duke from the Barren Court, but I came with the Royal procession to witness the Baths. I was a minor duke at the time. Sixty years old, although I looked to be about your age.

We *do* age, you know, though much more slowly than Pretties. Mada Vittora was a great beauty. She came from a seaside village in Italy, though it was the Parisian Court who enlisted her services after she survived the trials. She was so determined, so beautiful, so bold when she faced the flames. She'd seen nine other girls die before her, yet she didn't bat an eye. She clutched three long-stemmed roses and strode into the Coals and out the other side like it was nothing. We all knew she'd be a force to reckon with."

Anouk wandered down the length of the bookcase while he spoke, running her finger along the spines. "Why do you think she survived and not the other girls?"

"The simple answer is that she found her true crux. But cruxes are deceptive. They're only a symbol; there isn't any inherent magic in them. Does it matter if a girl walks into the flames holding an acorn or a feather? Not exactly. The Coals don't evaluate whether or not you've found your true crux—they determine whether you've found your true connection to *yourself*. *You* must believe you've found your crux."

Anouk reached the end of the bookshelf. Saint's perch was just a few feet away. The falcon was hooded and asleep, as best she could tell. The bell sparkled in the light of the study. "She wasn't a kind person," Anouk said.

"Heavens, no. She was a monster even as a young Pretty. But the Coals don't care if a girl is good or bad." He motioned to the books she was inspecting. "These volumes were written by the original Royals. They deal with the morality of magic. A complicated thing. It isn't like the morality of the Pretty World. Magic doesn't reward one for good deeds and it doesn't punish one for being bad. It's far more complex than that. It could take ten lifetimes to understand it."

She saw Saint out of the corner of her eye. "You've read them all?"

"Each one a hundred times."

She glanced at the door anxiously. She needed to stall for time. She blurted out, "Do they mention something called the Noirceur?"

This seemed to surprise the Duke. "That's quite an obscure reference, one I haven't heard mentioned in decades. It happened thousands of years ago, at the time of the Snowfire Court. Few Royals today know of the Noirceur. How does a beastie know of it?"

She sneaked another glance at the door. "Something I heard Mada Vittora say once."

He gave her a doubting look. "You have greater concerns than an ancient force. You came for my advice, did you not?"

A knock finally came, sharp and insistent. Anouk let out a long breath of relief.

The Duke grumbled but strode around his desk, adjusting his red cloak, to answer it. Petra was on the other side, staggering under a crate of fresh oranges.

"Ah! These just arrived," she said. "Where do you want us to put them? The pantries are full and there's a family of rats in the kitchen. I'm afraid if I leave them out, the rats will eat them."

He made a dismissive gesture toward the hallway. "Put them in the kitchen. I'll whisper away the rats."

"Thanks, and, um—"

"You're a clever girl, Petra. You can figure out where to put some fruit."

He closed the door and rubbed his nose, then turned back to

Anouk and dropped his hand, looking almost as though he'd forgotten she was there. Then he said, "You asked me about your crux."

Anouk's hands were deep in her apron pockets. "Yes. I . . . I thought that because I'm not a Pretty, my crux might be different. Something unique to a beastie. Maybe a bit of Beau's fur?"

She couldn't read the odd expression he gave her, but after a long time, he took off his glasses. "It sounds like you don't need my advice after all." He opened the door, clearly dismissing her. She was all too happy to hurry out.

She ran to the cellar, taking the stairs as fast as her tender feet could handle, and then threw open the door to Little Beau's cell and wrapped her arms around the dog. He sniffed at her pocket and she took out the bell she'd stolen while Petra had distracted the Duke.

"I made a fake bell out of an old brass cup in the kitchen," she told him. "I put that around Saint's neck instead of this one. We have to hope the Duke doesn't notice before the Baths."

In the faint light of the cellar, the bell glowed with soft green light.

Little Beau let out a low whine.

Anouk sighed. As tempted as she was to swallow it down to regain her magic, the Duke would know instantly that she'd broken the rules. Besides, Rennar had made it clear that magic wouldn't protect her from the Coal Baths.

"Everyone else's crux is something from the Pretty World," she mused. "But I'm not of the Pretty World, so why would my crux be? My crux is of the Haute. It's something magic."

She carefully stowed the bell in her pocket, then clipped off a bit of Little Beau's fur and tied it with thread; she would use it as a fake crux. Little Beau nosed her jacket again and looked at her with big eyes, letting out a heavy breath.

Over the next three days, the Cottage was a flurry of activity. Anouk barely knew when it was day and when it was night. The Royal procession was due to arrive at any moment, and the acolytes were kept busy preparing the guest rooms with fresh linens and sprinkling the requested rose petals everywhere. Anouk stayed in the kitchen with Karla and Jolie, organizing the new ingredients and planning a menu that would please eight Courts of Royals from across the near realms. She baked star-anise croissants and *pain aux raisins*. She selected a triple-crème Crémeux des Cîteaux for the cheese course, planned a winter salad with buttermilk dressing, began slow-braising the pork, set out the quail to thaw, selected brussels sprouts and pancetta to go with the salmon they were keeping on ice. And the desserts! Clafoutis fruit pie, cream puffs, upside-down tarts, chocolate gâteaux, and macarons colored with the dust from butterfly wings.

Her mind was always on the bell in her pocket. Whether she was in the ice pantry, the confectionery, or the roasting room, she checked for it obsessively. In the canning room, she was so distracted, she didn't see the shadow looming outside the door or the shovel that came rushing out of the darkness and slammed into the back of her head.

She blinked awake, coming into a blurry kind of awareness. The back of her head stung. She touched the area, and her fingers came away bloody.

Someone was dragging her.

The person pulled her down a hallway she didn't recognize until she smelled the reek of goats. She was in the cellar. She tried to lift her head but a bolt of pain shot through it. The hard ground bruised her back, ripping her muslin dress to tatters, but whoever was dragging her didn't seem to care.

She squinted through her blurry vision until a storm cloud of black hair became clear.

"Frederika! Let me go!"

She kicked, but Frederika's grip on her ankles was firm. No amount of twisting or kicking freed her. She heard fabric tearing on the floor. Frederika dragged her down a stone step, and her head smacked it, sending a starburst of pain across her vision. When the stars cleared, she found herself in the goat pen. There was a lantern on the milking table. And a knife.

Anouk scrambled to her hands and knees in the mud. The smell of goats was overwhelming. From the next stall, Little Beau started barking and scratching at his locked door.

Frederika picked up the knife with one hand and the lantern with the other.

"What are you doing?" Anouk cried, cradling the back of her head. "The Royals will be here any moment! Is this about the odds? One in ten surviving? Hurting me isn't going to help you!"

"It isn't about the odds. I need my crux before the ceremony."

"Poppy seeds?" Anouk felt dizzy. "There are some in the store-rooms . . ."

"My crux isn't poppy seeds." Frederika looked at her own reflection in the knife blade. "I knew my crux as soon as you arrived. The night before, I had a vision of a girl climbing a vine, and then there you were."

"So . . . the vine? That's what you want? Let me get my jacket. It's right in that stall. I have more seeds in the pocket."

"That's not what I need."

Anouk's stomach plunged. The cold mud was starting to make her teeth chatter. She could taste blood deep in her throat. The whole back of her neck felt tender, as if something were broken, and her ribs were just as sensitive. "If not the vine . . ."

"I dreamed of a girl who could wield magic. It's a simple idea. If I take the blood of something that changed from Haute to Pretty, and if I carry it upside down into the flames, then the opposite will happen to me: I'll go from Pretty to Haute. I'll become a witch."

"You think *I'm* your crux?"

"Not you. Your blood." Frederika removed a glass jar from her apron pocket and stepped forward with the knife. Anouk pushed herself to her feet, pressing a hand to her ribs. She felt for the bell in her apron—if there was ever a time to break the rules, it was now. But her eyes went wide. Her apron was ripped. The bell must have fallen out, into the mud . . .

She dropped to hands and knees and searched through the muck. The goats, sensing tension, bleated deafeningly. Was this why Frederika brought her here, to mask her screams?

Her hands came up empty. Her pulse raced. She'd left Rennar's mirror hidden in the trunk in her bedroom. What could she use for defense? There was the dung heap. A trough of kitchen scraps. No spare tools within reach, no loose boards . . .

Frederika lunged.

Anouk scrambled forward and braced herself against the trough. She pushed it into the center of the pen, keeping it between her and Frederika. Frederika moved left; she moved left. Frederika went right; so did she.

"Frederika, this is crazy! Beastie blood has never been a crux!"

"Only because there have never been beasties here before."

Anouk's legs, smeared with cold mud, felt sluggish. Frederika darted to the pile of tools in the far corner and grabbed a broom. Before Anouk could run, she slammed it over Anouk's shoulders. She collapsed. Frederika rammed the end of the broom into her ribs, knocking the air out of her. Her fingers slipped in the mud, searching for something, anything . . . a rock . . . a piece of wood . . . a nail . . .

Frederika slammed the broomstick down again. Anouk felt hot tears at her eyes. They mixed with the blood and mud in her mouth. She couldn't find the bell. She raised a hand to shield her head against the next blow, but Frederika slammed the broom into her shoulder. She fell back, out of breath. Tried to sit up. Her fingers found the trough, reeking with rotted vegetables for the goats. She tried to pull herself up but her arms gave out and she collapsed back.

Frederika raised the knife.

"Let. Her. Go."

Frederika turned toward the new voice. Anouk tossed her head up. Petra, crowbar in hand, stomped through the muck and knelt next to Anouk. She rested a hand on Anouk's back. Her fingers came away with blood and she grimaced.

"You're *complètement folle*, Frederika! This is a place for sane people! The Duke will throw you out when I tell him."

104

"This is a place for Pretties," Frederika said, her face red. "For *girls*." There was an edge to her words.

"For girls," Petra repeated with an equally sharp edge. "Not a place for me either, is that what you mean?"

Frederika's eyes blazed. "You weren't born a girl."

Petra let out a harsh laugh. "The Duke doesn't care about that."

"It isn't up to the Duke. It's the Coal Baths that determine who will live and who will die. What will happen when you step into the blue flames and the magic there senses that someone born as a boy has—"

"Shut your *fichu* mouth." Petra let go of Anouk, grabbed a rotten apple from the goat trough, and slammed it into Frederika's mouth before she could react. Frederika doubled over and coughed out rotted, wormy bits.

Little Beau continued to bark viciously from his stall.

"I've got your back," Anouk whispered to Petra.

"I've got yours."

Frederika raised her knife. Anouk grabbed a shovel from the tool pile in the corner, and a pitchfork for Petra.

A rumble began in the coal chute, though no coal had been delivered to the abbey in decades. All three of them whipped around. Something from outside was coming in with the sound of frantic movement and cries. Before anyone could close the coal-chute door, a storm of wings rushed in. Birds! There must have been hundreds. Crows. Ravens. Falcons. Even a few owls, their eyes round and yellow. Anouk clutched the shovel, staring, transfixed. The birds circled the goat pen, flapping their sharp wings, cawing their deafening cries.

Frederika ducked to cover her head.

And then as soon as they'd come, the birds circled and poured out through the coal chute again, leaving the goat pen in a thunderous silence. Anouk dared to raise her head again. The sound of cawing came from high above and they looked upward.

"They've moved on to the courtyard," Petra said, tracing the sound from room to room overhead. "And there . . . now it sounds like they've moved to the great hall."

The shrill whistle of Duke Karolinge's falcon call pierced the din, and Frederika jumped as though she was conditioned to respond to the whistle just as his birds were. Muttering a curse, Frederika sheathed the knife in her apron. "I have to have a crux before tomorrow."

Petra, blood trickling from her lip, waved her toward the stairs. "Well, there'll be no murder today, so *va se faire foutre.*"

Frederika gave them a long, unreadable look, then turned and climbed the stairs.

Petra snorted. Anouk fell to her knees, dug through the mud, and sighed in relief as her fingers at last closed around something small and hard. She wiped it on her apron. The bell.

"What's that?" Petra asked.

"Nothing." She pushed herself to her feet. "Those crows." She coughed. "I recognize them. They belong to Rennar."

"What does that mean?"

"The Royals are here."

Petra cocked an eyebrow. "From Paris?"

Anouk shook her head. "From *all* of the realms."

Chapter 14

PETRA AND ANOUK HURRIED UPSTAIRS, and Anouk cleaned her wounds as best she could; fortunately, the gash at the back of her head had stopped bleeding. They washed off the mud and changed clothes and then found the rest of the acolytes gathered in the enclosed cloister to watch the Royals' arrival, their breath fogging the glass.

The Royal procession descended upon the Black Forest like something out of a dream. The flock of birds was only the first herald. Next, the treacherous mountain path, normally accessible only by foot or by mule, smoothed and unrolled itself, carpet-like, into a meandering road that led across the bridge to the abbey's front steps. Birch trees curled their branches inward to form an archway. Snow swept itself to either side of the road and rose up in ice statues.

Anouk and Petra kept carefully to the back of the group of girls, placing as much space as they could between themselves and Frederika, who threw them wild-eyed stares.

"Look," Jolie cried. "That must be the Court of the Woods!"

They had all heard rumors of the various Courts, and it turned into a fabulous game of guessing which Court was which and trying to name the princes and princesses who stepped out. The Court of the Woods' delegation drove up in a hunter-green Daimler with spotless chrome and oak running boards. It purred as it stopped in front of the bridge, and a princess dressed in thick furs climbed out on the arm of a duke in an ink-black suit. Behind the Daimler, a pair of cream-colored coupes that the girls guessed belonged to the Crimson Royals pulled up, and a delegation of three—the queen and her sisters—climbed out, their eyelashes and brows dusted in butterfly wings. Next to arrive was the Lunar Court, composed of a gray-haired king and his brown-skinned son, whose barely tamed long hair was swept back in a loose plait. The Minaret Court came in a horse-drawn carriage that, no doubt, had been glamoured to look like something mundane to the Pretties in the valley—a trolley car, perhaps. A count and countess descended, both dressed in red capes and with garnets dotted around their eyes.

"Where's the Court of Isles?" Marta asked. "They're missing."

Anouk kept her mouth shut. She'd been careful since her arrival not to tell anyone but Petra about the Coven of Oxford's takeover of London. She liked most of the acolytes but that didn't mean she trusted them. They were all willing to risk their lives for magic— it wasn't a stretch to think they might try to seek favor among the Haute by warning the Oxford witches that Anouk and Rennar were planning their downfall.

A fleet of silver motorcycles that could only belong to the reckless Barren Court arrived, and the missing London Royals were forgotten.

There was one car left at the end of the procession, a sleek black Rolls-Royce with a gleaming hood ornament in the shape of a crow instead of a winged woman. Anouk drew in a breath. She'd seen it before, outside the townhouse and in front of Castle Ides. The door opened and there he was, Prince Rennar, dashing in his frost-gray suit and crown of golden briars. A few of the acolytes sighed. He limped only slightly. If you didn't know his right leg was made of stone, you might not even notice.

Two lesser Parisian Royals accompanied him: a young black man wearing a hat that shaded his face and a preteen girl in a silver gown and glass slippers with polished black claws affixed to each of her fingernails. She bore an uncanny resemblance to Countess Quine, who had been dead for months and whose body, as far as Anouk knew, was still at the Château des Mille Fleurs, decomposing in the rose beds. She hadn't known that Quine had a daughter, but the Royals valued family only as far as lineage. It was entirely possible the girl had wanted her mother dead as much as Anouk had.

"I thought Prince Rennar's entourage would be twice that size," Sam mused. Anouk felt a stab of guilt—it would have been twice that size if Anouk hadn't killed the other members.

Jolie let out a long sigh and stroked her braid dreamily. Seeing the glittering princes and princesses setting their fine shoes on the abbey grounds only highlighted how bleak their home truly was. Bare floors. Dust and the cobwebs. The eternal winter.

Anouk glanced again at Frederika. A bruise was blooming on the girl's left temple, although it was mostly hidden by her hair.

A car door slammed and Anouk's attention returned to the Royals. The Crimson Court delegation's vehicle seemed to have bumped fenders with another delegation's. Curt words were exchanged between the Court of the Woods and the Barren Court, and then, suddenly, the girls heard someone pointedly clearing his throat right behind them.

Several of the girls jumped.

Duke Karolinge gave them a stern look. "Girls. You've seen cars before. You've seen dresses and diamonds. Don't embarrass yourself by swooning over riches. Show the Royals that you are not impressed by their glamour; you didn't fight your way here to learn how to shroud yourself in luxury. You came with nobler aims." He added in a gentler voice, "Tomorrow you will have your chance to prove your worth."

A ripple of anxiety spread through the girls. As dazzling as the Royals' glitz was, it heralded the next day's deadly trials.

"Today, however," the Duke continued, "is just like every other day. There are chores. Responsibilities. *Go*." He barked the command and the girls leaped to attention. "Do a final check of the guest rooms. Freshen the rose petals. Glasses of champagne waiting in each room. Anouk." He rested a heavy hand on her shoulder. She flinched, all too aware of the bell hidden in her clasped palm. "They'll expect perfection from tonight's Eve Feast."

Her shoulders relaxed when she realized he was talking about her cooking. "They'll have it." *Not that they deserve it.*

His black eyes held hers for a long second, and she felt her cheeks burning as brightly as the stolen bell. She threw herself into a long, sweat-soaked afternoon over the kitchen stove.Sam and Karla were abuzz with gossip as they helped her chop and peel. They discussed which Royal lady wore the loveliest dress, which had the most enviable shoes, which young men they'd sneak into a closet with. If anyone knew about Frederika's attack that morning in the goat pen, it was forgotten, eclipsed by the Royals' arrival.

While preparing courses, Anouk stole glimpses out the kitchen windows, but she never caught sight of Rennar. He was likely in one of the elegant upper chambers with the other guests, sipping something sweet, speculating about which girl might survive the Baths. She wondered if he'd told the other Royals about her—the beastie girl he'd bargained with—or if their deal was a secret.

While the soufflé was baking, she grabbed the leftover ham scraps and stole away to visit Little Beau. When she reached the bottom stair, she made out a figure kneeling in the mud in front of Little Beau's stall. She slowed, uncertain, the memory of Frederika's ambush that morning still fresh. She grabbed one of the shovels. But from the clothes, she could tell that the person was a Royal. He was whispering something too low for her to hear. She curled her fingers around the shovel handle. If he tried to hurt Little Beau . . .

"Excuse me, monsieur." Her words were hard.

The man turned. She couldn't see his face in the shadows, but she recognized the hat. It was the baron who'd arrived with Rennar. He took a step into the lamplight.

Anouk's throat went tight. It was a face she hadn't expected. She was used to seeing his face dusted with potting soil, not rouge.

"Luc?" Her voice was breathy, uncertain. She felt as though she were seeing a ghost. Then he grinned and the spell broke.

"Dust Bunny."

"Luc!" She dropped the shovel, stumbled toward him, and tripped over a basket of eggs, but he caught her before she fell. Laughing, she ran her hands over his arms and the sides of his face. "You're here! You're . . . *you!*"

"I came with Rennar from Paris."

"But you were—"

"A mouse? Don't remind me. He changed me back six weeks ago. I've been at Castle Ides with Viggo and the Goblins, keeping them company. Yesterday, Rennar handed me these pretty clothes and said we were taking a trip to the Black Forest. You can imagine my surprise. Which was even greater when he explained he'd made a deal with you and that my humanity was the prize."

Anouk shook her head, confused. "But I saw you just this morning in an enchanted mirror. You were still a mouse in a cage."

"Ah. What you saw was a different mouse, not me. Rennar changed me right away, but it seems the cat and the wolf had gotten used to having a mouse caged next to them. It kept them from wanting to kill each other. So Rennar had the idea of putting a regular mouse in the cage to distract them."

Anouk groaned. "He might have bothered to send me a message. I spent weeks thinking he'd backed out of our deal, thinking you were still trapped!"

Luc rested his hands on her shoulders. "It's okay. I'm me. And I've missed you, Dust Bunny. I came down here as soon as I could slip away from the Royals because I knew that wherever Beau was, you'd be nearby. Anouk, you can't seriously be considering undergoing the Coal Baths."

She lifted her chin. "I'm here, aren't I? Of course I'm serious."

He muttered something under his breath. "You must have hit your head. You can't trust the prince."

She dropped her voice. "He claims he's tired of ruling. He's agreed to give up his power and put it in the hands of the other orders, even to let the Pretties make some of their own decisions."

Luc gave her an odd look.

"Look, I don't trust him either, but we're facing the same threat, and in a sense that makes us allies. Have you heard what's happening in London?"

Luc's face turned grave. "Yes. It's all the talk in Paris. As soon as Rennar turned me human, I heard it on the lips of every lesser Royal. It's all over the scryboard wires too. Double moons. Black rainbows. Apparently, when it first happened, the Pretties in London panicked. The witches cast a spell to convince them it was only an optical illusion caused by low-lying pollution. Still, the Haute is worried. There's never been anything like this before."

"That's just it," Anouk insisted, "there *has* been. I found something here in the Cottage library. The books are old, but the few pages I could salvage made reference to plagues that aren't so different from the ones happening now. Gray rainbows instead of black ones. Three moons in the sky instead of two. Rainstorms of worms instead of toads. All of this happened five hundred years ago, across all of Europe, from Dublin to Prague. These plagues occur whenever the balance between technology and magic is upset. It's referred to as the Noirceur, or the Darktime. Someone must have erased it from all the modern Royal records, but whoever it was overlooked the Cottage library. And the Duke has more books in his private collection, but I'm not allowed in."

"You've broken into locked libraries before. Why don't you use a whisper?"

She haltingly explained to him what had happened with her arrival and Saint's bell. Luc's face turned very grim. "Anouk, you've been here this whole time without your magic?"

She nodded reluctantly, then thrust a hand in her fresh apron and pulled out the bell. She smiled. "A few days ago, I stole it back. I'm going to carry it into the flames with me."

"*That's* your crux? Are you sure? The odds of survival are one out of—"

"I know." Her fingers closed over the bell as her smile disappeared. "*Alors,* don't remind me."

The bell, her crux, would keep *her* alive, but she didn't want to think about what that meant for the others. Petra. Esme. Marta. Jolie and Karla and Sam. Heida and Lise. Even Frederika. If she lived, odds were the others wouldn't.

"You have to be completely certain, Anouk. You aren't a Pretty, and the flames are designed to test Pretties. Who knows what they'll make of you."

She frowned at him. "Don't make it sound like I'm spoiled cabbage, Luc. I'm a beastie and you are too. That's nothing to be ashamed of."

"Of course not, but is it enough to protect you from the fire?"

She shoved the bell in her pocket. "I'm certain, Luc. I promise."

Music began playing in the great hall overhead. Luc didn't move, but Anouk tipped her chin up, listening keenly. It was a dreary dirge on violin and viola, but hearing any music at all at the Cottage was like stumbling on a coconut-cream cake in a cemetery.

"The Eve Feast is starting. *Zut,* I haven't finished mulling the wine." She eyed Luc's baron's crest more closely. "No one knows you're a beastie?"

He adjusted his hat. "Not a bad disguise, eh?"

"We can use this. If the Royals think you're one of them, you can listen in for any mentions of the Coven of Oxford or the plagues in

London. For all we know, some of the Royals might be in league with the witches. Could you do that?"

"Dust Bunny, I didn't just water roses for Mada Vittora. I've been a spy longer than you've been alive."

"Go, then," she said, giving him a gentle push toward the stairs.

The music stopped and was replaced by the Duke's muffled voice. He must have been introducing each of the delegations as part of his welcome speech. Luc reached the stairs but then raised a finger and circled back. "Ah. I almost forgot." He reached into his pocket. "I brought this for Beau. He loved cupcakes." He produced a slightly smushed miniature cake with dark brown frosting.

"Dogs can't have chocolate, Luc."

Little Beau, on the other side of the bars, whined low and insistently. Anouk knelt down and scratched his head, then fed him the ham scraps she'd pilfered from the kitchen. He wagged his tail.

Luc started for the stairs.

"Hold on." She snatched the cupcake out of Luc's hand. "Give me that. There's no rule that says *I* can't have chocolate." She took a hefty bite, and for a wondrous but too-brief second, she leaned against the stairwell and savored the taste.

She finished it, then dusted off her hands. "Right. *Now* we can face the most powerful people in the world."

Chapter 15

THE EVE FEAST TRANSFORMED the normally bleak great hall into a banquet room from out of a fairy tale. In lieu of musicians, Royals summoned music from the elements: piano from the snow hitting the windows, timpani from the stones that made up the church walls, violin from the flames licking the hearth. Delicious smells rose from the serving dishes Anouk and Jolie and Karla brought out from the kitchen, cinnamon and pineapple, orange and nutmeg. The twin dining tables, so rough-hewn that the girls got splinters while eating their porridge, were now draped in shimmering gold lace that caught the candlelight. The Royals' soft chatter, flowing in and out of a dozen earthly and magical languages, was pierced by laughter. The antler clock in the nave had changed its carvings to show depictions of fir boughs and stags.

The Parisian Court had the center of one of the tables, next to the Crimson Court princesses, one of whom kept purring in Rennar's ear, her long red fingernails tracing small circles against the sleeve of his suit. On Rennar's other side, Quine's daughter sipped watered-down wine, looking bored, waving a black-clawed finger in and out of the candle flame before her.

Luc was seated across from Rennar, next to a trio of empty places that should have belonged to the Court of Isles from London and that was marked with their crest of obsidian and diasporite.

"This makes me think of your story," Anouk whispered in Luc's ear as she served him a fat slice of blackberry pie. "'The Northland Maidens.'"

He raised an eyebrow. "The Northland Maidens" was a tale of seven beautiful girls selected each year by the village priestess in a land where the sun never set. There was a grand feast in the girls' honor with plum wine and venison steaks, the lion's share of the village's winter food stores. The girls' cheeks and shoulders were dusted with tinted sugar, and they were draped in garlands of fir; the villagers took turns serving them. At the end of the feast, the seven girls were thrown into the sea to appease the ancient gods.

Luc's dessert fork hovered over the pie. "That's a bleak comparison, Dust Bunny."

Anouk nodded toward the other acolytes, serving the Royals wine and dessert. "But accurate. Tonight a feast; tomorrow some of us will be dead." Bitterness filled her mouth, and she swiped the fork from his hand and stole a bite of pie. The taste of dark berries and butter lingered on her tongue. "At least in the story, the maidens were the guests of honor at the feast; they didn't have to be the servants." She jerked her chin at the Crimson princess flirting with Rennar. "Do you think they suspect they're dining with a beastie?"

"You think they'd still be sitting here if they did?" He took the fork back from her pointedly and dropped his voice even more. "Listen, do you really believe Rennar will give all this up? This glamour? This power?"

Across the table, the princess kept purring in Rennar's ear. A drunken smile teased the corners of his lips, but it didn't match the sober look in his eyes.

"I think there could be more to the prince than we know," she said noncommittally. In truth, the pie was sitting like a heavy stone in the pit of her stomach. The feast did feel eerily similar to the one for the ill-fated Northland Maidens. The end of the feast didn't mean certain death in a watery grave to appease ancient gods, but still, her odds weren't good. Then again, when had her odds *ever* been good? She'd defied the odds countless times. She'd survived Mada Zola's machinations. She'd battled topiary soldiers and Marble Ladies. She'd faced a frozen death in the Black Forest and lived. She touched the outside of her dress, feeling the lump of the bell for reassurance.

She became aware of a sense of being watched. Across the table, the Crimson princess with the red nails was entwining her fingers with Rennar's, whispering something into his ear, but Rennar's eyes were fixed on Anouk.

She tipped up her chin, put plates and cutlery on a silver tray, and took it back to the kitchen. She could still feel his eyes on her back. Was he also thinking of the unlikely odds? Wondering if he'd placed his bet on a poor choice?

Her mind was so absorbed with the story of the seven sacrificed girls that she didn't register the sound of a shoe scuffing the ground as she passed the confectionery. She squeaked as two hands tugged her into the dark pantry and shut the door behind her. The silver tray slipped from her hands and she cringed, awaiting the crash of broken plates and cutlery, but—

There was only silence.

Then: *"Incendie flaim."*

The voice was like crackling coals; a voice she knew. A flame sputtered to life in the palm of Prince Rennar's hand. It threw back the shadows and lit up both of their faces as well as the shelves, normally bare but now laden with chocolate bars and flour sacks and tins of marzipan.

She glanced down.

The silver tray, with its spilled plates and cutlery, floated six inches from the floor.

"Maigal doucie," he whispered, and the silver objects rested themselves on the ground as quietly as an exhale. Anouk realized she'd been holding her breath.

"That's a pretty trick," she said in a low enough voice that they wouldn't be overheard. The flame lit up a smear of pastel blue on his bottom lip — the powder he'd swallowed to cast the whisper. On instinct, she reached up and wiped it away.

His head turned slightly, following her finger.

She jerked back her hand. "You . . . had powder on your lips. It was bothering me." She swallowed. "Always the maid, I guess."

Her cheeks were warming. She started to pick up the fallen tray but, to her surprise, he cupped her chin and smoothed his thumb over her own bottom lip.

"And you have pie on yours." He licked the smear of blackberry pie off his thumb. "It doesn't bother *me.*"

For a moment Anouk was caught in the spell of the aromas surrounding them — spices and peppermint and warm flaky crusts, smells that she'd missed. Hard to believe that just steps away were the cold, dreary hallways of the abbey.

She cleared her throat. "And why, exactly, have you abducted me to the dessert pantry?"

His teasing eyebrow fell, and the look in his eyes grew serious. "Luc told me you found information about the Coven."

Curls of frigid air were drifting in from a crack in the door. Anouk shivered, wishing she could regain the spell of simpler times: warm, sugary delights. "Not about the Coven, exactly, but about the source of their magic. The Noirceur. Have you heard of it?"

He shook his head, but then stopped, as if he were remembering something from centuries ago. "Maybe."

"It's an ancient time, the Darktime. When plagues like what's happening today were common, when the balance between magic and early forms of technology was even more unstable than it is now. The Duke has books about it in his private library. Tomorrow, everyone will be distracted during the Coal Bath trials. You and I can't go missing—our absence would be noticed. But not Luc's. No one's even looked hard enough to realize he's a beastie you dressed up as a baron. He can break into the Duke's library and steal the other references to the Noirceur. If we can figure out the source of the Coven's magic, maybe we can stop it."

Rennar nodded. "Good." But he hovered near the jars of caramel, looking as though he had something else to say. He favored his right leg slightly.

The cold air bit at Anouk's bare heels. "What is it?"

He tipped his head toward her and said quietly, "Luc said you lost your magic."

She sucked in a sharp breath. "It was taken."

"Regardless, it's a problem. It changes things." He paused and then confessed, "I don't think you should undergo the Baths tomorrow. It's too much of a risk."

"Don't worry. I have it back—in a sense. It's my crux, in the form of a bell. I'm going to carry it into the flames in the morning."

He studied her carefully. "Are you sure?"

She gave him a hard look. "Is this just you trying to get out of our deal? Luc in exchange for Viggo and the Goblins. Hunter Black when I become a witch. Cricket for marrying you. I've kept up my side so far. The other beasties—"

"Anouk, forget the other beasties. You can have Hunter Black. You can have Cricket. Come back with me now and I'll change them before your eyes. Our bargain is just a silly game—don't you see that? I'll concede if it means you don't risk killing yourself." When she stared at him blankly, he added, "Every girl thinks she's found her crux. Every girl has some vision or dream. Every girl steps into the flames thinking she'll be the one to walk out the other side. You say you're sure, but you can't truly know."

The smell of cinnamon was starting to burn her throat. She rested a hand on her chest, taking slow, deep breaths. "What about the Coven of Oxford? I can't defeat them without strong magic. *Witch* magic. Otherwise, what does it matter if Cricket and Hunter Black and Luc and Beau are human or not? We won't be human or animal or *anything* if the Coven takes over Paris."

Rennar hesitated a second too long. His hand drifted to the toosmooth place on his neck, below his ear, where he'd been nearly cut in half. Then he moved his hand down his torso, as though tracing the injury. "We'll find another way."

She grabbed his hand. "What other way? You said it yourself—you need me, and you need me to be more powerful than the witches. The only way for me to do that is to undergo the Coal Baths. The other beasties can't do it; they can't cast whispers as well as I can."

"If the Coven takes Paris and the near realms, we'll flee to the far realms."

"The Coven will spread there too. It's just a matter of time."

He cursed in a mix of French, the Selentium Vox, and a language so ancient Anouk had never heard it before. He let go of her hand. "Fine. Kill yourself, if you're so determined to die."

"I'm not going to die." She balled her hand into a fist. "Why do you even care?"

His eyes smoldered in the shadows. "I've known princesses. I've known queens. I've never known anyone who was meant to be a monster but who baked pies instead, who danced with Goblins, who loved a witch, who never hated a single thing in the world. Except me, perhaps."

"I don't hate you."

"Well, wait until we're married."

He paced in front of sacks of marshmallows, dragging his right leg slightly, then turned sharply toward her. Impulsively, he took her face in his hands. Then he pressed his lips to hers. The pantry went dark — the flames in his palm had been extinguished by their touch. Surprised, she leaned back against the racks of cooling pies. Cherry. Pecan. Chocolate cream. The rich smells made her lightheaded. Rennar put his a hand on her waist and deepened the kiss. His fingers pulled gently against the fabric of her dress, inching her closer. She reached a hand up, thoughtlessly, to touch his jaw. He let out a small sigh and kissed her again. Had she gone mad? Every Royal in Europe was mere steps away. Luc was just beyond the door. Beau was in the cellar, even if he was, currently, a dog. But Rennar's lips tasted of powdered sugar. She'd missed such little comforts. The flavor of something sweet. The touch of another person.

She pulled back abruptly. The pantry was so dark that she couldn't see his face. "What was that for?"

He whispered another flame to light in his palm. There was an edge in his eyes again, that arrogant mask the Royals wore to hide what they truly felt. But as the flames danced in his hand, the mask slipped a little.

"In case I don't get another chance."

He closed his fist, extinguishing the light again. She heard uneven footsteps and then the door swung open and he disappeared back into the feast. The door shut behind him.

In the dark, Anouk sank onto a lumpy bag of flour. She gently touched her lips. They still tasted like powdered sugar.

Chapter 16

THAT NIGHT, ANOUK TOSSED and turned in bed. It was likely that every acolyte in the Cottage was lying awake, wide-eyed, minds heavy with what the morning would bring. Only the Royals, in their sumptuous guest rooms on the upper floor with their bellies full of Anouk's *soufflé au fromage*, would be getting any sleep. For them, the Coal Baths were little more than a game. Anouk imagined them as spectators betting on racehorses, watching some girls die and others live, distressed only by their failed wagers. To beings who had lived for centuries, what were a few more dead Pretties?

At dawn, the ten acolytes kept their heads low as they filed down the stairs to the bathhouse, where enchanted Pretty servants who had come with the Royals bathed them in herbed warm water, rubbed them with sweet almond oil, and gave them stiff, gray robes woven from Icelandic sheep's wool to wear. Anouk tugged the coarse fabric over her head. A Pretty fastened a crimson sash around Anouk's waist. Anouk ran her hands over the fabric, thinking once more of the Northland Maidens.

"Mada Zola wouldn't have been caught dead in plain wool," Petra muttered to Anouk. "I guarantee she found a way to line her robe with silk."

They began the procession back up the stairs, their bare feet quietly scuffing on the steps. Anouk stared numbly at the back of Petra's messy strawberry braid. Duke Karolinge was waiting for them. He threw open the nave doors to the cloistered courtyard.

Anouk shivered, shielding her eyes from the light, and hung back. A cold breeze siphoned off the warmth from her bath. It was a bright but gray day, threatening snow. Never a joyful place, the courtyard was usually full of frozen mud puddles, a few scrawny chickens pecking the ground, and Frederika doing pushups. Now the bed of coals was here, powder-fine and raked to perfection. Wooden planks were laid out over the mud beneath the aster tree. The other girls were already in the middle of the courtyard, lining up by height. Esme was at the head of the line, Heida next to her, then Marta, then Petra. Anouk was next to Petra, followed by Lise, Jolie, Karla, and Sam at the end. Frederika should have been in fourth place, in front of Petra — but she wasn't with the others.

Anouk frowned.

Before she could think, a hand shot out of the shadows and pain blasted through her side. She held in a cry. The ache felt like a spear straight through her ribs.

"It isn't personal," Frederika whispered, leaning out of the shadows. "But I need my crux."

Frederika dug the blade deeper into Anouk's side. Anouk fell against the doorway, breathing hard. Frederika pulled her breakfast napkin out of her robe and pressed it to Anouk's side, soaking up the blood, and before Anouk could even think to scream, Frederika palmed the blood-soaked napkin and went to take her place as fourth in line.

Anouk clutched at the doorway. The pain in her side was like fire.

Everyone's attention was on the other eight acolytes lining up in front of the bonfire. No one had seen her and Frederika in the shadows, but now Petra was standing on tiptoe, looking for her. Their eyes met. Petra gave her a questioning look. Anouk sucked in a breath. She adjusted the folds of her robe to hide the wound. If Rennar or Luc saw the blood, there was no way they'd let her go through with this. Weakened and bleeding was far from ideal. But they hadn't seen her vision the night of the firewalk. A wound didn't matter, not as long as she had the right crux.

She tried as hard as she could to ignore the pain and took a few careful steps to her place between Petra, who was an inch taller than her, and Lise, who was a hair shorter. Her stomach churned at the thought of watching Petra writhing in the flames, but then the pain in her side flared and it took all her strength to remain standing.

"Hey, you okay?" Petra whispered.

Anouk nodded. Sweat dripped down her temples despite the chill. Her eyes flashed to Frederika, who hid the bloody cloth in the palm of her hand.

The chapel bell rang, long and foreboding, piercing the winter quiet, and the southern doors opened. The Royals filed out, pulling up their fur-lined hoods and slipping on leather gloves. They chatted among themselves; one of the women even laughed. Anouk stared at them, speechless. Rennar was in the midst of them, a mug of some hot liquid in hand, the hint of a smile on his face, all of them looking as though they were preparing to ice skate, not watch girls die.

Nothing but a game to them.

Luc, at least, wasn't among them. Anouk glanced up at the Duke's library, searching the windows for his shadow.

One of the members of the Crimson Court stepped in a puddle and her boot broke through the ice. Mud splashed on her hem. She let out a cry, and the brooding Lunar Court prince dashed to assist her.

"Please, my lady. Allow me."

He touched powder to his lips and cast a whisper that turned the puddles into beautiful frozen ponds. Not to be outdone, the Court of the Woods delegates turned to the four corners of the cloisters and summoned roaring bonfires that chased away the worst of the cold. Then they all took their seats, sipping hot drinks.

Duke Karolinge swept out of the nave in his crimson cloak, Saint perched on his shoulder. The Duke looked enormous and daunting, the beast she had seen her first night. He'd tucked his quiet academic persona into his pocket along with his crooked spectacles.

"Acolytes, welcome. Royals of the Courts of the Near Realms, welcome. We gather today to observe an ancient tradition. The Coal Baths were founded fifteen hundred years ago, during the Merovingian dynasty. Prior to that, our realm was accessible only to those who had been born of magic." He tilted his head to acknowledge the Royals, and it irked Anouk that he didn't mention the Goblins, whose lineage was just as magical as the Royals', if not more. But Goblins weren't invited to the Baths unless it was to clean up afterward.

"There have always been the odd Pretties who discovered our existence, whether through honest trade with us or through accidental means. For millennia the Pretties were seen as simple folk, sheep in need of a shepherd. But the Merovingians believed they could be something more, that through hard work and sacrifice, some could even join our ranks. Many Pretties died in attempts to gain our magic. But with the help of the ancient creatures who call these woodlands home, a few bold women discovered the power of the Coal Baths. This abbey has, for centuries, been the seat of these ancient coals. You ten acolytes, like those first women, have risked much for a chance to enter our world. Your bravery is acknowledged by the Royals here today who have come to bear witness." He made a sweeping gesture to the Royals, who didn't bother to stop chatting with one another, indifferent to the dramatic presentation. The only exception was Rennar, who tented his fingers and watched with a hooded expression. Quine's daughter leaned toward him and spoke a few words. He shook his head quickly.

"If it were in my authority," the Duke continued, speaking to the girls, "I would grant each of you the powers for which you have labored so hard. But it is not up to me. The flames determine which girls have discovered their connection to magic. You have each selected a crux. I pray you have chosen wisely." He turned to the Royals, and, as if sensing the end of a speech they must have heard hundreds of times before, they stopped talking. "Royals, do you witness?"

"We witness," they replied.

"And acolytes, do you burn?"

"We burn," they said in unison.

"It is time for the Lighting of the Fires."

The cloisters grew very quiet. Even the wind stilled. The Royals straightened in their thrones, and all touched some powder from the vials around their necks to their lips, staining them vibrant hues of green and orange and blue. In unison they began whispering in voices that formed an eerie harmony, like a church hymn spoken in the Selentium Vox. There was strain in their faces. Despite the many times they'd performed this ceremony, it never became any easier. This wasn't any simple fire-casting trick. Gradually the raked coals began to smoke. Sparks caught, shooting out from the beds. A red glow began deep in the coals. The fire burned hotter and hotter, throwing off waves of heat that made sweat break out on Anouk's face even though she was twenty paces away.

The voices of the Royals rose. The Minaret Court stood, arms extended, then the Lunar Court, and then the Court of the Woods. Soon all of them were standing, chanting in a clash of loud whispers, and Anouk wanted to slam her hands over her ears. With a flash like lightning, the powder-like coals crystalized to glass. The red glow gave one final throb and then burst into a blue so bright, Anouk had to look away.

The Royals stopped chanting. Once more the courtyard was silent except for the crackling flames. One by one the Royals retook their seats and reached for a drink of something strong.

The wound in Anouk's side throbbed. She pressed a hand to it, feeling suddenly uncertain. She turned quickly to Petra and grabbed her hand.

"If only one of us makes it," she whispered fiercely, "promise that the one who survives helps the other beasties and the Goblins."

There'd been a time when she'd considered Petra her enemy. But after those long nights in their dormitory bedroom dreaming of magic, she'd come to see herself in the witch's girl, and vice versa. Two girls who wanted everything, and would do anything to get their hearts' desires.

Something passed over Petra's face. Anouk almost expected her to ask what was wrong, but instead, she said quietly, "I promise."

The sky was darkening overhead, threatening snow. The smell of tea and wood smoke was heavy in the air. Duke Karolinge laid a hemlock bough over the glass coals, and the brilliant blue flames dulled into a blue so thin and faint it was nearly invisible, but Anouk knew that the most dangerous things weren't always the brightest.

The bitter aroma of hemlock filled the courtyard.

"Esme," Duke Karolinge announced. "You're first."

If Esme was afraid of the flames, she did not show it. With bare feet she stepped onto the soft boughs of hemlock, and then, clutching a pearl between her palms, lifted her chin high and walked straight into the flames. Her face contorted but she didn't cry out. She clasped the pearl harder and took another step. The other girls watched from the line, riveted. The Royals observed with decidedly less interest. Esme took another step, wincing. The rippling flames distorted her figure so that Anouk couldn't make out the expression on her face. The flames ate away at her gray robe. But her body wasn't burning; there were no eyelashes caught on fire, no sizzling skin. And yet Esme clenched her jaw as though she were being ripped apart. Her mouth suddenly fell open as though she was screaming, but if she was, the flames ate the sound. The courtyard was deathly silent. She managed another step, though shaky, and then another. Five steps in all. Not even halfway.

She lost her footing and crumpled. Her robe was all but burned off her, exposing her soot-covered thighs and back. Jolie gasped. Anouk pressed a hand to her mouth. Esme was on all fours in the coals. The fire licked around her. She tried to stand but couldn't. Her mouth was open in silent screams.

And then, with another blinding flash of light, she was gone.

Anouk stared in shock at the empty glass coals. There was nothing left of Esme, not even a pile of ash. Lise let out a wail, but she was quickly silenced by Heida. The Royals turned away, disappointed and bored, and Anouk caught one of them saying something about a bet.

Duke Karolinge stoically turned to the line of girls. "Heida. You are next."

Heida—like the rest of them—looked utterly shaken. But she'd been at the Cottage the longest. And she was nothing if not determined. She clutched a lock of Lise's hair between both palms and stepped barefoot on the hemlock boughs. She glanced back at Lise, gave her a curt nod, then stepped into the fire.

Anouk clenched her jaw against the ache in her side. She felt dizzy from the pain. Her vision was starting to blur. Across the flames, Rennar was watching her with an odd expression on his face, as though he sensed the hidden wound in her side.

Heida made it three steps into the fire before crumpling. Her mouth opened in silent screams. The flames ate away her robes and then tore apart her body in one awful flash, and fast as a blink, another girl vanished from existence.

Chapter 17

❧

SME. HEIDA. MARTA.

All of them were gone after taking only a few steps into the flames. When Duke Karolinge called the fourth girl, Frederika, Anouk couldn't watch. She didn't relish watching anyone die, even someone as deranged as Frederika. She kept her eyes fixed on a clod of mud and thrust her hand in her robe pocket. When she'd changed clothes, she'd slipped Rennar's mirror into it. It felt solid against her shaking fingers, the mother-of-pearl back soothing. The frozen grass crunched under Frederika's feet as she approached the coals. All the girls tensed. Anouk kept her gaze low. Was Frederika clutching Anouk's blood between her hands? Was she sorry for what she had done? Was Frederika screaming silently, like Marta had? Had she tripped and fallen, like Esme?

At Anouk's side, Lise gasped. Anouk squeezed the mirror harder. When she looked up, the fires were empty. Another girl gone. She sucked in a breath, feeling like the air had been pulled out of her.

Beastie blood was nobody's crux after all.

"Petra," the Duke said calmly. "You are next to burn."

Petra twisted toward Anouk with wide eyes full of sudden panic. The jar of lavender ash in her palm trembled wildly. In a rush she said, "I'm ash in the wind, Anouk, I know it."

"Then don't go," Anouk whispered urgently. "You can forfeit. Wait until next year. Mada Zola wouldn't have wanted you to take such a risk."

At the mention of Mada Zola's name, the look in Petra's eyes cleared. She tilted up her chin. "Yes, she would have. She always hoped I'd join the Haute. The things she showed me, Anouk . . . the magic. I can't live a quiet Pretty life." She ran a shaking hand through her strawberry hair. "All Pretties die, right? Whether it's today or fifty years from now, what does it matter when immortality is at stake?"

"Petra, don't—"

But Petra had already started walking. She pressed the lavender ash between her palms and stepped barefoot onto the hemlock boughs. Before she could stop herself, Anouk reached out to snatch her back to safety, but it was too late.

Petra stepped into the blue flames.

"Ouch!" Petra said. She cursed. "This hurts like hell! No one said it hurt this—" Anything else she said was swallowed by the flames.

Anouk pressed her hand to her mouth. Through the flickering blue wall of fire, she could see Petra's mouth contorting.

One pace. Two. Three.

Anouk tore her eyes away. She couldn't watch. Her gaze fell on the abbey tower, and, for a second, she thought she saw a shadow in the Duke's library. Had Luc broken in? Had he found anything?

She looked back at the pyre—she couldn't help it. She had to know. Petra was five paces in, then six. Anouk felt hope rising in her chest—but then again, if Petra survived, it meant Anouk's chances were infinitesimal. And yet she couldn't help but silently cheer her friend on.

Eight paces!

"Keep going," she whispered. "Just a few more steps . . ."

Petra faltered. Karla cried out, but Petra caught herself before falling. Her robes were entirely burned away; only the red sash remained, hugging her narrow hips.

Nine paces through the coals and still going. Her fists were balled fiercely at her side. Her mouth twisted in a grimace. But she was still going! One more step and—

Anouk held her breath.

With a final lurch, Petra made it through.

Anouk cried out in shock and awe. How many nights had she and Petra lain in their room and discussed this moment? Even prepared for the end? And yet Petra had survived. She'd found her true crux. There were gasps from Lise and Sam and Karla and Jolie as Petra fell out of the Baths, naked. The impossible had happened! Her bare feet touched the grass on the other side and she crumpled into a heap in the snow. She curled into a fetal position, letting out small gasps as though she were still on fire. But there wasn't a speck of soot on her. She was still Petra, but somehow more beautiful. The bruises were gone from her knees; the perpetual shadows under her eyes had brightened. Her face looked fuller, her hair glossier. Even though she and Mada Zola hadn't been related by blood, there was now a resemblance, that certain something that united all the witches.

The Royals clapped with the first true enthusiasm of the whole day. A new witch was a valuable thing. New blood in the Haute. At the Witchery Feast tonight, they would all be vying to win the loyalty of the new witch, promising her every luxury in return for her service in their Court. Petra was French, but that didn't mean she'd be bound to serve Rennar in the Parisian Court. Already the Crimson Queen was arguing with a count from the Court of the Woods.

The Duke whispered something to Saint, who took off and vanished over the northern mountains, bearing the news.

Anouk felt herself grinning. It was miraculous to witness the birth of a witch. And Petra! She was so fiercely proud. But the other remaining acolytes around her now wore stony faces. Anouk's own smile fell as she remembered why.

Petra had survived, so what were the odds for the rest of them?

Anouk suddenly felt like she might throw up.

After the Pretty servants had draped a cloak around Petra and helped her hobble to a bench to recover, the Duke calmly turned toward the rest of them.

The remaining acolytes were staring in apprehension at the pyre. No—at Anouk. She touched her face and hair, wondering if she'd somehow smeared soot on herself. It took her a moment to realize that Duke Karolinge had called out a name.

Her name.

"Anouk," he repeated. "You are next to burn."

Her stomach plunged. The pain in her side flared.

I'm going to die.

She knew it like she knew the sun rose in the east. She dropped the twist of Little Beau's fur. Fear roared in her head, deafening her. Lise wasn't smirking now. None of the girls were. They all looked as pale as Anouk knew she was. The odds were now equally poor for all of them. Dimly, Anouk became aware of someone calling her name from across the courtyard. Rennar was shouting, but her senses had gone numb. And then he was standing, pushing through the other Royals to speak to Duke Karolinge, his limp far more pronounced in his rush. He was pointing to Anouk, saying something to the Duke that Anouk couldn't hear, something about an unfair wound. Somehow, he'd figured out what had happened to her. But the Duke kept shaking his head. A man of honor, but not a man of sentiment. The kind of man who could spend a year patiently, even kindly, training a girl and then not blink as he watched her burn.

"Anouk." The voice came from the bench by the rectory. Petra, still shivering in the blanket, met Anouk's eyes. "Damn the odds, Anouk. Do it. I know you can."

Anouk started to protest. There hadn't been two witches in the Coal Baths in decades.

Petra jerked her chin toward the coals. "Girl, *go.*"

Her feet started to move as though someone else inhabited her body. With a shaking hand, she took Saint's bell out of her pocket and pressed it between her palms. Rennar watched with an intense look of dread, but then, as she stepped into the flames, he vanished. Everything vanished. The courtyard. The Royals. The Duke. Petra. Lise and Sam and Jolie and Karla. Her world had suddenly become nothing more than blue, blue as far as she could see, blue in hundreds of different shades, and no one had ever told her that as painful as the Baths would be, they would also be heartbreakingly beautiful. But then pain sliced up her leg and she let out a cry. The coals underfoot were sharp as glass. The heat seared up her legs, and she felt as though the soles of her feet were charring, but when she looked down, she was untouched.

Take a step, she told herself.

Now one more.

How many paces had she taken? Shrouded in the blue flames, she lost a sense of time and place. All she felt was pain. It felt as though each cell in her body were being ripped apart, as if a child had broken her up like a puzzle and was trying to put it back together again to form a completely different image even though the pieces wouldn't fit. Her skin itched and burned. Beneath it, the muscle rippled as though someone was tearing it from her bone.

Another step.

Was this what it felt like to be reborn as something else? But she had already been reborn as something else. Suddenly she was back on the floor of Mada Vittora's attic in a puddle of blood with the other beasties standing around her. She'd gone from owl to girl. Now from girl to witch.

Another step.

The pain was almost unbearable. Her hands were shaking. She wasn't even certain she was still clutching the bell. The audience outside the Baths couldn't hear her screaming, but she could. Her own screams pierced her ears. The flames were pulling her apart, remaking her. Testing her blood and her bone. Determining whether she'd found her crux. If it was possible for a beastie to become a witch.

Another step. She lost her footing and barely caught herself. The pain in her side flared. The flames were too strong. The wound had weakened her too much for her to take another step. Where was her bell? There, on the coals. Just a useless piece of metal. What if a beastie couldn't become a witch? What if she was what they said she was —an animal? A base, lowly thing? Rennar had believed in her. So had Petra. But they didn't make the decision.

And the flames were turning.

She fell to all fours, wincing against the pain. The flames no longer felt like they were trying to put her back together into something new. They were only tearing her apart. Piece by piece, burned so cleanly not even ash remained. Her vision wavered. The world turned darker. She sucked in smoke. And then an odd image appeared before her.

Black smoke covered the ground. A group of what looked like witches in black robes were chanting. The smoke obscured them so that they were only hazy outlines, and Anouk couldn't tell if there were five or ten or twenty of them. Their faces were nothing more than blurry ovals of various skin tones, but they were all crying black tears. The smoke rose higher and higher. It looked like they were summoning the smoke. Commanding it. And then, out of nowhere, an owl skimmed over the darkness. It twisted its head, cawing into the void, and she gasped. It had no eyes.

A fluttering of wings erupted in her heart and the vision of witches and smoke shattered. Suddenly she was back in the Coal Baths. On her hands and knees. The pain in her side unbearable.

And she *knew*.

She knew.

Her crux wasn't the bell.

The flames burned away the last of her robes. Something clattered onto the coals in front of her. The blue world was fading away, but with her last ounce of strength, she managed to reach out a hand and grab the object.

The round mirror.

A face looked back at her. Not her own, but Rennar's.

She whispered.

The last thing she felt was a drenching rain like a late-fall shower, but if it was rain, it was thick and heavy as tar, coating her skin and her eyes until everything was black.

PART II

Chapter 18

❦

"ANOUK."

"She's still asleep."

"Look—her eyelids are twitching."

"They've been twitching ever since the Black Forest. That's what happens when you're nearly torn apart by ancient magic. She'll be lucky if muscle spasms are the worst thing she suffers."

Voices faded in and out of Anouk's ears. In her hazy state she wasn't sure what was a dream and what was a memory. She remembered the blue of the Coal Baths and glass slicing at her palms. The clatter of a mirror and Rennar's face—or had that been a dream too?

Someone threw water on her face and she shot up with a gasp. Blinking, wiping water out of her eyes, she tried to focus, and in a moment, she was looking at two familiar faces.

"Luc! Viggo!"

They stood at the end of the bed she was in. Viggo's cane rested against the footboard but he was standing without it, his arms crossed over his chest. There was a healthier color to his face. His dark eyes were bright and clear. Best of all, his slouchy hat was nowhere to be seen, replaced with a slick of hair gel and a trace of gold eyeliner. The Goblins must have gotten to him.

Viggo slapped Luc. "I told you she was awake!"

A sudden wave of nausea hit Anouk and she doubled over in the bed, clutching at her stomach.

Luc's smiled faded. "Easy, Dust Bunny. You've been through a lot."

The burning sensation reached Anouk's temples but she dismissed it and tried to throw off the covers. "The Baths . . . I was burning . . . the whole forest was on fire . . ."

Her gaze fell on a basket of fruit on the nightstand. A bright yellow note told her to GET WELL SOON ALREADY! Next to it was a bouquet of lilies that looked more than a few days past their prime. She ran her fingers over the bed's silk duvet, confused. The bed was monstrously luxurious, not at all like her simple cot in the Cottage room she shared with Petra. This bedroom was glittering with crystal lamps and golden wall sconces, mahogany furniture and paintings of regal-looking people on regal-looking horses.

"It's clean in here. Too clean." She tilted her head to the side. "This isn't the Cottage, is it? Not even the guest quarters are this nice."

"You're in Paris," Luc told her.

"Castle Ides," Viggo added.

Anouk pressed a hand to her temple. The pain wasn't going away. Hazy daylight came from a pair of windows. She shifted to look outside. A gray city skyline, rain falling. In the distance, the sloping point of the Eiffel Tower.

She collapsed back against the pillows with an exhale and kneaded her hands against her forehead. "This is all wrong. I should be in the Black Forest. The Coal Baths . . ." Her throat seemed to close up as she remembered the agonizing sensation of being torn apart. She had no idea what had happened after that.

Luc sank onto the edge of the bed, gently taking her hand between his. "You fell, Anouk. Into the flames. It was awful to see. You looked like you were screaming but I couldn't hear you. I tried to run to help you but Duke Karolinge wouldn't permit it. Petra kept yelling for you to get back up, but you didn't. You couldn't. Your robes burned off, and your skin started to burn. And then—" He cocked his head as though he was still uncertain about what occurred next. "And then Rennar started whispering. At first none of us understood what he was doing. Once the Royals realized what he was summoning, it was too late to stop him."

She sucked in her breath. Rennar must have heard her call for help through the mirror. "What did he summon?"

"A storm," Luc continued. "A black rain strong enough to put out the flames. I worried it was too late—you were curled in a ball, looking for all the world like a charred scrap of toast. The Royals were furious that he'd interrupted the Baths. The rest of the acolytes weren't able to undergo the trial. They're still alive—Lise and Jolie and Sam and Karla. In the chaos, Petra and I were able to pull you off the coals and get you back inside the Cottage. Duke Karolinge practically sent Rennar into exile. We barely made it back to Paris before the other Royals conjured up pitchforks. Metaphorically speaking."

He gently placed the bell in her lap. Her pulse quickened.

"I found this."

Her hands started shaking. It was melted and misshapen. One look told her there was no green orb of light trapped in the metal leaves anymore. The magic inside must have burned away in the flames. Now it was nothing more than a useless lump of metal. She wanted to grab it and throw it across the room. "It's just a piece of junk."

Her pulse was thundering now. Someone had dressed her in pajamas with long sleeves. She shoved up the sleeves, grimaced to find bruises and burn marks. Her skin should have been as preternaturally smooth as Petra's. She shook her head fiercely. "It . . . it didn't work. I'm not a witch. We have to go back, Luc. I have to try again!"

"We can't. We're banished from the Cottage. Anyway, the Royals couldn't light the coals again. They won't hold any Coal Bath trials until next year."

She felt as though she were falling. She clutched the sheets. Banished from the Cottage? It was a cold, desolate place, and yet it had also been the one place where her wishes could be granted. And now she'd never set foot there again. She leaned forward so her hair curtained her face. The smell of rotting flowers turned her stomach. She glanced at the fading lilies. "How long have I been here?"

"A week."

Her stomach twisted. Luc squeezed her hand. "It's not all bad. I found those books you told me about in the Duke's library. They reference plagues similar to what's happening in London, just like you said they would. I was able to steal the books when we left the Cottage in such a hurry. I'm hopeful they'll contain some answers."

Books?

She stared down at her clasped hands. She felt hollowed out like a pumpkin, her insides gutted and tossed into the slop pile for goats. She was supposed to have been the most powerful creature in all of Europe right now, and instead they were telling her to be hopeful about some *books?*

146

She balled up her hands and stuffed them under her thighs in disgust. "I have to talk to Rennar. There must be some way I can fix this. I chose the wrong crux. But I could choose again . . ."

Choose what? she thought. She'd been so certain about the bell. The night of the firewalk, when Little Beau had barked up at Saint, she'd felt struck by lightning. What had she gotten so horribly wrong? She touched her side, which didn't hurt now. Rennar must have healed the stab wound she'd gotten from Frederika.

"Rennar's been working around the clock to win back the favor of the other Royals," Luc continued. "Ever since the Coal Baths didn't, ah, turn out as we hoped, he's changed his strategy. If we can't go to London and defeat the Coven through force, we can at least attempt to keep them out of the other realms. He wants to conjure a defense spell to prevent them from spreading beyond London, but for that he needs the other Royals' cooperation. Their borders are intertwined; if one falls, they all fall. And after he wreaked havoc on the Coal Baths, more than a few of them are inclined never to speak to him again."

She grimaced. "A border spell? That will slow the Coven down, but it won't stop them. What about regaining the Goblins' home city? And the Royals who disappeared? And all the Pretties who live there? We can't cut off an entire city and leave it to fend for itself."

Cities falling one by one . . .

White to Red, White to Red . . .

"I'm not sure we have a choice," Luc said quietly.

All this heavy talk seemed to unnerve Viggo, who tore open the plastic wrap of the fruit basket and thrust a banana at her. "Eat something, Dust Mop. You're skin and bones. The Goblins packed this for you."

She pushed away the banana and he frowned.

"At least have a grape."

"I don't want fruit right now! I don't want anything!" She grabbed the fruit basket and chucked it onto the floor. "Don't you understand? I failed. I missed something. I thought I knew myself and my connection to magic. I was so sure. But it turns out I don't know myself at all. All that time at the Cottage studying spells and reading about other witches and I still got it wrong. I had to beg Rennar for help." She groaned and squeezed her eyes shut. "I want to go home."

"Ah. Yes. About the townhouse..." Viggo started. Her eyes snapped open again. Viggo looked fairly sick. He turned to Luc for help, but Luc just stuffed a grape in his mouth, leaving Viggo to answer alone. Viggo grimaced. "It's, ah, it's gone."

Anouk blinked, thinking she couldn't have heard him correctly. *"What?"*

"Burned," Viggo clarified in a nervous rush. "An awful accident. Just a few days after we left. You'd already gone to the Black Forest, and the Goblins and I packed up and moved to Castle Ides. December and I went back for my hat. The whole building was already on fire. Pretty fire trucks were on the scene, even some news reporters. But they couldn't put it out. You can imagine my horror. I nearly choked on my own tongue. December practically had to perform the Heimlich."

Anouk was speechless. The townhouse was *gone?* It didn't feel possible that she would never again go back to her old turret bedroom with the playbills pasted on the walls and her collection of found objects from the Pretty World that Beau had brought her—baby shoes, toupees. She'd never again set foot in Mada Vittora's wondrous closet of shoes. Never whip up buttercream frosting in the kitchen and smack Beau with a wooden spoon when he tried to lick the bowl. Never curl up in a chair in the library to read tales of the world beyond the windows.

There was no going back now. There was nothing to go back *to*.

"How?" Her voice was hollow.

Viggo looked away, ashamed. "Turns out I'm not such a good Goblin babysitter after all. One of them must have left some toast on the stove."

She narrowed her eyes. There was something Viggo wasn't telling her. He'd always been a terrible liar. "There was no more bread left. The pantry was bare." She turned to Luc. "What do you make of all this?"

Luc's face was as serene as always. If she hadn't known him so well, she would have missed the ripple of suspicion in his eyes. "Seems like too strange a coincidence for Rennar not to be behind it. I think he wanted you to have no home except his."

Her mood turned even nastier. "Well, the joke is on him. He didn't know that I'd fail in the Baths and be useless, townhouse or no townhouse."

Viggo and Luc didn't respond. Their silence might as well have been an accusation. *Failure. Disappointment.* What right had she had to think she could do anything grander than sweep the floors?

An awful idea took hold of her. "Beau! He's still at the Cottage!" Before the Baths, she had left him in the stables in the Cottage basement, locked in the muddy stall with only a few ham scraps and her Faustine jacket, and that had been a week ago!

She pitched forward, tossing off the covers. "Shoes . . . I need shoes . . ."

"Calm down." Luc pressed his palms gently against her shoulders, easing her back into bed. "Beau is okay. Petra has him. When she and I got you out of the Coal Baths, she promised to get the dog and bring him here as soon as she could."

Anouk's muscles relaxed slightly. Petra was a witch now. At least that was a ray of light in the darkness. If the Duke or anyone else tried to stop Petra from taking Little Beau, she'd be a force to reckon with. And then Anouk's thoughts turned dark. *She* was supposed to be a witch too. She should have been able to free Little Beau herself, even turn him human again. He should have been in bed with her; they should have been whispering dreams and plans to each other and nibbling on the goodies in the fruit basket. "I've ruined everything."

Viggo and Luc were silent. Rain pelted harder at the window, icy and loud, threatening to turn to snow. The city skyline was a growing smear of gray on the horizon.

"Get some rest," Luc said at last. He nudged Viggo and motioned at the door. As soon as they'd left, a deafening silence filled the room, and Anouk wanted to call them back. The bedroom was too empty without them; the luxury gave her no comfort. Her thoughts bumped around the high ceilings and echoed back to her. She palmed the melted bell angrily. She lost track of time. She had no townhouse to return to. No magic sparking at her fingertips, not even the simplest tricks and whispers. No clue what she'd gotten wrong when she'd chosen her crux. No idea how to make it all right again.

At least she could rid herself of the bell. On an impulse, she ran to the window, preparing to hurl the bell to where she'd never have to see it again.

But she froze.

The last thing she'd expected to see, eight stories up, was a face. She nearly fell over. "Jak!"

He was crouched on the exterior sill. He tapped one long fingernail against the pane. "Let me in, lovely?"

She hesitated, then decided that things couldn't get much worse. She twisted the brass lock and opened the window. He unfolded his nimble limbs, climbed in, and took a look around at the opulent décor. Though his eyes glittered with curiosity, he didn't move more than a few feet from the window; he was bound to the cold.

Frigid air gusted in and she went back to the bed and tugged the blanket around her shoulders. "What on earth are you doing here?"

"We Snow Children travel where the snow goes."

"Yes, but why did you come *here*, and why now? It must be snowing in hundreds of other places at this exact moment."

"Only Paris has you."

She gave him a hard look. She wasn't in the mood for games. "Are you after more gin?"

He laughed. "That's not why I'm here, though I wouldn't say no to a dram. I saw what happened at the Coal Baths."

Of course—it had been snowing then, just a few flakes, but enough for Jak to spy on her. Her face warmed with shame and she turned to a cabinet with glasses set out on the top. Sure enough, when she dug through it, she found a bottle of gin. She filled a tumbler and gave it to Jak.

He drained the glass and wiped a finger along the rim for the last traces and then said slyly, "Poor girl. Not a Pretty. Not a witch. Not a thing of wings and feathers either." He popped his finger in his mouth.

She stiffened. "How did you find out about that? The owl?" She had no memories of that time when she'd been an owl, nothing but a dim awareness of feeling hungry and frightened.

The Dark Thing. The Cold Place.

"As far as riddles go, it was not overly difficult to solve," Jak said. "I told you, we Snow Children have been around since long before beasties, or Pretties, or witches. We've seen it all." His black eyes glistened.

She rolled the melted bell in her hand. "Do you know what was wrong about my crux?"

"The crux is merely a symbol. The other girl, the one who lived, chose a crux that connected her to her past, to her tragedy, to other witches. Lavender ash."

"This bell contained my *own* magic. How could I have found a stronger connection?"

"You weren't looking in the right place."

She groaned and slumped into the window seat. "Fine. Speak in riddles. But tell me this: If you've existed so long, have you heard of a time called the Noirceur?"

Jak froze, then lowered the glass in his hand. His eyes were still playful, but there was a hint of danger in them too. "What does a beastie know of the Noirceur?"

"Just tell me what you know," she said, then jutted her chin toward his empty glass. "I'll give you the whole bottle."

He leaned in, the snow blowing in at his back. His icicle locks hung in his face. "The Noirceur. You're wrong—it wasn't a *time*. It was a *force*. Chaos itself. It's very old, perhaps the oldest thing there is, from before time, from before life, even. Only a small remnant of it remains: the vitae echo. The rest of it faded away over the ages." He gave a mirthless smile. "Or so the Haute would have you believe."

"It never faded, did it?" Her voice was hushed. She thought of the books in the Duke's library that Luc had brought back, the ancient references to plagues that were happening all over again.

Jak shook his head slowly. "No. It was merely contained."

"What do mean, contained? Where?"

Jak grinned devilishly. "Do you wish to know badly enough to give me a kiss?"

She scowled. "Your kisses bring death."

"Very well." The corners of his blue lips curled up. "I solved the riddle of your origin, and so now it is your turn to solve a riddle of mine. The Noirceur was contained in . . ."

"Yes? In what?"

"Ah, that's the riddle." He blew a breath of frost to cloud the window and traced a symbol there, a circle containing two small lines and broken rays, like an incomplete sun.

"That isn't a riddle," she said. "It's a picture. And a nonsense one at that."

Jak grinned. "The riddle is simple. Its portrayal is not." He began to fade away with the lessening snow, and she thrust her head out the window, calling for him, but he didn't return.

"Snow Children," she muttered under her breath.

She still held the bell in her palm, but she no longer wanted to throw it out the window. What had Jak said? *You weren't looking in the right place.* She found a gold chain in a drawer, strung the empty bell on it, then fastened it around her neck. A reminder to keep looking for the right place.

She jumped when a knock came at the door.

It was Countess Quine's green-eyed daughter, carrying a large rectangular cardboard box.

"It's you," Anouk said in surprise.

"My name is Mia."

Anouk's fingers plucked uselessly at the chain around her neck. "Mia, listen, what happened in Montélimar to your mother—"

Mia shoved the box into her arms. It was heavier than Anouk had expected, bulky and flat, and tied with a cream-colored ribbon. "A package from Prince Rennar. With his most sincere hopes that you're feeling better." If the girl felt any anger over her mother's murder, her face did not show it. She just drummed her black-clawed fingernails against her arms.

Anouk tried again. "You must hate me."

The girl gave a sigh that conveyed annoyance. "Countess Quine wasn't my mother. She was my twin sister." Mia looked no older than ten, whereas Countess Quine had been in her thirties. Mia smiled

154

flatly. "I took herbs to age more slowly. It was always a point of vicious jealousy for her. I'm not sorry she's gone. One of these centuries, one of us would have killed the other. You just beat me to it." She shrugged. The girl's heart was even colder than her late sister's.

With a tip of her small chin, Mia left, and Anouk, feeling even more lightheaded, tossed the package onto the bed. Her mind whipped in dizzying circles. How could she regain her magic? What was her crux? And what of the Noirceur? It seemed like blankness over the world, not unlike what she called the Dark Thing.

The Dark Thing . . .

The Noirceur . . .

Was it possible they were different terms for the same void?

Her bare toes—all eight of them—curled anxiously against the rug. She sat on the corner of the bed, twisting a strand of hair around one finger. Her eyes fell on the package. She tugged off the ribbon distractedly, threw aside the lid, and dug through what must have been a hundred layers of tissue paper.

"Oh!" She covered her mouth with one palm, but a small gasp escaped anyway. *"Merde."*

Chapter 19

A WEDDING DRESS.

Tucked amid the layers of tissue paper was a garment made of textured silk as fine as frost on a windowpanes; it was the same silver-gray color as the suit Rennar wore when he was feeling princely. Anouk pulled it out and held it up to the light. Hundreds of crystals were embedded in the bodice in a snowflake pattern. The train was just long enough to graze the floor. Soft white feathers spilled out from the bustle in the back. To a casual observer, the feathered detail would look like a soft adornment. Only those who knew her past — like Rennar — would recognize the subtle pattern as wings and understand its significance. Two glass shoes were also tucked in the box, clear as crystal and molded to fit perfectly around her missing toes.

Angry and a little embarrassed, she crammed the dress back into the box, fighting the sea of tissue paper. She paused before tossing in the shoes; they *were* lovely — but no. Into the box they went. She slammed the lid shut, picked up the box, and threw open the bedroom door.

Mia was still in the hallway, pretending to admire a portrait, a snicker on her face as Anouk strode by. Anouk's cheeks burned. Did everyone in Castle Ides know what was in the box? She stomped down the maze of hallways, muttering under her breath. She turned a corner and stopped at a dead end. A grandfather clock ticked tauntingly before her, reminding her that every hour on the hour, the floor plan changed.

She tried a different hallway. Cricket had been the one to memorize each of the changing blueprints, not her. Two Pretty maids were sweeping the hallways but she didn't bother to ask them for directions. Their eyes were glazed over with enchantment; they'd be no help. At last she turned a corner and found the beautiful doors of the spell library. Directly across the hall from them was the unassuming wooden door that led to Rennar's room. It was slightly ajar.

Struggling under the unwieldy shape of the box, she threw her shoulder against the door and burst in, a string of expletives poised on her tongue, but the room was empty. She shifted the awkward-shaped box. The sound of running water came from another interior room. She walked toward it. "Rennar? Where are you? You must have lost your mind if—oh!"

She was in a master bathroom. Rennar was standing in front of an ornate mirror, naked from the waist up, a razor blade in one hand. Shaving cream that smelled of vanilla, citrus, and pine coated half his chin. Anouk dropped the box. The crystal shoes tumbled onto the bathroom rug.

In the mirror, Rennar's reflection raised an eyebrow, the razor hovering over his neck. "I take it you received my gift?"

The only men she'd ever seen shirtless were Beau, when he washed the car in summer, and Hunter Black, when Luc was stitching up his wounds. Never a prince. Though Rennar's body looked a twenty-year-old's, a map of scars interlaced with faded ink spoke of centuries of life. His chest and stomach were lean and hard from the physical demands of spell work.

She managed to close her mouth. She picked up the shoes and stuck them back in the box with the dress that was spilling out of it, then shoved the whole mess at him. "What is this?"

"It's a wedding dress."

"I know it's a wedding dress! Of course it's a wedding dress! You've lost your mind if you think we're still getting married."

He wiped his blade on a towel, then returned to shaving. "Oh?"

"Of course! Our deal is off. There won't be a wedding. There won't be a coronation. And . . . and . . ." She cocked her head as he continued to painstakingly shave his neck. "Why don't you just whisper your chin smooth?"

He gave a wry half smile, sliding the blade over the last streak of shaving cream and then rinsing it in the sink. "I like the feel of real things, things that take work. Tricks and whispers don't make me feel alive anymore." He dried the blade and ran the towel over his neck. "If you'll excuse me," he said, "I should get dressed."

He slid past her into the bedroom, bending stiffly because of his stone leg as he rummaged through drawers for a fresh shirt. Anouk, speechless, gritted her teeth and stomped after him, still holding the box. "Rennar, answer me."

"What do you want me to say? Why on earth should our deal be off?"

Her cheeks burned. In a quiet voice she said, "You know why."

"I haven't the faintest idea." He put on a crisp white shirt and began buttoning it up, hiding the scars and the ink.

Anouk felt tears pushing at her eyes. He looked at her in alarm. "Anouk, what's the matter?"

He knew. Of course he knew, and it was cruel of him to pretend not to. He'd been in the courtyard. He'd seen how she'd fallen into the coals. *He had heard her beg him for help.*

And she hated that he'd answered.

She turned away sharply, hugging the box to her chest as though it were a shield. "I chose the wrong crux. You were there. If you hadn't summoned the storm to put out the flames, I would have died. I'd be nothing now, not even ash."

And that was it, wasn't it? Now it was said. That nasty toad that kept creeping and crawling around in her chest was now croaking away for all the world to hear.

"I failed." Her voice was urgent. She needed him to agree and stop pretending everything was okay. "It's over, Rennar, why can't you admit that? You and Mada Zola and Cricket and Luc were wrong. You might have created beasties to be powerful, but you must have messed up, because I'm useless now. I lost my magic. It's gone forever, burned in the flames! I can't turn my friends back. I can't help the Goblins. I can't stop the Coven of Oxford. And apparently I have no idea who I am."

She was hugging the box to her chest so hard that it dug painfully into her ribs. She frowned grimly. Pain was what she deserved.

Rennar finished buttoning his shirt very calmly, infuriatingly calmly, as though she'd confessed to stealing a sip of his gin, not destroying the future of the near realms and maybe even the entire world.

"Say something, Rennar. The truth. It's over."

He came to her, smelling of citrus and vanilla and pine, and she was half afraid he would brush away her tears and half afraid he wouldn't. But he only stroked a long white feather poking out of the box.

"The truth? You're going to look beautiful in this dress."

He started fastening a cravat around his neck and she stared at him, open-mouthed, so angry that her tears dried up. He looked at himself in the mirror, combed his fingers through his hair, then went out into the hall, moving fast for a man with a leg of stone, leaving the door open behind him. She stared, and then, clutching the box, followed him. "Rennar! Wait!"

He didn't slow as he adjusted his cufflinks. She had to jog to catch up with him, the box jostling in her arms. "There's no point anymore, don't you see? Why do you even want me? I'm not a witch and I can't do magic at all now, not even spells to mend a button!"

"Believe it or not, not everyone marries out of a cold-blooded pursuit of power. Some people actually marry for love."

She gave him a hard look. "We shared *one* kiss. And besides, Beau is my—"

"Pet?"

"*Friend*. I love him and he loves me. You want me only because I can move mountains for you, or at least you thought I could, before I disappointed everyone." He abruptly turned into another hall. "Slow down! Where are you going, anyway?"

He didn't slow down.

"Why the dress? Why go through with a marriage and coronation if it's pointless? And *don't* say anything about love."

"Fine." He sighed as if she'd ruined his game, but then flashed

160

a sidelong look at her. "Though, for the record, you didn't seem to mind that kiss. But yes, there is another reason to go through with the marriage. The Code of Courts."

"Is this tied to the old laws you told me about? The Nochte . . . ah . . ."

"The Nochte Pax." A clock on the wall chimed, and he instinctively spun and went back the way they came—he knew the changing floor plans by heart—and went down another hall. "The Code of Courts was established twelve hundred years ago, when the Royal families of the near realms warred with one another." He spoke mechanically, as though reciting ancient history. "A peace alliance was formed, and it included a pledge to come to one another's defense if any of the other Courts were attacked. And the Court of Isles is under attack now. The problem is, with the Coven's spell keeping us out of London, I can't prove it."

They were walking through the artifact hallway, the various objects from the Pretty World under glass, everything from crystal scepters to humble pairs of scissors, things that had been imbued with magic to influence history.

"That is a problem," he continued. "After the Coal Baths, the other Royals were, shall we say, less than willing to entertain the idea of the Code of Courts. I interfered with something ancient to save your life, I broke a lot of rules, and for that, they believe that the entire Parisian Court should be ostracized. *Except.*"

"Except what?" Anouk said breathlessly as they turned down another hall. The box was nearly forgotten in her arms. Sounds of clanking silverware and soft music came from a distant room. Probably the Goblins—except there was no rock music.

"You really should change into something more festive. And are you certain you want to carry that around with you?" he said, nodding toward the box. "If anyone sees it now, it'll ruin your entrance on our wedding day."

"Forget about the dress! Rennar, what happened? What were you going to say?"

"Ah." His eyes gleamed darkly. "The Parisian Court was ostracized, yes. Stricken from our position as head of the Haute. Not even the Crimson Queen would speak to me at first, and Queen Violante and I have, ah, a *history*." He smirked, but it soon faded. "But then something happened to the Lunar Court. Just two days after the disaster that was the Coal Baths, King Kaspar's eyesight started to go. His tongue started to blacken. Prince Aleksi reluctantly came to me for help. He alone believed me when I said that the Coven of Oxford was dangerous and might even be behind his father's sickness, though no one knows how they're getting to him. Aleksi and I have been researching long-lost traditions to invoke the Code of Courts. If the other Royals won't voluntarily agree to help, we will force their hand."

"What does that have to do with me?"

"The Nochte Pax. I told you that it's a wedding gift. More specifically, it's a request the wedding couple can make and that the others can't refuse. Once we're married, I'm going to use the Nochte Pax to invoke the Code of Courts. The other Royals will have no choice but to help Prince Aleksi and I put up a protection spell to keep the Coven from spreading beyond London."

"That doesn't sound like much of a solution," she said.

"It *isn't* a solution," he said gruffly. "At the moment, I'm just trying to keep us alive." His hand went instinctively to the glossy mark on his neck where the border spell had nearly split him down the middle. His expression soured. "The rumors coming out of London are bleak. The smoke has filled the catacombs and the subterranean tunnels. Whoever breathes it in chokes."

The artifact hallway ended in a set of double doors, but instead of opening them, he turned to a plain door in the corner that looked like a closet. It had a knob like an old man's bulbous nose. He opened the door and she stopped behind him abruptly. On the other side, as the clocks chimed a new hour, it transformed into the double-door entryway of the Castle Ides ballroom. It looked like something out of a dream, grander than anything she'd read in books about Versailles or royal palaces. There was no single crystal chandelier but hundreds of lit crystals suspended from the ceiling like falling stars.

Dancing couples in beautiful gowns swept across the floor. Anouk saw the few remaining Parisian Royals, Mia and some lesser dukes and duchesses. Prince Aleksi of the Lunar Court stood alone by the fireplace; his ailing father, King Kaspar, was slumped in a chair, wearing a crown of lustrous black stone. The beautiful Crimson Queen, Violante, and her two sisters were there. Goblins had taken over the balconies of the ballroom and were drinking and eating and dancing jigs. Viggo was chastising one who'd climbed on a table. Luc was there, still disguised as a Royal in his baron's crest, at a table set with fine china. There were a few young men of questionable background, probably Pretty brokers. One had a series of zeros and ones tattooed on his neck, and he wore black gloves that ran past his elbows; he clutched a live golden hare in the crook of his elbow. Another was bedecked with exotic flowers in every buttonhole.

If Mada Vittora were alive, she would have died all over again out of jealousy. The part of Anouk that remembered being a maid couldn't stop looking at the chandeliers (not a speck of dust!) and the polished silver (spotless!) and the dishes of perfect food that a whole fleet of cooks must have spent hours preparing. She turned to Rennar in bewilderment. "Goblins . . . Pretties . . . Royals . . . Viggo . . . Luc . . . what *is* this?"

"This, my dear, is why you should have changed into something else."

For the first time, she thought to wonder why he was so meticulously groomed, with his fresh-shaved chin and cravat and cufflinks, and now she dreaded the answer. He touched the mark on his neck one final time, then took her hand.

"This is our engagement party."

Chapter 20

BEFORE SHE COULD SPUTTER a reaction, she saw a dark shadow flying toward her. She dropped the box and ducked, and it narrowly missed her head before sweeping out into the hallway.

"Saint!" she whispered, her eyes following the falcon.

Prince Rennar motioned to Duke Karolinge, who was somberly eating sugared plums at a table by himself. But Luc signaled her to catch her attention, then surreptitiously pointed to a cage sitting on a chair two tables away. It held a small white cat that was hissing at anyone who dared come close; not far from the table was another cage that held a muzzled wolf.

"Cricket!" Anouk gasped. "And Hunter Black!"

She pushed her way through the crowd. Music and laughter deafened her.

Women wore gowns of gold and silk that fanned out wide, blocking her path. She bumped into a Pretty servant carrying a tray of champagne. She pushed her way between the two princesses of the Crimson Court only to find herself stumbling into a clear area surrounded by the crowd. In the middle of it were two acrobats suspended by silken ropes that hung in midair, not attached to anything. One of them gracefully slid down the rope and threw his weight backward, which made the rope arch toward Anouk. He grinned and reached out for her.

She shrieked and dived back into the crowd.

After a few minutes of fighting her way through dancing couples, she managed to get to the banquet table. She grabbed the cage and dragged it close. "Cricket. Oh, Cricket. You poor thing." The cat inside was hunched on a velvet cushion that she'd shredded with her claws until it was nothing more than stuffing and threads. "I'll turn you back, I promise. I'll find a way."

The cat's green eyes looked at her in disdain. Just a cat. Not her friend. Though the flick of the cat's tail *did* remind her a little of Cricket when she was pissed off.

"Can't we let her out of the cage?" Anouk whispered to Luc. He was disguised as a Royal, and she was careful not to look directly at him. The crowd was impatient enough with Rennar's fondness for her; they'd never tolerate another beastie at their tables.

He picked up his water glass, pretended to take a sip, and whispered from the side of his mouth, "We tried. She ran away and hid in the vents and ate half the Goblins' pet rats. There was a mass funeral. Better to keep her here, where at least we know where she is."

Anouk stroked the cat through the bars with one finger. She glanced around the room at the partygoers. "Have you found out anything else about the Noirceur?"

"Not yet. I still have half the Duke's books to read through."

She remembered her vision and that uncanny feeling that maybe the Noirceur and the Dark Thing were one and the same, but before she could mention it, Luc said in an odd tone, "I've heard some disturbing rumors."

Anouk's eyebrows rose. "What rumors?"

His eyes skimmed over the room, his expression hooded. "A few days ago I was in the stairwell headed to the roof. The Minaret Court was ahead of me. They didn't know I was just one flight below them. They were gossiping about a traitor. Someone among the Royals who helped make the Court of Isles disappear."

Anouk tried to keep her face still. "Who?"

"They didn't mention the name." He paused. "I did overhear one of them say, 'What do you expect from a boy who shares a roof with witches?'"

She frowned as she considered this. It was clearly a male and clearly someone who had a close relationship with a witch. Her expression turned dark. "Viggo?"

Luc shook his head. "He wouldn't. I know him better than that."

"He isn't one of us," Anouk countered, though it made her sick to think about. Viggo was many things, most of them awful, but nevertheless, in the past few weeks he'd become dear to her.

Luc hesitated. "It sounds like a witch's boy, but it could also be a man who enjoys the company of witches. Someone who was once betrothed to one. Someone who, even at hundreds of years old, would still be considered a boy by the older Royals."

She leveled a look at him. "You mean Rennar."

He didn't deny it.

"You have to find out," she whispered urgently.

"There's a princess from the Minaret Court who . . . fancies me. I've danced with her, but she hasn't let anything slip yet. I suspect I'll have more luck as your wedding celebrations continue and the wine keeps flowing."

"There you are!" A black-haired princess sidled up to Luc with a grin and rested her hand on his arm. "You're drinking plain water? How positively monastic of you. Come, let me introduce you to the rest of the Minaret Court."

Anouk pretended not to know Luc as the princess dragged him away. She turned back to her caged friends. In addition to putting the muzzle on the wolf's mouth, someone had fastened iron chains to his feet.

"Oh, Hunter Black. Poor thing. I take it from those chains that you've been a handful."

Viggo caught her words as he sauntered over. "Wolf or human, it's still Hunter Black. Still an irritable bastard." He patted the top of the cage affectionately. "Rennar insists on keeping him muzzled. There were some accidents . . ." He trailed off. "But naturally he's tame with me." Viggo reached through the bars, unbuckled the muzzle, and offered the wolf a turkey leg, but the wolf snapped at his fingers.

"Ow!" He clutched his thumb.

"Yes, he obviously adores you," Anouk said dryly. She wondered how much Viggo knew about Hunter Black's true feelings. After the siege of Montélimar, Hunter Black had confessed to Anouk that he was in love with Viggo, and Anouk felt certain Viggo knew it, even if it had never been spoken of between them.

Saint flew overhead and her thoughts circled back to the Coal Baths. Her heart faltered, and she was overcome by the memory of flames and failure. Her legs went weak and she collapsed in a chair. She touched the melted bell around her neck. *What a fool.* Her mood turned bleak until she felt a presence at her back and turned. Rennar stood with that arrogant expression on his face. He set the box she had dropped on the table.

"What's this pretty thing?" Viggo said, plucking at the silk spilling out.

Anouk shoved the box away. "Nothing. Rennar, change the cat and the wolf back. I can't bear to see them like this." She lowered her voice. "You said we were past games."

He glanced at the caged animals with little sympathy. "Perhaps I decided to take the game more seriously after I expended every ounce of social capital I had on saving you from the flames." He motioned to the insanely elaborate party. "But you can still have Cricket. The deal was that I free her and turn her human in exchange for you marrying me."

"So if I go through with this wedding, you'll hold up your end of the deal? You'll turn her back?"

He nodded once.

In a whisper, she said, "We have to agree it will be a strictly political union. That means no romantic entanglements. No wedding night, no ripping each other's clothes off, no more stolen kisses. After we invoke the Nochte Pax, we'll be free to fall in love with whoever we want outside of the marriage."

"Those are rather chaste rules."

"Do you want a princess or don't you?"

"Touché." He handed her a glass of wine. "I don't like it, but I'll agree to your terms." He poured a glass for Viggo too and then motioned with his own glass across the ballroom to the tables where the Lunar and Crimson Courts sat. Prince Aleksi was leaning over his father, a hand on his shoulder as he coughed. Like all the Royals, King Kaspar must have been hundreds of years old, but unlike the others, he actually looked his age. He coughed harder.

Rennar said, "Prince Aleksi and Queen Violante are the only ones on our side, at least for the time being. The Lunar Prince and I have never gotten along, but his father's illness has put our feud on hold. He's here because he doesn't know how else to help his father. And the Crimson Queen . . . Well, as I said, we have a history. The two of them will make certain that the rest of the Royals fall in line with our Nochte Pax invocation."

King Kaspar doubled over, pushing his son away to keep him from ministering to him. His sleek black crown slid down his head. A team of acrobats took to the center of the ballroom in beautiful blue costumes that were enchanted so they'd change color with every somersault and tumble, and Anouk lost sight of the Lunar Court.

She sighed. "I suppose the show must go on, then."

Rennar raised his glass. "To the future princess of the Parisian Court."

Viggo gave Anouk a doubting look, but when she shrugged and picked up her glass, he did the same.

"To me," she said.

They all clinked glasses.

The sound rang out like a bell and she flinched.

As soon as she pressed the glass to her lips, a commotion came from the hall. The music stopped. A dog came charging in, followed by Petra, who was wearing sunglasses and the most fabulous coat Anouk had ever seen, charcoal-black wool with gold embroidery that caught the light and looked like live coals. Anouk wasn't entirely sure it wasn't enchanted to be *actually* smoldering.

"Have room for a couple of late arrivals?"

Little Beau ran to Anouk, and she dropped to her knees and pulled him into a hug. The smile vanished from Rennar's face. He muttered something about fleas and drained his glass of wine.

"Oh, I missed you, sweet fellow!" Anouk cupped the dog's face and kissed his snout. She looked up at Petra. "Thank you for watching out for him. I guess . . . I guess you couldn't make him human?"

"Sorry. That spell is beyond my ability." Petra was already pouring herself some wine. She looked different, and it wasn't just the beautiful coat. Once she'd made it through the blue flames, it had been impossible not to notice her smooth skin and her lustrous red hair, even though she'd been naked and dusted in soot. Anouk touched the gold studs on the coat's shoulders and gave Petra a questioning look.

"It's a Faustine original," Petra said.

"I wondered." Anouk felt a stab of loss at the thought of her own Faustine jacket, which she'd left at the Cottage.

"Speaking of which . . ." Petra reached into a black leather handbag draped over one arm. Though it was a small bag, she whispered and drew out of it a silk jacket. Anouk gasped.

"My jacket!"

"It was in Little Beau's stall. He clawed up some of the embroidery. I can whisper it fixed for you, but personally, I like the distressed effect."

Anouk ran her hand down the jacket lovingly. Beau had clawed through the creature's widespread wings. Multicolored threads hung loose and dangled like fringe. She pressed her face into it, breathing deep. For a second, she felt hopeful. She'd gotten her jacket back. Maybe there was some way she could regain magic too.

Petra's long lashes blinked lazily behind champagne-colored sunglasses. "You missed the Witchery Feast. Jolie and Sam and Karla and Lise were there. Since Rennar put the coals out, we couldn't continue with the trials. I think the girls were secretly relieved. The Minaret Court and the Barren Court both wanted me in their region — you should have seen them clamor! The things they offered me — estates, cars, servants, horses." She tossed back some wine and sighed contentedly. "Naturally I told them to go stuff themselves. My loyalty is with Paris. Montélimar is the closest thing I have to a home. So I cast a whisper, took Little Beau, and stole one of the Crimson Court's cars."

"I suppose congratulations are in order," Viggo said, tossing back his black hair. "It doesn't feel like so long ago that you and I were playing chase in the lavender fields. And now look at you, so different, so . . ."

"Not a little boy anymore?" Petra gave him a droll look.

"I was going to say how powerful you look."

"Sure you were. Now, are we ignoring the fact that a coven of insane witches have awoken an ancient dark magic, or are we coming up with a plan?"

"Wedding first," Rennar said. "Plan after."

Petra raised her glass again. "So we have a few final days of revelry before we're all destroyed. Great." Her eyes fell on Anouk and she got up and pulled her by the wrist to the privacy of the next table, where she leaned in close. "Are you okay?"

Anouk squeezed her jacket and looked away. "You saw what happened at the Baths."

"You're alive, that's all that matters." She saw the melted bell around Anouk's neck and grimaced. "You really want to hold on to a failed crux? I didn't think you were that morbid."

Anouk gave a bitter laugh, clutching the bell. "If I ever get a second chance, I have to start by understanding where I went wrong before." Then she dropped her hand and peered closely at Petra. "How did you know what your crux was? What did you do differently?"

Petra held out her hands and shrugged. "I haven't a clue. Ten girls who were all clever and deserving. Ten girls who all wanted it as bad as I did. You all seemed somehow *complete* to me. I don't know if that makes sense. Even Frederika, crazy as she was, seemed true to herself. It was like you all belonged there, at the Cottage. I always felt like an impostor, in a way, like I never belonged anywhere. Maybe that's what happens when you're abducted by a witch as a baby. It didn't really bother me—I accepted that feeling a long time ago—but I'd have thought one of you would have chosen the right crux, not me." Petra pressed a quick kiss onto the top of Anouk's head. "For what it's worth, you would have made a great witch. Maybe you'll get a second chance." And then she grabbed Viggo's hand and pulled him toward the dance floor.

Anouk sank back into her chair and rubbed her temples. The wine was already going to her head. She took another sip and a few drops sloshed onto the wedding dress on the table. "Oh, *merde.*"

Rennar took the chair next to her, picked up the dress, and, with a gentle whisper, made the stain vanish.

"Why must you be so infuriatingly calm about all of this?" she snapped, and she wasn't talking about the dress. "You heard Petra —we're facing ruin and you just dance and drink!"

He swirled the wine in his glass and looked moodily into the liquid. "I've been alive five hundred years, Anouk. This isn't the first time someone has shrieked about impending doom."

"It's the first time someone cut you in half." Her eyes fell on the glossy mark where he'd repaired himself after being cut in two. "I don't buy this nonchalant act of yours. You're frightened. You've just never learned how to look afraid."

He flinched. He set down the glass and took her hands in his. For once, the arrogance was gone from his face, and his blue eyes searched hers. "Very well. You want me to tell you that for the first time, I'm uncertain about the future? I am. But I'm certain about you."

He kissed her knuckles. She bristled at the intimate gesture, then relaxed. Maybe they *were* in this together. Maybe his centuries of experience did count for something. He let go of her hands, but on impulse, she grabbed his hands and pulled him even closer.

He looked surprised.

She whispered, "Rennar, turn them back. Please."

His hands tightened in hers. His features were just as tense. "You'll get Cricket in a few days, after the wedding."

"What about Hunter Black and Beau? Forget the deal. It was just a game, like you said. *I* failed the Baths—that doesn't mean Hunter Black should be doomed to a lifetime of being muzzled. And Beau was always supposed to stay human, not me."

"Beau," he said slowly, "is in love with you. And *I* am marrying you. Only a fool would bring him back. At a minimum, he'd stop the wedding. He'd probably try to poison me."

She couldn't argue with that.

But Rennar had been grumbling with the reluctance of someone who hated to concede but knew he was going to. He filled her glass with champagne. "You're impossible. Drink this."

She looked at him in surprise. "Why?"

"Because I'm going to turn Hunter Black back for you, purely out of the goodness of my heart, and the least you can do is make a toast to my honor."

A smile crept onto her face. It felt good to smile again. She clinked her glass against his and downed the champagne in one heady sip. As the bubbly warmth spread through her, making her the slightest bit tipsy, she thought back to the kiss in the Cottage's confectionery. Before she knew what she was doing, she leaned forward and brushed her lips against his cheek.

"To you," she said softly.

Chapter 21

A NOUK'S KISS LEFT a drop of champagne on Rennar's cheek. He wiped it away, as flustered as she'd been by the kiss in the dessert pantry. He drained his own glass and then stood, snatched up a fork, and tapped it loudly enough against the crystal to silence the surrounding chatter. The Goblin drummer, oblivious in his headphones, still pounded away. Rennar cast a quick whisper to silence his instruments. The Goblin's eyes shot open in surprise when his drumsticks turned to putty.

All eyes were fixed on Rennar. Queen Violante gave him an unabashedly flirtatious look, and Prince Aleksi listened respectfully, but most of the Royals watched with the stiff faces of guests who were forced to listen to something they'd rather not hear.

"A speech? Now?" Luc whispered as he surreptitiously came to stand behind Anouk.

"Not a speech." Anouk shivered as she looked around at the cold stares in the ballroom and found that more than a few sets of eyes were focused on her. She'd nearly forgotten this party was to celebrate her own engagement.

"Ladies and gentlemen," Rennar began. "Royals and witches of every realm—and Goblins—today, as you know, we come together to celebrate my impending nuptials. The last time we all gathered for a Royal wedding was eighty years ago, when Prince Sorin married Princess Marieta of the Barren Court. It is my hope that this wedding will unite not only my bride and me, but all of us. There are still those of you who refuse to acknowledge the threat posed by the Coven of Oxford and what has befallen the Court of Isles, but I promise you, a great danger hovers at our doorsteps. The only way we will protect our realms is if we unite our forces."

The Royals' faces remained eerily still. No smiles. No smirks. No frowns. Over hundreds of years, they had learned to perfectly hide their emotions, and they gave no reaction now. Standing in the center of his palace, Rennar, too, wore a mask of indifference. He cut a striking figure in his frost-gray suit. Every person in the room hung on his every word, though they all pretended otherwise, and it was hard for Anouk not to fall under his spell too. She snatched up her champagne glass and sniffed it, feeling suddenly uneasy. Had he enchanted it?

Luc leaned down and whispered, "Not exactly the tone I'd expect from someone planning to surrender his power once all of this is over."

Anouk whispered back, "*He's* willing to step down. It doesn't mean the other Royals will do the same without a fight. He's not a fool."

Luc made a noncommittal snort.

"But let us not dwell on such troubles tonight," Rennar continued. "There are times for war and times for power, but let us put such times aside."

"See?" Anouk whispered to Luc.

"Tonight, we celebrate." Rennar smiled. "Relish the wine. Savor the cake. Enjoy the entertainment. In fact, I have a special perfor-mance planned. I am rarely one for spectacle, but this is to oblige my bride."

All eyes shifted to Anouk. Queen Violante stared at her with bald curiosity, doubtlessly wondering how such a simple girl—a girl who even now had a dust streak on her cheek—had won a prince.

Anouk's face warmed under the scrutiny. She clutched the bell around her neck.

"You," Rennar commanded to a group of butlers surrounding the wolf's cage. "Bring the wolf."

The butlers, despite their enchantment, weren't quick to oblige. One of them, who had a bandaged hand, took a step away from the cage, and Anouk could guess what had happened. One started to hold a trembling key to the lock, but the wolf snarled and leaped at the bars, and the butler fell back with a cry.

Viggo, sulking by the balcony, gave an exasperated sigh. "Out of my way, cowards. I'll do it. He's just a pup." Stumbling slightly—he'd had a lot to drink—he pushed through the butlers, grabbed the key, and unlocked the cage. The wolf bared his teeth and growled but Viggo reached in, grabbed him by the scruff of his neck, and growled back. The wolf, as surprised as everyone else, went quiet. Viggo unlatched the chains and led the wolf toward Rennar.

Perhaps no one else would have caught it, but Anouk saw how Rennar eyed the wolf cautiously. The last time bars hadn't separated them, in the bell tower of the Château des Mille Fleurs, the wolf had nearly killed him.

Rennar touched yellow powder to his lips and whispered, *"Des skalla animaeux . . ."*

A ripple of interest came from the audience as magic began to swirl around the wolf. The bonds circling his neck and his feet clattered to the floor. The muzzle disintegrated into a puff of dust. As soon as he was free, the wolf lunged at Rennar, but with a quick whisper, bonds of golden rope replaced his chains. Enraptured, Anouk pushed through the crowd. She'd seen her friends turned to animals, and it had been the worst experience of her life. This felt topsy-turvy, like history reversing itself. The magic in the air tasted sweet and tart, like gingersnaps.

"Des skalla animaeux . . ."

A sheen of sweat broke out on Rennar's forehead. To turn a man into an animal was a simple thing, but the reverse was no easy feat. Even Rennar, who had *written* the beastie spell, struggled to control the chaotic ribbons of magic that swirled around the wolf. A hush fell over everyone except King Kaspar of the Lunar Court, whose cough became more violent by the minute.

"Fiska ek forma humane."

With a dramatic flick of his wrist, Prince Rennar summoned a flash of light so bright that at least one Goblin shrieked. Plates and glasses shattered around the room, table by table, like miniature dynamite blasts. The windows shook in their frames. The Pretty broker with the long gloves and pet hare jumped backward and smacked into an hourglass perched on the mantel behind Anouk. It tottered, and he reached for it but couldn't catch it in time. It fell and shattered into a mess of broken glass, sand going everywhere. The hare leaped out of his arms. Anouk jumped up too, pressing a hand to her heart, dodging the mess.

"Sorry about that." The broker hastily swept up the sand into a napkin. "I owe you a favor for nearly slicing you apart. I'm Sinjin. Hacker extraordinaire and rabbit enthusiast."

"Forget it," she said.

He carried the spilled sand toward the door but tripped and dropped it all over the Lunar Court's table, and then he turned the other way and spilled it on Mia's hair. He started apologizing profusely to them too.

When Anouk looked back to the center of the room, the wolf was changing. His thick fur was falling off in clumps; pale skin and taut muscles and a smear of charcoal hair replaced it. And then two smoldering eyes appeared—human eyes, eyes she knew—and Hunter Black shed the rest of the fur like he was shrugging out of a coat. His pelt fell to the floor. He stood upright on two feet.

Entirely human.

Also entirely naked.

A few gasps came from the crowd, along with more than one appreciative whisper from a woman in the room and perhaps from a few men; Hunter Black *did* cut quite the figure. His eyes were unfocused. He fell to his knees again. Luc grabbed a nearby tablecloth and draped it around Hunter Black's shoulders. The motion made Hunter Black blink hard a few times and then shake his head as though waking from a drugged slumber. He looked at his bare knees and roared, "What the devil?"

The crowd erupted in cheers. "What a performance!" Queen Violante stood, clapping uproariously. Her sisters followed suit, though not quite as enthusiastically.

"Magnifique!" cried a princess from the Minaret Court.

"I thought it was only a rumor!" said the hacker, Sinjin, who'd come back from the Lunar Court's table and had managed to catch his pet hare again.

Rennar ignored the crowd. He held himself wearily, especially the leg that had turned to stone, as though the magic had exhausted every bone in his body. He searched the crowd until his eyes fell on Anouk.

She rested her fingers on the table to steady herself. What had she just witnessed? *A miracle.* The opposite of the cruel magic that had reduced her friends into things with tails. Rennar's spell had taken an animal and evolved it into something that could rationalize, feel complex emotions, dance a jig, bang a drum, kiss. A grin stretched across her face and she felt like that dreamy, hopeful girl she'd once been. This was the kind of magic she wanted. The kind she'd been so close to winning. And maybe it was what Rennar wanted, too. Maybe everything he'd said wasn't so far-fetched. Her head fizzed like the champagne cocktails that butlers were now serving on golden trays throughout the ballroom. Could she possibly get magic back?

"Hunter Black! Move aside, you devils, let me near him!" Viggo shoved through the crowd, then fell to his knees beside the assassin. He rested a hand on Hunter Black's back. Sweat dripped from Hunter Black's hair and soaked into the tablecloth over his shoulders. "Someone get this man a coat, for the love of God. And a comb!" When no one listened to him, Viggo grumbled under his breath and helped Hunter Black to his feet. Anouk set down her glass, intending to go help them, but then someone screamed.

She spun toward the sound. It came from the direction of the Lunar Court's table, but with the throngs of attendees, she couldn't see what was happening. One of the Minaret Court women seated at the next table cried out and stumbled back against her chair, sending china crashing to the floor. Anouk stood on tiptoe but still couldn't see. What had happened?

Hunter Black, ever the warrior, stumbled toward the nearest table and grabbed a knife from among the silverware, but his eyes were still glassy, and Viggo thrust himself in front of his friend, brandishing his cane.

Petra shrugged off her Faustine coat and climbed onto a chair. She pulled out a flask that, by its anise and sooty smells, held a powerful potion, and threw back a swig. She wiped her lips with the back of her hand. Her body was tense, ready to battle.

Anouk pushed forward, nearly getting trampled by the Goblin musicians who were dragging their drum kits and guitars toward the door. At last, she reached the front of the crowd.

It was King Kaspar.

Only moments ago, during Rennar's performance, his hacking cough had been impossible to ignore. He was a hunched old man whom she'd barely have noticed if it hadn't been for Prince Aleksi's concern. Now the king's normally curved back was ramrod straight, grotesquely so, as though someone had thrust a metal pole through his spine. He must have stood over seven feet tall, towering over even the tallest partygoers. His head was tilted toward the ceiling as though he'd been suspended on invisible wires from his eyes; his crown slid backward, and his arms contorted behind his back.

Anouk's stomach turned. Bodies weren't meant to move like that.

All the Barren Court delegates fled, clearing her view completely, and she gasped. The king wasn't naturally that tall; he was floating about a foot off the floor. Thin ribbons of satiny black smoke curled from his mouth and ears.

She clapped a hand over her mouth.

Black tears—just like the ones from her vision—were pouring down his face.

Chapter 22

"HE'S POSSESSED."

The man who spoke was Baron Winter, a Court of the Woods delegate. He was one of the few Royals who hadn't fled to the edges of the room.

"It's witch magic," Marquesa Ana spat.

Several sets of eyes turned to Petra, the only witch in attendance. The three Crimson Court sisters turned on her like a pack of wolves, wrestled her to the ground with violent whispers, and held her in place with spells. Tablecloths bound themselves around Petra's wrists and stopped her from reaching for her flask of lavender ash.

"It isn't me!" she cried.

Before she could get out another word, the tablecloth wedged itself in her mouth as a gag.

Anouk clutched at the bell, wanting to rip it from her neck. She was useless! The Lunar King's contorted body rose higher. The ribbons of smoke poured out of his mouth. Black tears rolled down his face, dripping into a puddle of tar. Suddenly she was back in the flames, having her body pulled apart, burning without burning at all, and sweat broke out on her brow.

"Let her go," Rennar ordered the Crimson Court sisters, motioning to Petra. "She wouldn't do this. She's a new witch, anyway. It takes decades to master a possession trick."

"It must be her," Marquesa Ana insisted. "She's commanding that smoke. There's something unnatural about it—I can feel it making my skin prickle. It's poison."

The smoke twisted toward the Marquesa as though drawn to her voice, and the Marquesa recoiled.

A chill ran up Anouk's back. She grabbed Rennar's arm and dragged him a few feet away. He frowned when he saw how her hands were shaking.

"Anouk, what is it?" Concern laced his voice.

"It's the Coven." She gestured toward the puddle of black tears. "I saw all of this in a vision during the Coal Baths. I thought it was just delusions, but the Oxford witches were there, somehow, *in* the flames. A group of them were summoning smoke that curled just like this. It rose so high that I couldn't see them anymore." She shivered. "They were crying black tears too."

He pursed his lips. "You're certain?"

"I know I disappointed everyone before, but I'm positive. They're *here*."

Although she sounded crazy, he didn't argue. Before he could act, Prince Aleksi shoved to the front of the crowd and touched silver powder from the vial around his neck to his lips. He began to whisper. Threads of magic wove themselves together into golden ropes that wound around his father's limbs and tried to pull him back to the floor. The king's head twisted unnaturally to observe him. Blankness filled his eyes. Something was looking through them, but not King Kaspar.

The threads of golden magic pulled the king back, but each inch was a battle. The Lunar Prince was straining under the pressure. Rennar reached for his own powder vial, but then the king's eyes began bubbling with tar. His mouth hinged open and a blast of bright light bolted out. Prince Aleksi was struck. He fell back into a chair, clutching at his chest.

Words began pouring out of the king's mouth along with more ribbons of smoke. They grew from low, unintelligible hisses into fragments spoken in the Selentium Vox.

"Previso . . . rivet . . . morfin . . ."

"What's that?" Viggo grabbed her shoulder. "What's he saying? I don't speak that damn language."

"Get back, Viggo," Luc snapped. "Don't breathe in the smoke."

The Royals and Goblins who hadn't yet fled the room all listened uneasily. Anouk translated for Viggo in a hushed voice. "It's strange —he's speaking as 'we,' not as 'I,' like the witches are a collective voice speaking through him. His words are broken. He's threatening an . . . an impending darkness. A deathless death."

Rennar lowered himself to one knee beside Prince Aleksi, who still clutched his chest. Queen Violante knelt at his other side. They helped Aleksi stand.

"You see?" Rennar yelled to the crowd. "The Coven of Oxford is upon us. They've even found their way into our midst. There can be no more doubt about the threat they represent." His face grew serious as he looked to Aleksi and Violante. "We must cast them out, them and their poison smoke. A kindred spell."

They nodded.

The three of them began whispering in unison. Anouk had heard of kindred spells—the kind that took two or more magic handlers working in unison—though Mada Vittora had always preferred to work alone.

As they cast the spell, the smoke seemed to tremble and flow toward their voices. The possessed king shot out more light from his mouth but the Crimson Queen cast a spell to cloud the light while Rennar and Aleksi worked spells to cast out the witches. Powerful energy surrounded them and the king, making the few remaining dishes shatter. A marquesa from the Minaret Court stepped forward and joined in the kindred spell. Baron Winter joined next.

The king's body began to jerk and twist in mid-air. The ribbons of smoke curled tightly, constricting around his body.

"It's working," Petra said as she finally managed to shimmy out of her tablecloth bindings. She shoved herself to her feet and cast her own whisper into the mix.

Anouk's arms hung at her sides. She'd never felt so helpless. Petra fought alongside the others. Luc and Viggo were helping Hunter Black, who was still disoriented from his transformation. Even the Goblins were spitting whispers to keep the witches' magic at bay.

But Anouk could do nothing.

She felt hollow inside. She turned her hands palms up and then curled them into fists. Her nails dug painfully into her palms. *Useless!*

Someone cried out behind her. She spun around. The Royals had managed to surround the possessed king with a sphere of glass cobbled together from broken pieces of crystal and stemware. It trapped the bursts of light, but a thin thread of smoke still snaked out and oozed around the room in the direction of the Goblins. The king continued to cry black tears, which now pooled in the bottom of the glass sphere. Rennar, Violante, and Aleksi redoubled their efforts, but their brows were heavy with sweat. Violante looked on the verge of passing out. The vitae echo prevented them from outright killing the witches or the king; the best they could hope for was to banish the witches' astral projection from the king's body, but even that was proving to be an impossible feat.

Anouk let out a frustrated cry. *She* could kill a witch. *She* wasn't bound by the vitae echo. If only she hadn't lost her magic! But was she totally helpless? A line of black smoke snaked toward her, drawn to her cry, and she flinched and moved away. It came from a small hole in the glass orb. The Royals had enchanted the glass shards to melt together with no gaps or cracks, but the tip of the king's little finger was caught in the glass, leaving the tiniest opening for smoke to escape.

Here, at least, was something she could do that didn't take an ounce of magic.

She grabbed a butter knife.

In a few strides, she was at the glass sphere. It took three slashes to sever the king's little finger. The finger fell with a gush of blood. With a flash of light, the barrier was sealed, the glass sphere complete, the smoke trapped inside where it couldn't poison anyone.

Rennar threw a look over his shoulder and gave her a nod of gratitude.

The sphere started to glow. The king began screaming, his voice as contorted as his body, and with a flash of light, the glass barrier shattered. Shards of crystal rained down. Rennar, closest, took the brunt of it. It carved deep gashes into his face and chest. He threw out whispers to seal his wounds but smoke, now freed from the orb, was snaking into his body.

When the last of the smoke dissipated, slithering out through the window or into Rennar's cuts, all signs of the witches were gone.

So was the king.

Chapter 23

◆

PRINCE ALEKSI KNELT by the fallen shards of glass where the king had vanished. "Father!"

"He's gone," Luc muttered under his breath. "Dead. You don't come back from something like that."

"I guess we know what happened to the Court of Isles," Viggo murmured.

Rennar remained on the ground, groaning as his body convulsed. The ballroom was in terrible shape. Shards of crystal and broken plates littered the place. Chairs had been overturned in the commotion. Tables were upended. The floor was slick with spilled champagne.

"You see?" Queen Violante twisted toward the other Royals. "There is no denying now that we are under attack."

Anxious grumbles came from the few remaining Royals. Aleksi, eyes rimmed in angry red, pushed himself to his feet. "It's true," he spat. "This is the Coven of Oxford's work. This is why we must come together. Only then can we protect our borders and ensure what happened to my father doesn't happen to any of you."

"You mean protect *your* borders," a prince from the Barren Court replied. "Your borders are closest to the Court of Isles. If the witches spread, they'll spread to your territories first."

"They'll be your problem soon enough, Sorin," Violante hissed.

Anouk leaned close to Luc. "Did you learn anything else from the Minaret Court princess?"

He shook his head. "We were interrupted. I'll try again. I know she's frightened by this King Kaspar business—she was sobbing on my shoulder. I'll see if I can't take advantage of that."

Anouk nodded. "Find out what you can, then meet us. We need someplace safe. Someplace private."

"There's a billiard room down the hall," Viggo offered in a whisper, overhearing them. "I've never seen it used. The Royals hate games—they find them utterly dull."

"Meet us there as soon as you can, Luc," Anouk said.

Luc nodded and disappeared into the crowd, looking like just another rattled Royal in velvet and silk.

Anouk knelt by Rennar's side. His breathing was labored. His eyes were glassy. His muscles twitched involuntarily, threatening to convulse. Anouk touched a shard of glass that was buried deep in his chest. Black blood pooled over his skin and she hissed and pulled her hand back. If she tried to remove the glass, he might bleed to death.

"Petra," she whispered loudly, motioning her over. "Can you help me carry Rennar out of here?"

"Are you sure it's safe to move him? I could cast a trick. Enchant that table to grow wheels like a hospital stretcher."

Remnants of smoke were still rising toward the ceiling. Anouk eyed them warily. She hadn't liked how the smoke seemed to respond to the sound of their voices. "Save your magic until we're farther from that smoke, and keep your voice down too. Who knows how the Coven got in here. We'll just carry him. I'll take his arms. You get his feet. Careful, one leg is made of stone."

A few feet away, near the wreckage of the engagement cake, Viggo rested a hand on Hunter Black's shoulder and said gallantly, "And you lean on me, my friend."

Hunter Black swatted away Viggo's hand with a growl. "I don't need rest."

"Of course you don't. You're made of piss and steel. But humor me." He dragged Hunter Black's arm around his shoulder despite the assassin's protests.

As Anouk prepared to stand, the Crimson Queen met her gaze, her eyes filled with mistrust. Anouk froze. The queen squeezed the vial around her neck and took a step toward Anouk, but then one of her sisters started coughing and the other sister screamed, afraid she was possessed, and Violante's attention was dragged back to the other Royals.

"Now. Hurry." Anouk and Petra slowly made their way through the ballroom and into the hall, grunting under Rennar's weight. Viggo followed closely, Hunter Black leaning on him for support. They all stopped at a massive grandfather clock that sat where the corridor forked.

"Which way?" Anouk asked.

"Take a left. It's almost always a left after midnight. Here, let me go first. I told you I'd be good for something." Viggo led the way, counting doorways as he supported Hunter Black, and then toed open a blue door that was slightly ajar. "Aha! I told you. Smell that. Cigars. Whiskey. Cue chalk."

The curtains were drawn, casting the furniture in shadows. Petra whispered the gaslights on, and they flickered to life one at a time, illuminating twin billiard tables lined with black felt, a fireplace flanked by massive leather chairs, and a wall of shelves laden with chessboards from every corner of the globe.

"There. Lay him on that billiard table." Anouk nodded toward the closest one. Groaning, she and Petra hoisted him onto the felt and rolled him onto his back. His eyes were closed, but he was whispering feverish things in a language Anouk didn't know. She pulled up one of his eyelids and her breath stilled—his irises were black with swirling smoke. She swallowed back her panic. Fingers shaking, she focused on easing open the buttons of his shirt to reveal the worst of the cuts. He smelled of sweat and that citrus-vanilla-pine aftershave. It did something to her, smelling that. She felt a tug in the pit of her stomach.

She couldn't afford to lose him.

She toyed with one of his buttons, uncertain whether she wanted to touch his skin. Black smoke marbleized the blood dripping down his side. She fought the urge to wipe it away with her hand. "Petra, the smoke got into his cuts."

Petra leaned in to inspect the poisoned blood and then cursed. "I'll need a potion to draw it out." She looked helplessly around the room. "There's nothing alive in here. Just chessboards and cue sticks." She grabbed a cue from the rack, sniffed it, then recoiled. "The wood's been treated too much. What's wrong with these people? Don't they keep ingredients around the house? Mada Zola stuffed acorns in every spare drawer and hung herbs from every rafter."

"They keep their life-essence in vials around their necks."

Petra bit hard on her lip. She turned to Anouk. "We need Luc. He knows potions better than anyone."

"I'll find him." Anouk started for the door, then returned to the billiard table and rested her fingers gently on Rennar's brow. "Stay strong, you idiot."

She went into the hall and followed the dizzying maze of corridors back to the ballroom. When she found no sign of Luc, she checked the salon, then a washroom, and she eventually found him hidden in a coat closet with a blond count from the Court of the Woods. Luc was murmuring reassurances that the count would never be possessed like King Kaspar. The boy's blue-tinted powder streaked Luc's cheeks.

"Luc! Er, Baron von . . . um . . . we need you." Anouk ignored the surprised look on the count's face as she tugged Luc out of the closet by his shirt cuff. "Hurry, please," she hissed. "If the clock changes, we'll never find our way back."

He wiped the blue kisses off his cheeks with the back of his hand. He smelled of rosewater cologne. She gave him a hard look. "I thought you were interrogating a member of the Minaret Court."

"I . . . *interrogated* her too."

"Ugh—boys. Zip up your trousers and come on."

They raced back to the billiard room, where Luc finished straightening his clothes and then set about inspecting Rennar's wounds. "I need something for expelling smoke," he muttered. "Petra, fetch me that arrangement of fresh hydrangeas in the hallway. And try to be quiet, everyone. The smoke looked like it was responding to vibrations from sound."

While Petra went after the flowers, Luc started rifling through the supplies on a bar cart. "Mint . . . lime . . . it's for cocktails, not spells, but one must do what one must do." He pulled out bundled mint and cherries and citrus rind, snatched a pawn from one of the chess sets, used it as a pestle to grind everything together, then emptied the concoction into a cocktail shaker. The sound of rattling ice jangled Anouk's nerves.

She combed her fingers softly through Rennar's sweat-soaked hair. "Hang on. You've survived centuries. You can pull through another few hours."

He coughed, and the gashes wept more black-streaked blood. She ripped off a scrap of his cloak and dabbed it around the glass shards. Rennar couldn't die. She needed him. She rested a hand gently on his chest, felt his heart struggling to beat beneath her palm.

Luc peered into the cocktail shaker and muttered a prayer. "This is either a delicious potion or a terrible martini. Here." He thrust the shaker at Petra, who sipped it hesitantly.

Her eyes lit up. "Delicious potion, definitely. Do I detect a trace of amaretto—"

Anouk smacked the empty shaker out of Petra's hand, and the room filled with the smell of mint and cherry. "Petra, cast the spell! He's dying!"

"And we're certain we need him alive?"

"Petra!"

Petra rolled her eyes but set to work. She rested a hand a few inches above Rennar's heart and whispered. There was a gravitas to her movements that hadn't been there before the Coal Baths.

Rennar suddenly let out a sharp cry. His eyes moved rapidly back and forth beneath closed eyelids, but he didn't wake.

Petra frowned. "The smoke is tangled up with some kind of dark magic I'm not familiar with. I can't expel it."

"But you're a witch now," Anouk said.

She rubbed the back of her neck uneasily. "For less than a week! Give a girl a break. I just figured out what I want my moniker to be. I don't even have an oubliette yet. That leather bag is on loan."

Anouk tried not to let her frustration show. It wasn't Petra's fault that Rennar was dying amid the billiard balls. And yet, if Rennar died, she'd never be able to keep her promise to the Goblins, and the Coven would spread . . .

"Silly little things," said a voice at the doorway. Queen Violante strode into the billiard room with that easy grace, eyeing Rennar on the table.

"Violante!" Anouk exclaimed. "The smoke . . . it's in his body. It's poisoning him. Can you—"

"Of course I can." The queen gave a pensive frown. There was arrogance there, as Anouk was used to from the Royals, but also a wrinkle of concern. Rennar had alluded to a history between them. Anouk could only imagine. Decades traveling the world together, enchanting waves to rise and fall at their beckoning.

Anouk ran her finger over her lips. She still tasted the champagne Rennar had served her.

"Move aside," the queen said emphatically.

Anouk, Luc, and Petra took several steps backward. From the leather seats, Hunter Black and Viggo watched. Anouk tossed a billiard ball from one hand to the other anxiously. Violante picked up the spilled cocktail shaker and sniffed at it.

"Who made this?"

Luc's hand snaked toward the ceiling.

"It's good," she said begrudgingly. She eyed his baron's crest and then let out a harsh laugh. "For a beastie, you pass well as a Royal.

196

Was that you who absconded to the coat closet with the Minaret girl?"

Luc thrust his thumbs through his belt loops, turning a little red.

Queen Violante tipped up the glass to drain the remnants. She considered the taste, supplemented Luc's elixir with her own powder, and then began to whisper. She sang, more than spoke, the Selentium Vox. The billiard ball went still in Anouk's hand. She'd never heard anyone pronounce the Silent Tongue like that. She knew what an opera was but had never heard one; Beau sometimes sang show tunes while he washed cars, but *angelic* wasn't exactly the word to describe his voice.

The smoke began to work itself out of Rennar. His skin rippled and his body buckled, convulsing until Anouk was afraid he'd break the table, and then he suddenly eased back with a strange sigh as ribbons of smoke curled from his ears and mouth. Queen Violante pitched her voice upward and the smoke pooled itself tidily into the empty cocktail shaker, then she quickly screwed on the lid, trapping it. She leaned over Rennar's body and traced a long fingernail over the bridge of his nose, inspected his eyes and gums for any lingering trace of smoke. Her fingers seemed to know every dip and rise of his face.

"He'll live." She signaled to Luc. "You. Potion-smith. When he wakes, he's going to be weak. Give him fresh blood from that one." She jabbed a long fingernail in Viggo's direction; he rested a hand on his hip and snorted. "Oh, sure, drain the witch's boy."

But if he thought he'd get sympathy, he was wrong. Luc started digging through the bar cart for a sharp knife.

Anouk pressed her hands together and stepped toward the queen. "I don't know how to thank you—"

Violante cut her off with a sharp look, but then it softened. "Ah, it's you. A shame, what happened at the Baths. You could have been great."

Could have been. Three little words like three little daggers to her heart. *Could have been* a witch. *Could have been* strong. *Could have been* more than a maid.

Her cheeks flushed with shame. She cleared her throat. "Now that the other Royals saw what happened, will they help us?"

The queen sneered. "You are a hopeful thing, aren't you? No, little beastie. The attack on King Kaspar has only driven a wedge further between the realms. Now that the Court of the Woods and the Barren Court have witnessed the Coven's power firsthand, they're even less inclined to risk their lives to protect other realms. But I suppose they won't have a choice when you and our prince marry. Not even the Barren Court would dare defy the Nochte Pax." Violante's gaze roamed over Anouk and she mused, "Perhaps you'll be good to him." Then she laughed. "Better than I was, in any case. I was a monster to him."

Anouk ran her hand over Rennar's forehead, hoping for a sign of recovery. His skin was cold. His lips were pale.

By the fireplace, Viggo tried to press a glass of water on Hunter Black, urging him to rehydrate. The assassin pushed it away. Hunter Black's cheeks burned crimson. "You should have left me as a wolf, Viggo. I failed you."

"Shh. Say nothing, my friend." Viggo set down the glass and made as if to reassure him with a touch on the knee, but his hand hesitated and fell back into his own lap instead. Hunter Black bristled. Anouk felt as though she was watching something she shouldn't. She knew that Hunter Black was in love with Viggo. Judging by the careful silence of Luc and Petra, *everybody* knew it, just as they also knew that Viggo wasn't attracted to boys.

Viggo rested his palm on the assassin's shoulder. "Our lives are intertwined, don't you know that, Hunter Black? Where you go, I go."

Hunter Black looked moodily at the lace tablecloth he was wrapped in and mumbled, "Even to hell?"

Viggo flicked a lace edge between his fingers. "Even there."

"Even to Liverpool?"

"Oh God, no."

That elicited a half smile from the assassin. Viggo tsked and plucked a few stray pieces of long gray fur off the tablecloth Hunter Black was wrapped in.

"You'll catch your death in this ugly thing." He twisted to face the group. "A penthouse full of magic handlers and no one can conjure him some clothes?"

Violante was offended by the idea that she would trouble herself with such simple magic. But Petra came over to the leather chairs. Luc's elixir was still in her veins, unused on Rennar. Her gaze raked over the curtains and the billiard tables and then settled on a deck of cards with a black spade design. She gave them a quick shuffle and tossed them toward the ceiling. Quick as a flash, she threw out her hands and cast a trick that froze them in midair. Fifty-two cards hung like a lazy cloud over Hunter Black's head. Petra began to whisper in the Selentium Vox, and the cards, one by one, exploded into fibers that wove themselves together into a dark fabric and then stitched themselves into sleeves and a collar and pants, and soon black trousers, a black shirt, and a coat floated over the coffee table. When the coat caught the light from the fire, an impression of spades shimmered. As a final touch, she whispered toward a paperweight of cut glass that had fallen on the floor. The paperweight floated across the room, then shattered apart and reformed into three smooth clear buttons that sewed themselves onto the shirt.

Hunter Black snatched the clothes out of the air and pulled them on, seeming not to be concerned that everyone got a good glimpse of his bare backside in the process. He tugged up the trousers and buttoned the coat's glass buttons.

"Thanks," he growled with a nod.

Anouk tugged off her socks and handed them to Hunter Black. "Here. They're torn, though," she said. "And, um, covered in soup."

"I've seen worse. I've *worn* worse."

"Anouk."

She spun toward the billiard tables. Rennar was lifting up his head; his eyes were rimmed in red, but his blue-gray irises were clear and fixed on her.

Chapter 24

A T THE RASPY SOUND of Rennar's voice, Queen Violante turned too, but Anouk climbed over an ottoman and beat the queen to the prince's side. She touched his forehead. "Rennar! Are you all right?"

"Of course he is," Violante declared. "*I* cured him."

He pushed himself up on one arm and with his other hand, he touched his lips, his nose, and his ears, then looked at his fingers as though expecting blood. "I'm surprised to be breathing, to be honest."

Anouk sat on the edge of the table. "Whatever that smoke was the Coven used to possess King Kaspar, it nearly got you. The king's gone. Vanished just like the entire Court of Isles. The other Royals are nearly at war with one another, arguing over what to do next."

He sat up halfway, shaking his head. "Never mind them at the moment." He coughed, his whole body trembling with the effort. He ran a shaky hand over his face. "Where are the animals? The cat and the dog?" His voice was hoarse.

"Still in the ballroom."

"Get them."

She gave him a questioning look. Impulsively, she leaned forward and felt his forehead again. But he pushed her hand away and sat up fully, wincing with pain, and then wincing with the effort to hide it. He had to use both hands to swing his stone leg down from the table.

"What are you doing? You nearly died! Sit!" She gently tried to push him back down.

"I'm fine." He was clearly not fine, but the look in his eye dared anyone to contradict him. "You saved my life. Now, do you want me to turn your friends back or not?"

She stared at him as though he were muttering in a fever dream. "You said you wouldn't turn them back until our wedding night," she said. "It was our deal."

He coughed a mirthless laugh. "Anouk, Anouk, forget our deal. It was all just a stupid game, like you said." He swept a weak hand toward the collection of chessboards lining the shelves.

"You can't possibly be strong enough." She instantly regretted her words when he bristled. She let out a puff of air. "Don't growl at me like that! It's the hardest spell there is. It would be challenging even if you were well."

He thrust his hand toward Violante and beckoned for the vial around her neck, which she handed over after a long moment of reluctance. He uncorked it and poured the entire contents down his throat, then followed it with the contents of his own vial. Anouk gasped. That much powder would have taken the powdersmiths in the basement half a century to produce.

"Do you still doubt me?" Rennar's eyes practically glistened with power.

Anouk felt a thrill spread from the pit of her stomach to her throat. "You'll really change them both back? Even Beau?"

Instead of answering, he eased himself to the edge of the billiard table and tested his weight on his leg of stone.

She gave his chest a shove. "And Beau?"

He winced and she clapped her hands over her mouth, afraid she'd hurt him, but he waved off her concern. "Yes! Yes, damn it. Beau too."

Hope surged like the sugary rush that followed the first bite of something sweet, but she swallowed it back down. The Shadow Prince did nothing for free. People would have razed entire cities for the amount of powder he'd just poured down his throat. "Why?" Her voice was hard.

"Just get the animals before I change my mind." It came out as a snarl. He added, softer, "Please."

She felt several sets of eyes on her. Hunter Black and Viggo by the fireplace, Luc and Petra near the bar cart. The only person who seemed bored by the exchange was Queen Violante, who had made herself a mimosa.

Anouk wanted to press Rennar further, but there was a slightly unhinged look in his eye. His offer was fragile. Push him, and he might change his mind. She hurried back to the ballroom, where a fleet of maids were already mopping the floor. The Royals were gone. A few Goblins picked through the fallen trays of food for anything worth snacking on.

She spotted Cricket's cage overturned beneath a table. She dropped to her knees and fished it out. The white cat inside yowled.

"*Zut.* Sorry we left you, Cricket." She peered under the rest of the tables. "Little Beau? Where are you?" She whistled softly and the tablecloth over the dessert table rustled. A blond snout poked out, followed by big brown eyes. "Come on, Little Beau, it's all right! You can stop hiding. The witches are gone."

Anouk dusted off a piece of ham that had fallen on the floor and coaxed him out with it, then she tied the end of a tablecloth around his collar and led him back to the billiard room, holding the cat's cage a safe distance away from him.

Rennar was standing, though he looked unsteady. When he saw her, he motioned to the animals. "Take the cat out of the cage. Put her there, in the center of the rug. Hold her so she doesn't run away."

Anouk gingerly reached into the cage and grabbed the cat by the scruff of her neck.

"Here, give her to me. Cats love me." Luc took her. He sat cross-legged on the rug with the cat struggling in his lap.

"Anouk, take the dog," Rennar commanded.

The dog sniffed at the magic still sparking in the air from Rennar's healed body and Hunter Black's playing-card coat. Then he licked Anouk's nose.

"Just wait, Beau," she whispered into his floppy ear. The dog couldn't know why her hands were shaking. That this was what she'd worked so hard for.

The hush over the billiard room felt sacred as Rennar began to whisper. Something tugged inside Anouk. She knew the words like she knew her own name.

"Des skalla animaeux, fiska ek forma humane . . ."

She closed her eyes. Her lips moved silently in unison with Rennar's voice. The pit of her stomach ached with longing. It should have been her turning them back to human. Like a rash, the shame of failure spread up her neck.

She opened her eyes. The air began to swirl around the cat and the dog. White fur floated off the cat like dandelion fluff. The cat twisted and snarled in Luc's lap, green eyes flashing. Little Beau trembled beneath Anouk's hand. She muttered reassurances in his ear, stroking his back. Handfuls of blond fur came away in her fingers. And then suddenly pale skin showed and she jerked her hand back. The magic was swirling faster, whipping her hair around her face. The cat yowled. Luc hissed — the cat had clawed him. *So much for cats loving him.* But he didn't let go.

In the next moment, with a flash of brilliant light, there was a boy on the floor and a girl in Luc's lap. Two pelts fell to the rug like fur coats sliding off hangers. Beau was crouched, his blond hair hanging in his face, light reflecting off his naked back and thighs. Cricket's tea-brown limbs were tangled in Luc's arms as she sputtered and shrieked, scratching him with fingernails. Luc caught her wrists.

"Cricket! It's me! It's Luc."

Cricket was breathing so fast that Anouk was afraid she'd pass out. Her head whipped around the room, blankly taking in the unfamiliar wall of chessboards, the billiard tables, Rennar, Queen Violante sipping her cocktail, Hunter Black, and Viggo.

"What the . . ." Cricket pressed her fingers against her temples.

Anouk felt a gentle touch on her shoulder, and she spun around. Beau squinted at her with dazed eyes. He rubbed the back of his neck groggily. "Anouk?" His voice was hoarse, as though he'd been asleep for days.

She threw her arms around him, knocking them both completely over. "Beau!" She couldn't touch him enough. His hair. His cheeks. The off-center bridge of his nose.

He looked around the room, bewildered. "I'm . . . confused."

She laughed and buried her face against his shoulder. She drew in the very human smell of him, sweat and stale breath and *boy*.

"What happened?" he muttered.

Petra whistled low. "How much time do you have?"

Anouk pressed her palms against his cheeks and turned his head to face her. She grinned so hard it hurt. "Beau. You're back. You're really back."

His eyebrows knit together as he looked at his bare limbs. On impulse, Anouk kissed him. His lips against hers were big and clumsy, but he kissed her back. She leaned against his chest, slid a hand around his side. His lips were like honey. His pulse was quick, almost too quick, but so was hers.

"Dust Bunny?"

"Yes, it's really me, Beau. You're back."

He touched her face. His thumb brushed her cheek and she leaned into it, closing her eyes. Waiting for him to kiss her again. Her lips parted.

But the kiss never came. He pulled his hand away, and her eyes shot open in alarm, but she saw that he was grinning and holding up an accusatory finger smeared in frosting. She touched the part of her face that must have collided with the engagement-party cake during the commotion.

He gave a lopsided grin. "Some things never change." He popped his thumb into his mouth.

"What. The. Hell. Is. Going. On?" Cricket's eyes were glassy. "My head is killing me."

"Welcome back." Luc released her wrists and she massaged them, scowling, but then she saw the bleeding claw marks on his arms and made a small squeak.

"Christ, did I do that?" She peered at her fingernails.

"Cricket!" Anouk let go of Beau, crawled over to Cricket, and swept her into a hug. She smelled like cherry Pop Rocks. Her hair tickled Anouk's cheeks. Luc wrapped his arms around them both, and then pulled Beau into the embrace as well. Anouk wasn't sure where she ended and they started. She only felt marvelously warm in her heart. They were together again.

Well. *Except.*

Hunter Black, still weak, leaned back in the armchair and scowled at their public display of affection.

Anouk rolled her eyes.

But even Hunter Black couldn't keep up his moody pretense for long, and his scowl, despite his best efforts, changed into a smile as Cricket and Beau both stretched out their arms and tested their fingers.

"How did this happen?" Beau asked.

Anouk twisted around to point to Rennar, whom she'd halfway forgotten about in her excitement. Her grin vanished. He was slumped against the billiard table. His face had lost its color. Queen Violante was dabbing a silk handkerchief against his brow. Anouk shoved herself up from the rug.

"Rennar! Are you okay?"

He mumbled something that sounded like the opposite of okay.

"It's a difficult spell, that one," Violante said. "Even with all that powder, he was already weak." She went to the bar cart and rummaged around for something to strengthen him.

Anouk fought the urge to comb back the hair falling in his eyes. "Rennar," she said softly, shaking his shoulder gently. She kept her voice low, only for the two of them. "Tell me why you did this. Why you were kind."

His blue eyes were piercing. He licked some moisture back into his lips as he rasped, "Call it a sign of faith that we can trust each other. I don't want you to marry me because I'm holding your friends hostage. We enter into it freely or not at all. No more games. No more bargains."

She gave him a slow nod.

Luc handed Cricket and Beau blankets to use until they could conjure them up some clothes. "A lot has happened," Luc explained to them. "I'm afraid we haven't brought you back with good news."

"That's okay." Beau caught Anouk's gaze from across the room and smiled, though his eyes flashed briefly to Rennar. "We're back. That's enough good news for one lifetime."

Chapter 25

THE BEASTIE SPELL was taxing not only for the caster but also for Beau, Cricket, and Hunter Black. Their bodies had stretched, and so had their minds; evolving from animal to human in the blink of an eye would have fatigued even the strongest physique. When Mada Vittora had first transformed them years ago, she'd prepared pallets for them to rest on, strengthening herbs, and good hearty meals. At Castle Ides, there was no shortage of places to rest and sustaining suppers, though it still took them days to fully shake off the stupor. A near-constant stream of Pretty servants brought them chilled water and lavender-scented pillows and drams of pain-relieving elixir for their aching heads. Viggo oversaw their recovery with all the confidence of a boy who'd more or less successfully babysat a houseful of Goblins.

Anouk, meanwhile, ate cake.

Red velvet cake and raspberry cheesecake and tiramisu paired with champagnes and rosé wines and chocolate-infused merlot. She sampled roasted venison, baked Camembert, *moules marinière*. Rennar kept her so busy rushing from one wedding preparation to the next that she barely had time to pop in and check on her friends before it was time to taste-test more entrées.

A fleet of Pretty tailors took up an entire afternoon measuring her for a wedding wardrobe, but when December peeked in and saw the subdued fabrics they had chosen, she chased them out in disgust and rounded up the most fashionable Goblins to dress Anouk instead. The hours flew by in a flurry of black bows and long feathers and jagged-edged lace. The Goblins whispered the dress together, creating elaborate stitching that not even the most skilled Pretty could match. They added a few inches to the heels of her glass slippers along with a dash of enchantment so that they would leave glittering prints behind wherever she walked.

And the hairstyles! Elaborate braids plaited with magic, and updos that took the Goblins' punk styles to a sophisticated polish. As soon as they had settled on a chignon shaped into a bow, Rennar appeared to whisk her away to the spell library, where a jeweler waited in the hazy blue lights to measure her for a ring. There was talk of fire opals and diamonds, of palladium metals. She'd barely selected a cut before Rennar paraded a stream of musicians past her, every type from jazz quartets to folk bands to punk rock and even a singer who—December whispered in her ear—was all the rage in New York after winning a televised singing competition. By the time she selected flowers, her mind was spinning. Florists carried in buckets of the most beautiful flowers she'd ever seen, all of them wildly impossible colors, and pressed her hard to pick a color scheme. She finally cried out, *"Blush!"* in a panic, and then everything from flowers to dresses to cakes were delicate shades of rose, pink, red, crimson. The cake was red velvet. The flowers were pink dahlias. Even her dress had pale roses woven in with the feathers.

"Please tell me this is the last of it." She was seated on a throne by Rennar's side, posing for a portrait by a Muscovite artist.

An arrogant smile flickered over Rennar's face. "Come now, you enjoy it. You were drooling over the cakes."

Her stomach groaned, betraying her. "I'm just saying that it's an awful lot of work for a sham marriage."

"My dear, all marriages within the Courts are shams. In the history of the near realms, I don't think a single marriage has been a love match. That doesn't mean they're spared from tradition. In fact, some would argue that tradition is all the more important when the Royal Courts are nearly at war with one another, not to mention when the bride can't stand the groom. You *do* still loathe me, don't you?" His eyes dared her to contradict him.

"You're fortunate that I'm good at pretending," she said noncommittally.

And she *was* good at pretending. Pretending to enjoy his company. Pretending her smiles were real. Pretending to savor the luxury of royal life. She'd spent her life as a maid, so what was the harm of letting others wait on her for once? Of being the princess of her own fairy tale?

Pretending, it turned out, wasn't difficult at all.

The night before the wedding, exhausted from dancing lessons and stuffed full of beignets, she dragged herself into the billiard room, which the other beasties had staked out as their own space, and flopped down on the long leather sofa. She gave a tired but satisfied sigh and took the last of the beignets out of her pocket. Music still chimed in her ears.

Beau and Cricket and Hunter Black had recovered enough to spend the evening poring over the Duke's books from the Cottage. Judging from the small piles of moth wings on the table, Cricket had been practicing spell casting. And judging from the singe marks on the carpet, Anouk wasn't sure if it had been successful.

Viggo sent her a wry glance over top of his book. "Nice of you to spare a moment from being pampered to come see us. We're only staying up all night trying to figure out a plan for saving the world here."

Anouk was poised to shove the last of a beignet in her mouth. She paused and guiltily wiped her hand on the sofa. "Rennar says I have to make it look convincing."

"Yeah," Beau mumbled, not taking his eyes off his book. "You could have fooled me."

Beau's face was still winter-pale, but the glassy sheen was gone from his eyes; he was himself again, minus the memories from the past few weeks. Yesterday morning, she'd brought him fresh coffee in bed and crawled beneath the covers and told him about traveling to the Black Forest and about him being locked in the stables. He'd gone moody and quiet until she'd mentioned how she'd sneaked him ham scraps, and that had mollified him.

She moved to perch on the armrest of his chair and run a hand through his messy hair, but he bristled. She stopped and turned to the stack of books instead. "Have you found anything?"

Petra slammed a book closed. "Black tears."

Anouk raised an eyebrow. "You mean a reference to them?"

"No, *real* black tears. This morning while you were trouncing around sniffing bridal bouquets, Quine's sister started crying black tears."

Anouk's face went slack. "Mia?"

"Yes. And it gets worse." Petra went to the window, leaning on the sill. Sleet pounded against the glass. "Duke Karolinge sent Saint into London this afternoon on a reconnaissance mission."

"I didn't think birds could get through the border spell."

"The spell prevents anything enchanted from crossing into London. That includes Rennar's crows and the Castle's messenger doves. But Saint isn't enchanted. He's a regular falcon. The Duke used Pretty falconry methods to train him, not magic. Saint made it across the border and brought back a message from a contact there that the plagues in London are getting worse. There are reports of time slips. Pockets of the city getting trapped in thirty-second loops. Men and women walk into a time slip and repeat the same gestures again and again until their bones wear out and they die of exhaustion. The Pretties are starting to realize this is more than just 'atmospheric irregularities' caused by 'pollution excess.'"

Luc suddenly sat upright, eyes wide at the book in his lap. "Look at this. Here. It mentions something called the Dark Chaos, but I think that's a mistranslation. I think they mean Noirceur. Anyway, it says it originated with the formation of the Earth. It came about from natural elements. Fire and water."

"Fire and water don't go together," Viggo said.

"Yes, they do," Luc said, eyes dancing. "In a sense. They make *smoke*."

Anouk raised an eyebrow.

"That still doesn't help us with Jak's riddle," Beau said. One of the first things Anouk had told them about, once they were human again, was her talk with Jak.

Luc sank back in the leather chair, took off his wire-rimmed glasses, and massaged the bridge of his nose. "If we want to solve his riddle, we have to first figure out what the symbol means. There are books here on pictographs and iconography, but there's nothing that looks like what he drew."

Anouk joined Petra at the window. The sleet painted the city in messy gray strokes. If only it would snow—then maybe Jak would come and give her another clue.

"You never said what it was," Anouk said quietly.

Petra raised a questioning eyebrow. "What *what* was?"

"You said you decided what your moniker will be, but you didn't say what it was."

A coy smile flickered over Petra's face. "Didn't I?"

A gray shadow rippled through the rain and landed on the bust of Rennar in the front yard.

"There's Saint," Cricket commented, "back from London again. Maybe he's brought better news."

Petra gave a gasp and sat up straight. Her eyes were wide. "That's it! The falcon!"

Anouk stared blankly. "What about him?"

"You asked how he got into London and I told you about the border spell. How he's just a regular bird."

"And . . ." Beau said.

"*And* that means the Coven's border spell doesn't block animals. Regular, unenchanted animals." Petra's eyes gleamed darkly. "Don't you get it? Really? No one? I can get you in! Well, not *you*. But you. You know."

"No," Luc said flatly. "I don't."

"Animals," Petra continued with shining eyes. "The five of you are enchanted when you're in your human form, not in your animal

214

form. The cat and dog and such were just plain animals that Mada Vittora found around the city. If I turn you back into your original selves, you'd be just as unmagical as you were then. You could get through the border and into Britain. I can do it—the contra-beastie spell isn't as difficult as the beastie spell." She tapped a jagged fingernail over her lips. "Let's see. A boat won't take wolves or owls, and neither will an airplane. Ah! There's a service tunnel that runs alongside the Chunnel, the tunnel that runs beneath the English Channel. It's only ever used in emergencies. You can travel through it into Britain and hop a commuter train the rest of the way to London."

The room was quiet, but Petra was so electrified that she didn't seem to notice.

"One problem," Viggo pointed out. "Cats and wolves and owls are predators. If they aren't in cages, what's to stop Cricket from eating Luc?"

Petra's face fell momentarily, but then a grin spread across her face. "*You'll* stop her, Viggo. You're just a plain, boring Pretty, which means you can cross into Britain too. You'll lead the animals through the Chunnel and make sure no one eats anyone else."

Viggo glowered. "I wouldn't say *boring*."

Anouk turned away from the gleam in Petra's eyes. Petra was so proud of herself for the plan—and it *was* a decent one—but Petra thought changing from human to animal was like changing into a new set of clothes. She'd never experienced the Cold Place. The Dark Thing. Petra had always been human and so she'd taken for granted her ability to reason, to laugh, to feel, to cry.

The other beasties were silent too. Then Luc shifted and said patiently, "You don't know what you're asking, Petra."

Petra's face scrunched up. "This will work."

"Maybe." Luc pressed his hands together. "But it's no small thing, giving up our humanity. After everything we've fought for, the idea of returning to our origins, even temporarily, feels like defeat."

Petra's lowered her eyelids slightly. She was beginning to understand, but she still frowned. She spun on Anouk. "I get it, I do, but there's no other way. What, we're supposed to trust in Rennar's plan? Even if he manages to get the Royals to cooperate—which is a big *if* —they'll only be slowing the Coven down. That isn't a solution, it's a Band-Aid." When Anouk just chewed on her lip, unsure what to say, Petra turned to Cricket. "Come on, Cricket. You know that this makes sense."

Cricket folded her arms tightly. "Do I? My whole life, I've day-dreamed about beasties being able to cast magic, and now we can. We have libraries full of spells, people who can teach us. Yesterday I learned how to make myself invisible. But I can't do magic if I have *paws*."

Petra groaned and turned to Beau, but he cut off whatever she'd been about to say.

"I've been human all of three days, Petra. Let me live a little! I want to race a car down the Boulevard Saint-Michel. I want to shop at Galeries Lafayette. I want to eat— *mon Dieu*, do I ever want to eat. And—" He stopped short. His eyes rested on Anouk, and he looked at her in a way that didn't need words for everyone in the room to understand exactly what he wanted to do with Anouk.

Petra slumped against the windowsill and threw her hands up. "I'm trying to help. Trying to save the world, you know."

Anouk rested a hand on Petra's shoulder. "Your idea's brilliant,

Petra. But even if we went through with it, how would we turn back to humans once we reached London? Only a few Royals are powerful enough to perform the spell, and none of them can cross into the city. Viggo certainly can't turn us back. Viggo can't do anything."

"Hey," he protested. "I'm feeling very ganged up on at the moment."

Petra was quiet. She clearly didn't have an answer. But a deep voice spoke from behind them.

"I might know someone who can help."

Rennar stood in the billiard-room doorway. How long had he been listening? He wore casual loose gray pants, a white cotton T-shirt that hugged his biceps, and a crimson terrycloth robe. Anouk glanced at the grandfather clock. It was nearly dawn.

Despite the pajamas, he strode in with a princely air. "Sinjin."

"Sinjin? Oh, from the party? Black gloves? Tattoos around the back of his neck? A golden hare?"

Rennar nodded. "He deals in information. He was a hacker before the Court of Isles got their hands on him—hence the tattoos of zeros and ones. Binary code. He'd been dating a Goblin girl who talked in her sleep. He found out about the Haute and went to Lady Imogen, begged to be let into our world. Normally she'd have wiped his mind, but hacking skills are useful to people like us, people who can't use advanced forms of technology, like the internet, without losing our magic. He's a Pretty, so the border spell has no effect on him. He can come and go freely in London. I sent him back to the city a few days ago to do more reconnaissance. He's there now, based in Omen House in Piccadilly."

"But if he's a Pretty," Cricket countered, "he can't change us back."

"He can't, no. But I can. There is a way that we could . . . *arrange* . . . to have you turned back." He went to the wall of chess pieces, selected one hewn from purple amethyst, and waved it enticingly in the air.

Cricket groaned. "He's talking in riddles again."

"Dear Cricket, sometimes riddles are preferable to reality. Did you know that the Haute can store magic in certain gemstones? Emeralds for beauty. Amber for love. Blue diamonds for transformation. With the proper tools, a skilled Pretty can release the spells they hold. Amethyst," he mused, toying with the chess piece, "has always been one of my favorites. Give me a few days. It'll take time."

Beau grumbled again about wanting to use his thumbs for a while longer. Cricket had drawn out one of her knives and was twirling it absently, a scowl on her face.

"It's an awful plan," Hunter Black said gruffly, breaking the silence. "But it's the only one we have."

Petra raised a glass to that.

Anouk chewed her lip, turning back to the window. Paris was beautiful at night in the rain, the streets like glass, the lights and headlights like streaking stars. Could she really turn back voluntarily? She'd fought so hard to keep from turning back. And there were deeper worries. Worries she hadn't yet fixed a name to. Worries that those dark shadows might be made of the same magic as the Noirceur.

"Anouk?" Beau touched her shoulder and she jumped. Everyone was staring at her as though they'd been trying to get her attention.

He searched her face. "Are you okay?"

She tore her eyes away from his and gave a shallow nod.

"We don't have much time," Cricket said unhappily. "If Quine's sister is crying black tears, who's next? We don't know how the Coven is reaching them, what King Kaspar and Mia and the entire Court of Isles have in common. I hate the plan, but Hunter Black's right. We don't have anything better."

"Then it's decided?" Luc asked. "I'm in, but it must be unanimous."

"I'm in too," Cricket said glumly. "But I don't like it."

"And I." Hunter Black nodded.

"No one asked me, but I'm in too," Viggo interjected.

"Anouk?" Beau asked softly. "I'm in only if you are."

She hugged her arms around her chest. "If we're going to do it, we do it tomorrow after the wedding and coronation. As soon as the Royals swear fealty to the Nochte Pax. That way, even if we fail, the Royals still stand a chance of protecting the rest of Europe."

Beau's face had gone dark at mention of the wedding. Anouk placed a hand on his cheek and smoothed out his worried wrinkles with her thumb. "I told you," she said quietly. "It's only a marriage in name. After we stop the Coven, I don't have to be faithful to him. You and I will be together."

"I'm not sure your fiancé knows that," he grumbled, sliding a look at Rennar.

"Speaking of fiancé," Rennar interjected. He sauntered over and took one of Anouk's hands. "If you haven't forgotten, we have a wedding to prepare for. Our own." He glanced at the clock. "It'll be daylight in an hour and you're in desperate need of a bath. You can't show up at your own wedding with ink stains on your fingers and crumbs on your chin."

She wiped at her mouth guiltily, then turned back to Beau. "The wedding will be over in a day, we'll have the support of the Royals, and then you and I will stuff our faces with fistfuls of that cake, okay?"

Beau still looked glum. "Before rushing to our dark fates?"

"Yes, before that."

She placed a soft kiss on his cheek. He reluctantly smiled.

The clock chimed six. Rennar tugged Anouk toward the door, calling for the servants. December and the Goblin beauty squad swept into the room and tugged her out by wrist and skirt, scrubbing cloths over her sticky fingers. She sniffed her armpits surreptitiously. She sighed and gave in.

Even if this wedding was a sham, Rennar was right—a bath first wouldn't hurt.

Chapter 26

A S SOON AS DECEMBER and the other Goblins got her to the penthouse salons, they gave her a bath, and then they began to work their magic. Pulling combs through her hair, casting whispers to smooth out the tangles, then styling it into a chignon bow at her nape. They swallowed June bugs and spat out tricks to erase the odd pimple here and there and bring a permanent blush to her cheeks. It took four of them to lower the wedding gown over her head, and when Anouk looked in the mirror, she was surprised to see that the downy feathers covering the train had multiplied yet again so that the wing effect was exaggerated; she looked like she was about to take flight. She tapped at her reflection in the mirror, almost expecting it to move independently of her.

"Stop looking so surprised," December said. "We can make the ugliest duckling look like a swan. Er, of course, you were a nice-looking duck to begin with. Pretty, even. For a duck." She grabbed Anouk's arm in an attempt to change the subject. "Are you sure you don't want me to ink some tentacles on your arms?"

"No, thanks. Really."

"I could use pink ink. It would fit the color scheme."

"This is fine as it is."

"Just one little tentacle?"

Anouk shook her head. The Goblins exchanged looks. "Boring," one of them whispered.

But Anouk smiled at her reflection. She was going to be a princess. From owl to girl to princess. Not many people could claim to have achieved so much. The only person who'd risen equally high was Rennar. Spell-scribe to prince. Now they were going to prove that those who started from humble beginnings were capable of great things. The greatest of all? Turning over their power and putting it back into the hands of the people.

A knock came at the door.

December opened it for Beau, who had also bathed and was dressed for the occasion in a black suit. He took one look at Anouk and swallowed, then wiped his mouth with the back of his hand. He started to loosen his tie. "Are you sure you don't want to run off together? We could go back to the Black Forest. Find that castle full of candy and grow fat together."

She lifted the heavy train of the dress and waded over to him in a pool of feathers and silk. She placed a hand on his cheek. "First we save the world. Then candy."

His soft eyes practically consumed her whole. "What about a kiss? When does that come in?"

She grinned. "Right now."

She touched her lips to his. He smelled like fresh soap, and his skin was smooth and clean. He slid his hand around her back, crushing the feathers, and December gasped in horror and slapped his hand away.

"You beast!" December cried. "No touching the dress!"

His mouth curled into a grin over Anouk's. He picked her up by the waist and swung her around in a twirl of feathers, out of range from December's slaps, and kissed her again. She leaned into him, laughing, resting a hand on his chest. His heart was beating steadily. The smell of him was driving her wild. She nipped at his bottom lip. He captured her own and leaned her back into a dip, one hand behind her head to keep her from falling.

Several Goblins stylists gasped.

"Not the hair!" December wailed. She smacked Beau's broad shoulders with a hairbrush.

He put Anouk down and held up his hands in mock surrender. "I'm going! I'm going!" He gave Anouk one final look. A corner of his mouth turned up, but something about it didn't quite reach his eyes. "You won't kiss him like that, will you?"

"Impossible," Anouk said honestly.

December started smacking him again with the brush until he fled.

The Goblins frantically fixed her fallen hair and smoothed the wrinkles from her dress, and when the clock chimed noon, they opened the same door that Beau had walked out of, but the hallway beyond had vanished with the changing of the hour. Instead, a set of frosted glass doors with white ironwork stood before them: the entrance to the rooftop garden. Anouk twisted her hands in the folds of her dress, hoping the Goblins couldn't see how they were shaking. With a grin, December threw open the doors.

Anouk braced for a blast of winter air. Her shoulders and arms and décolleté were bare, but instead of a harsh chill, she felt buttery warmth. Her muscles eased as she blinked into the sunlight. *Summer* sunlight, rich and bright. Just moments ago, snow and sleet were pounding against the windows. The rooftop garden, the last she'd seen of it, had been dreary and wet, the furniture covered with tarps, frozen puddles on the stone paths, rosebushes scraggly and bare. She tipped her head up and nearly tripped on her hem. It *was* still snowing. Someone—Rennar, probably—had cast a spell to create a dome of summertime over the rooftop garden. Beneath the spell, it was all flowers and the trills of birdsong. The rosebushes now burst with soft pink blooms the same color as her blush.

She felt eyes on her.

The rooftop garden was filled with more Royals than she'd ever seen in one place. She'd met the leaders of the various Courts at the Coal Baths and again at her engagement party, but in the days since, lesser Royals had also arrived. Dukes from the Minaret Court dressed in a bold vermillion. Ladies-in-waiting from the Barren Court with their arms overflowing with cherry blossoms. Knights bearing the crest of the Crimson Court dressed in shades of blush. Court of the Woods nobles in flowing coral robes. Duke Karolinge, a reluctant-looking officiant, stood at the front of the assembly in a red suit so dark it was almost black. The Goblins huddled in attendance around the edges of the garden, crammed in amid the rosebushes. They'd each donned a pink hat or a pink scarf or put on a smear of pink eye shadow. The only one not dressed in shades of red was Petra, who was wearing her black coat and champagne-colored sunglasses.

No one told a witch how to dress.

Rennar stood beneath an archway of vines in the center of the garden, dressed in red, a crown of gold antlers on his head. His eyes, normally such a cool blue, seemed to crackle like embers.

Anouk took a step forward and promptly tripped on the hem of her dress.

"Careful!" Cricket, standing by the doorway, moved to help her. Her hands were cool against Anouk's burning skin. Cricket was wearing her ripped jeans but she'd put on a pink lace top for the occasion. A bouquet of roses was balanced in the crook of her arm.

Cricket gave her a dry smile as she helped her stand. "Try to make it down the aisle in one piece?" Her voice dipped low. "If we must go through with this ridiculous ceremony, at least let's not make a fool of ourselves in front of the entire Royal Court." She shoved the bouquet into Anouk's arms. "Here. This is yours. I'll hold your train. Apparently, I'm your maid of honor."

Anouk blinked down at the roses. Someone had removed the thorns and wrapped the stems in lace. A wave of doubt suddenly washed over her. "Cricket, I'm not sure about this."

"Me neither, but it's too late to get out of it now." Cricket prodded her in the backside. "Hurry up so we can at least eat cake."

Anouk's glass shoes wobbled on the uneven stones. On either side of her, the Royals observed her with cool indifference. She wondered what was going through their heads. Just months ago she'd been sweeping floors. What did they think of the leader of the Parisian Court marrying a maid? A *beastie*? Not the most likely individual to button up in a feathered dress and march down the aisle. Not the kind to lead a realm.

She could feel their judgment beating down on her. She swallowed, swaying slightly, then gripped the rose bouquet in determination. Well, she'd never asked to join their ranks. She was going to save their necks—ungrateful though they were—but she was doing it to save her own. None of them were risking their lives to set foot in London and face the Coven. They'd be here, in their protected penthouse palace, drinking rare wines and bemoaning the decline of the Haute.

She tipped her chin up.

Rennar watched her with an unreadable expression as she approached and took her place beneath the arch. Duke Karolinge loomed over them, looking uncomfortable in a suit instead of his robes. He adjusted his wire-rimmed glasses.

Rennar leaned forward to whisper, "You have grass stains on your hem."

She looked down. *Zut alors.* If anyone could manage to ruin a magic-infused couture dress in thirty steps, it was her.

Cricket artlessly arranged her dress around her, kicking at the lace train to make it cooperate, and then joined Beau, Hunter Black, Luc, and Viggo, who made up the motley wedding party. Beau tugged on his tight collar. His eyes flickered to Anouk but he couldn't seem to make himself hold her gaze. Cricket gave him a sideways hug.

Duke Karolinge slammed his staff against the ground and Anouk jumped.

"Let us begin."

Those were the only words spoken in an earthly language. He switched to the Selentium Vox, rattling off a litany of oaths from a dusty volume he cradled in one hand. He seemed to be the only one interested in the ceremony. The other Royals looked bored. One of the Minaret Royals stifled a yawn. Queen Violante didn't even bother to hide hers.

Anouk, with her basic knowledge of the language, tried to follow along, but it was so dry that when he launched into the history of Haute rites in the twelfth century, her mind wandered. Was she truly doing this? Marrying a prince? She thought of the wrinkled playbill she'd once pasted to the wall of her bedroom. Princes and princesses, daring rescues and sword fights. At the time, she'd dreamed of such things as she darned Mada Vittora's socks into the late hours of the night. Such lives had belonged to other people. *Special* people. Not maids or gardeners or chauffeurs.

Overhead, the sleet turned to snow that pitter-pattered on the dome that Rennar had conjured. She let her gaze drift over the crowd. Viggo had moved to stand with the Goblins, slapping away their mischievous hands as they tried to steal things from the Royals' pockets. Hunter Black in his suit, Luc, and Beau — a trio of misfits. Cricket beside them, prettier but no less out of place.

And then, without warning, Rennar took her hand. She realized Duke Karolinge had stopped talking. The entire rooftop garden was silent, heavy with anticipation.

"What's happening?" she whispered urgently.

"This." He drew her toward him and, before she could take another breath, pressed his lips to hers. Her pulse leaped to life. She felt like she was in the sky on downy wings, snow falling on her while she watched the scene happening below. Rennar's lips were soft. Beau stood just paces away. Would Rennar do something crass to humiliate him? Paw her bodice? Kiss her like he had in the dessert pantry?

But almost as soon as his lips had touched hers, they were gone. A quick, chaste kiss. He released her hands.

She blinked, not sure what to do with her hands. "You . . . you promised no more stolen kisses."

"That wasn't a kiss. That was ceremony. Trust me, if I *kiss* you, you'll know it."

She flushed and glanced at Beau to make certain he hadn't overheard. "So . . . is it finished? We're married?"

"Not quite."

He crooked a finger at Duke Karolinge, who blew his whistle for Saint. The bird took wing from a rosebush and landed on the Duke's shoulder. In his beak he held an achingly beautiful crown, as fragile as gold dust held together with spider silk. Rennar gently placed it on her head.

"Princess of the Haute," he whispered. "Ruler of the Parisian Court."

The crown was so light that she had to reach up to make sure it was real. Duke Karolinge said a few final words in the Selentium Vox, but her head was spinning and she couldn't hear them. She hadn't expected to feel anything. The marriage was a sham. But a maid who became a princess—it meant something.

Rennar took her hand once more. The rooftop garden was a sea of pink and crimson and blush. The Court of the Woods delegation approached and knelt at her feet. She barely had the sense to lift her grass-stained hem for them to kiss her toes. She almost laughed deliriously. It wasn't long ago that Mada Vittora had cut off her toes to make her a better plaything with smaller feet to play dress up. Now kings and queens were on their knees to kiss those toes.

"Princess Anouk," the Woods Queen said. "We welcome you to the Haute. We swear our fealty to you."

Rennar prodded her, and she remembered what she'd been

instructed to say. She fought with the billows of her skirt to kneel down and kiss her toes in return. "And I to you."

One by one, the Royal delegations approached, knelt, and swore fealty in exchange for her own. They all viewed her with cold glares. None of them were pleased about this marriage, except perhaps Prince Aleksi of the Lunar Court, who was the only one to give Anouk a wink.

By the time the last of the Royals had sworn fealty, Anouk felt dead on her feet. She had that wobbly sensation that time had either frozen or sped up. Several Goblins were glancing at their pocket watches, holding their forks, eager for the feast.

"With all of you as witnesses," Rennar said, clutching Anouk's hand, "it is our right to invoke the Nochte Pax. A wedding gift that you are bound to honor. Our wish is to activate the Code of Courts, which states that if any one of us is under attack by an outside force, the others must come to that party's aid. Few of you were willing to admit that the Court of Isles was under attack, even after you witnessed the Coven of Oxford possess King Kaspar. But now each of you is bound. Tonight, we will meet in the spell library and negotiate how to protect our borders. Until this is done, none of you may leave Castle Ides."

The members of the Barren Court looked daggers at Rennar. Anouk worried suddenly that Rennar might not know what he was doing. Forcing the others to cooperate might lead to even more enemies.

He touched fresh champagne-colored powder to his lips and whispered a spell. The dome over the rooftop garden burst like a soap bubble. Soft snow began to fall over the garden. Thick flakes landed on her eyelashes. It dusted the roses and the Royals, who didn't bother to brush the snow off their shoulders. Goose bumps sprang up over her bare arms. She hugged her shoulders and looked over the crowd to catch Beau's eye. Snowflakes dusted his hair. He looked as handsome as everything else in the garden, but there was an uneasiness in his eyes that matched her own.

Tension was thick in Paris.

Disgruntled Royal Courts were Rennar's problem now. They had their own problems. There would be no feast for them. No venison or red velvet cake. (Well, maybe a bite.) No rosé wines or champagne. No first dance beneath the stars while the famous American contest winner sang a ballad. No toasts to love and good fortune. The party would happen, of course—every Goblin was already hopping from one foot to another—but Anouk wouldn't be there.

The snow fell harder.

She'd be somewhere dark. Somewhere cold. Somewhere she had run from her whole life, somewhere she'd promised herself she'd never return.

Beau held open an umbrella for her against the snow. He didn't need to remind her of what came next: beastie spells, the Dark Thing, tunnels into an unfamiliar city, a coven they didn't know how to defeat. For now, he needed only to hold the umbrella over their heads. She rested her cheek against his chest and felt the beating of his heart match her own.

Chapter 27

AS SOON AS THEY COULD, Anouk, Beau, Cricket, and the rest of their troop stole away from the rooftop garden. The sounds of the feasting were audible throughout Castle Ides. The other Royal Courts might resent the Nochte Pax, but they were still Royals, and Royals never turned down an opportunity to dress well, eat well, and flaunt their cruel beauty in front of one another.

"This way," Cricket said, leading them through the maze of hallways. They all had a slightly giddy air, or perhaps it was delirium. There was a point at which reality was so unbelievable that the most rational thing to do was to give in. Anouk couldn't quite believe that she was truly a princess, married to Prince Rennar—let alone that the two of them weren't trying to kill each other! And she couldn't believe that she'd made an absurd promise to fight the witches of Oxford when she couldn't even cast a simple whisper. She was no closer to knowing what her crux was now than she'd ever been. It was madness. But then again, what in her short life hadn't been?

Cricket threw open the door to the billiard room and they tumbled in, full of a manic kind of recklessness. Viggo went straight to the bar cart to make himself a drink. Luc joined him. Hunter Black paced before the empty fireplace with tight, silent steps, his fingers toying with the glass buttons of his shirt. Petra shook the snow from her hair and, with a whisper, enchanted a fire in the hearth to warm her hands.

Anouk pulled the crown from her head, though it tangled in her hair and she had to tug it free with a squeak. She tossed it onto the coffee table. They all stared at it. Hunter Black stopped pacing.

"I never thought I'd see it," Luc said quietly. "A beastie become a Royal."

"And here I was, proud just to have my own apartment," Cricket said.

"Along with power," Hunter Black said darkly, "comes more danger."

"*Aaaand* there it is." Beau rolled his eyes. "I was waiting for Hunter Black to say something bleak." He came up behind Anouk and circled his arms around her waist. He whispered in her ear, "Don't listen to them. You did what you had to."

She leaned back into him. "I'm sorry about the wedding, Beau."

"I'm not."

She raised her eyebrows in surprise and twisted around to face him.

"To see all those queens kissing your feet? I'd have paid any price for that." He ran a hand gently through her hair; she'd undone the elaborate chignon. "You know," he said quietly, "when I turned back in the fountain alleyway on Rue des Amants, there was a second before my memory faded when I was caught somewhere between human and animal. I can't quite describe it; it was like being in a dream. Like I could sense things I couldn't when I was human, but I was still human enough to think. And do you know what I thought?"

"What?"

"If I was cursed to spend life as an animal, at least I'd known you."

She smiled so wide she thought her heart might break.

Cricket started pulling out her knives and arranging them on the billiard table. Then she went around the room plucking various blunt artifacts off the walls and adding them to the pile. Viggo, drink in hand, watched her with a bemused look.

"How exactly are you going to carry all of those weapons?" he said. "Tied to your tail? Hidden in your fur?"

"*You're* going to carry them for me." Her sharp grin bared her teeth. She checked her watch. "We need to leave within the hour. The entrance to the Tunnel sous la Manche is at the Coquelles terminal. It's a two-hour drive from Paris. We need to arrive when the tunnel shifts change over. With a few tricks, we can get past the guards."

Beau looked wary until Cricket tossed him a set of keys. "Perk up, Beau. Rennar agreed to lend us his car for the drive."

His jaw dropped. "The Centenario Roadster?"

"With alligator interior."

His hands closed around the keys and he pumped his fist in the air.

Anouk shook her head, though she smiled.

"We need to make the potion for the contra-beastie spell," Luc said. "Petra, what do you need?"

She rattled off a list of herbs and then slid a look to Viggo. "And blood."

Viggo sighed as he rolled back his sleeve. "Leave me enough so I don't pass out while I'm dragging these animals from France to England."

While Luc, Petra, and Viggo worked on the potion, Anouk fought with the billows of her dress. "I'm going to change out of this parachute. I'll meet you all in the lobby in fifteen minutes."

She gave Beau a peck on the cheek, kicked off her glass slippers, lifted her skirts to her knees, and made her way to the bedroom she'd been sharing with Beau. She wondered if, assuming they got back from London in one piece, she and Beau would move into a different room. The terms of the marriage allowed her to love someone else, and they didn't forbid her to share a room with someone else either. Rennar had his own apartments—a master bedroom fit for, well, a prince. And it wasn't as though there was any space limitation in Castle Ides. Rennar could take an old broom closet and enchant it into a sprawling master suite for her and Beau. She'd paint the walls a midnight blue with stars on the ceiling. A giant bed big enough for them both to stretch out on and never reach the edges. A whole wall of windows looking out onto the Parisian skyline, and a balcony lined with grimacing gargoyles.

She shuffled into her temporary room and fumbled with the buttons on the dress. She was relieved when she heard Beau's footsteps behind her. "Would you help me with the buttons?"

She felt his presence at her back along with an odd moment of hesitation. He didn't touch the buttons. She looked over her shoulder and paled when she saw Rennar standing there.

"Oh! I . . . I just came to change."

"Do you still want help?"

"Um, sure." She turned around and lifted her hair for him to unfasten the row of pearl buttons, and then she dragged the heavy dress behind the privacy of a dressing screen. Through the latticework, she could barely make out his shape. She struggled to get the dress over her head.

"You're leaving." He said it as a statement, not a question.

"Yes." They'd already been through this. He knew their plan, uncertain though it was. She bent over, trying to shimmy out of the dress. "The others are waiting for me downstairs. Saint can get through the border spell, so once we've left, have Duke Karolinge send him into London. If we have any messages to convey, we'll send them back through him. I don't think we'll be gone longer than a few days. By then, one way or another, this will all have come to an end. We'll either find a way to defeat the Coven or . . ." She didn't need to finish the thought.

"Prince Aleksi and I are gathering the senior Royals at midnight to begin drafting the protection spells."

"Good luck. If we fail, your spell will be all that protects the near realms." She finally managed to shed the dress and left it pooled in a puddle of feathers on the bedroom floor. She glanced in the mirror and cringed at the mess that was her hair.

Through the lattice screen, she saw him move to the window, pick up a seashell she'd left on the sill, and toy with it absently. "You don't have to, you know." His tone had changed.

"Don't have to what?" She dragged a comb through her hair.

"Come back."

She froze with the comb in her hand. She glanced toward the dressing screen. His back was turned to her so she couldn't see his face.

"You and your friends are human now," he continued. "You are bound to no master. You've gotten everything you've ever wanted.

You could run away. Take off in the Roadster and never come back. Go to Prague. Go to Timbuktu, if you like. Leave us to our fates with the Coven. You owe me nothing. You made the terms of our marriage very clear."

She frowned as she slid back into her old tuxedo pants and T-shirt. "I gave the Goblins my word that I'd help them retake London. They sacrificed everything to help us in Montélimar. I'm not going to walk away from my promise." She tucked in her shirt and then pulled her hair into a ponytail. "Besides, beasties are the only things that can kill witches. You think the Coven would let us run off to Timbuktu? If we don't stop them, they'll come for us next. Even me. Even though I can't cast a single whisper."

She slid on the Faustine jacket and instantly felt better, like a lock had clicked into place. She sighed. She thrust her hands in the pockets and came around the dressing screen. Rennar's gaze flickered over her. He didn't seem to mind her like this, dressed in pants instead of a gown.

"Why are you saying all of this?" she asked softly.

"Because I need for it to be said. I have no hold over you anymore. None of your friends are caged or tied up with chains. We are married, but we've agreed that it doesn't mean you must remain at my side."

She leaned against the bedpost, arms folded. "I'm not going to betray you, Rennar."

"You could. We aren't friends."

"Like you said, we aren't enemies either."

He walked toward her with a smoldering look. "What, exactly, are we?"

She was lacing her oxford shoes; she paused and looked up at him.

She didn't have any kind of answer for that question, and she told him as much.

"For the first time in my life," he continued in a softer tone, "I have something I don't want to lose. Some*one* I don't want to lose. I'm worried for you, Anouk."

"Rennar, it's a sham marriage."

"I don't care about you because a piece of paper tells me I must." He was close enough to her that she could smell his cologne. "Anouk, you're . . ."

She made a show of rolling her eyes, but the truth was, his look was shaking her. "Beautiful? Charming?" she suggested.

"Unexpected." He reached up to untangle a knot in her hair. He was close, and his head turned, and so did hers, and before she knew it, he was kissing her. How? She again got that sense this was happening to someone else. His hands gripped her waist. His fingers dug into her sides. His lips were urgent. Her pulse flared to life. This wasn't like the kiss at the wedding. There was nothing chaste about the way his lips crushed hers now. He ran a hand up to the back of her neck, cupped her head to deepen the kiss. His other hand fumbled with her jacket for a moment and then found her hand and wove it into his own hair, as though he were silently begging her to touch him.

She pushed away, took a step back, and wiped her mouth with her hand. She was breathing hard. "Don't do that again, Rennar."

He stared at her. His hair was mussed from where he'd run her fingers through it. His lips were parted, and she thought he was going to do something stupid like try to kiss her again or even say that he loved her, but then his lips twisted into that arrogant smile.

"I won't. Not until you come to me, admit that you regret the ridiculous terms you set for our marriage, and beg me to kiss you again." For all the show of superiority, he seemed wounded by her rejection.

She gave a sharp laugh. "You'll be waiting a long time."

He shrugged carelessly. "I *do* have eternity."

She gave him a long look and then left, closing the door firmly behind her, wishing she could lock it and barricade it and push a dresser in front of it, just to keep him from saying such things again. She paused in the elevator foyer, her legs wobbly, and sank onto a bench.

What a foolish thing it was for him to remind her of her freedom. What a foolish thing, too, for her not to take it.

Then she took a deep breath, slid on her sunglasses, and pushed the elevator button.

Chapter 28

THE OTHER BEASTIES were waiting in the lobby, along with Viggo, whose pale face and bandaged arm said he'd given the blood they needed for the spell. His long dark hair was pulled into a ponytail. He shouldered a backpack that sagged heavily—Cricket must have packed it with more than ample weaponry.

The five Marble Ladies, stone guardians of Castle Ides, blocked the turnstile that allowed access to the building's exit. Cricket paced in front of them, tapping them provokingly on the ears and noses, but of course, none of them would move an inch until compelled to.

"Good. You're here." Petra nodded approvingly at Anouk and then gestured to the Marble Ladies. "Shall I whisper them out of our way?"

"This is one thing I can do," Anouk said. She made a gesture toward the Marble Ladies like she was shooing away a fly, and they roused themselves from their stone slumber and stepped away from the turnstile. "I'm the princess of Castle Ides now. They have to obey me whether I wield magic or not."

"Have a nice journey, Princess," the closest Marble Lady said with a carved smile.

Cricket snorted as she passed through the turnstile. "We could have used that the last time we tried breaking into this place, Princess."

Anouk paused at the front door to adjust her jacket. The embroidery under her fingers was like a talisman, giving her strength. She shook away the thoughts crawling around in her head about Rennar's kiss, Rennar's confession.

Someone I don't want to lose.

"Is the car ready?" She peered out the glass door at the snowy city streets.

"December's pulling it around now," Beau said.

In another moment an engine roared and headlights shone into the lobby. They pushed outside into the shelter of the porte-cochère, where a spotless Roadster purred with its windshield wipers going.

"*Si belle.*" Beau sighed contentedly. He tugged on his old leather driving gloves, flexing his fingers.

The car shook a little as though someone was bouncing around inside, and then the driver's-side door opened and December tumbled out. Anouk wondered if she was drunk.

"December? Is everything okay?" she asked.

"Perfect!" With outstretched arms, December jerkily made her way around the car, and it became apparent that her strange movements were because she was wearing roller skates. They looked ancient, worn white leather and rainbow trim, grungy laces, and scuffed wheels. She grinned uneasily.

"What are those things?" Luc asked.

"Roller skates!"

Beau looked toward the car in alarm. "You drove the *car* wearing those?"

"Don't you get it?" December struggled to push herself from the car to one of the porte-cochère columns. "I'm coming with you." She tromped awkwardly on the skates. "I'm not setting *foot* in London. That's the spell, isn't it? That no living creature imbued with magic can set foot in England? It doesn't say anything about not setting *wheels* in England."

"That's insane," Cricket muttered.

"Technically," Luc pointed out, "she's not wrong."

"So I can come?" December beamed.

The beasties all exchanged hesitant looks. December had saved Anouk's life at the Château des Mille Fleurs with a handful of glitter, so maybe rainbow roller skates would rescue them this time. But December lost her balance and tumbled to her knees. She winced, rolling onto her bottom.

"Um," Anouk said. "You're . . . needed here is the thing. Someone has to look after the rest of the Goblins. We can't have them burning down Castle Ides like they burned down the townhouse."

December, still wincing, gave her an odd look. But the clock in the church steeple across the street chimed six, and Cricket smacked Anouk lightly.

"Time to go, beasties."

Anouk knelt down and helped December to her feet. Then she gave her a push toward the doors, and December wheeled her arms forward and caught herself on the door handles.

The rest of them piled into the car, Beau in the driver's seat, Anouk in the front passenger seat with Cricket in her lap, and Luc, Viggo, Hunter Black, and Petra in the back. "There'd be more room," Viggo said, "if Cricket hadn't brought so many knives."

"I brought toasted-cheese croque-monsieurs too," she said.

"You took the time to pack sandwiches?" Luc asked.

"Have you *had* British food?"

Beau threw the car in gear and stomped on the gas. He roared down the narrow streets, throwing up puddles of icy slush. The windshield wipers fought against the snow.

Anouk gazed at the city. Leaving France altogether, even leaving the continent! She'd never traveled through a tunnel before, especially one that ran thirty kilometers beneath the English Channel. What would London be like? In Germany she'd wandered into fairy-tale land: Black Forests, Snow Children, eternal winters. Would London be a fairy tale too? All Anouk knew of London was what she'd read in books and seen from the enchanted windows of the fourth floor of Castle Ides, which looked down on Piccadilly Circus. She wondered if the bakeries would rival Paris's patisseries. If there were wishing fountains down secret alleyways. If there were Saturday bird markets and poets by the riverbanks.

"I don't suppose we'll have time for shopping?" Cricket said as though reading her mind. "There's Debenhams. And Fenwick of Bond Street."

"Harrods is better," Hunter Black muttered.

Beau gave the assassin a questioning look in the rearview mirror.

Luc laughed. "Let's focus on, first, getting into London. Second, hoping Sinjin can turn us human with that amethyst chess piece that Rennar enchanted. Do you have it, Viggo? Good. Third, recovering from the change. And fourth, stopping a coven of evil witches who can wield technology that we can't."

This plunged everyone into a thoughtful silence for the remainder of the drive. Night came early in winter, and the roads between the city and the coast were cast in murky darkness. Streetlights lit up orbs of falling snow, but beyond that, the world was black. After some time Beau pulled off the highway at a sign for the Coquelles train terminal and followed the arrows to a nearly empty parking lot. Snow was still coming down heavily. The train station itself had a small lobby, ticket booth, and coffee shop. The station was mostly quiet. According to Cricket's timetable, they were in the lull between departures. Passengers for the next train to England wouldn't start to arrive for at least a half an hour.

The seven of them stared through the windshield at the train yard behind the station.

"That's it?" Beau asked.

Luc pulled out the guidebook he'd taken from Castle Ides. "'The Chunnel is thirty kilometers long,'" he read. "It'll take us most of the night to walk that far."

"Longer," Petra added, "if one of you decides to go chasing another one's tail instead of following Viggo."

Viggo dug around in his backpack and proudly held up a fistful of leashes. "Already thought of that."

Luc eyed the leashes, then sighed and rubbed the bridge of his nose.

"Just *try* to put one of those things on me," Cricket said to Viggo.

"It's that or stuffing you in one of the boxes in the trunk. I don't have time to go chasing after a white cat."

She sulked in the front seat. "Fine, but I can't help it if I claw you to shreds while you're trying to put it on."

"Well, you'd do that as a human, too."

243

She smirked. "Good point."

"Okay, look." Petra, who'd been watching out the side window, pointed to the guard station. "There. Only one guard on duty." She swallowed a sip of her elixir and began to whisper. *"Latinka, latinka . . ."*

The guard put down the paperback he was reading, stood, hopped awkwardly from one foot to the other, then ran toward the terminal to what Anouk assumed was a badly needed bathroom. Petra whispered again and, one by one, the floodlights shining on the train yard turned off. With another whisper, all of the CCTV security cameras slowly panned upward, filming only the night sky.

Petra dusted off her hands. "I'm getting good at this witch thing."

They climbed out of the car and crept from parked car to parked car to the chain-link fence surrounding the train yard. Petra whispered and the lock fell off the gate. She held the gate open and they dashed across the long expanse of rail and gravel until they reached the rear of the station. A single light shone down on an access door.

"Now watch," Petra said. "I'll put out that light." She hunted through her black leather oubliette for whatever life-essence she intended to use. *"Merde,* where is—"

Her head jerked up at the sound of glass shattering. Hunter Black was no longer in their midst. In just a few seconds, the assassin had crept across the train tracks and thrown a perfectly aimed rock at the light bulb. He was now waiting for them in front of the door.

Petra muttered a curse.

They crossed the train tracks quickly and joined him.

"Okay," Petra snarled, "but you can't unlock that door with a rock, can you?" She went to the door and wiggled the deadbolt for proof. Then she made a big show of consuming some aspen leaves from her oubliette and enchanted the deadbolt. When she twisted the knob, the door swung open. She gave Hunter Black a toothy smile.

They passed through the doorway into a dimly lit cinder-block room with nothing but a staircase and a bulletin board filled with train timetables and a pinned note telling someone named Jacques to stop stealing lunches from the break room. Anouk hugged her arms across her jacket. The access rooms were dank, and she didn't like the odd clicking sounds and smell of standing water. Not all of Paris was glittering lights.

"Down the stairs," Luc said.

They followed him down three flights of service stairs and through a few more locked doors. It was loud down here. Machinery rumbled in unseen rooms. The trains overhead squealed. At last Luc opened a door marked No Access and they were out of the station. An enormous subterranean tunnel stretched as far as Anouk could see and then disappeared into darkness. Her footsteps echoed. The ground began to tremble. Dust rained down from the pipes overhead and she steadied herself.

"The trains," Luc explained, motioning to either side. "This access tunnel runs between the two lanes, one from London to Paris, one from Paris to London."

As soon as the train passed and the rumbling stopped, Anouk squinted down the tunnel. "So that's England on the other side?" She took a curious step forward and smacked into something hard. "Ow!" She bounced back, rubbing her head.

She stared at the place she'd just hit. It was thin air, no different from the rest of the empty space around it. Luc approached, holding out his hand, and then he, too, stopped as if he'd encountered a glass wall.

"The border spell," he said in a hushed voice. "That's it." He jerked his head toward Viggo. "Viggo, go over there." He pointed beyond where he and Anouk stood.

Viggo took a few cautious steps forward as if he were walking over a barely frozen lake, afraid to put his weight in the wrong spot, but he passed through without any obstruction.

"See?" Luc said. "He can cross. The spell stops us because we're magical in our human forms. But it won't stop us once . . ." He cleared his throat. "Once we turn."

His words cast a dark shadow over the tunnel. Another train rumbled by, loud enough to drown out anything anyone would have said, and Anouk was glad for the pause. Panic was starting to crawl up her throat. Nothing about this dank, utilitarian tunnel felt heroic. This didn't feel like the kind of place where magic happened. If she had to turn back into an owl, she would have preferred to do it amid the beautiful bones of the Goblins' catacombs or in some charming glen in the Black Forest.

And that dark end of the tunnel . . . it felt impossible that England actually lay on the other side. A crazy fear came to her that there was nothing at the end. That the blackness was complete. She would willingly walk straight into the Noirceur, which waited for her, ready to swallow her whole.

"Are you ready?" Beau rested a gentle hand on her shoulder.

She jumped and spun toward him. She saw herself reflected in his eyes: frightened, bedraggled, nothing like a princess.

She clutched the melted bell around her neck, then grabbed his hand. "Beau, I'm afraid."

One of the lights flickered behind him, throwing shadows over his face. In that moment, she would have given anything for them to be back at 18 Rue des Amants, cuddled up in Mada Vittora's library with a bowl of popcorn. She hadn't been free, but life had been simple.

Her stomach tightened.

The townhouse was gone. Mada Vittora was dead. There was no going back. There was only one way forward, and it was through this dark tunnel.

In only moments, she would become an owl. Petra was already digging through Viggo's backpack for the vials of blood and other supplies that she needed to perform the contra-beastie spell. Anouk looked at her hand clasped in Beau's. Soon his hand would be a shaggy golden paw; hers a talon. It would have made her feel sick to think about it, if she could have brought herself to think about it.

She let out a cry. Beau swept her into his arms and held her tightly. "Don't be afraid, Anouk. We'll be together."

"We won't know each other! You know what it's like. So dark, so cold, and everything shrouded in fog. What if we don't make it to London? Or what if Sinjin can't turn us back? We could be trapped like that forever, Beau."

"I don't care what the spell says," he said, smoothing her hair. "I'd know you anywhere, Anouk. If I lived forever as a dog and you as an owl, I'd spend the rest of my life with head upturned, searching the night sky for your silhouette."

She buried her head in his chest. She wanted to believe him. Wanted to feel that, regardless of what happened, they'd recognize each other's souls. She knew it was foolish . . . but maybe she hadn't given up on fairy tales just yet. She clutched the bell again. Maybe she wouldn't give up on magic either.

He brushed some dust off her temple and pressed a kiss on the center of her forehead.

She closed her eyes.

Something hard snapped around her ankle.

Her eyes shot open and she kicked involuntarily at a rope Viggo was tying to a plastic ring around her foot. Her toes connected with his nose.

"Hey!" he complained. He rubbed his nose as he unrolled the rope connected to the ring around her ankle. "I can't have you flying away. You'd perch up somewhere in those pipes and I'd never get you down. I'd have to use Luc as bait."

She felt sick. "That isn't funny."

"It's a *little* funny."

None of the others looked amused either. Viggo had already tied a rope around Luc's wrist. He had a third fastened to a collar around Cricket's neck, and a fourth attached to a chain around Hunter Black's. They all stood with their hands on their hips, shooting daggers at Viggo with their eyes.

Anouk moved to stand next to Petra and said quietly, "If you're ever going to tell me your moniker, it might as well be now. I might be an animal forever. If it's a secret, it'll be safe with me."

Petra smiled mysteriously. "When—not if—you're human again, I'll tell you."

Viggo held up another collar. "Your turn, Beau."

Anouk couldn't watch, even though she knew Viggo was only doing what they had all agreed to. She wondered if he had any idea what it felt like to be anything other than rich and beautiful, if he knew how often she had craved even a day of his lavish life.

Hunter Black, attached to the chain, also eyed Viggo closely, but with a different look of longing.

"Does he know how you feel?" Anouk asked quietly.

Hunter Black's dark eyes flashed to hers, and for a second she was afraid he might growl at her, but then his eyelids lowered. "He knows."

Anouk felt her heart sink. They all knew that Viggo was attracted to girls only, but she still wished the best for Hunter Black's doomed love life.

He continued, "All that matters is that he knows I'd kill for him. I'd steal for him. I'd die for him." Hunter Black paused before adding, "As I would for any of you."

This surprised her so much that she nearly stumbled. "Hunter Black, do you mean that?"

He slowly nodded.

Before she knew what she was doing, she wrapped her arms around him and squeezed him hard. If she could, she'd spare him all the pain they were about to endure. If she could, she'd spare them all.

"There." Viggo interrupted them by clicking a chain to the collar around Hunter Black's neck. "Now, try not to kill each other, everyone. And remember, I'm your friend. You don't need to bite me or scratch me or piss on me."

"No promises," Cricket said.

Luc touched Cricket's shoulder reassuringly, then went around to all the beasties, pressing his forehead to each of theirs, giving each of their shoulders a good squeeze.

"Okay." Luc turned to Petra. "Do it."

The five of them joined hands, their five ropes connecting them all to Viggo. He pulled on the backpack and took out an umbrella with a sharp point. Clearly, it wasn't meant for rain.

"This is going to work," Petra said, sounding like she was trying to reassure herself as much as anyone else. "I can do this, and Viggo has that amethyst chess piece that Rennar imbued with the beastie spell. As soon as you can, send word through Saint that you're human again."

A train rumbled by in the next tunnel over. The utility lights flickered. Dust rained down again. The train's roar was so deafening that Anouk couldn't hear the words Petra began to whisper. Suddenly it all seemed to be happening too fast. What if Petra got a word wrong? What if they'd botched the elixir? The train began to squeal. The lights flickered faster. Beau was squeezing her left hand tightly, and Cricket her right. Her vision began to swirl as she twisted to look down the far end of the tunnel. So black. Nothing was that pure black. Except the Noirceur.

She was about to scream for Petra to stop, but suddenly the squealing and rumble of the train disappeared, and the flickering lights vanished, and the pressure from Beau's and Cricket's hands was gone, and the blackness had swallowed her whole.

PART III

Chapter 29

❧

ANOUK WOKE WITH THE SOUND of wings beating in her ears. She blinked groggily. Overhead, orbs of light swayed from side to side like a sky hung with pendulum moons. Walls pressed in on every side, giving her the unnerving sense that she was waking up in a coffin. She sat up with a gasp for air.

At first everything was blurry and she took in only strange, whimsical shapes—figures with no arms or heads, lumpy bones twice her size, vibrant sprays of oranges and blues. When her vision cleared, the shapes still didn't make sense. Marble statues that *were* missing heads and limbs. Fossils of femurs that must have belonged to prehistoric creatures.

With a yelp, she realized she *was* lying in a coffin.

It wasn't like the tombs in Paris's catacombs that the Goblins had used for makeshift dining tables. This one was curved in the approximate shape of a person and was covered in flaking red and gold paint. A sarcophagus.

A chill ran through her. She tipped forward, trying to climb out, but she wasn't prepared for how weak her limbs were. She collapsed back.

"Hey, watch out, you'll hurt yourself!"

Viggo appeared by her side with a damp cloth. He dabbed at her forehead with a tonic that smelled of rosemary and sweet orange, then thrust a steaming cup of tea in her hands. "Here. The tea will help ease the lightheadedness. You're the first one awake."

She stared dimly into the cup. Tiny leaves floated in dark brown liquid. She blinked and looked around the room. It was filled with bizarre antiquities. A suit of Japanese armor made of chain mail and lacquered iron. Masks with beaded headpieces. One whole side of the room was taken up by a stage set: a frozen lake made of glass, a painted backdrop of a forest that was only half finished, ballet costumes, buckets of artificial snow.

There were three more sarcophagi. Like hers, the heavy stone lids had been pushed back. In them were Cricket, Luc, and Hunter Black, one in each, their hands folded over their chests, which rose and fell with their breathing. Next to the last sarcophagus was a cardboard box filled with crumpled newspapers. Beau slumbered in that, one arm thrown clumsily over his eyes.

Viggo gestured to the box sheepishly. "We ran out of sarcophagi. Found that carton in the back."

"Viggo, stop talking, please. This is all too much." Anouk set down the tea with a shaking hand. A thousand questions appeared in her head but she chose just one. "*We?* Who is *we?*"

"Sinjin and I. He popped upstairs for a moment. There's a café. It's closed now, but they keep microwave pizzas in the freezer. The egg-salad sandwiches aren't bad either. If you want pastries, though, you're out of luck. We ate all of those yesterday."

Her head ached so badly that everything Viggo said felt like it had happened to her in a dream. Sinjin—that was the hacker who supposedly knew what to do with the amethyst chess piece to turn them human. She looked down at her feet and saw a fine powder of purple-tinted crystal. Was that what was left of the amethyst? Then her gaze fell on a taxidermied lion with worn fur in need of repair.

"What is this place?"

"The British Museum." Viggo perched on the edge of her sarcophagus and sipped his own cup of tea. "Part of its basement. It makes for a brilliant base of operations. The Pretties closed it when the plagues began, so we have it to ourselves. Lots of ancient magic here. Old herbs and charms. Plus the café—well, I already told you about the café." He motioned to a stack of greasy paper plates that bore the British Museum's logo. She noticed that over his usual black shirt, he was wearing a fleece jacket from the museum gift shop.

She sat up straight and gripped the edges of the sarcophagus. "So it worked? We're human again?" She pressed a hand to her face, feeling for a beak, for feathers, almost crying in relief to find her own nose.

"Yes—didn't you hear what I told you?"

"Tell me everything." Her voice was breathy and quick, but as soon as she said it, she wasn't sure she wanted to know.

"*You* were the least of my worries." Viggo leaned back, swirling his tea. "As soon as Petra's spell took effect, you perched on my shoulder for most of the walk through the Chunnel, except once, when the mouse slipped out of my pocket and you dived for it. You nearly ate Luc."

Queasy, she pressed a hand to her stomach.

"Beau was Beau—even as a dog, he's deliriously happy. But

Cricket! And Hunter Black! Naturally, they were awful. She got loose and hid in a drainpipe and Beau had to sniff her out. The wolf was insufferable, even though I eventually got the muzzle on him." As evidence, he held up his arms, which were covered with bite marks.

"But I got all five of you through," he continued proudly. "Took all night to walk the tunnel. Sinjin was waiting on the other side with a taxi. He'd gotten our message." He gestured to a spot behind her, and she turned to find an entire wall of taxidermied animals, a lion and a badger and a falcon. The falcon's head suddenly turned in her direction. Not taxidermied after all.

"Saint!"

Viggo nodded. "Saint got through first and delivered Rennar's message to Sinjin, so everything was set up."

Her headache worsened at the thought of Rennar. She collapsed back in the sarcophagus with a sigh. The lights overhead made her wedding ring gleam. She worked it anxiously between her fingers. Did Rennar toy with his ring too? Did he think of that last kiss before she left? She shook her head to banish such thoughts and then sat back up. Her gaze again fell to the glittering purple powder on the floor. "Is that the amethyst chess piece?"

"You should have seen it," Viggo said, guessing her thoughts. "Sinjin had tools to extract the spell. It took a special kind of hammer, nothing magical, but a technical one that could shatter the amethyst in just the right way so as not to damage the spell inside."

"And it worked?"

He reached out and pulled on her ear and she winced. "What do you think? As soon as the amethyst powder landed on the five of you,

you turned human. I dressed you all. Didn't think you'd mind. Look, I even remembered that jacket you like."

She was relieved to see she was wearing her Faustine jacket. She rubbed her sore ear. "And the others?"

"Should be waking up soon. Sinjin warned it would take a while for all of you to recover. You've been out for two days." He opened a greasy pizza box, but it was empty, and he frowned. "I'll go upstairs and get you something to eat. You'll feel better."

Before she could stop him, Viggo grabbed a flashlight branded with the British Museum security logo and disappeared into the cavernous basement. His footsteps echoed. Anouk hugged her jacket around her. It was eerie down here. What she'd mistaken for swinging moons were, of course, overhead lights. The whoosh of wings was the air-conditioning unit. They must have been in the portion of the basement used for constructing exhibits. Cautiously, she climbed out of the sarcophagus. She checked on the others, but they were deeply asleep, their pulses slow and steady. All around her were tables full of cataloged bits of broken ceramic, hunting spears, bronze vases. An assortment of long white feathers that, judging by the size, had belonged to an owl; they made her shudder and she quickly stepped away. She moved to a table that held a collection of Victorian clocks in various states of repair. The smell of polish and oil laced the air. She picked up a massive pocket watch that was bigger than her palm. It ticked softly.

A dream pulsed at the edge of her memory. Only it hadn't been a dream, had it? When she'd entered the Coal Baths, reality and the dream world had merged—instead of a bed of coals in the Cottage courtyard, she'd been thrust into a den of witches with an eyeless owl overhead.

She found herself absent-mindedly tracing the shape of Jak's symbol in the dust on the clock-repair table. A circle. The two lines. It looked like the owl from her vision, a face with a mouth and nose but no eyes. An idea rustled at the back of her mind.

A face with no eyes . . .

"Well, well. The sleeping beauty awakens."

She spun around so fast that the pocket watch slipped from her hands and fell to the ground. Viggo was back with the Pretty broker she remembered from the engagement party. He held his golden hare in the crook of one gloved arm.

"Sinjin," she said. "It's nice to see you again."

He was holding two paper plates of pizza. He thrust one at her, and she found that she was ravenous. She perched on the edge of her sarcophagus, stuffed pizza in her mouth, and groaned contentedly. Greasy perfection.

Sinjin leaned over Cricket's sarcophagus and lifted one of her eyelids. "This one's waking too."

Viggo leaped up to pour another cup of tea. Cricket sat up with a jolt, reaching instinctively for the knives she kept tucked in the folds of her clothes. But her hands came up empty. Viggo must have taken the blades. She gave a growl.

Viggo held up the tea.

"Hi, Cricket. Welcome back. You'll find your knives on that table over there. Forgive me for taking them from you, but you did enough damage to my skin as a cat."

She looked disoriented until her eyes settled on Anouk and a little of her panic faded. Anouk swallowed a mouthful of pizza, tossed aside the plate, and threw her arms around Cricket.

"It's okay. We made it."

"Is this hell?" Cricket was staring at the threadbare taxidermied lion. "We died, didn't we? This has to be hell."

"Not quite, but it is a basement."

Cricket's gaze caught on a collection of pearl-handled boxes that looked valuable and immensely stealable, and the worry lines around her mouth disappeared. She straightened, her fingers already stretching toward the treasures.

Sinjin went to check on the status of things outside while Anouk explained to Cricket what Viggo had told her. Cricket scarfed down some pizza and then went snooping through the museum's collection of shiny treasures with a glint in her eye, and then Luc jolted awake, and Hunter Black a few minutes after him; an hour later, Beau started snoring loudly. Anouk couldn't wait any longer. She poked him in the side until he sputtered awake.

Once they had all eaten and cleared their heads, Sinjin returned. His face was grave.

"You look like you've seen a ghost," Luc said.

"Close enough." Sinjin jerked his chin toward the ceiling. "It's gotten worse out there."

"How could it possibly get worse?"

"You know about the plagues? The black rainbows? Double moons?"

"We've heard the rumors," Luc said.

Anouk got a sudden shiver. Here in the basement, amid all the artwork and artifacts, at least they were protected. Bolted doors, security systems, locks. She scanned the ceiling, wondering what was happening outside.

"It's a nightmare out there. Pretties coughing up blood and black smoke and dying in the streets. Car accidents everywhere. Madmen on lawless sprees, driven wild by the double moons. Time slips so big that entire buildings have disappeared into the past."

"Why would the witches do that?" Luc asked.

"They wouldn't," Sinjin said, stroking his hare. "The plagues are as much a problem for the witches as they are for us. They're an unintended consequence of dabbling in magic they shouldn't."

Anouk asked, "Why didn't anyone try to stop the witches when they first took over?"

His hand went absently to the ruby stud in his left ear. "They did. Prince Maxim fought them, but it was a battle he could never win; the witches were only projections. Kill one, it didn't matter—it was only smoke and magic. Lady Imogen knew better. She sent a fleet of lesser Royals to search for their den, the source of their magic. But those Royals disappeared. If they found the den, that knowledge died with them."

The air conditioning turned on overhead with that *whoosh* like flapping wings. Prince Maxim and Lady Imogen had been looking for the same thing she was—the answer to Jak's riddle. The object that bound the Noirceur.

Her eyes fell to the clock-repair table where she'd drawn Jak's riddle in the dust, the circle with what might be a nose and mouth but no eyes.

A face with no eyes.

Hesitantly, she stretched her hands out over the drawing. A small thrill ran up her limbs as she realized the shapes on either side of the circle weren't meant to be sunrays—they were more like fingers. Ten in all, though the hands lacked arms.

Hands with no arms.

She pressed a palm to her mouth.

"I know it." She could hardly believe her own words. "I know the answer to Jak's riddle."

Chapter 30

CRICKET MADE HER WAY out of the back storage rooms, her pockets bulging suspiciously. Always the thief, even now. Cricket said nothing about her stolen treasure and simply said, "Well, don't leave us wondering."

Sinjin raised an arched eyebrow. "What's this about a riddle?"

Anouk pointed to her drawing in the dust and said in an excited rush, "A face with no eyes. Hands with no arms."

Luc and Beau stared at her blankly.

"A blind man?" Viggo attempted. "A blind man with no arms? A victim of some freak accident? Anouk, this is getting grisly."

She groaned. They were all staring directly at the answer. It was right in their faces, ticking away, big ones and small ones and broken ones and repaired ones.

Luc started laughing. He grinned and picked up the oversize pocket watch. "I get it now. It's a clock."

Cricket perched on the edge of her sarcophagus, picking at her fingernails with a blade. A few scraps of dusty parchment stuck out of her back pocket, nothing nearly as valuable as the gold vases and statues all over the basement shelves. Anouk felt a ripple of curiosity. If Cricket wasn't lifting valuables, what was she taking?

The papers crinkled in Cricket's back pocket and she casually shoved them down deeper. "The Noirceur is trapped in a clock? Oh, great. There must be millions of clocks in London. How are we supposed to find and destroy the right one?"

Anouk set aside her curiosity about Cricket's pilfering and paced across the basement to the stage set under construction. Her foot scuffed a brochure.

SPECIAL EXHIBITION.
Tchaikovsky's The Nutcracker Ballet.
Original set and costumes.

She turned to Cricket abruptly. "Can you summon snow?"

Cricket's eyebrows shot up. "It's not safe outside. The plagues strike without warning. You really want to go out there?"

"I don't mean outside." She pointed to the painted backdrop of the forest and the frozen lake. "I want you to summon snow here."

"Indoors?" Cricket grunted. "That's harder. But yeah, I think I can."

She took out a pouch of eucalyptus. The others drifted closer, watching. Both Viggo and Sinjin eyed the scene hungrily—as Pretties, they'd never cast a whisper. Cricket swallowed the eucalyptus and closed her eyes. Her lips moved slowly. The whisper was so quiet that Anouk felt it more than heard it. She was used to seeing the Goblins' magic, insects and spat whispers, or the Royals' spells, with their elegant flourishes. Cricket wielded magic differently. It seemed to come not from her fingertips or the end of her tongue, but from her core. She rooted her feet firmly on the floor. Flexed her fingers back so that she could cast with her palms.

A chill spread around Anouk's ankles. Slowly, as though someone had slammed a door and loosened dust in the rafters, a light snow began to fall over the *Nutcracker Ballet* set. No snow fell anywhere else in the museum basement. The entire snowstorm was six feet across, as though suspended within a giant snow globe. Anouk stepped into the enchanted diorama, holding out her hands. Real snow landed on her palm and dusted her eyelashes and hair. The others looked nervous, like they were afraid that the costumes of *Nutcracker* soldiers might come to life.

Anouk turned in a slow circle. The snow was thickest near the Nutcracker throne. Slowly, piece by piece, a boy with icicle hair took shape amid the flakes, perched on the throne.

He grinned.

Quick as a flash, Hunter Black threw one of his knives, but it soared right through the snow, straight through the boy, and lodged in the wall on his other side.

"Hello, Jak," Anouk said.

"Hello, lovely." His black eyes glistened. "You've solved my riddle. Well done. You've earned yourself a story."

"A story?" This wasn't what she'd expected. "What story?"

"The only one that matters."

Snow Children could exist only where snow fell, so Jak was restricted to the six-foot orb that made up the *Nutcracker* set. Cricket continued to hold the spell with her left hand and circle her right, whispering soundlessly, keeping the snow falling steadily. The others dragged over medieval ottomans and plywood crates as makeshift chairs.

Jak leaned forward in the Nutcracker throne, a theatrical crown perched on his head, his black eyes shining.

"My story begins ten thousand years ago, before the Age of Order, a time now lost to scholars. The Noirceur was loosed on the world like a spark in a dry forest. But its aim was not to destroy. Did you know there is a certain kind of pine tree that requires fire to reproduce? The cones are sealed with wax and will only open and spread their seeds when the wax is melted. The Noirceur was thus — to some it brought destruction, to others life. There was no logic to it. No rules or order. All that came much later. The Noirceur evolved as the world evolved. As early humans, Royals, and Goblins began to shape their world, the Noirceur changed too. It fractured into three forces: Magic, the controllable force that could be commanded by the Selentium Vox; the vitae echo, which keeps magic from being overused; and, last, technology. Less potent than magic and bound by rules of the Pretty World, technology still springs from the same force, which is why it and magic cannot be handled together."

He sank back into the throne, tossing a costume ermine stole around his shoulders. Cricket continued to whisper and cast with her hands, and the snow continued to fall.

"If the Noirceur fractured into magic and technology and the vitae echo, how can it still be present in the world?" Luc said.

"Ah, yes. Consider the tree that produces three apples: The tree does not vanish once it has fruited. Neither did the Noirceur. It lingered in the form of chaos, like the roots of a tree. The legendary King Svatyr and Queen Mid Ruath of the Starfire Court came together, dressed in enviable cloaks of bearskin—so the rumor goes—and led a spell that uprooted the remaining Noirceur. They trapped it in a clock five thousand years ago."

Viggo snorted. "There weren't clocks that long ago." He turned to the others. "Are we sure this kid is right in the head?"

Jak considered Viggo with an unimpressed air. "It is best to shut your mouth, lovely, if you do not know what you're talking about." He stood, threw off the ermine stole, picked up several of the Nutcracker dolls, and arranged them on the set. He cast a whisper and the dolls began to move on their own in a stiff dance.

He spoke faster, a thrill flashing in his eyes as he commanded the dolls. "As long as there have been people, there have been ways to track time. Even the earliest Pretties learned to thrust a stick in the ground and use it to follow the sun's movements. The early Royals, of course, had more sophisticated means." He twisted his hands and the dolls began to pick up the rectangular presents under the artificial Christmas tree and arrange them in a circle. Most of the presents stood upright, and a few pairs were joined together by a third present on top.

Cricket was still whispering to keep the snow falling, but her eyes were heavy-lidded. She was getting tired.

"That looks like Stonehenge," Luc said.

"It *is* Stonehenge." Jak leaned over his creation, cackling in delight. He cast another whisper, and the flashlight that Viggo had been using switched on by itself and levitated into the air. It created an effect like the sun rising over the model of Stonehenge. Shadows elongated and shrank as the flashlight-sun crossed the sky.

"Stonehenge already existed at the time of Queen Mid Ruath and

King Svatyr, and it was already shrouded in mystery. They used tricks and whispers to trap the Noirceur within the circle of stones. Even today, Pretty tourists who wander into the ring say they can feel its odd energy."

"But we felt the Noirceur at Anouk's engagement party," Luc pressed. "The witches used it to get in and possess King Kaspar. If it's trapped in Stonehenge, how is that possible?"

"Ah." Jak wagged a finger at Luc. "For a gardener, you're clever." His finger drew a line in the air until it reached Viggo. "For a witch's boy, you aren't."

"For a Snow Child," Viggo said coolly, "you're full of sh—"

"Viggo!" Anouk chastised him. Viggo grumbled and sat back down on his medieval ottoman.

Jak leaned on the arm of the throne, the crown dangling from the sharp locks of his hair, and asked Luc coyly, "Say, not to change the subject, but would you care for a kiss?"

Anouk saw the hungry look in Jak's eyes and shoved herself between the two of them. *"Don't,"* she ordered Jak, and she gave Luc a warning look over her shoulder. "You know what happens if he kisses you."

Jak sank back in the throne with a downturned mouth. "You're spoiling all my fun." He crooked his head to flash a smile to Luc. "Some things are worth the risk."

Luc took a step backward and bumped into the clock-repair table.

Jak sighed and continued, "That handsome gardener is correct. Stonehenge was only the original vessel—it is still a place of immense power, a place of transformation and blue flame, but it was *time itself* that those ancient Royals bound the Noirceur to, not the ancient stones. It can move, in a sense, from timepiece to timepiece. As the world evolved, there existed sundials, hourglasses, candle clocks, pendulums, pocket watches, digital clocks. The Noirceur resides in all of them. The Coven awakened the Noirceur in the timepieces that rest within the London city borders."

"Isn't the Noirceur in the black smoke too?"

"The smoke is a symptom. Poisonous, yes, but only a result of the Noirceur, not the Noirceur itself."

Luc paced in front of the *Nutcracker* set with his hands tented in thought. "So we know that the Noirceur is trapped in time and that the Coven of Oxford has taken control of the Noirceur. It's strengthening their power and letting them use technology but releasing chaos in the process." Luc paced back the other way, tapping his fingers together. "If we don't stop them, that chaos will spread from London to other cities. Black rainbows over Paris. Double or triple moons over Prague. For all we know, next the ocean will rise up and swallow us all whole. It stands to reason that to accomplish their grand aims, the witches would need an enormous vessel to contain the Noirceur. Something much larger than a single clock. Something the size of the original vessel. Stonehenge."

"But in London," Beau added.

Sitting over by the sarcophagi, Sinjin snorted. Anouk spun to face him; she had almost forgotten about the information broker. He was feeding his hare small pieces of pizza crust and wiping the grease on his white coat.

"Why do you laugh?" She didn't like his tone.

"You don't know London well, do you?"

Anouk leveled a cold look at him. "No. But then again, I've only been alive one year and I already seem to know more about the Haute than you do." She tilted up her chin. "If you have information for sale, we can arrange a price."

"Don't pay him a cent," Viggo said. "The answer is easy, if you know the city." He jerked his chin toward a framed map of England among several other artworks being restored. "Look there, at London on the map . . . Big Ben."

Anouk dragged the map away from the stack of paintings, coughing as a cloud of dust rose around her. She traced a finger over the antiquated writing until she found London and then a reference to Big Ben.

"It looks like a giant bell."

"It *is* a giant bell," said Viggo. "Big Ben is the nickname for the bell *and* for the clock tower that holds it." He gave Sinjin a sharp look. "Tell them."

Sinjin closed the pizza box. "The whole area around Big Ben has been roped off for days. It's under construction. Closed for repairs."

Luc was eyeing the broker curiously, as though he'd seen something odd in the tattoos that stretched across the back of his neck. "The witches must have set up Big Ben as their base of operations," he said.

"So what do we do?" Beau said. "Blow it up?"

"Oooh." Cricket's eyes glittered.

"That wouldn't work," Luc said. "You can't destroy something that cannot be destroyed. We can only hope to contain the Noirceur again in a new vessel. Something extremely unique. Something highly protected. But first we'd have to gather every clock in the city and consolidate them all in a single location. Then, maybe, we could trap it for good." His eyes glistened. "That would take powerful magic."

Cricket continued to whisper. Her voice was getting hoarse, and the snowfall came in jerky waves. She couldn't maintain the spell forever.

Anouk turned to Jak. "How do we get the witches to consolidate their power? We'd need to threaten them with a whole army of magic handlers, Goblins and Royals and witches on our side, but none of them can enter London."

Jak reached out and stroked her cheek. "That, lovely, is a riddle not even I can answer."

Sinjin laughed. "I like you, beasties, but you'll be lucky to make it through the night." He popped a piece of pepperoni in his mouth and added, "Especially not *this* night. It's cursed. Two moons. By tomorrow, there'll probably be five."

Luc stopped pacing. His hand fell away from his chin as a look of dawning realization crossed his face. "Five moons?" Then, to everyone's surprise, he turned on Sinjin and said it again. *"Five moons."*

The broker appeared confused. It wasn't lost on Anouk, though, that he picked up his hare and was now very gradually moving toward the door.

Luc's expression turned hard. "I knew there was something odd about your tattoos. No self-respecting hacker would get zeros and ones tattooed on his neck; that's advertising you're a criminal. Not unless you were trying to cover up *other* tattoos."

Now Sinjin glanced at the steps that led to the door, but he was smiling oddly, trying to play it off. "I don't follow." His hand went to his ear, and he toyed with the ruby stud there.

Luc was moving to block the exit as stealthily as Sinjin was moving toward it. "London witches are known for tattooing their marks on their boys," Luc continued. "Parisian witches think it's crass—Viggo used to talk about it, didn't you, Viggo? You wanted a tattoo but Mada Vittora would only ever let you get temporary ones. But it's tradition here in London. Your tattoos aren't zeros, are they? Before you *covered them up* to look like zeros, they were moons. A row of five moons. The symbol of the Worm Moon Witch. The leader of the Coven of Oxford. *You're her witch's boy.*"

"That's a lie!" Sinjin's fist was tight on his ruby earring now, his knuckles white. He turned to Cricket, who was sweating, struggling to keep up the snow spell. "Use a truth spell on me. I'll prove it. Ask me if I'm a witch's boy and I'll be compelled to tell you the truth."

Anouk stood straighter. At her engagement party, Luc had told her that the traitor was someone who shared a roof with witches. They'd been afraid it was Viggo or Rennar.

"Luc," Hunter Black said quietly. "We researched all the Coven's associates back in Paris. There were records of the witches' boys in Castle Ides. They're all accounted for. Five boys for five witches. None of them are Sinjin."

Luc's gaze was steady. "A count from the Court of the Woods once whispered in my ear that truth spells are nothing but a clever trick. Use a truth spell and then ask you? You would tell us honestly that you aren't her boy. But you *were.* How long ago did she cast you out for a younger boy?"

Sinjin's fingers toyed hard at the stud in his ear; he almost looked like he was twisting it off. Awareness of danger flashed in his eyes. He kept darting gazes toward the blocked doorway.

Luc folded his arms across his chest. "Your gloves aren't a fashion statement, are they? They're hiding scars on your inner elbow. Blood-letting scars from your time as her witch's boy."

Viggo's hand drifted mechanically to his own inner elbow.

"In Paris, there were rumors of a traitor. No one thought to consider a Pretty."

Anouk pressed a hand to her head. It was making sense now, but so fast that she couldn't hold it all in her mind at once. "The party!" When they all stared at her, she explained in a rush, "The broken hourglass—that's how the Coven got into my engagement party. How King Kaspar was possessed."

Cricket shook her head. "The hourglass was a Parisian timepiece and the witches only awakened the Noirceur in London ones."

Anouk turned on Sinjin. "You brought it from London with you, didn't you? You knocked it over intentionally. Pretended to spill sand on King Kaspar and Mia. It was a trap. Anyone who physically touches the sand could be possessed. You were working for the Coven."

The broker's smile came quick and mean. In the next second, three things happened:

First, Cricket stopped whispering so she could pull her blades.

Second, Sinjin opened his palm to reveal his ruby earring stud.

Third, the golden hare leaped into his arms and ate the stud in one quick swallow.

It happened so fast and was so unexpected that at first Anouk wasn't certain she had seen it correctly. But before she could wonder what such a strange thing meant, the hare leaped out of Sinjin's arms onto the taxidermied lion's back, then onto a vase, and then down to Cricket's feet, where it started hopping in a circle around her.

Saint cawed and took flight, wings flapping wildly.

The vase teetered precariously before falling in a spectacular crash.

Cricket twisted in circles, trying to catch the hare. She said, "Stop Sinjin!" and threw one of her blades, but all the spinning threw off her aim. The blade flew an inch from Sinjin's ear and lodged in a totem pole. The snow started to lessen and Cricket cursed and began the whisper again.

In the chaos, Sinjin pulled an amber stone from his jacket pocket and hurled it at the floor. It broke into clumps of resin, emitting a smell that was musky and rotten. Beau and Luc pulled their shirts up over their mouths against the smell.

Anouk didn't know what kind of gem or jewel could smell like that, but it couldn't be good. She could feel magic spreading through the room, warm bilious clouds of the reeking smell floating toward the vents. Something groaned high up in the upper floors of the museum, as though the entire building were waking from a long slumber.

"Don't follow me," Sinjin warned. "They aren't human anymore —and they haven't eaten in a thousand years."

He ran out the door before anyone could stop him.

Chapter 31

⚜

"THEY?" BEAU ASKED. "Who are *they?*"

Everyone's head tilted upward as the building groaned again. A fine dust rained down. There was the sound of stone scraping. Luc consulted the map. "That sound's coming from the Egyptian Wing."

Jak, reclining in the throne, clapped his hands together in delight. "Ah! Frankincense. It has the ability to hold necromancy spells, but I haven't seen it used in centuries."

Anouk whirled to face him. "Sinjin woke the *dead?*"

"He didn't, but the spell stored within the frankincense did, yes."

Cricket, in shock, stopped whispering again. The last flakes fluttered to the ground. A second before they landed, Jak turned to Anouk with a flash of urgency in his eyes.

"It's snowing in Wiltshire, lovely."

Then he was gone.

The fallen snow blanketed the *Nutcracker* set as though a ballet production had just ended and janitors would soon come sweep it away. But it was real snow, not cotton, and it melted into a puddle that soaked the presents and other props.

She turned to Beau. "What's in Wiltshire?"

Beau shrugged, and before she could puzzle out the meaning of

Jak's final words, another one of Cricket's blades whizzed just over Anouk's head. She ducked. The blade sank into the leather of Viggo's jacket sleeve. He let out a wail. "You stabbed me!"

"Cricket, be careful!" Anouk cried.

"I was aiming for the rabbit! I just woke up in a sarcophagus and now there are dead Egyptian kings after us. Sorry if my aim is off!"

"It's fine." Viggo staggered backward and collapsed on the ottoman. "I deserve it. I deserve this and more. Impale me again, Cricket!"

Anouk grabbed him by his jacket collar, looked at the wound, rolled her eyes, and tossed the knife to the floor. "It barely scratched you. You'll live. Now knock it off!"

Viggo whimpered, cradling his bleeding arm.

She sighed, knelt in front of him, took his face in her hands, and said kindly, "You can help us, Viggo. You're a witch's boy too. You must know something. That ruby earring—what was it? One of the jewels that can store magic?"

He blinked fiercely. "The ruby. Yes, it's enchanted. Gems like that are extremely rare. Londoner witches particularly favor gems. Rubies are for . . . *merde*, I forget. Oh! Safe passage!" He seemed very pleased with himself.

"Why would a rabbit need safe passage?" Anouk asked.

"The ruby isn't for the rabbit." Viggo was so excited by the fact that he had valuable information that he had temporarily forgotten about the bleeding scratch on his arm. "It's an old Goblin trick. They've been known to feed their pet rats talismans that they want to hide. They get the talisman back eventually. You know." He raised his eyebrows suggestively.

Cricket made a face.

"When it craps it out," Viggo finished.

"Yes, we all got it without you having to explain," Anouk said dryly.

"Anyway," Viggo continued. "The rubies work only for witches. He must be safeguarding them for the Coven."

"Then we can't let the witches get them." Anouk started after the hare, but Cricket grabbed her sleeve.

"We need to stop Sinjin first, before he goes to Big Ben to warn them!" She tugged Anouk in the direction of the loading-dock door, and Anouk dug in her heels.

Luc shoved between them. "Listen, we'll split up. Beau, Hunter Black, you two go after Sinjin. Cricket, Anouk, catch the hare. I'll stay here and stitch up Viggo."

Beau's eyes lit up with an idea. "Hunter Black, remember how we stopped that Pretty who tried to steal the Benz on the trip to Lisbon?"

Hunter Black's mouth drew back in a grim smile. "Let's go."

The two of them disappeared in the same direction as Sinjin. Cricket prodded Anouk's shoulder and handed her a bag of eucalyptus. "Take this."

Anouk bristled. "I can't use it. I lost my magic, remember?" It pained her to put it into words.

"Just hold it for me, okay? In case I lose my supply. Grab some of those white feathers too."

Anouk shrugged off her jacket and hung it on the back of the throne for safekeeping, then followed Cricket as she weaved around the crates that formed a maze through the basement. It had only been a few hours since they'd woken up in the sarcophagi, and her limbs still felt stiff. The pizza was a lump of grease in her stomach. They darted past workrooms filled with specimens and half-constructed exhibits. They peered in boxes of dinosaur bones and checked behind ancient tapestries brought to the basement for cleaning. There was no sign of the hare. Cricket ran past a roped-off staircase, but Anouk grabbed her sleeve.

"Wait!" Anouk picked up a clump of fur that was stuck in a crack in the stairs. It shimmered with golden strands. "The rabbit must have gone up the stairs."

"Good thing you have a knack for spotting dust."

"Thanks. I think."

They climbed over the velvet rope and up the stairs, then through a door that opened into the museum's main entry. The overhead lights were off, and with the eternal night outside, not much light came through the glazed windows. A round ticket counter sat in the center, flanked by two curving staircases. An enormous banner hung from the ceiling and proclaimed: *Special Exhibit Coming Soon: The Original* Nutcracker *Set Comes to London!* Anouk grabbed a pamphlet that included a map.

Something creaked in another room.

"That was too loud to be a hare," Anouk said darkly.

Cricket grimaced. "The dead?"

"I don't want to find out." Anouk bolted the basement door behind them, and they ran in the opposite direction, past a giant stone head and into the Early Greece wing. Shards of pottery and replicas of mosaic artwork were encased in glass displays, forming a maze that they navigated as fast as they could, searching under exhibits for the rabbit. They checked the World of Alexander, the Mausoleum at Halicarnassus, the Nereid Monument.

Another creak came from an adjacent room; it was followed by a scrape of stone, then a dry, hollow moan.

Cricket shuddered. "Let's head upstairs. Hurry."

They carefully checked around corners until they found a staircase and made their way to the second floor. Here were artifacts from Iran and ancient Mesopotamia, Anatolian and Assyrian tablets and pottery. A hum of magic emanated from some of the objects. Cricket eyed a carved bowl covetously, her long fingers twitching, but then something else caught her eye.

"Over there!"

She pointed to the entrance to an exhibit on the Heart of Alexandrite, a forty-five-carat color-changing gemstone rumored to be the most valuable jewel in the world. Anouk looked just in time to see a flash of gold fur. They chased the hare into the special-collections room, where the walls were painted in all the hues that alexandrite could take on: purple, blue, yellow, green, pink. Heavy iron bars surrounded the glittering jewel. Security cameras pointed at it from every direction. They darted between informative panels after the hare.

"Rapi blok," Cricket whispered.

The hare leaped into the next exhibit, the history of illuminated manuscripts, before her trapping spell could grab it. Cricket and Anouk raced to the end of the darkened room and then froze.

A few steps ahead of them, a shadow stretched across the floor in the light of the moon. It moved haltingly, dragging its feet like the flesh had long ago worn off the bones. The smell of decay was thick in the air. The figure loomed in the doorway. Anouk held in a scream. Desiccated flesh. Rotted brown teeth. Tatters of fabric and a bead necklace tangled in exposed ribs. Anouk felt another scream building in her throat.

Cricket shoved her hand against Anouk's mouth to keep her quiet.

"Come on," Cricket whispered. She yanked Anouk toward the Mesopotamian exhibits. They ran through the displays of Assyrian tablets but stopped short when another figure lunged in the darkness ahead. Cricket pressed a hand to her nose against the stink of rot and sulfur.

"It's another one," Anouk whispered.

"Damn Sinjin." Cricket shuddered. "How many mummified bodies does this museum have?"

Anouk fumbled to read the pamphlet in the faint light. "Counting the ones on display and the ones in storage . . . one hundred and twenty." She looked up from the pamphlet, feeling sick. "And one mummified bird and one mummified cat."

"Oh, great. Our distant cousins. Well, let's not join them in the afterlife."

They ran into the next room and hid behind the curtains of a tall window, trying not to make a sound. Cricket swallowed a few eucalyptus leaves and whispered a spell to make them as unnoticeable as possible. Anouk's heart drummed in her chest.

Cricket adjusted something in her pocket—one of the carved bowls from the Assyrian exhibit, Anouk saw.

"You stole that," Anouk whispered.

Cricket shoved the bowl farther down in her pocket. "Forget it."

Anouk gave her a suspicious look. Cricket took pride in her thievery, but why risk it *now?* "What do you want with some bowl? And the parchments from the basement? It's just old junk."

"*Shh!*" Cricket nodded toward the sounds of more footsteps, and Anouk shut her mouth reluctantly. Cricket had been snooping through the artifacts at Castle Ides back in Paris too. What was Cricket looking for? After the siege of the Château des Mille Fleurs, Cricket had talked about tearing down the Haute, throwing the whole system into chaos so that the four orders might start afresh, with Royals and witches and Goblins and beasties on a more even playing field. Maybe that's why she'd been snooping around Castle Ides—maybe she intended to whisper a spell on Rennar's shoes so that he'd slip on the stairs and break his neck. Anouk had to admit she'd had similar thoughts. That arrogant look in his eye. His insistence that there would come a time when she'd beg him to kiss her.

She realized she was toying with her wedding ring again.

Anouk shifted so that she could look out the window. *Nightmare* was the word Sinjin had used, and he was right. She could barely make sense of what she was seeing. Fallen toads and the bodies of cats and dogs that had choked to death from the black smoke curling out of sewer grates littered the streets. Traffic was a mess; cars were bumper-to-bumper, blocking the roads. The convenience store on the corner kept flickering in and out of reality, trapped in a time loop. The Noirceur had driven the whole city mad.

Hunter Black and Beau were out there in the chaos.

Cricket tapped her shoulder and whispered, "Um, Anouk?"

Anouk thought she saw Sinjin's white coat below and she pushed the curtain back farther—but no, it was just a Pretty running in terror. "Yes?"

Cricket ripped the curtain from her hands. "Run!"

Chapter 32

A DOZEN DEAD WERE COMING for them. The pale light of the double moons shone on their hollow eye sockets, rotted teeth, and desiccated fabric.

Anouk screamed before she could stop herself. The dead roused themselves at the sound. They lurched in her direction with snapping jaws and outstretched fingers. Their steps grew more certain. They began to move faster.

"They're remembering how to run," Cricket moaned.

Cricket and Anouk took off. The pamphlet's map was useless —Anouk's vision had gone blurry from terror. Cricket grabbed her hand and they tore past exhibits of Iron Age tools and Celtic jewelry, a twenty-foot-high statue of the Buddha and tiny jade figurines. They ran over benches and under velvet ropes. It seemed that around every corner, they could hear the dragging of desiccated feet on museum tile.

"I'm going to kill Sinjin!" Cricket yelled as they sprinted toward signs for the museum restaurant. "I'm going to kill him, bring him back with his own necromancy crystals, and then kill him all over again!"

They reached the restaurant and threw open the glass doors. Anouk grabbed a tablecloth and used it to tie the door handles together to buy them a few extra minutes. They ran between the tables, knocking over glassware in their haste.

"Hey, wait!" Anouk grabbed Cricket a second before she darted into the kitchen. "Look!"

The golden hare was just on the other side of the glass wall that separated the restaurant from the rest of the museum. Its nose was twitching and its eyes rolled anxiously, as though it could sense the unholy magic that had taken hold of the museum.

"We can't go out there," Cricket said. "We'd have to go back through the restaurant doors. There are dead people out there wanting to eat us!"

"We don't need doors. You can cast magic, Cricket!"

Anouk plucked a fistful of petals from a wilting arrangement of spider mums, pulled out one of the long white owl feathers, and shoved all of it over to Cricket. Cricket grabbed the supplies and swallowed them whole.

"What do I say? I mostly only know cutting and stealing spells."

"Try *Ax aguis*."

"Ax aguis," Cricket repeated in a whisper in the direction of the glass wall. The right intonation didn't come naturally to her, but she'd been practicing diligently, and it sounded correct to Anouk's ears. The spell was one to make the nature of glass waver briefly—

"Now! Grab the hare," Anouk said breathlessly.

Cricket looked hesitant but thrust her hands toward the glass wall, giving a yelp of surprise when her hands passed through it like water. She swiped at the hare. It lunged away and hopped toward the curving stairs to the ground floor.

"Merde! So close!"

Behind them the restaurant doors shook violently. Anouk whirled around. Rotted bodies pressed against the glass doors three and four rows deep. The tablecloth wasn't going to hold for long.

"Quick," Anouk said. "Let's go through the glass."

Cricket grimaced. "What if my spell doesn't last? We'll be sliced in two."

"We don't have a choice . . . sorry about this!"

She shoved Cricket. Cricket tumbled through the wall as easily as her hands had gone through it, and then Anouk thrust herself through after. She patted her head and chest and hips to reassure herself that she was whole. A crash came from inside the restaurant as dozens of the dead stumbled in through the doors. They picked themselves back up with alarming speed.

"Down the stairs!" Anouk cried. "Hurry!"

She and Cricket scrambled toward the staircase. Anouk caught a flash of golden fur again—the hare. It was scampering down the stairs, as anxious to get away from the dead horde as they were. Did she have time to catch it? The dead were already sprinting through the enchanted glass wall behind them. The spell ended abruptly and the glass returned to glass, trapping half the horde in the restaurant, but two dozen were still headed for them.

Cricket threw a leg over the banister. Anouk got the idea and did the same on the other side. They slid on their stomachs down the banisters, rushing so fast that Anouk squeezed her eyes shut. But that was even scarier, so she opened them again as she hurtled toward the ground floor. She passed the hare, still hopping down the stairs. The end of the banister came all too fast and her shoulder and then her bottom connected hard with the tiles. She winced.

The hare hopped down the last step. Anouk lunged for it on her hands and knees, gasping when her hands closed around its foot. But it kicked hard and slipped from her grasp. It hopped toward the main entrance, which someone—Sinjin or Beau or Hunter Black—had left ajar. It hopped straight out of the museum.

"No!"

"That rabbit has the right idea, if you ask me." Cricket grabbed Anouk's arm and dragged her to her feet. The dead were almost at the bottom of the stairs. "We're getting out of here!"

"We can't! It's a mess out there!"

"It's a mess in *here*."

They dashed across the cavernous entryway. The moans and shuffling feet of the horde echoed from the high ceilings. The *Nutcracker* banner rippled in the breeze from the slightly open door. Cricket threw the door wide open and they shot out into the city, then heaved their weight against the heavy door to close it.

Cricket ran, dodging a police officer on a motorcycle weaving in and out of stopped traffic. Horns blared wildly. Screams and sobbing filled the city.

Dizzy, Anouk looked up at the double moons. The shift in gravity had caused waves to rise on the normally placid river Thames. It looked like a churning ocean, splashing over the banks, pulling in Pretties and drowning their screams. Across the street a fight erupted between two well-dressed women; they clawed at each other, drawing blood, driven mad. Something hurtled out of the sky and slammed into a boy running away from the two women: a toad. He fell to the ground, smacking his head.

"Cricket, get out of the street!" she yelled.

If they didn't stop this plague, Paris was next.

Cities falling one by one, White to Red, White to Red . . .

Anouk started to run after Cricket but a flash of gold caught her attention. The golden hare was at the crosswalk on the corner. Its attention was fixed on the lettuce in a half-eaten hamburger by a trashcan.

A man with blood pouring from his ears started toward Cricket. Her blades appeared in her hands, flashing in the moonlight. Anouk tiptoed closer to the hare until she was right behind it, partially hidden by the trashcan. She held her breath.

A car's horn blared. Brakes squealed. A woman screamed and a man cried out—he'd been hit. There was a terrible smash of metal, followed by a long string of cursing.

The hare's head shot up at the sound of the accident.

Anouk lunged. "Got you!"

Her hands closed over it and this time it didn't slip away. She wrestled the hare to her chest, hugged it tight. She looked up triumphantly, but then her face fell.

Cricket was in the middle of the street, straightening up after throwing a knife. She looked untouched. Safe. Someone had darted across the street, and a black town car had driven up onto the sidewalk and hit him. Sinjin! He was moaning. Blood stained his white coat.

Anouk jogged over to Sinjin, clutching the hare. From the looks of it, Sinjin hadn't been hit fatally. One of Cricket's knives protruded from his shoulder. The car doors opened and people climbed out, and Anouk jumped in surprise to see familiar faces. "Beau! Hunter Black!"

Beau ran around the car and checked for Sinjin's pulse—they

needed him alive so they could question him—then grinned up at Hunter Black. "Just like in Lisbon."

Anouk scoffed. "*That's* what happened in Lisbon? You ran some-one over?"

"It worked, didn't it?" Hunter Black smoothed a hand over his black shirt with its gleaming glass buttons. There was a note of satis-faction in his voice.

Cricket came over and nudged Sinjin with her toe. "He wouldn't have darted into the street if I hadn't wounded him first with my knife. So it counts as my catch."

"What? That's not fair!" Beau protested.

Anouk crouched by Sinjin. His forehead was slick with a yellow-ish sheen. She glanced warily at the smoke drifting out of a nearby sewer grate. "We need to get him inside. Quickly. Beau, Hunter Black, carry him through the loading dock straight into the base-ment. It'll be safe there. I bolted the door to the upper levels—let's hope it holds."

"What's in the upper levels?" Beau asked.

Cricket snorted. "Trust us."

They picked up Sinjin and carried him toward the museum, Cricket and Anouk right behind them. Anouk still clasped the hare firmly. She whispered reassurances in its ear—then made a face as she thought about what they were going to have to do to get that ruby back.

Chapter 33

THE FOUR OF THEM brought Sinjin in through the exterior loading dock. Beau checked the rest of the basement doors to make certain they were locked against the dead upstairs, while Cricket searched for a place to put their prisoner. She settled on a wire storage locker currently filled with artwork from one of the museum's rotating exhibits. She shoved aside some paintings, pausing to appraise the expensive gold frames, and then they dumped Sinjin into the makeshift cage.

"Careful." Luc stood up from where he'd been tending to Viggo, who'd gained a few stitches in his arm. "Those are priceless paintings. Part of Monet's Water Lilies series."

"*How* priceless?" Cricket stroked her chin.

Her pockets, Anouk noticed, were no longer bulging with stolen goods. At some point in the past few minutes, Cricket must have hidden the Assyrian bowl somewhere.

Luc felt Sinjin's forehead. He lifted both of Sinjin's eyelids and checked the pallor of his lips with a frown. "Cricket, were your blades poisoned?"

"Of course. I'm not an idiot. I use every means I have."

He carefully drew Cricket's knife from Sinjin's shoulder and sniffed the blade. He suddenly dropped the knife to the floor. His eyes went wide. "This is nightrose poison! Once it gets to the heart, nothing can stop it, not even magic."

Cricket nodded. "That's the point."

"You stabbed Viggo too! When were you going to tell us so that we could cure him?"

She rolled her eyes. "That knife didn't have poison on it. *Unfortunately.* Look—he's fine." Viggo had turned a shade paler, but it was true, he didn't look poisoned.

Luc shook his head as he fetched his herbalist bag and started to make an antidote for Sinjin out of various elements preserved in dark bottles. He handled every flower with grace, every set of wings with care. In Mada Vittora's service, he'd made love potions for Goblins, obedience potions that he soaked into clothing, tonics that sometimes smelled divine, sometimes reeked, sometimes were the electric color of heat lightning, sometimes were blacker than night. Anouk suspected that half of Mada Vittora's power had come not from her magic but Luc's skill.

Anouk sidled up to Cricket, the hare clutched in her arms. "What did you do with that carved bowl?"

Cricket gave a dismissive wave. "Don't worry about it."

"If you're planning something against Rennar, I don't blame you, but tell me."

Cricket looked mildly annoyed. "I'm not *completely* obsessed with revenge, you know." Then she sighed. "Look, it's . . . it's just a new spell I've been working on. A stealing spell. There are plenty of spells for masking intention or distracting security guards, but there are no spells for making an object disappear from one place and reappear elsewhere, regardless of walls or vaults or anything between it and a thief."

"A transference spell? You're writing it yourself?"

"Trying to."

Anouk was about to prod her again—she was clearly not telling the whole truth—but Luc gave a satisfied grunt.

"There!" He swirled the antidote, then touched a few droplets to Sinjin's lips, the edges of his nostrils, and the inside of his ears, using every last drop.

On the floor, Sinjin let out a groan. Luc gathered up his supplies, exited the locker, and slid the bolt closed behind him. Sinjin sat up and squinted at them through the wire mesh.

"Guess what?" Cricket said, sneering. "You're going to live, but you and your bunny belong to us now."

Hunter Black said bleakly, "I say we feed him to the dead upstairs."

"Hunter Black gets cranky," Cricket informed Sinjin, "when he goes more than three days without assassinating someone."

Hunter Black spun on her. "I never said I enjoyed killing."

"Ha! I've seen you kill. You look like you're having really good sex or really bad indigestion."

He growled, "Mada Vittora made me to kill and so I kill. Not because I enjoy it. Sometimes difficult things must be done, and I'm the only one who has both the stomach and the skill to do them."

Cricket threw up her hands and exclaimed dryly, "Oh, noble you."

Before Hunter Black could retort, Viggo pushed between them and gripped the bars of Sinjin's cage. "Look, ignore these two," he said to the broker. "One witch's boy to another, tell us how we can defeat the witches. They must have weaknesses. All witches do. Certain organs that haven't yet turned to wood and can still bleed."

Sinjin scowled. "Organs? What are you talking about?"

Anouk joined Viggo at the cage. "Tell us how many witches there are. What their monikers are. What they use as oubliettes."

Sinjin stared at them oddly.

Luc came over, dusting herbs off his hands. "Listen, you'd best tell us everything. I have it on good authority from a Crimson princess that one of the Royals is in league with your witches. That's the only way the witches could have gotten into the Castle Ides ballroom. Tell us how. In exchange for the information, we'll spare your life and even keep your secret. You can go back to Paris and hack whatever Pretty websites you want."

Sinjin's expression slowly cracked into a cruel smile. He started laughing.

Beau slammed his palm against the wire cage. "It's no use. He won't betray his witches."

Sinjin's laughing tapered off. "You don't understand, any of you. There are no monikers or oubliettes. There are no *organs*. Not anymore," he spat out sourly. "There's nothing left to betray."

Anouk considered him carefully. "What are you saying?"

"There are no more Oxford witches. The entire coven is dead."

Viggo barked a laugh. "Yeah, right."

Anouk added, "We saw them at the engagement party when they possessed King Kaspar."

"They possessed King Kaspar not to *threaten* you. They were *warning* you. Begging for help! When your Royals killed King Kaspar, they killed the final spirit of the witches too."

Cricket shot up from a crate and waved her knife. "I've got a whole city plunged into chaos out there that would disagree with you. Chaos *your witches* awoke."

Sinjin shook his head. "You have no idea what you're up against."

Anouk crouched next to the cage and said softly, "Then tell us."

He looked up with cruel words poised on the tip of his tongue, but then he met her eyes and the fight seemed to go out of him. He sighed. Sank back heavily against the water-lily paintings.

Luc winced. "Ah, the paintings really are quite delicate—"

Beau elbowed him quiet.

Sinjin rubbed absently at the line of tattoos spanning the back of his neck. "They *were* witches, once. Women who, decades ago, were turned away from Oxford University, back when women weren't allowed to be students. One of them found a reference to the Coal Baths in a book that a Royal had left behind in the university library. She saw it for what it was: a chance to learn more than they ever would at Oxford. She convinced the others to go to the Black Forest. Close to a hundred went; only five survived and came out witches. They named themselves the Coven of Oxford. One of them was Mada White, my mistress. She stole me as a baby and raised me as her own until I turned twenty-five. Then she found a younger boy and kept me on as a spy."

"You hated her," Anouk concluded.

His eyes flashed. "I loved her. If she were alive, I'd be at her side. But she's gone. All of them are. It's the Noirceur, don't you get it? They woke up something they couldn't control. It destroyed all five of them. Women who had shaped the world, gone like that." His snap echoed. "The Noirceur destroyed the entire Court of Isles too, and King Kaspar." He pointed in the direction of Big Ben. "Anyone who's gone up against the Noirceur is now part of it. You aren't fighting people, you're fighting that smoke. It can't be stabbed with knives. It can't be poisoned. It can't be bribed or reasoned with—it doesn't *want* anything. It's simply a force. A void. And it'll destroy you too."

Anouk's heart thundered in her chest. She thought of the glimpses she'd gotten of London, the escalating chaos, the plagues that were getting worse. Most of all, the black smoke that had sunk into the streets, dirtying everything it touched with soot, swarming toward the vibrations of screams.

She stood and paced by the ballet set. "This changes everything. I thought we were up against witches. Women we could bargain with or, if it came down to it, kill. But how do we stop chaos?"

"We round it up," Luc said. "Jak said the only way to stop it is to transfer it to a new vessel. The first step is to collect every clock in the city."

"That's impossible," Beau argued.

"Not if we had reinforcements," Luc said. "Not if we had teams in every borough of the city that could use tricks and whispers to gather every clock, street by street."

"It would take hundreds of magic handlers," Anouk said. "We would need every Royal in the near realms."

Luc nodded. "And every Goblin and every witch too."

"We'd have to break the border spell to get them into London."

"Exactly, Dust Bunny."

"I lost my magic—I can't do it. And Cricket isn't powerful enough."

He sighed. "Well, I didn't promise a perfect answer. And then there's the question of what the new vessel would be."

Anouk's mind raced. She paced through the artificial snow on the *Nutcracker* set, thinking. Luc said the vessel needed to be something unique, something secure. The original Royals had placed it in an abstract concept—time—before they knew how ubiquitous clocks would become. She tapped her chin. If only she hadn't failed in the Black Forest. If only she could get a second chance. She knew so many spells, but none of them could help her now.

She gasped softly. "I might know a good vessel—"

But as she turned, Luc cried out. He'd stepped too close to the art locker. Sinjin had reached between the wires and grabbed him, and he now held one of Cricket's poisoned knives to his neck, the one Cricket had stabbed him with earlier, that Luc had thrown to the floor.

"Sinjin!" Anouk felt the blood drain from her face. "Let him go."

"Let *me* go."

"I've got your rabbit. I won't hesitate to hurt it."

He shook his head. "You might be partial to things that creep and crawl, but I am not. Go ahead. Kill it." He pressed the blade to Luc's neck. "I have to get out of London. That darkness is growing and it's going to kill us all. Plagues, smoke—one way or another, anything breathing in this city will be gone soon. *I have to get out.*"

"Easy, Sinjin." Anouk held out one hand. She could feel the desperation rolling off him like cold sweat. "Easy . . ."

"I have to get out!" A mad sort of fever overtook him. He jerked the knife. Luc dodged the full impact, but the blade scratched his neck.

"No!" Anouk cried.

Luc staggered away from Sinjin, one hand pressed to the scratch on his neck. A small scratch, barely bleeding. But . . .

"The nightrose poison!" Cricket breathed.

Anouk gave the hare to Viggo and knelt next to Luc. Her hands were shaking. Her lips felt so cold. She tapped her fingers against them, wishing for that fizzy warm spark of magic, but they didn't warm. Hunter Black, brooding over by the dinosaur fossils, had been so silent that Anouk had almost forgotten he was there. But in a few steps, he threw open the bolt of the locker, grabbed Sinjin by the shoulder, twisted his head, and, with a sickening crack, broke his neck.

"Hunter Black!" she cried.

Sinjin's body slumped to the ground. Anouk started to run over, but then stopped. There was no point in feeling for a pulse. His chin was practically touching his spine. She spun on Hunter Black with hot cheeks. "I thought you said you didn't enjoy killing!"

"Luc is family," he said grimly. "And I make an exception when someone hurts my family."

Should she feel grateful or disturbed? "Luc." She picked up a cloth and pressed it to his neck, but he waved it away—the bleeding had already stopped. "Cricket, get his herbalist kit."

Luc shook his head. "Dust Bunny. No." His face was slick with sweat. It smelled sharp and astringent. "I used the last of the antidote on Sinjin."

"Then we'll get more. It's a big city. We'll get flowers and . . ." She turned helplessly to Cricket.

Cricket looked like she'd seen a ghost. "The poison I used is from

Mada Zola's stash in Montélimar. It contains a cultivar of lavender found only on the estate. The antidote has to come from there too."

Anouk staggered to the nearest seat, the throne from the *Nutcracker* set. She felt numb. Luc was poisoned. They had no antidote. She had no magic to save him. They had the golden hare, which meant they had the ruby stud. Theoretically, if they could get the ruby to Paris, Petra could pass into London — but she'd never arrive before the poison reached Luc's heart.

At her feet lay the Nutcracker dolls that Jak had commanded like puppets. She kicked one, watched it roll across the stage and bump into the presents that had been set up to look like Stonehenge.

Her spine went rigid. An idea was forming in her head, a valiant one, and those were the most dangerous. She closed her hand instinctively around her Faustine jacket, still hanging on the back of the throne.

Cricket stopped pacing and gave Anouk a searching look. "What are you doing?"

"Leaving."

"*Leaving*? Why? Where?"

Head spinning, Anouk pulled on the jacket, letting the silk slide over her like battle armor.

It's snowing, Jak had said before disappearing, *in Wiltshire.*

Her eyes fell to one of the paintings in the art locker, a landscape of a field of heather beneath a brilliant blue sky. For all she knew, it was a field in the Russian countryside, not in Great Britain, but regardless, something about the field reminded her of Jak's words. "I'm going to Wiltshire."

Cricket stared at her as though she'd gone mad. "What's in Wilt-shire?"

Anouk flipped up her jacket collar. She checked the security cameras trained on the exterior steps, noting with satisfaction that a light snow had started.

A place of immense power, Jak had said. *A place of transformation and blue flame.*

"Stonehenge," she answered.

Chapter 34

❧

"ANOUK. WAIT."

She was halfway up the stairs. Hunter Black, his face cast in shadows, took a single, halting step toward her.

"You're leaving," he said. "You're going to do something dangerous. At the least, you're going to fight your way through the dead up there."

"If you're going to tell me not to go—"

"I'm not." He took another step toward her, closing the distance. "You wouldn't listen to me anyway. But I want to tell you . . ." He cleared his throat, and she found herself curious and a little worried. It was rare to see Hunter Black flummoxed. Rarer still that it didn't have to do with some poor soul he'd just killed. "Be careful."

She let out a laugh without meaning to. "Careful?" How many times had Hunter Black *himself* threatened her? He was Mada Vittora's loyal wolf, there to do her dirty work. In the case of Anouk, that had meant making sure she was too scared to ever leave the townhouse.

He gave something like a growl, coming up the rest of the stairs until they were just a few steps apart. "I know I . . . I've been a monster. But it isn't like it was before. I meant what I said about us being . . . being . . ."

That ugly feeling inside her softened, and she hesitantly took a step down. "Family?"

After a second, he muttered a word that resembled *yes*.

A smile flickered at her lips. "And you're worried for my safety?"

"Hmm."

She smiled wider at his obvious discomfort. "And you care if I live or die?"

He scowled again. "Don't mock me." But then he tipped up his chin. "All things considered, your survival would be . . . preferable to your death."

"Hunter Black! How sweet."

He turned and went down the stairs so quickly that for a moment she thought she'd imagined their conversation. Hunter Black, caring about whether they all lived or died? She'd never have believed it. He was right, though—the beasties were family. The thought made her feel both tender toward and fiercely protective of the others.

She climbed the rest of the stairs to the museum. She ducked and dashed her way up four floors, dodging undead hands, running from hollow undead eyes, and finally reached the roof. She went through the doors and thrust a flashlight through the door handles behind her, barring it against the mummies trying to get through. Moans came from the other side. She was breathing heavily. She dusted bits of desiccated fabric and skin and an errant tooth off her clothes with a shudder.

"Damn it, Sinjin," she muttered, even though it was bad luck to curse the dead.

The roof of the British Museum was largely taken up by a glass dome. She extended her arms for balance and carefully stepped across the glass tiles toward the cupola. Clouds had moved in, darkening the skies, and the double moons threw strange light over the city. Anouk's heart drummed wildly. From this high, she could see all of London. The churning waves of the river Thames. Entire buildings flickering in and out of time. A Ferris wheel that rose like the blackened bones of the city. To the right of the Ferris wheel rose a tower with a glowing clock face.

Big Ben.

The clouds hung low around it. Black fog swirled at its base. It was roped off for construction, but in the chaos of the plagues, Pretties staggered straight past the barricades and disappeared into time loops.

She shivered. The wind was savage this high.

A snowflake bit at her face, and she looked up at heavy clouds. Alone on the rooftop, Anouk felt topsy-turvy, as though she were standing on a frozen lake high over the city, and she thought of the Schwarzwald and the Cottage. The snow began to fall more heavily. The wind blew in an odd circle with a whistling sound and then, just as she knew he would, Jak materialized.

He crouched like a gargoyle, perched effortlessly on the glass tiles.

"Jak." It was darker now, the city skyline lit only by headlights and streetlights. "Take me to Stonehenge."

The smile he gave her was sweet, not like his usual sharp-toothed grin, and it made him look suddenly like an impish boy who'd only ever wanted someone to play with.

"You figured out my other riddle." His voice brimmed with cheerfulness, but then he seemed to think of something grave, and he said more seriously, "Do you know what waits for you there?"

She nodded. "I do."

"You failed once. What makes you think it will be different this time?"

She paused. Heart-pounding feelings of failure flared up again. But courage, she'd decided, was forging ahead when things went wrong, not when they went right. "I've been thinking about what Petra said after the trials," she said carefully. "She said she felt like she never belonged anywhere—at the Cottage or anywhere else—but that she'd accepted it. The rest of us were searching for our connection to magic as if we were looking for the place we belonged. But I think that's why Petra succeeded when we all failed. Because you *never* find the place where you belong. Duke Karolinge said it himself—the cruxes are only symbols. There's nothing inherently magical about, say, leaves or moths. The trick is to accept the hole in yourself. Accept that it will never be filled, not with flowers or herbs or anything. Like Petra accepted herself."

Jak cocked his head. "So you think you've learned the morality of magic? That the Coals will honor you now when they didn't before? If cruxes don't matter, will you walk in empty-handed?"

"I didn't say that cruxes don't matter. Even symbols have power. I won't be empty-handed."

She felt certain this time, but she'd felt certain before. She could fail again, and this time Rennar wouldn't be there to save her. "I think that sometimes it takes a spectacular failure before you can rise to incredible heights. I think that I've never accepted the fact that I'm not like the Pretties out there. That I have a hole in my heart shaped like an owl. That no matter what I do, that hole will never be filled. I'll never be a Pretty. I'll never be normal. And that's okay."

She reached into her pocket and pulled out one of the long white feathers she'd taken from the museum basement. "*This* is my crux. I should have known from the start. I was blind to my own soul."

The glint of mischief returned to his eyes. "Take my hand."

The wind swirled around her, pushing her toward Jak. This time, there was no magic mirror in her pocket, no Rennar to save her, no Petra and Luc to catch her if she fell.

She stepped onto one of the dome's glass panels.

And she was falling. Falling. Falling.

But Jak caught her hand, and they were falling together.

For a few moments, Anouk felt trapped in time. The snow swirled so thick around them that the city was gone, the lights and the traffic and the smell of burning chestnuts on the air. Her feet no longer rested on the museum roof. If the dead still pressed at the door, their groans were very far away now. She felt burning cold as Jak clutched her hand, but he was gone—at least his boyish form was. He was simply snow again. She wondered if this was what it felt like to be a bird. To ride the wind. To soar with the snow. She had the sense that the world was passing far below, that they were skipping over towns and valleys and roads as easily as Beau would trace his finger over one of his road maps. Up high, they didn't need to bother with traffic circles and detours. They could fly as straight as a bird, and almost as though no time had passed at all, Anouk felt solid ground once more beneath her feet.

She crouched, breathing heavily. The snow and wind swirled around her. Her fingers dug into the earth. The grass was stiff with frost. She stood, squinting into the snow and fog. There were no sounds of the city. No sounds at all except the wind. The fog continued to lift until she could make out colossal stone slabs rising around her. There was a hum that was almost deafening and yet somehow didn't make a sound. It was like the hum she'd felt from some of the enchanted ancient objects in the British Museum, but it came from every direction. An ancient song of the stones.

Jak materialized on the other side of the circle, sitting on one of the stones. She tilted her head up.

"I thought there'd be tourists," she called.

"Not at night, lovely." He pointed far off, where she could see a faint light on the horizon. Dawn was coming, but for now, she had Stonehenge to herself.

"What do I do?"

"Wait," he said cryptically, "and watch."

As the sun rose, its rays caught the frost on the grass like light concentrated through a magnifying glass, and mystical blue sparks began to appear. Anouk stepped back as if she'd stumbled onto a beehive. The song of the stones grew.

"It won't last long," Jak warned. "Once the frost melts, it'll be over until the next midwinter dawn. It was Pretty women who first discovered this, one thousand five hundred years and a day ago. They saw and understood the power of the stones. And so the Coals rewarded them for their insight. It gave them the chance for greatness. It still does today. But do not mistake a *chance* for a *promise*. There is just as great a chance that the Coals will burn you alive, as it has so many women."

The sparks began to catch and spread. This was no ordinary

flame. It took on the blue tinge of the frost. Flames rose, licking at the falling snow. Anouk got the sense she was watching something rare and special. The stones, the frost, the winter dawn—it had all come together in just the right conditions to create a naturally occurring Coal Bath.

The flames formed a circle bound by the stones. She was starting to feel cold coming from them, a cold so intense that it was burning. She glanced in the distance. The fog was rising, and she could make out a wire fence and vast fields stretching toward the horizon. There was still time. She could run. Break out of the circle.

But then it was too late, even if she'd wanted to. The flames were too high. Her chance to give up was gone—but she didn't want it anyway. The blue flames rose three feet, then six, then nine, almost as high as the tops of the stones. On his perch above, Jak crouched, his icicle hair hanging in his face and hiding his expression. Another ray of sun burst from the horizon, and he called through the snow: "Now, lovely. It must be now."

The frost was already melting. Her shoes and socks were soaked with dew. The flames burned brightly. No Royals watching now. No Duke Karolinge and his rituals. No acolytes. No robes.

She kicked off her shoes, clasped the owl feather in both hands, and stepped barefoot into the flames.

Immediately, she was burning. Her throat closed up as she remembered the pain from before, the courtyard and all those watching eyes as she screamed, as the flames licked at her skin with their barbed tongues. Burning into her flesh. Scalding her blood. Hot and cold became one: pain. She felt her body being torn apart again. Dimly, she blinked down at her bare toes. The flames had eaten off her trousers. Her underclothes were in tatters, rapidly burning off of her skin. Oh, the jacket! Her beautiful Faustine jacket was falling apart and turning into ashes. She cursed herself for not taking it off. But then the flames rose and she didn't care about the jacket. She could barely remember what the jacket looked like. The flames were turning *her* to ash now. Skin and bone and blood and eyes and hair and throat and toes; she was ash, all of her. She waited for the blackness to come. That awful, encompassing, yawning blackness. It licked at the edges of her vision. She felt nothing—she had no more fingers or toes with which to feel. She heard nothing—her ears were no longer ears. The blackness overtook every one of her senses and she knew the end was coming.

But then, with a brilliant burst, the blackness shattered. Lights crackled and then the darkness was replaced by the full spectrum of light. Reds and blues and greens and oranges. All the colors of her jacket, all the colors of the world, the colors of frost and grass and dawn and sky, all at once in a single beautiful burst.

So beautiful it ached.

So beautiful it healed.

PART IV

Chapter 35

WHEN ANOUK OPENED HER EYES, she was staring into the frowning face of an old man dressed in a navy-blue coat, Wellington boots, and a tweed cap. He prodded her gently with his cane.

"Oy there, girlie. No sleeping in the stones. I don't have to tell you crazy pagan types that. Now, scamper off and there's no harm done, eh? Don't want to have to call the police."

She stared blankly at the old man. A patch on his jacket declared him an employee of the Stonehenge Visitors' Center. She must have looked more than a little bedraggled because he cocked his head and said, "Girlie? You okay? Didn't eat any special mushrooms, did you? I was young once. I remember the thrill of sneaking into a forbidden place after lights-out. Lucky you didn't freeze to death out here."

Dazed, she sat up and looked around her, but Jak had vanished from the top of the stones. It wasn't snowing anymore. Dawn had come and gone, and the sun had burned the frost from the fields. She pressed a hand to her head. Last she remembered, she was being roasted alive. Her skin had sizzled like butter in a pan. Her blood had bubbled like broth brought to a rolling boil.

"Missy?" The elderly man was holding out a hand to help her stand. Instinctively, she took it. He pulled her to her feet and then brushed lightly at her shoulder. "Oops, you have a bit of grass on you. Don't want to stain such a pretty jacket."

She jerked her head at the word. *Jacket?*

To her supreme shock, she was fully dressed. She was wearing the black dress she'd gotten from Galeries Lafayette—never mind that she'd left it in Mada Vittora's townhouse—and her oxford shoes, and her hair was pulled back in a black ribbon. Nothing was burned or singed or even wrinkled; it was as though every piece had come straight off the hanger. And the Faustine jacket! *She'd watched it burn!* Now it was draped over her shoulders like a cape. She shrugged it off and ran her fingers over every inch, checking the stitching, the red satin fabric, the cuffs and collar. Everything was perfect—almost. It wouldn't be *her* jacket if it didn't have a few errant streaks of dust.

She hugged the jacket to her chest and then ran her hands up her arms, marveling at how the bruises she'd collected when she'd hit the floor after sliding down the museum banister had vanished from her skin. Even her knuckles, which had been perpetually chapped since the Black Forest, were now buttery smooth.

She laughed aloud. "It worked!" She threw her arms around the first thing she saw, which happened to be the visitors'-center employee.

Puzzled, he laughed off her embrace and readjusted his cap. "Hop off now, girlie. Howl at the moon somewhere else tonight, eh?"

She spun in a circle in the center of the stones. They weren't humming like they'd been the night before, but she still sensed magic in them. She felt connected to the stones and the grass and the visitors'-center employee in a way she never had before, as though the world were now an extension of her own body and she might make the grass ripple as effortlessly as she tossed her own hair. Was this what it felt like to be a witch? Not just small sparks of magic at her fingers, but as though the whole world were a warm glittering dream that until this point she'd been merely sleeping through?

The smile left her face as she remembered London. "I have to save Luc!"

The bewildered old man called after her as she leaped over the guard railing and sprinted down the path to the visitors' center. An awful idea hit her and she stopped abruptly. Without Jak, how was she supposed to get back to London? She needed a bus schedule . . . a ticket . . .

"Idiote!"

She groaned. She was a witch! She thrust a hand into her pocket and found the bag of Cricket's eucalyptus. At the Cottage, Esme had told her that, with the right combination of life-essences, doorways could be altered to lead to different destinations. It was tricky magic. Flowers alone wouldn't suffice. She swallowed three dried eucalyptus leaves along with a handful of fresh dewy grass from within the circle. A glittering, warm fizz spread through her body. Why hadn't Mada Vittora told her that magic could feel like this, like the tickle of a feather on the back of her neck, both delicious and bothersome at the same time? Raising her hands toward the nearest bathroom door, she whispered the words that were bumping around in her mouth. *"Abri nox."*

Creating doorways was far more advanced magic than sewing on buttons. She'd expected the magic to explode from her like water from one of Luc's garden hoses set on high, but instead it simply was there when she needed it and wasn't when she didn't. It reminded her of "The Goat Lottery," one of Luc's fairy tales, about a poor goatherd girl who'd bet her family's flock in the village's annual lottery and won a magical coat from the meadow sprite who ran it. Every time the girl needed money, she reached in her pocket and there it was. Exactly as much as she needed, no more, no less.

She held her breath as she twisted the bathroom doorknob. The last thing she wanted to see on the other side was a commode—and to her delight, the bathroom beyond had indeed disappeared. The door now led into the grand entryway of the British Museum, with a banner over the ticket booth advertising the upcoming *Nutcracker Ballet* special exhibit.

She paused to smile over her shoulder at the old man.

"Thanks for not calling the police, monsieur."

The door now led into the grand entryway of the British Museum, with a banner over the ticket booth advertising the upcoming Nutcracker Ballet special exhibit. The ancient stones had worked their magic again--the border spell was no match for their mysterious energy. The elderly visitors'-center employee would doubtlessly run after her though the door, but he'd find only the usual row of urinals. A shiver of magic ran through her as she crossed the enchanted threshold. No trains, no buses, not even any help from Snow Children. That warm tickle ran through her whole body, but there was a scalding-hot edge to it too, and she pressed a hand to her stomach as if she'd gotten a sudden cramp. Magic wasn't limitless. She could open a doorway across half of England, but she couldn't travel that far that fast without a hefty bout of motion sickness.

Her shoes echoed on the museum foyer floor as the door shut behind her.

"Anouk!"

Cricket was on the stairs, skipping down the steps two at a time to join her. "We've been looking for you all night! Beau's tearing up exhibits to find you. Luc is barely hanging on. The dead have completely taken over the upper floors—we had to barricade the basement to keep them out. You . . . whoa. *Arrête un moment.*" Cricket stopped on the last step. Her features twisted as she looked Anouk over. "You don't look like you."

Anouk knew what Cricket meant, even though on the outside she looked like she always did, dressed in the Faustine jacket, tawny hair pulled back in a messy ponytail.

"I did it," she breathed. "Cricket, I'm a witch."

The caution in Cricket's face intensified. She was a thief, after all, and thieves had a sharp eye for traps. But then Cricket's gaze settled on the grass stains on Anouk's shoes. Her frown vanished.

"Like, *seriously?* Anouk, that's incredible!"

She ran over, touched a lock of Anouk's hair, rubbed the silky strands between her fingers, and laughed. Anouk beamed until a rasping groan came from the top of the stairs.

Both girls tensed.

"The dead," Cricket warned. "We'd better get out of here. Luc's still downstairs. Hurry."

The sound of multiple sets of alarmingly fast footsteps came from the upper level. The dead had heard them. Anouk and Cricket ran to the basement, pushing aside the crates the others had used as a barricade. Anouk used the last of her eucalyptus to cast a barrier spell to keep the dead from following them, and then they raced down the stairs.

Had a tornado swept through the basement? Crates were thrown open. Packing straw littered the floor. Viggo was knee-deep in a storage box. Saint was high in the rafters as if he'd been spooked by something. Luc was laid out in one of the sarcophagi, his brow beaded with sweat, his eyelids fluttering.

"Anouk!" Viggo collapsed onto a pile of packing straw. "Finally! We thought one of the dead had gotten you!"

"Anouk? Where?" Beau appeared from a back room with a broom in his hand, a layer of dust on his hair and shoulders as though he'd been poking the broom through the rafters looking for her. When he saw her, he dropped the broom and went to wrap her up in bear hug, but then he stopped. A shadow wavered in his eyes.

"It's me, Beau," she said softly. "I know I look different. Jak took me to a place where the Coal Baths occur naturally on midwinter dawns." Her voice danced. "I did it this time. I survived."

He didn't seem to trust his own eyes until Anouk pushed up her jacket sleeves and showed off her smooth skin, free of bruises. When her skin caught the light, it even glowed with a golden undertone.

His eyes widened. "Mada Vittora's skin gleamed like that. I thought it was makeup."

"Not makeup. Magic."

She knelt next to Luc and touched his burning forehead. "Luc?"

His lips moved soundlessly. Beneath his fluttering eyelids, his eyes rolled wildly.

"He's fading," Cricket said.

Anouk stroked Luc's forehead. Being a witch came with great power, but it didn't come with obvious answers. She'd thought that once she was a witch, casting spells would be as automatic as breathing. That she'd somehow simply *know* what life-essence to consume and what words to utter. But as she took Luc's weak pulse, she felt almost as uncertain as she always had. She knew dozens of spells, but she didn't know which one would work best, and she didn't have time to try them all.

"Anouk?" Beau asked softly.

She cleared her throat. "Where's Luc's stash of herbs?"

Cricket hunted up Luc's knapsack, and Anouk dug through his jars of herbs and dried flowers. She thought back on all she'd read in the Cottage library about poison. There was one particular spell that drew out poison like salt drew out moisture, but it required a complicated combination of life-essences.

Something breathing, something bleeding, something blue.

It was time to be a witch.

Chapter 36

❧

"VIGGO, GET ME a few drops of blood," Anouk ordered. "Put it in that mug. Beau, there's a stuffed peacock in the storerooms. Bring me one of its feathers. A blue one. And someone catch one of the flies buzzing around the pizza box."

Her friends set to work. Hunter Black searched for something to prick Viggo's finger with and found a safety pin attached to a nineteenth-century gown. Beau disappeared to the back rooms and returned with the feather; it smelled like a musty sweater, but the iridescent barbs hadn't lost their blue sheen. Cricket, with her nimble hands, made quick work of trapping one of the flies. She cupped it in her hands. "Do you need it squished or still buzzing around?"

Anouk felt a flutter of regret. "Squished."

Cricket smacked her hands together and then dropped the dead fly in the mug. If they'd been Goblins, they would have poured out a sip of tea in honor of the insect's sacrifice, but as it was, Beau just let out a small sigh. Viggo added his blood and Anouk mixed it with cherry blossoms, then used one of the long white owl feathers to paint a line of the mixture from Luc's heart to his left hand, whispering as she went. Finally, she pricked the center of Luc's palm with the safety pin. A black, putrid-smelling liquid oozed out.

Slowly, Luc's fluttering eyes calmed. He blinked hard a few times before turning his unfocused gaze on Anouk. He squinted at her healed arms.

"Dust Bunny?" A weak smile, followed by a faint knowing laugh. "You brilliant thing. *You're magic.*"

She took in a sharp breath. To the others, it must sound like a simple enough comment, but it went beyond that. Just over a year ago, days after she'd been made human on the floor of Mada Vittora's attic, she'd found Mada Vittora's collection of wands in the back of the witch's closet. The delicate one made of ivory. The heavy one of iron. The wooden ones, some of which still had knots and forked branches. She'd played at being a magic handler herself, pointing the ivory wand at the shoes in need of cobbling, the clothes in need of mending, the dresses in need of washing, pretending that magic would spring forth and do her work for her. Mada Vittora had caught her, of course. Anouk had frozen, terrified. But the witch had only laughed at Anouk's silly games, stroked her hair, then taken the wand out of Anouk's hand and replaced it with a feather duster.

Here's your *wand, my pretty little beastie.*

Luc had been watering the houseplants at the time. He'd overheard it all. That evening, he'd found Anouk dusting the library, took the feather duster out of her hand, and replaced it with one of the books from the shelves.

What's this? Anouk had asked.

You don't need a wand to cast magic, he'd replied. *This is all you need. Books. Stories. Imagination. You're magic, Dust Bunny, as long as you have those.*

And now here he was, one foot in the grave, and those words meant just as much to her now as they had then.

She cupped his cheek. "Luc, you're safe. I drained the poison."

He closed his eyes for a long time. A pained look crossed his face before he said, "Of course you did. Of course you did."

He opened his eyes and smiled.

She tried to help him up, but he winced and shook his head. "Wait. *Attends*. It's going to take me at least as long to crawl back to life as it did to get so close to death." He eased himself back into the sarcophagus. His breathing was labored. When she gave him a concerned look, he responded with a weak laugh. "I just need rest." He eyed her closely. "You've got dust on your face. No, don't wipe it off. I like that you're still you, even as a witch."

She told them about Jak and Stonehenge and enchanting the bathroom door into a portal back and how it felt to be remade top to bottom by magic and how she now understood why Mada Vittora had been so arrogant (the sheer potential at her fingertips) and yet so callous (because no power was limitless, and not even witches were spared from making mistakes).

"You need a moniker," Luc said.

Beau and Cricket and Hunter Black turned to her, interested to hear what she would say. Mada Vittora had been the Diamond Witch of Paris. Mada Zola had been the Lavender Witch of Montélimar.

Anouk lifted her chin. "The Gargoyle."

"The Gargoyle Witch?" asked Hunter Black.

"No, just the Gargoyle." She hesitated. She wanted to put in words the complicated feelings in her heart: That she didn't *feel* like a witch. There was being a witch in the sense that she could handle magic, which was true, but there was also being a witch in the sense of a cadre of ambitious women, hungry for power, ruthless in their means, whose hearts, in many cases, were quite literally made of stone. She was determined never to be like the latter.

"Was 'the Cabbage' taken?" Beau asked.

Anouk gave him a shove.

"Don't forget about an oubliette," Cricket said. "You need one of those too."

Anouk picked up the Faustine jacket from where she'd laid it at the foot of Luc's sarcophagus. She stroked the fabric and felt an answering spark of magic.

"Hunter Black, can you hand me that safety pin?"

He passed it over wordlessly. Anouk pricked her own finger, then ran a line of blood around the rim of the jacket's right pocket, then the left, speaking a spell under her breath.

"Mada Anouk," she whispered.

As soon as the words were spoken, the spots of blood ringing the pockets soaked into the fabric so deeply that they disappeared. Hesitantly, aware of the many sets of eyes on her, Anouk reached a hand into the left pocket. Her arm disappeared up to her armpit.

"What are you going to keep hidden away in there?" Beau asked.

"Herbs. Wands, if I ever find one. Maybe a boyfriend, if he gives me any trouble."

Beau held up his hands in mock surrender.

Cricket took the jacket and thrust her own hand in the right pocket. She frowned when her fingers came away with nothing more than lint.

"It works only for me." Anouk took the jacket back and slid it on one arm at a time. It fit her body so perfectly, so right. In a way, that was what it felt like to become a witch—it was like slipping into a set of clothes that had been tailor-made for her.

She motioned to Sinjin's body. "We need to find out if he was telling the truth about the Noirceur." She turned to Luc. "Do you have herbs for astral projection?"

He was too weak to get up, but he gave Anouk directions, and she and Cricket worked to concoct an elixir. At Anouk's request, Beau and Hunter Black dragged out one of the Monet paintings. Anouk whispered softly and the painted water began to ripple. She grinned. Beau and Luc and Cricket all looked at her oddly; they couldn't see what she could through the painting. As she continued to whisper, the water stilled like glass, and she could make out the glow of Big Ben's clock. She blurred her vision so she could see into the projection. She felt herself floating around the outside of the tower. Construction cones and police barricades surrounded the base. She floated past them, soared like a bird to the glowing clock face, and felt herself perching on one of the giant hands. She peered through the number three into the chamber within, and gasped.

It was entirely filled with coal-black smoke. It swirled like a slow-moving tornado trapped in a glass ball. She made out the shape of the bell in the center of the smoke. It was turned upside down like a cauldron. Standing around it were murky shapes, but to call them human would be inaccurate. They swirled with the smoke, more like wisps of ash than people. Perhaps the figures had once had faces, but now their features were merely dips and rises of smoke. Sinjin was right—the witches' identities were very nearly gone. The Noirceur had been destroying them at the same time that it had been bringing them great power. Anouk continued to whisper into the painting, changing the angle of her view so that she could peer inside the cauldron. It was filled with smoke so thick it was only blackness. The Nothing. The Chaos.

She whispered again and her projection pulled out of the cauldron, then out of the tower entirely, and then it was all of London she was seeing, sometime in the near future. The city was in complete ruins. Smoke blackened the streets in a deadly fog. The river had overflowed its banks. The ground was littered with bodies of Pretties, blood dripping from their eyes and ears. And then, with a flash, the clock hands met, and with a spectacular crack, Big Ben's clock face shattered. The clock stopped. A deafening rumble spread through the city as lightning crackled through the unnaturally dark smoke. Bolts came faster and faster until the entire city was on fire. The Pretties were decimated. The streets were fractured, buildings reduced to rubble.

The ultimate plague: the Noirceur let loose on the city.

Anouk pulled out of her vision with a gasp. Beau caught her before she stumbled. She blinked hard, her body twitching, as she slowly took in the familiar surroundings of the basement, reassuring herself that what she had seen was only a vision. The city — for now — was still standing. She drew in a ragged breath.

"Is what Sinjin said true?" Hunter Black asked darkly.

"No," she whispered. "It's much worse."

She told them about the destruction of the city, which would happen when the clock hands met unless they found a way to stop it.

Beau gave her a searching look. "What are you thinking, cabbage?"

Anouk dragged a hand through her hair. "I can't do this on my own, even as a witch. We need reinforcements."

Her eyes settled on Viggo. Determined, she went to him and took the golden hare he held in his arms by the scruff of its neck.

Chapter 37

MERCI À DIEU, Anouk thought, *for magic.*

Instead of waiting for the hare to expel the ruby the natural way—or, as Viggo crassly put it, waiting for it to *démouler un cake*—Anouk consulted with Luc and then gathered a concoction of gorse, owl feathers, a snippet of the rabbit's fur, and a splash of Viggo's blood. She swallowed it down and, while Cricket held the hare steady, whispered a spell she'd learned at the Cottage, a version of the one Cricket had cast in the museum restaurant, that could temporarily transmute a substance into water. As soon as she finished the whisper, the hare's golden fur turned translucent. They could see through its skin like peering through glass: its clear heart beating and clear lungs breathing and, in the pit of the hare's stomach, a red ruby.

Fast as she could, Anouk thrust her hand through the enchanted fur—her fingers sinking into the watery substance, through fur and skin and stomach lining—grabbed the ruby stud, and pulled her hand back out. The watery substance molded itself back into place as her spell faded, and within seconds, they were looking at fur again. The hare, unharmed, twitched its nose and leaped out of Cricket's arms.

"Hey!" Cricket ran after it, but Anouk shook her head.

"Leave it. We don't need it for anything else. Anyway, it'll be safer down here than anywhere else in the city." She held the ruby in her palm and watched its polished facets catch the light.

She peered into the empty rafters. "Where's Saint? We need him."

They poked through the back storerooms until Hunter Black found Saint perched on the frame of a Degas painting, a freshly killed mouse in his beak. Cricket and Beau kept their distance but Hunter Black enticed the falcon onto his arm and carried him back to Anouk.

Saint cocked his head. A drop of blood rolled off the point of his beak.

"Easy, fellow. Remember me?" He had a new golden bell dangling from a cord around his neck. She thought briefly of how anguished she'd been when the Duke had taken her magic, how desperately she'd wanted it back. Carefully, Anouk unfastened the bell, pried back one of the metal leaves, and inserted the ruby stud inside. She refastened the bell around Saint's neck and treated him to a scrap of pepperoni. He hopped onto her arm. "Hunter Black." She called over the assassin and delicately passed him the bird. "Take him and try not to terrorize each other.

"We need to get to the roof," she told the others.

"The floors between here and there are still overrun by reanimated corpses," Beau said.

Anouk turned to Luc. "Do you have any more gorse?"

With a pinch of herbs and a whisper, Anouk enchanted a janitor's closet door into a portal to the roof. When she twisted the doorknob, mops and buckets had been replaced by the exterior rooftop dome.

Frigid air carried in the chaotic sounds of the city. Cars honking. People screaming. Alarms that never ended.

Anouk held the door open for the others. They filed through, but Anouk grabbed Cricket before she crossed the threshold and motioned for her to hang back.

"That ruby has me thinking about jewels," she said. "How good they are at containing spells. Did you see the exhibit for the Heart of Alexandrite downstairs? It's the rarest jewel in the world. It had every manner of security guarding it. Bars. Cameras. Alarms. It seems like the perfect vessel to contain the Noirceur."

Cricket cracked her knuckles. "I'll just need a few hours and a screwdriver."

"There's . . . something else."

Anouk hesitated, and then discussed the situation with Cricket in a quiet voice. Cricket's eyes went wide, but she nodded.

They joined the others on the roof. Beau supported Luc under one arm. Viggo propped open the door with one of the Nutcracker dolls in case they needed to get back into the basement quickly. Anouk walked to the edge of the roof. Beau joined her on one side, Cricket on the other. Hunter Black, with Saint still perched on his wrist, veered dangerously close to the edge, peering down at the tumultuous city with an unreadable expression. Viggo hung back in the warmth of the doorway, blowing into his hands.

"*Merde,*" Cricket muttered as she gazed over the rooftops. "It's gotten even worse."

In just a day, the city had become unrecognizable.

Twin moons shone on roof tiles littered with toads — some alive, some dead. Wisps of black smoke curled toward the sounds of the city in arcs too perfect to be regular chimney smoke. The time slips had multiplied. Cars drove into them and simply vanished. Pretties running from crazed mobs took wrong turns and disappeared.

Luc, still weak, sank onto an air-conditioning unit.

"What happened?" Beau's voice was halting. His eyes were wide as he took in the Pretties circling, repeating the same motions again and again.

"The plagues," Anouk said. "And they're only going to get worse. I saw it in my vision. The time slips will accelerate until the city is completely consumed by the Noirceur. Once those clock hands reach midnight, it'll be nothing but smoke." They looked at the clock face and saw they didn't have much time.

Anouk motioned Hunter Black and Saint over.

"Go to Castle Ides," Anouk told the bird. "Fast as you can."

She nodded a signal. Hunter Black went to the edge and launched the bird off of his wrist. Saint took wing and glided into the air, soaring over rooftops until he'd disappeared into low-lying clouds.

Cricket peered incredulously down at the city. "How long until Saint gets to Paris?"

"He's fast, even without magic, and he's strong enough to fly high above the time slips. He'll make it within the hour," Hunter Black said.

"He'd better," Beau muttered, "otherwise there won't be any city left to save."

Luc was shivering. Hunter Black shrugged off his heavy coat and rested it over the gardener's shoulders.

Cricket folded her arms tightly. "So how exactly are we supposed to stop the Noirceur when we can't walk two steps beyond the museum without getting caught in a time loop? We'll never make it to Big Ben. We'd get hit by a falling toad or struck by lightning."

Anouk thought about this, then jerked her head toward the clouds. "Snow."

"Um, cabbage, it isn't snowing," Beau pointed out.

"Not yet." Anouk felt the magic tingling in her palms. This time, she didn't have to rely on anyone to cast magic for her. She needed a big storm, big enough to cover the whole city. She began to whisper. She spun her left hand in a circle, and the clouds lowered and darkened. Flakes started to fall.

"You're summoning Jak," Cricket realized.

Anouk muttered between whispers, "Not just Jak—all the Snow Children. They can't stop the plagues, but they might be able to interrupt them. Buy us time before the city is torn apart."

The snow fell like the gods were sugaring the city. In the chaos below, the few Pretties not caught in time loops raised umbrellas. Snow fell thick on Anouk's head and arms. It caught in Cricket's hair and in Beau's eyelashes. Hunter Black pulled up the collar of his shirt, hunkering low. Soon a light coating of snow dusted the glass dome of the museum roof.

Anouk heard a cruel chuckle behind her and spun.

"Miss me so soon?" Jak asked.

He was clutching the spire at the top of the dome.

Behind him, more faces appeared, all of them pale with black eyes and icicle hair. Dozens of Snow Children perched on the glass dome. A girl with jagged frosty curls. A cluster of boys with clothes made of ice. Even as a witch, Anouk felt uncertain. These were ancient creatures. Older than Goblins, older than Royals, so old that they weren't even an order of the Haute.

"Jak," she said. "The Noirceur is spreading too fast. I need you and the other Snow Children to freeze the city. Coat it all in ice temporarily. Cricket and I have a plan to transfer the Noirceur to a new vessel—the Heart of Alexandrite—but the plagues are going to destroy the whole city and everyone in it before we can."

Jak didn't seem concerned about the bedlam below or her anxiety. "Cities rise and fall. It is the way of things. Why should we intervene?"

Her cheeks burned. She was desperate. "You want a kiss. I'll . . . I'll give you one once all of this is over."

Hunter Black growled his disapproval.

Beau spun on her. "Cabbage, are you crazy?"

Viggo, in the doorway, looked deeply troubled. "You can't, Dust Mop. Think of those dead girls in the forest you told us about. You want to join them?"

She ignored them. "I'll do it," she told Jak. "I promise. I'll risk it." She held her chin high, but to her surprise, Jak sadly shook his head.

"No, lovely."

Her eyes widened. "Why not?"

"You've changed. You're no longer warm—*you're burning*. The blue flame inside of you would burn me too."

Anouk let out a cry. She'd become a witch to defeat the Coven of Oxford, only to find they'd ceased to exist, swallowed by something even more daunting. Now she couldn't even kiss a Snow Child. "Then what *do* you want?"

"A kiss, just not from you."

His black eyes skimmed over Cricket, who gave him a scowl, to Beau, who straightened quickly, to Viggo, who leaned in the doorway and picked carelessly at his fingernails, to Hunter Black, who looked like a sullen shadow even without his coat, to Luc, where they finally settled.

Jak smiled.

Luc tensed. He pulled the collar of Hunter Black's coat higher around his neck. The other Snow Children crept forward over the dome, soft and graceful as spiders, leaving no prints behind.

Hunter Black moved defensively in front of Luc. He cracked his knuckles. "Try it, and you'll kiss my fist."

"He's right," Anouk said. "It's me or nobody."

Strangely, Luc hadn't said a word. She shot him a worried look. He looked awful. She crouched next to him and asked quietly, "Luc? You okay?"

"Yes, it's—" His gaze flickered to her eyes briefly, then to Hunter Black's, and he closed his mouth. "Nothing."

Jak took a silent step forward and Anouk snapped her head around. "No. He was poisoned. He's still recovering. A kiss from you would kill him immediately."

Jak gave Luc a long look, and Anouk got the sense she was missing some understanding between them.

"It's all right," Luc said quietly. "I'll do it."

Hunter Black barked a quick *"No."*

Anouk dug her fingers into Luc's arm. "Luc, you can't. You know what a kiss means."

Beneath her fingers, his skin was burning up. Shouldn't her antidote have worked by now?

"It's okay, Dust Bunny." He clapped his hand over hers. Then he faced Jak. "Freeze the city and when all of this is over, I'll give you what you want."

Anouk tried to protest again. Cricket pulled out her knives, hurling threats at Jak and the other cold bodies behind him, but the Snow Children only blinked their black eyes languidly.

Jak pivoted toward Anouk. "We can do as you ask, but only if we are present, which means as long as the snow falls. As soon as your snow spell ends, we vanish, and your city returns to chaos. Do you intend to keep whispering forever?"

Anouk felt a moment of panic. But she wasn't some maid anymore with minor tricks at her fingertips. She was a witch. The Gargoyle. She swallowed a pinch of snow with downy-soft owl feathers and whispered, *"Ombra ja."*

She took an exaggerated, theatrical step forward. A copy of herself, nearly translucent, remained behind. A shadow self. She'd never tried this spell before, and she marveled to see her own ghostly double hanging back. She stopped chanting the snow spell, but her shadow self continued. The snowfall continued too.

"That's amazing!" Cricket said. "How long will it last?"

"Not long, I'm afraid. Shadow selves are unpredictable. A few hours, maybe. Right now it's the best I can do. We'll have to work fast."

Jak turned to the other Snow Children and spoke a few words in a language she'd never heard. They gathered on the dome, clinging like frost. They needed no life-essence to cast magic; it was easy for creatures made of snow to command ice and frost. The glass beneath their hands began to frost over. The doves that were perched at the edge of the museum froze in place as though they'd been encased in glass; not a single movement of their eyes, not a flutter of their feathers. Anouk ran to the edge of the rooftop. The frost rapidly spread down the sides of the museum, stopping leaves from fluttering, pausing birds in midflight and leaving them fixed in the sky, immobile. The frost spread to the next block, where it froze the churning waves of the Thames, froze the pedestrians and the cars, froze billowing coats and scarves, even froze the flickering gas-lamp flames outside of tourist pubs. There were no more screams, no honking cars, no twisting of metal, no deafening flutter of wings. Only the patter of snow.

Anouk pressed a hand to her chest to feel for the rise and fall of her breath, reassuring herself that she was still able to move. Beau stretched and folded his fingers. Cricket tapped her shoe on the rooftop to hear it echo.

"The whole city's standing still," Beau breathed.

Hunter Black pointed grimly to the horizon. "Not all of it."

The black smoke that clouded at the base of Big Ben was still swirling. The clock hands still ticked, echoing in the quiet city, and the smoke vibrated in time with it.

"We cannot freeze what cannot be frozen," Jak explained. "That tower is commanded by the Noirceur, and the Noirceur is an oblivion, an emptiness. There is nothing *to* freeze. The city now belongs to you and to it." He jerked his chin toward the tower. Then he flashed Luc a grin. "And soon, you will belong to us. We'll come to collect."

Hunter Black darted between them in a flash, his fists raised. The wind blew stronger; the snow was so heavy it was hard to see more than a foot or two in any direction. Hunter Black twisted, hanging close to Luc in case the Snow Children tried to grab him. When the wind finally eased, Jak and the rest of the Snow Children were gone. Hunter Black spun in a tight circle, fists high, ready to fight a foe who'd vanished.

Anouk threw her arms around Luc. "You shouldn't have made that promise!"

The city was eerily quiet. She could hear Luc's heartbeat, Cricket's pacing footsteps, Beau's anxious hands stretching his leather gloves, Viggo spitting over the roof edge onto the motionless Pretties below.

And then there was an odd crackle in the air. The hair on the back of her neck stood up, like it did when electricity was building before a lightning strike. But the clouds overhead weren't threatening a storm. The crackling sound thunked and whirred like machinery gearing up, and she peered at the air-conditioning units on the museum roof. A half an inch of frost coated the fan blades. They were as frozen as the mummies that had just moments ago been pressing and moaning against the stairwell door.

Suddenly, the crackling noise came from behind her, and she twisted around. Little sparks erupted in the air around the skylight. The others heard it too. They all gathered close. Cricket drew her knives. Hunter Black balled his fists.

With a blinding flash, a figure appeared on the skylight.

Anouk slapped her hands over her eyes. When the spots cleared from her vision, she saw a girl dressed in an enviable black couture coat and champagne-colored sunglasses, holding a box.

Petra.

The witch coolly slid the sunglasses up into her hair, squinting at the double moons with a distrustful glower. She dusted a few

330

snowflakes off of her coat. Then she caught sight of Anouk and grinned. She stepped off the skylight, shifted the box to one arm, and held out her palm.

The ruby.

"Thanks," Petra said, folding her fingers back over the ruby, "for the ticket into the city. We got your message from Saint. Congratulations on walking the coals, my fellow witchie." Something glittered in her eyes, a deep pride. She leaned close to kiss Anouk's cheek and whispered, "Ash."

Anouk raised an eyebrow. "Ash?"

"The Ash Witch. That's my moniker. Born of fire, heart of coals, cozy but dangerous if you get too close. I told you that I'd tell you my moniker when you survived."

Anouk grinned. "It's perfect."

Petra slid her sunglasses back down. She turned to the others. "Rennar sends his regards along with something that I think we'll find exceptionally helpful. Who's in the mood for a present?"

She shook the mysterious box tantalizingly.

Chapter 38

THEY USED ANOUK'S ENCHANTED DOORWAY to pass directly from the roof to the basement, bypassing the museum's floors overrun by the dead. (Even frozen, Petra said, mummies were creepy.) Once they'd settled in amid the artifacts and half-finished dioramas, Petra devoured a few slices of pizza, then set Rennar's box on the clock-repair table and removed the lid with a flourish.

"Voilà," she proclaimed. "Our problems are solved. Well, one of our problems."

Anouk held her breath. The last time Rennar had given her a gift, it had been her wedding dress. She twisted the ring on her finger anxiously. Curse him if it was some other trinket meant to tempt her or mock Beau—but she frowned when she peered into the box. It contained two ancient brass doorknobs and a collection of rusty hinges carefully tucked into silk handkerchiefs.

Anouk picked up a screw. "Rennar sent hardware?"

"Not just any hardware." Petra reverently unwrapped a hinge. "They're *Objekte*."

Anouk's eyes widened. One of the long nights studying in the Cottage library with Marta, Anouk had come across a reference to *Objekte*. Now she considered the hinge in her palm with more awe.

"What are *Objekte*?" Beau seized a doorknob and poked around at the latch to see how it all fit together.

Petra gasped and knocked the doorknob out of his hand. "Careful, *imbécile!*" She sighed toward the ceiling. "*Objekte* are permanently enchanted objects. They're rare and fabulously valuable. Each one is worth more than ten of your lives, Beau." She shooed him away from the box as she nestled the doorknob back into the silk and explained, "Most objects, like doors or brooms or motorcycles, can be enchanted, but only for a few minutes. Enchantments have a short half-life. But over the ages, a few casters have figured out how to imbue certain items with deeper magic. Judging by the style, this set of door hardware comes from the Prussian Empire. Used correctly, the knobs can open doorways to anywhere in the world, bypassing border spells and other protection enchantments. Once we got your message, Anouk, Rennar consulted with Duke Karolinge and they went poking around in the cellars of Castle Ides and came back with this. They made me promise on the fate of my oubliette not to lose any of the pieces." She shot Beau another warning look.

Anouk peered closer at the hinge in her palm. Now that she knew it was *Objekte,* it felt almost alive in her hand. "How does the spell work?"

"Well, for starters, we need to get to Omen House."

Omen House. Anouk had heard of it, of course. In each of the most magical cities in the world, there existed a facsimile of the exact same building, a stately eight-story edifice of stone and brick. In Paris, it was called Castle Ides, and the Parisian Royals claimed the honor of inhabiting the penthouse. In London, the building was called Omen House, and the Court of Isles had their offices on the fourth floor. Not long ago, Anouk had peeked into a fourth-floor boardroom when the elevator accidentally stopped there. She'd met the irresistible Tenpenny, with his broken-heart tattoo and his pet rat. Thinking of him brought on a stab of sadness. Tenpenny had fought hard to regain the Goblins' hold on London. He should have been with them, plotting to take back his city.

But he hadn't made it. Neither had the rat.

"Omen House is near Piccadilly Circus," Anouk said, still feeling mournful. She set the hinge back in the box. "I saw it from the fourth floor of Castle Ides. Beyond the windows, there were double-decker buses circling the square."

Petra closed up the box of hardware. "Then we're taking a walk."

Luc had been leaning heavily on the corner of one of the sarcophagi. Now he stood, but the effort seemed to cost him. He leaned back and pressed a hand to his heart.

Anouk felt his forehead. "Maybe you should stay here."

He waved away her hand and stood up straight again, this time more steadily. "I can make it."

But Anouk knew him better than that. There was a knot of fear in his face. He wasn't telling her everything. Was this about his deal with Jak? The impending kiss? Her thoughts began to spiral someplace dark, and before Luc could see the worry on her face, she turned to the box of hardware.

What if she lost Luc like she'd lost Tenpenny? She'd known the Goblin for only a few days but had found much to admire in his quirks and mettle, so losing him left her feeling unfinished, like a dish in need of salt and pepper. How would it feel if she lost Luc, who'd been with her almost every day of her life?

Petra poked around through the odd assortment of tools on the clock-repair table and found a screwdriver and a wrench. "We might need these for the spell. And who knows what else we'll encounter out there in the city."

They made their way up the basement stairs. Cricket pushed aside the crates they'd used to barricade the door, eased it open, and, head cocked, listened for any activity. After a second, she gave the others a nod. "It's quiet. But stay on the alert, just the same."

They entered the museum cautiously. The dim security lights were still on but coated in thick slabs of ice that gave the rooms strange shadows. They made their way down a hallway with bathrooms and then turned the corner into the main section of the museum.

Beau, in front, saw a figure and jumped. "Argh!" Instinctively, he threw a punch. Anouk and the others rushed to his side. There was a mummy there, its hollow mouth open in a silent roar, but it was as frozen as everything else. And now there was a fresh dent in its skull where Beau had hit it.

Beau made a face. "Ew. I think I touched brains." He wiped his hand on his pants.

There were more mummies behind the one that had startled Beau. One had been frozen as it crawled across the carpet. Another one had been frozen while scratching stumpy fingers against a display case. A third one had been frozen while tangled in a velvet rope.

Petra raised an eyebrow in a silent question. "About these mummies . . ."

"Long story," Anouk told her.

As they made their way through the museum, Anouk filled Petra in on everything that had happened since they'd arrived in London:

335

Sinjin's confession, the visit to Stonehenge, her vision of the Noirceur and calling upon the Snow Children to freeze the entire city. They made it to the museum's entry hall, which was perfectly still. The banner proclaiming the upcoming exhibit was frozen mid-flutter. A moth was suspended over the ticket booth, its wings coated with ice. Anouk and the others were silent, as though a single word might break the spell. Luc, wheezing, leaned heavily on the ticket booth. His eyes were unfocused. But when Anouk gave him a worried look, he wiped the sweat off his brow and stood straighter.

"Ready?" Cricket said, hand on the front door.

"Wait," Viggo said, fumbling in his pockets. "Let me get my camera." He dug his phone out while Cricket gave him an impatient look. "It's not every day I'm part of saving the world."

Cricket mumbled under her breath and shoved open the door. One by one, they stepped across the threshold into London. Other than the light snowfall commanded by Anouk's shadow self from its position on the roof, the whole city was encased in an unsettling silence. A teenage Pretty girl was frozen as she ducked to avoid a brick another Pretty had hurled at her. Pigeons were frozen midflight above the corpse of a toad. A car had driven halfway into a time slip and was half gone—the driver and half of the passenger in the back had vanished; the other half of the passenger was frozen. Overhead, perfectly still clouds hung in front of the twin moons. Other than the falling snow, there wasn't a hint of movement.

"Follow me," Viggo said. "We should go along the river. It's a little out of the way, but we'll get a close view of Big Ben. Better to see what we're up against."

"Lead the way," Anouk said.

As they headed down Bow Street, Petra explained what had been happening back in Paris. Ever since the beasties had left, Rennar'd had his hands full with the other Royals. The Barren Court and the Minaret Court deeply resented that the Nochte Pax bound them. Rennar, along with Queen Violante and Prince Aleksi, had gotten them in line, although any agreements between them were shaky at best. Anouk found herself dangerously curious about Rennar's safety. What if the other Royals turned on him?

"All the Royals are on standby," Petra explained as she stepped on a smooshed toad in the middle of the road and grimaced. "As soon as we open a doorway for them, they're prepared to enter London and fight the Oxford witches."

"Yeah," Beau said, swerving to avoid the toad, "except there aren't any Oxford witches *to* fight."

"Um. *What?*"

Once Anouk had explained the situation to her, Petra gave a heavy sigh and said, "So how do we fight something that has no physical presence?"

Anouk glanced in the direction of Big Ben, though it wasn't yet visible over the rooftops. "Leave that to me."

Petra raised an eyebrow but didn't question her. They continued to make their way through the silent city, past the Opera House and the Strand junction. The snow was light, melting almost as soon as it landed. Hunter Black seemed particularly troubled by the silent city, his dark eyes darting to every shadow, checking every Pretty they passed for signs of breath. Luc moved slowly too, wincing as though in pain, but whenever Beau offered to help, he shook his head. They reached the walkway that followed the Thames River — the water frozen in motionless waves—and then passed Victoria Bridge. Viggo stopped at a police officer, pilfered the woman's pistol, and tucked it into his own waistband.

Cricket shot him a look. "Are you that stupid?"

"It's not like she's using it."

"*You* can't use it either. Guns have moving parts. It'll be frozen like everything else." She sighed and handed over one of her sheathed knives. "Take this."

He slid it into his back pocket with an easy grace, looking as though that was what he'd been planning all along. How some Pretty boys got away with such unearned self-assuredness, Anouk would never know.

They passed another bridge and Anouk stopped in the middle of the street. Ahead, through a gap in two Parliament buildings, she could make out the tower of Big Ben. With the two moons hidden now behind clouds, the illuminated clock face glowed bigger and brighter than anything else on the skyline. The pair of elegant clock hands kept moving, unaffected by the Snow Children's spell. Smoke clumped thickly around the tower as though the entire structure were encased within a thunderstorm, with tendrils of smoke reaching out into the street, settling low over the river, and extending toward the Parliament buildings and a nearby department store, Pickwick and Rue's, that had banners out front announcing its recent grand opening. Once the snow fell into the smoke, it disappeared.

Petra slid up her sunglasses. "That's the Noirceur?"

Anouk nodded. The pit of her stomach turned colder just looking at it. The dark ancient magic that conjured that smoke wasn't so different from the Dark Thing inside her.

Beau rested a hand on her shoulder. "We should keep moving."

They plunged back into the thick of the city, away from the river, passing government buildings until they reached Piccadilly Circus. An enormous open square, it was normally a boisterous tangle of tourists, vendors, honking cars, and pigeons going after crumbs, just as busy at night as it was during the day. Even now, lights were on in all the shops and restaurants, car headlights blazed, and Pretties congregated in the square, but nothing so much as quivered, all of it encased in ice.

Anouk knew Omen House immediately. It was identical to Castle Ides, down to the brick. The same exterior gate and sign for a private club—written in English here, naturally—the same porte-cochère in front that Beau had pulled Mada Vittora's town car up to countless times in Paris, even the same marble busts on the front lawn, though instead of Prince Rennar, these portrayed a young couple Anouk recognized from portraits as the missing Prince Maxim and Lady Imogen.

Cricket unlocked the gate with a touch of mint leaves to her lips and a whisper.

Viggo rested his hand on the front door. "Here goes nothing."

They stepped into the foyer. On the outside, Omen House was identical to Castle Ides, but inside, instead of glittering crystal chandeliers and a glass wall divider, Omen House's entryway looked like it belonged to a much-loved but musty old hotel. There was a small check-in desk in front of mailboxes filled with dangling keys, a threadbare rug, and a few mismatched tables and chairs next to a bar.

"No Marble Ladies," Cricket observed, eyes darting to the corners, fingers brushing the hilts of her blades. "Unless they're hiding."

"That's not how Omen House works." Viggo walked behind the reception desk like he owned the place. He dinged the bell a few times, and Anouk cringed as it echoed loud enough to wake the dead, but nothing happened. "Eight boxes and eight keys," he explained. "You sign your name in that fat old ledger there, and then you can take a key. The keys operate the elevator. You can only access the floor you have the key for."

He signed his name in the visitors log, and the key to the penthouse suddenly seemed to take on a life of its own, sparkling as though begging to be picked up. He plucked it off the nail, went to the elevator, and jammed his thumb on the button. Nothing happened. He frowned and pushed the button again and again, at least twenty more times, but still nothing happened.

"Stop before you break it!" Luc said. "It's frozen, just like everything else. Nothing mechanical works."

"So how are we supposed to get to the penthouse?" Beau asked.

"We aren't." Petra set the jangling box of hardware on the reception counter. She turned to Anouk, lowered her sunglasses briefly, gave her a knowing look, and passed her a brass doorknob. "Leave this to the witches, friends. Step back. Way back. Farther. Viggo, you might as well go outside."

Viggo didn't look amused, but he did step behind the bar and eye the closest bottles.

The spell to open a door between the penthouse in Paris and the foyer in London was relatively straightforward, though it did require preparations. Petra explained that they needed two doors, one in each city, and for that they needed two witches working at the same time. Under Petra's orders, Luc and Hunter Black cleared the artwork off the wall until it was nothing but plain wallpaper and a few empty nails. Petra ran her hand over the wallpaper, nodding, measuring with the width of her hand, and then directed Beau to use a piece of chalk to draw in the approximate shape of double doors to her measurements. Finally, Cricket climbed on a chair and hammered in the hinges and other hardware on the edges of Beau's drawing.

"Now." Petra took one of the doorknobs and handed Anouk the other. "Ready?"

"*Jamais.* Never. But let's do it anyway."

Mada Vittora had rarely worked with other witches, and maybe that was a mistake. It felt good to perform a kindred whisper with Petra. Their words spoken at the exact same speed, their movements simultaneous as they pressed the knobs to the drawn-in doors. Beau's chalk outline started to glow. The hinges produced a long creaking sound. The knob began to warm in Anouk's hand and vibrate a little, as eager to be handled as the enchanted key that Viggo had collected behind the reception desk.

"Okay," Petra breathed. There was a thrill in her voice. Magic was as new to her as it was to Anouk. "Whisper the opening spell. Now!"

Petra whispered the final word of the spell in English and Anouk whispered it in French, and they twisted the knobs at the exact same time and threw open the doors. A blast of sound and light erupted from the other side. In a city that had been stopped in time, Anouk had gotten used to perpetual silence, but now the sounds of music and footsteps and voices assailed her ears and she staggered back, pressing a hand to her chest.

A figure came hurtling through the doorway fast as a blur; it crashed into Anouk and toppled them both to the threadbare old rug.

Anouk caught sight of bright yellow braids and garish makeup. Grinning, December flashed her golden teeth.

"Anouk! Hello again!"

December was lying on top of Anouk, her knees digging into Anouk's stomach, still wearing her clunky vintage roller skates. The wheels slowed to a stop, and December frowned. "Sorry. Still getting the hang of these things. I accidentally enchanted them to my feet and now I can't get them off." December pushed herself to her feet, wobbling precariously, hands extended for balance. She started wheeling backwards and nearly crashed into a chair before Hunter Black caught her.

More figures crossed into the lobby through the enchanted doorway. Queen Violante and her sisters Carlotta and Ludovica; the Minaret Court Marques and Marquesa, Prince Sorin of the Barren Court, Duke Karolinge with Saint perched on his shoulder; and behind them a motley group of Goblins who were practically skipping as they returned to London. A Goblin boy with brown skin and golden dreadlocks petted the paisley wallpaper fondly. Two Goblin girls in short skirts poured themselves gin from the bar. A third grabbed the bottle and cried in joy at the label written in English.

The last Royal to come through the doorway was dressed in a frost-gray suit, though he'd left his crown behind. He leaned over Anouk, who was still on her back on the ground, massaging her bruised rib cage. His hair was perfect. His eyes devastatingly blue-gray. His lips dusted with fine white powder that made her think of sugar and dark, private dessert pantries. Her pulse throbbed to life.

He offered her a hand up. His wedding ring gleamed. "Anouk."

"Oof. Rennar." She clasped his hand, and as he pulled her to her feet, he gave a half smile down at her ring. Then he raised an eyebrow. "Do you know that you have roller-skate grease on your socks?"

She looked down at the black marks streaking her clothes, then shrugged. "Welcome to London."

Chapter 39

❧

RENNAR WAS ANOUK'S HUSBAND NOW—that was the wildest part. The thought made her laugh deliriously, which earned her a disdainful look from the Royals. She stopped laughing. Dirty socks be damned. She was a princess now and they were bound to her commands.

"Everyone out," she ordered. "Into Piccadilly Circus. We have work to do."

They obeyed, though not without a few lingering looks of contempt, and gathered in the streets that surrounded Piccadilly Circus. Hours had passed, but the moons hadn't moved an inch. Dawn would never come unless they vanquished the Noirceur.

The Royals' arrogant looks wavered as they took in the frozen city. The Snow Children's spell was a level of magic beyond even their own. The Goblins, however, were less perturbed. Twin Goblin girls stuck their tongues out to catch snowflakes. A Goblin girl with rose tattoos down her arms ran up to a red telephone booth and hugged it. The rest viewed their city with stars in their eyes, even if it was plunged in the middle of a frozen chaos.

Anouk said sotto voce to Rennar, "I'm glad the Goblins are home, but Prince Sorin and the Marquesa of the Minaret look ready to murder you."

"I imagine that's precisely what they're planning."

"They can't, can they?"

"Not while they're bound by the Nochte Pax. Even afterward, it would take some cunning to get around the vitae echo and find a way to destroy me. Then again, they're resourceful, and they feel as though I've made fools of them, which makes them particularly dangerous. If you and I come out of this alive, we'll be facing a royal war."

"I take it they don't agree with you that power needs to change hands."

"Not unless more goes to *their* hands."

"So what do we do?"

"Try not to die now so that we'll be alive to deal with them when the time comes."

He was teasing, wasn't he? She frowned. He didn't laugh it off and tell her that he'd faced royal wars before and come out in one piece. Instead, he looked perplexed.

"You've been busy." His gaze scoured the frozen streets and then her. "I've seen many girls turned to witches. They may look like the same girls who entered the Coals, but they're different."

She straightened, touching a lock of her hair. "Don't I look different?"

"In some ways." He paused. "But I think the flames liked what they found in you. They left part of your soul intact. I can see it."

"You once said that beasties don't have souls."

"Perhaps I misspoke. If such a thing as souls exist, then mine and everyone else's is made of salt, and yours is made of air. We are creatures of thought and sin. Your kind is tied to nature in a way we will never be."

She didn't have an answer for that. It was possibly the kindest thing he'd ever said to her, maybe the kindest thing anyone had ever said to a beastie. He must have seen her eyes growing big because he ran a hand over his face, and when he was done, he was back to wearing a cruel twist of a smile.

"Hopefully being a witch won't rot you out over the centuries like it does the others."

Just like that, any charitable feelings she'd had for him were gone. She sighed. *Royals.* But then she wondered if Petra's soul would rot like the other witches'. Over the decades, as the vitae echo ate away at her insides, would Petra become as cruel as Mada Vittora and Mada Zola?

The snow was growing lighter. Worried, Anouk glanced toward the roof of the museum. She couldn't see her shadow self, but she could feel a shift in the air, as though the magic was fading. In a few minutes, her shadow self would vanish. The snow would stop. The city would erupt in chaos again.

Anouk grabbed Rennar by the sleeve and pulled him toward the smoke that clung around Big Ben's base. "I need you to keep it snowing."

"Simple enough, but that requires full concentration. I'll be useless when it comes to anything else."

She paused. That would be a problem—she needed him to convince the other Royals to help them and to fight the Noirceur. She glanced over her shoulder.

"Duke Karolinge!" She hadn't seen him since her wedding. "I need your help."

He looked at her closely, then took off his glasses, wiped them, and gave a nod. "Mada Anouk, I am yours to command."

The words took her breath away. *Mada Anouk.* The honorific of a real witch.

She told him about the Snow Children and the spell, and he agreed to take up a position on the museum rooftop and maintain the snow spell. Anouk and Rennar led the rest of the group back down White-hall Street, past the British War Offices and 10 Downing Street, and toward the park that faced Big Ben. Just before they reached it, Beau backpedaled at the sight of a glistening motorcycle frozen in traffic. A Pretty boy was sitting on the back of it, coated in ice.

"I don't believe it," he breathed.

"Is it a fast one?" Anouk guessed.

He grinned. "Sure, it's fast. But it's a Genevar. There were only a few ever made. They're *Objekte* too, in a sense. Made by Pretties but charmed by Muscovite Royals who could do wonders with engines. How did you get ahold of this, friend?" he said to the frozen boy riding it. He poked him, then dropped a hand to the handlebars. Unable to resist, he cranked the bar, and the motorcycle roared. "Ah! You see. Not frozen. I guess the Hammer Court knows a thing or two that even the Snow Children don't."

Anouk eyed the motorcycle closely and said, almost to herself, "Luc said the smoke is drawn to sound. At the engagement party, it clustered around anyone screaming, and even now, it's clumping at Big Ben because that's where most of the sound is."

"What does sound have to do with anything?" Beau asked.

"Nothing—for now. But I might have an idea."

The others were already far ahead. Anouk nudged Beau, and they joined the others at the base of Big Ben. The grass in the square was brown and, like everything else, coated in frost that crunched beneath her feet. The smoke had spread out over a five-block radius around the tower, hovering up to their ankles. Anouk could barely see her oxford shoes. Several Goblins climbed on top of the park's marble monuments as though they thought the smoke might swallow them.

"It's poisonous," Rennar said, gesturing to the smoke with a grimace, doubtlessly remembering his brush with the smoke in Castle Ides. It was billowing out of the upper windows of Big Ben, pouring steadily down into the street. "The more of it we breathe, the more it's going to poison us. If we try to go in there, we'll die."

"We aren't going in Big Ben." She turned on her heel to the building opposite the clock tower. It was the department store that had just had its grand opening, Pickwick and Rue's, taking over a former government office building above the Westminster Tube station. The banners out front boldly proclaimed it to be London's best new shopping destination, with a confectionery and coffee shop and gourmet market on the ground floor, and upper levels packed with exclusive Chanel, Burberry, and Dior treasures. "We're going in *there*."

"Shopping?" Cricket looked puzzled but not altogether against the idea.

"Not exactly."

Rennar raised an eyebrow but didn't question her. With a few commands, he ordered the Royals to follow Anouk through the crystal-studded front doors. Inside, the store was frozen in brand-new perfection. Glass jars of sugared plums tied up in ribbons. Gorgeous displays of boxed pears. Earthy-smelling coffee bundled in beautiful packaging. Everything was untouched, sparklingly new. Since no amount of magic would make the elevators work, Anouk led them up a spiral staircase in the center of the store that rose all five stories and was connected by balconies to the many departments: Menswear on the second floor, Accessories on the third, Home Goods and Lingerie on the fourth, and, at the very top, Ladies' Shoes. They wound past displays of heels and golden sneakers and studded boots until Anouk stopped at the building's most ambitious architectural feature: a one-story-high domed window that looked out across the park, directly at Big Ben.

She pushed a pair of fireball Louboutin heels off a display table, climbed on top, and addressed the crowd.

"I know many of you are here against your will," she announced. "But this is bigger than what any of us want. The ancient Royals trapped the Noirceur in time, and the Coven of Oxford awakened it in every clock within the city limits of London. But they couldn't control what they unleashed. So it's up to us to contain the Noirceur once more. This is an effort that requires all of us, the four orders of the Haute, working together." She gestured behind her at the clock. "I've seen what's inside that tower. It's an enemy like you've never faced. Something that can't be manipulated. Can't be stabbed. Can't be charmed with spells."

Prince Sorin's expression was tight. "Can it be swept up with a broom, little maid?"

Beau turned on the prince and gave him a smart clip on the jaw. Sorin stumbled back into a display of ballet flats, clutching his chin.

"There's nothing wrong with being a maid," Beau said.

"He's right." Rennar folded his arms. "Anyway, she's your princess now. The beasties are our allies. Disrespect them again and I'll throw the next punch."

This silenced the Royals, though Beau went broody, not liking Rennar stealing his thunder. Anouk ignored their pissing match and laid out the plan as concisely as she could: They would divide into teams, go through each of London's inner neighborhoods, and use Cricket's new stealing spell to transfer every clock to a pile at the base of Big Ben. Grandfather clocks, church-spire clocks, wristwatches, alarm clocks, ovens with digital clocks. Once all the clocks were gathered, they would join in a kindred spell to trap and contain the Noirceur into the Heart of Alexandrite. At the same time, to protect them from the worst of the poison smoke, Hunter Black would scale Big Ben and seal the windows. Meanwhile, Beau would ride the Genevar motorcycle with one of the Goblin's portable audio players strapped to the back, drawing the noxious smoke out of the city with music blaring. They didn't need to contain the smoke, just get rid of it.

December's eyes grew wide at the idea of saving the world with rock music. "Consider the Goblins in."

Rennar turned to Cricket. Under his breath, quietly enough that only Anouk and the others gathered closely could hear, he asked, "You truly penned such a stealing spell?"

Cricket looked offended. "You don't think I can?"

"It doesn't matter what I think if it's true."

Cricket rolled her eyes, but he'd challenged her, and to prove it, she quietly whispered the spell to him while the rest of the group argued about which neighborhoods they'd take.

Suddenly, the Goblin with golden dreadlocks cried out, "My watch!" Then the Goblin girl with the rose tattoos did the same.

Soon all of the Goblins were grabbing for their pocket watches in a panic, finding nothing at the end of their watch chains.

"Calm down! I'm just proving a point!" Cricket pointed to a display table near the stairs. Every one of the Goblins' watches was stacked in a tidy pile amid the Chanel loafers. A few Goblins cried out in relief. "See? The transference spell works."

Rennar's expression was unreadable, as though something about Cricket's performance had troubled him. "It's a clever spell, but there's a problem. The spell requires the caster to know *what* is being stolen. An easy enough feat when it's limited to all the pocket watches in a single room. But we cannot possibly know where all the clocks in London are."

The chatter in the crowd turned sharper. Dissenting voices began to grow louder. Sweat broke out on Anouk's temples. Those old fears came back to her.

Failure.

It sounded almost like a real whisper, and she twisted around sharply and stared at the bright round clock face across the street. The two clock hands kept inching forward, and with each tick, she felt her muscles tensing. Suddenly she was back in the Cottage, feeling Frederika's wild eyes on her, inescapable. Reliving the awful final moments of Esme and Marta and Frederika and Heida. How Lise had cried out when her sister burned.

"We need a sister spell," she blurted out, surprising the others so much that they quieted.

Unlike what she'd first assumed, a sister spell didn't involve a pair of related witches—it involved a pair of related *spells*. Sister spells weren't common. They required not only a team of magic handlers working together—and when had magic handlers ever managed to coordinate on anything?—but also more than one spell. Casting two spells simultaneously was dangerous work that involved weaving together the spells word by word.

Queen Violante stroked her chin. "A sight spell to pair with the stealing spell. A spell that would allow us to see every clock so that we could then bind it with Cricket's spell." She waved over Prince Aleksi to discuss the possibilities, then called in Petra for her advice, then brought Luc over so he could tell them about available forms of life-essences.

While they were conferring, Rennar moved to stand next to Anouk and said quietly, "What has Cricket told you about this spell of hers?"

"What do you mean? It's just as she said, a stealing spell. I've seen her use it. Here, with the watches, and in Castle Ides and at the British Museum."

He peered at her intensely. "What was she stealing?"

Anouk shrugged. "Meaningless things. Old artifacts. Pottery bowls. Some artwork. Why? I assumed she was practicing her spell on anything at hand." Even as she said it, though, she knew how unlikely it sounded. Cricket wasn't the kind to steal worthless trifles when treasures abounded.

"You don't see what I see," Rennar warned. "She has a reason for creating that spell that she's not telling you. It goes beyond merely stealing for the joy of it. She used the words *Ut vol fer rein ut deux*."

"That just means 'move from one place to another' in the Selentium Vox."

"Not exactly. *Fer* is used only in reference to people. *Pas* is for objects." He paused and looked at her, as though that meant something serious. At Anouk's blank expression, he explained, "It's people she wants to find and move, not objects."

Anouk knit her brows together. "She just doesn't know the Selentium Vox as well as you do. She hasn't spent centuries casting whispers. It's a simple mistake. What does it matter, anyway? It worked on the Goblins' watches, didn't it?"

"I'm not concerned with whether or not it worked, I'm concerned with *why* she chose the words she chose."

"You think she's up to something?"

"You don't?"

She frowned. If she was being honest, then of course she did. Cricket was always up to something. But Cricket was also clever and smart and fair and would never do anything to harm anyone who didn't deserve it. If Cricket was keeping her spell secret, it was for a good reason. "She's my friend," Anouk said firmly.

Before Rennar could suggest anything more, the arguments among the Royals rose in tenor. Queen Violante scoffed at Prince Aleksi and asked, "And who is going to be willing to do *that?*"

"If you want the sight spell," he told her, "that's what it will take."

Anouk's ears perked up. "What will it take?"

"Sight," Prince Aleksi replied.

"He means that literally," Violante explained. "The prince wants one of us to give up our vision. The Selentium Vox requires it as part of the elixir. Someone must voluntarily go blind. Any takers? Ah, you see? I thought not."

Aleksi said haltingly, "It would be only temporary. Once the spell is finished, we will return the vision to its owner." He paused.

"Of course, no one's ever performed this spell before. So that's theoretical."

Anouk felt sick. "If it isn't certain, then we can't ask anyone to—"

"I'll do it," a voice at her side said.

Anouk closed her eyes. She wished she could turn back time. She opened her eyes and gave Beau a hard look. "Beau, you can't."

"It's my offer to make."

She let out a groan. "There's no guarantee they'll be able to return your sight to you."

"There's no guarantee we won't all be swallowed by the Noirceur," he said. "Life doesn't come with guarantees, cabbage. What choice do we have, anyway?" He went over the logic of his plan. "Everyone who can cast a half-decent whisper is needed to gather the clocks and join in the kindred spell. That includes you and Petra. We need Cricket to steal the Heart of Alexandrite. We need Luc to mix enough elixir for hundreds of magic handlers. We need Hunter Black to scale the tower. What magic can I do? That one blasted sleeping spell? That isn't going to get us out of a bind this time." His face darkened. "It has to be me."

She shook her head. "We need someone who can ride that Genevar motorcycle around the city to draw out the smoke."

"Yeah," he said plainly. "You, cabbage."

She blinked, shocked. "I can't drive."

"Well, not yet."

She pressed her lips together. Outside, across the park, the storm clouds surrounding Big Ben were rumbling. She went to the window. The smoke below was now three feet high, swallowing sidewalks and shrubs, bumping up against the revolving door. She crossed the shoe department to the balcony that looked down over the five-story atrium. As she feared, black ribbons of smoke were seeping through the revolving door into the store.

She felt Beau's presence at her side. He wordlessly looked over the balcony, and Cricket did too, both of their faces tight with apprehension.

"Okay," Anouk said haltingly. "I don't like it, for the record. Cricket, stay here. Teach the others how to cast your stealing spell."

Cricket looked at Anouk and Beau. "Where are you going to be?"

Anouk let out a long breath. "I'll be outside, breaking my neck on a Genevar."

Chapter 40

THE GENEVAR MOTORCYCLE STOOD where they'd left it, on a side street between the British Museum and Piccadilly Circus. The boy straddling it wore a chrome helmet and a navy-blue pea coat with a scarf frozen mid-billow behind him. Ribbons of black smoke had spread even this far and now swirled in and out of the motorcycle wheels and around Anouk and Beau's feet. She kicked at the street curb anxiously.

"We'll have to get him off of there." Beau attempted to gently pry the Pretty's fingers off the handlebars.

Anouk kicked once more at the smoke. They were running out of time. She gave the Pretty a good solid shove. He tumbled off the seat and crashed onto the sidewalk, where he was nearly swallowed by the smoke. His hands and legs were still posed for driving, like a doll whose limbs only moved when repositioned.

"Anouk!"

"Well, we need his ride, and we don't need him." She threw a leg over the motorcycle, hoping she looked like she knew what she was doing. "Show me how this works."

Beau knelt by the Pretty and patted the poor boy's shoulder, then unfastened his helmet and handed it to Anouk. "Wear this. I've never heard of witches dying in traffic accidents but stranger things have happened."

She buckled the helmet under her chin as he climbed on behind her. His body was solid. Settling against him felt like leaning into her favorite chair.

"First, take the handlebars."

She gripped them with sweating palms. She tried not to focus on the smoke rising up to their knees.

"Not so tight. Easy. Like . . . like you'd hold a plum. Light enough not to bruise it, hard enough for a solid grip."

She closed her eyes. She could almost taste the plum he was talking about. It made her think of summertime in the townhouse kitchen. Fruit tarts and jams. Sweet as the first time they'd kissed.

"Beau, I don't like this," she confessed, opening her eyes.

"You'll get used to it."

"No, I don't mean the motorcycle. I mean this plan. You handing over your vision for the sake of a spell we aren't even sure will work. You could be blind forever."

He was quiet for a moment. The smoke at their feet was so thick she couldn't see her shoes. Anouk couldn't help but feel something tug inside of her—the dark thing that she'd tried to hide from her whole life. Even as the Gargoyle, she wasn't free of it. If beasties had souls, as Rennar had said, then what was hers? Was it air? Was it wings? Or was it the same substance as the rising smoke?

Beau pressed his lips to her ear. "I don't need vision. I told you when we crossed the Chunnel. My heart would know you anywhere."

She felt tears at her eyes. She turned her head toward him. "Beau. Beau."

Words couldn't express what was in her heart. She tilted her mouth to fit against his. He leaned forward. He cupped her face with his hand, his palm rough against her cheek. She leaned into him, her back pressed into his chest. One of his hands curled around her middle and held her there against him, like he was afraid she might float away. She twisted around another inch to deepen the kiss.

"Anouk," he breathed. "Be careful. The darkness . . . it calls to you. I see it."

She pressed her forehead against his. At the sound of their voices, the smoke rose in tendrils around their knees.

His thumb traced over the apple of her cheek. "I'd give anything to be out there with you, protecting you, holding you back when it calls to you. But I can't be by your side this time."

She swallowed. "I don't know what it is, Beau. Something in the Noirceur pulling at me. Like two magnets pulling together, like the fastener on Mada Vittora's ostrich clutch. Rennar said something about our souls being tied to nature, and the Noirceur is also nature, in a sense. Don't you feel it too?"

He nodded. "I think I know what you're talking about. I don't remember being a dog in the Cottage cellar, but in a strange way, I remember a *feeling* of being there. Like it was a dream. I have a sense of girls telling me their hopes. Their fears. I think it was the other acolytes coming to visit me and give me treats—they needed some-one to talk to. But out of all of us, you're the most deeply connected to magic. You're the one it attracts the most. Just be careful. I don't plan for our story to end here."

His lips found hers again. Beneath her hand pressed to his chest, she could feel his steady heartbeat. She ran her hand down his arm and rested her head against the crook of his neck. He turned to kiss her temple. Then he took her hand, placed a kiss on her knuckles, guided both of her hands back around, and clamped them firmly onto the motorcycle handles.

She sighed. "We really have to do this?"

"Make me proud, cabbage."

In a few brief moments, he taught her how to start the ignition, how to use the clutch and front and rear brakes, how to signal, how to lean in to curves. His love for engines was palpable. Driving had been his greatest pleasure working under Mada Vittora, and he was a good teacher. When the lesson was finished, they climbed off the motorcycle, smoke swirling up to their knees, and she took his hand. She opened his fingers and laid his rough palm against her cheek.

"The blindness will only be temporary, Anouk," he said softly.

"That's what they say, but they wouldn't hesitate to lie if they thought it's what you needed to hear."

He didn't answer right away. Big Ben kept ticking away, the only sound in the city. He flicked an errant piece of ash off her cheek.

"My beautiful gargoyle."

"What happened to 'cabbage'?"

"I was wrong. You're fierce and strong and terrifying and nothing to make soup with."

She smiled and kissed him again.

Anouk drove them back to Pickwick and Rue's on the Genevar motorcycle, a little wobbly at first, but by the time they pulled up to the revolving glass door, she'd more or less gotten the hang of it. Smoke had risen above their knees, and the entire park was obscured beneath it except for the tallest monuments. Upstairs in the department store, they discovered that everyone had been busy mastering Cricket's transference spell. They'd stacked high heels on one table and were whispering them to another table on the other side of the department. Steadily, the shoes transferred locations pair by pair.

Cricket set up the pair of fireball Louboutins and motioned for one of the Goblins to practice again. "Welcome back," she said to Anouk. "The Goblins picked up the spell right away. It took the Royals longer. They've spent their lives mastering how to get other people to do their dirty work." She gave a long eye roll. "But they got it in the end."

Anouk felt a figure looming behind her and turned to find handsome Prince Aleksi. His eyes were fixed on Beau.

"It's time, Master Chauffeur."

Hunter Black and Cricket dragged an armchair up from the Home Goods department and placed it by the window, where, even without his vision, Beau would be able to hear the ticking of Big Ben and know if their attempt had been successful. Beau took a seat hesitantly, his fingers clutching the armrests.

Prince Aleksi placed a heavy hand on his shoulder. "Do you have a high tolerance for pain?"

Beau's face paled a shade. "Just do it."

With a touch of orange powder on his lips, Prince Aleksi whispered the spell to capture Beau's vision. His words were uttered as solemnly as a prayer, and Anouk felt like she was back in the Cottage's great hall with its vaulted ceiling that had once been part of a church, Esme praying softly by the fireplace. Oh, Esme. It was horrid to think of her gone. Marta and Heida and Frederika too.

Beau kept his eyes fixed on Anouk while Prince Aleksi performed the spell. The other members of the Haute stood at a distance, watching silently. Halfway through the spell, she noticed something strange about Beau's gaze. His head was turned in her direction but his eyes were fixed a little too far to her left. She took a step toward him and he didn't track her movement.

She felt a sharp tug in her stomach. "Beau?"

He swallowed hard. His hands felt for the armrests as though he needed to reassure himself they were still there. "It's okay," he said, though it didn't seem like it was okay at all.

Prince Aleksi continued his whisper and a gleam appeared at the corners of Beau's eyes, marbled with iridescent colors like a shimmering puddle of oil. Without breaking the whisper, Aleksi waved over Luc, who came with a pitcher — pilfered from Home Goods — and held it up to each of Beau's eyes, catching the rainbow-streaked tears, until Prince Aleksi stopped his spell.

"That should be sufficient. Combine it with the other ingredients. Three sips apiece. The first for an open heart. The second for an open mind. The third for open eyes. Everyone, drink deep."

Luc poured the elixir into three wine goblets that they'd also found in the Home Goods department. The members of the Haute passed one among themselves. The Goblins took another. Anouk went to stand next to Cricket by the window.

"About your spell," Anouk said haltingly. She thought back to what Rennar had said about Cricket's wording referring to stealing people, not objects. She lowered her voice. "I thought you just wanted to be a better thief, but there's more to it, isn't there?"

Cricket slid her a guarded look. "Nope."

"Then why'd you steal those artifacts from Castle Ides?"

Hesitancy flickered in Cricket's otherwise normally cool eyes. She pressed her lips together and then took Anouk's hand and pulled her into a private corner behind a rack of shoes. "Do you remember at Montélimar when Mada Zola showed us those portraits of the ancient selkas? The original beasties?"

Anouk tilted her head, curious. "Of course."

"Well, I know this sounds *complètement fou,* but when Countess Quine turned me into a cat at the château, I had something like a vision. It happened again when Petra turned us into animals to pass through the Chunnel."

Visions? Anouk's eyebrows shot up.

Cricket mistook the reason for her surprise and quickly rolled her eyes. "I know you're probably thinking that I drank too much of Viggo's absinthe. But it's true. It was more than a dream."

"No, I believe you." Anouk's mind filled with hazy pieces of her own strange vision of the Coven and the eyeless owl. She could almost kick herself. Why hadn't she guessed that the other beasties might have had visions too?

"I dreamed of the selkas," Cricket whispered. "That they hadn't all been killed off. I had a vision of the ocean and cliffs and women who could shift into seals. It felt so real, Anouk. And then in Castle Ides, I found maps of coastlines with pictures of mermaids—it was the selkas. *That's* what I was stealing."

"And in the British Museum?"

"In the Greek Wing, I found a hammered-tin bowl with pictures of women turning to seals. Don't you see? They're all clues that point to the existence of more of us. If I can figure out the maps and arti-facts, I might be able to find the others." Her eyes danced. "We might not be alone, Anouk. There might be more beasties that escaped the Royals' purge. Ones that can shift on their own. Haven't you ever wondered what our place in the world is? What it could be?"

Anouk's lips parted. So that had been Cricket's secret. Not revenge on their creators. (Though, to be honest, the Royals deserved it.) Anouk could see the desire sparkling in Cricket's eyes. *To not be the only ones.* To know that there were more of them out there, unbound by the rules and requirements of the Haute. It was a lonely existence, being a beastie. Why shouldn't they try to find others?

"I was going to tell you," Cricket added, "and the others once I was sure. But there are still a lot of unanswered questions. Besides, we have more pressing matters." She turned to the window with a tight look on her face. "All those Pretties down there. I feel sorry for them. They don't know their fates are in the hands of a couple of misfits and dreamers."

"And Viggo."

Cricket snorted. "Oh God."

Throughout the shoe department, the last of the Royals and Gob-lins finished drinking from the goblets of elixir. Rennar came over to the window with the final goblet and extended it to Cricket, who took her three sips with a grimace, and then to Anouk, who drained the dregs.

Rennar motioned to the various factions. "Aleksi, Violante,

December, and I divided the city by neighborhood. The Lunar Court is going to take Covent Garden and Soho. The Barren Court is taking Islington. The Court of the Woods will cover Camden and Hampstead. The Crimson and the Minaret Courts are taking Wandsworth and Lambeth. I'll handle Westminster on my own. December's leading the Goblins to take the East End. Petra's insisted on taking both Chelsea and Kensington, since you'll be otherwise occupied, Anouk."

"And I'm going to procure the Heart of Alexandrite," Cricket said, cracking her knuckles. She threw Anouk a quick look and cleared her throat. "It'll make the perfect vessel. Very rare. Extremely protected. The Noirceur will be safe there. I'll get it and be back here before Viggo says another stupid thing."

Anouk gave her a knowing nod.

The three of them turned to the window and looked out over the clock and the rising smoke. Snow steadily drifted down. Anouk pressed her fingertips against the frosted glass. She wondered how Duke Karolinge was faring out in the cold, whispering a spell powerful enough to span an entire city. If his spell failed, even for a moment, they'd be thrust into chaos once more.

Anouk went to the armchair and rested a hand on Beau's shoulder. He'd taken one of the Goblin's handkerchiefs and tied it around his eyes as a blindfold.

"It's time for me to go, Beau."

He gave her hand a squeeze. "This is our world, Anouk," he said. "Fight for it."

Chapter 41

T HE ENTIRE COMPANY of the Haute left Pickwick and Rue's. London remained as still as some terrible painting. Except for the rivers of smoke moving through the streets, not a single blade of grass or lock of hair wavered. The Snow Children's frost encased the world, and as she gathered with the others in the park as they prepared to split up into the different neighborhoods, Anouk got the topsy-turvy impression that the entire city was nothing more than displays at the British Museum — or perhaps a haunted house. Two teenage Pretties cowered behind a phone booth. A dog paused mid-snarl at a man with blood soaked into his shirt. The glass of a bookstore's broken windows hung suspended in time. And the magic handlers were like the museum's midnight custodians, there to sweep up the mess and put things back in order before dawn.

One by one, the teams broke off from the group and departed, all heading in opposite directions — the Goblins to the east, Petra to the south, the Royal factions to the north and west — until only Anouk, Hunter Black, and Viggo remained in the square, standing by a fountain frozen in time.

"Hunter Black, you're up." Anouk's stomach did flip-flops as she scanned the full height of Big Ben. Smoke steadily poured out of its windows and plummeted to the streets. "Are you sure you're okay with this? It's a long way to the top."

"I've scaled the Eiffel Tower blindfolded," he said. "This is nothing."

She'd never get used to hearing such staggering arrogance from such a sullen boy. She decided that he'd make an excellent Royal. "Well, try not to breathe in too much smoke." She gave him a sly grin and recited the same words he'd said to her: "All things considered, your survival would be preferable to your death."

He turned to her with a surprisingly touched look. "Thank you, Anouk." He gave her an oddly formal nod and then crossed the park. She'd seen him scale walls before; there was the time Viggo had stayed out past curfew and Hunter Black had had to throw him over his shoulder, climb the townhouse exterior, and come in through Anouk's turret window. He'd moved like a shadow, even carrying Viggo's bulk. Now he was twice as stealthy. Without his coat—Luc had returned to the museum to check on Duke Karolinge and he had it with him—Hunter Black looked shockingly lithe. Anouk and Viggo watched him ascend the limestone blocks at the tower's base as easily as if he were walking up a set of stairs.

Anouk watched until he was almost at the top, then turned and shaded her eyes to peer into the dome window on the fifth floor of Pickwick and Rue's. She could just make out the shape of Beau, sightlessly looking out over them. "Viggo, you'll keep an eye on Beau, won't you?"

"After a houseful of Goblins, he'll be a piece of cake."

Deep rumblings came from the east, followed by matched sounds from the west. The smoke wavered slightly as something within the city shifted. Anouk climbed to the top of the park's fountain and stood on tiptoe. To the east, Covent Garden glowed with a faint blue light. To the west, Soho crackled with orange.

"It's the different factions. Their spells are working. Look." Anouk clapped a hand on Viggo's shoulder and pointed to the base of Big Ben. Orange and blue sparks crackled amid the smoke. A grandfather clock suddenly appeared by the bushes at the base of the tower. With a colorful blue flash, a television set with a built-in clock appeared. The colored lights they were seeing in the distance were the teams performing the transference spells, sending the clocks here, to Big Ben. A small alarm clock with silver bells. A wristwatch. A giant clock that looked like it belonged to a church, and lots of identical round clocks that must have been from a school.

Viggo seemed riveted. "I'm impressed. I have to admit, I gave us only a fifty-fifty chance of even surviving the mummies."

More clocks appeared, pouring in from different neighborhoods, all accompanied by matching colored flashes.

The smoke was up to their waists now. Viggo coughed. "How much can we breathe before we're poisoned?"

Anouk turned to the Genevar motorcycle parked outside of Pickwick and Rue's. "I don't know, but it's time for me to take care of it."

They'd tied an audio player on the back of the motorcycle with Hermès scarves from Pickwick and Rue's and wired it to the motorcycle's working engine. She jabbed her finger on the Play button. The Clash erupted from the speakers. Around her, the smoke swirled in tight little eddies that moved toward the sound. She braced herself before cranking the volume to 10.

The rock music blasted out the back of the speakers. She could feel the vibrations spreading up her legs, and the smoke must have felt it too, because the wisps curved sharply toward the motorcycle. Big thick billows of it floated toward them, rising around Anouk and Viggo, moving up to their chests. She could barely even see the motorcycle.

Viggo pressed his sleeve to his face, though a scrap of fabric wouldn't protect anyone. "Godspeed, Dust Mop."

"Thanks, Corkscrew."

"Corkscrew?"

"If we're naming each other after the household items we use most . . ."

Viggo snorted. He saluted her before returning to the department store. Anouk took a seat on the motorcycle, already feeling wobbly. She flicked the ignition on and set the clutch as Beau had taught her, then twisted the accelerator. The motorcycle lurched forward so suddenly that she let out a shriek. Damn Beau and his noble sacrifices. But as it roared ahead, she got it under control and aimed it in the direction of the river. Pellets of snow stung her face. The blaring music pounded behind her. In the silent city, The Clash's beats reverberated against the tall buildings, booming back at her even louder.

When she dared a glance behind her, the black smoke was following in billows. It moved the way she imagined a sandstorm would, rising and falling in ominous waves. She swallowed a lump in her throat. She could feel the smoke at her back, moving faster than her. She bit her lip and cranked the motorcycle to its full speed, but the low layer of smoke ahead obscured the streets, and she was sure that any second she was going to collide with a curb or a bicycle and then be consumed by the smoke entirely. Her heart thundered.

She spotted Westminster Bridge and veered toward it sharply. The smoke rushed with her, rising in another awful wave, but as soon as she hit the bridge, the smoke fell off on either side, plunging into the frozen riverbed below.

"*Et voilà!*" she cried out.

She tore across the bridge, throwing glances at the river below. The smoke was gathering on the water, and as soon as she hit the other bank, it surged up in a twenty-foot wave behind her.

"*Merde!*"

She'd bought herself some time, but not much. She roared past the Lambeth North station and onto the A201. Here she could go faster, trusting that the street was wide enough that she was less likely to hit any objects hidden by low-lying smoke. Down every side street, she glimpsed fresh waves of smoke hurtling toward her, drawn to the pounding beats of the Clash. It rushed at her in twenty- and thirty-foot swells, spilling out into the wider highway. She cranked the engine. Sharp pellets of snow bit at her. Ahead, she caught a glimpse of green lights crackling like lightning. She was nearing the Westminster neighborhood, so it had to be Rennar performing the transference spell. She thought of the other teams spread throughout the city. The more noxious smoke that followed on her heels, the more likely it was that the others would succeed.

That was little comfort as she hit a roundabout, wasting precious time circling when the smoke didn't have to obey traffic signals. It burst into the roundabout, clouding everything in sight. The full force of the wave slammed into Anouk and she coughed violently. Her throat burned. All she could see was smoke. Her eyes stung. It was so thick that the street completely disappeared beneath her. Pain throbbed in her throat and eyes and she thought of King Kaspar crying black tears. She revved the engine as hard as she could and burst out of the dense smoke and back onto the A201.

She swerved sharply to avoid a city bus frozen in the middle of the road.

Her hands were shaking. She was pretty sure she'd screamed a time or two, but she couldn't hear anything between the blasting Clash and the pounding blood in her head.

She just had to make it to Gravesend. Twenty miles from the city center, Gravesend was a port where the Thames joined the start of the ocean. There, outside of the city limits, it wouldn't be snowing. The world wouldn't be frozen. Everything would be untouched by witches and Royals alike. If she could get the radio onto a boat—something viciously loud, like a barge—the smoke would follow it toward the North Sea, where it would dissipate into the vast wide-open air, diluted enough to be harmless.

The Genevar tore through Southwark, past a golf course plunged in shadows, past a sprawling grocery store with its lights lit, even though the people in the parking lot were frozen. Flashes of red light appeared in buildings on either side of the street. The Crimson Court was in Southwark. That was their magic, flashing block by block, as they cleared out the clocks. She adjusted her rearview mirror and instantly regretted it.

The smoke was now a tidal wave behind her, towering fifty feet and rushing fast as it gained more volume. Sweat broke out on her brow. She leaned in to the curves on the highway. The motorcycle was already going as fast as it could. She narrowed her eyes against the stinging snow. With a curse, she twisted the mirrors around so she couldn't see the dark wave behind her.

A tiny flicker of hope hit her as she neared the city limits. Snow was barely falling here. The Pretty World was beginning to move again, though sluggishly. Once she crossed onto the A2, the snow stopped completely, and shockingly, the world went from night to day in the blink of an eye. A bright sun hung in the sky. Cars were moving beside her at normal speeds. A station wagon carrying a large family. A couple kissing in the back seat of a taxi. Didn't they see the tidal wave of smoke behind her? None of these Pretties knew about the plagues just across the city line in London, where it was eternal night. They didn't know that their fates rested in the hands of a witch on a motorcycle.

She roared forward amid honking horns and swerving cars, and then there it was: Gravesend. The river. Ahead, a bridge spanned the port, and she searched the ships until she saw a barge about to depart. She skidded onto the bridge and slammed on the brakes in the very middle. The barge below was headed toward her. She pulled out a knife and freed the audio player and then hurled it over the bridge as the barge passed underneath; it caught in some of the machinery. The wave of smoke swerved to follow the music. She shrieked and covered her head as the smoke rolled toward her, but at the last moment it diverted sharply to the barge below, trailing the ever-more-distant sounds of The Clash.

She collapsed against the motorcycle, breathing hard. Cars honked and swerved around her.

"You're welcome," she cried out, though no one could hear her above the traffic, "for saving all your lives!"

She drew in a few deep breaths of wonderfully fresh air and leaned back against the motorcycle. Closed her eyes. Tried to calm her heart. And then groaned and stood up.

London awaited.

Chapter 42

SHE DROVE BACK to the city at less of a breakneck speed. As soon as she crossed the city limits, night descended again, as though someone had turned off the lights in a bright room. Likewise, the world came to a standstill. Frozen cars were coated in ice. Birds hung in mid-flight. Snow was falling, to her relief—Duke Karolinge must still have the energy to continue casting his spell, but she knew he wouldn't be able to last much longer. She crested a hill and saw flashes of colored light: purple in Belgravia, blue in Kensington. Her heart soared. The lights were at the outer edges of the neighborhoods. The teams were almost finished.

She drove back toward Big Ben on streets that were almost entirely clear of smoke. A few wisps curled after her, but they were too small to be harmful. She neared a figure standing at the base of the tower.

She cut the engine and smiled at Cricket. She tumbled off the motorcycle, her legs shaking badly, and let it crash to its side in the street. Beau would be horrified, but scratched paint was the least of her worries.

"You got rid of the smoke!" Cricket exclaimed. "And you didn't break your neck. Bravo!"

Anouk grinned. "And you? The Heart of Alexandrite?"

"Mission accomplished." Cricket held up a paper bag from the museum gift shop. Then her expression turned secretive. "Are you sure about this? About . . . the other plan you told me on the rooftop?"

"As sure as anyone can be."

A rustle came from the tower. Big Ben's lancet windows were now sealed, the smoke contained except for the few harmless wisps slipping out from the cracks.

Hunter Black jumped into the mountain of clocks at the base, cursing as he made his unsteady way toward them. His hands were bleeding. There were traces of downy moth wings on his lips. Whatever had been involved in sealing the tower's windows, it had taken magic and a risk of physical impairment. But the assassin only wiped his hands on his dark pants.

"You scaled the Eiffel Tower faster," Cricket teased.

She got a scowl in return.

Anouk rolled her eyes and pointed toward the east. "The Court of the Woods is almost finished with Islington. And from what I could see, Petra's cleared all of Chelsea. I think—incredibly—we might actually live."

Her confidence wavered as she looked at the pyre of clocks and the few remaining wisps of smoke curling around her ankles. The ticking of clocks—powered by the Noirceur—was deafening. She wished she could see the rooftop of the British Museum. How much energy did Duke Karolinge have left? Could he keep it snowing much longer?

"If I tell you something"—Hunter Black's voice was uncertain, but he pushed forward, clenching his bleeding hands—"do you promise to keep it secret?"

Cricket and Anouk exchanged a surprised look. Hunter Black was known for his secret keeping, but it was usually *them* he was keeping secrets from.

"Yes," Anouk said slowly.

A muscle jumped in his jaw. "This sounds like something from one of Luc's stories, but I swear that I'm not making it up. When I was at the top of the tower, looking into the smoke . . . I had a vision."

He jerked his head as though he expected them to laugh. But nobody laughed. Anouk and Cricket exchanged another look, and Cricket said in a hollow voice, "It wasn't your first vision, was it? I bet you had one too when you were turned into a wolf."

His eyes snapped to hers. "How did you know that?"

"Anouk and I had visions too."

His tense shoulders eased in visible relief. "The first one happened when Mada Zola turned me into a wolf. I didn't trust it then. Wasn't certain exactly what I saw." His hand anxiously toyed with the buttons on his shirt. "But up there in the tower, I saw it again."

Anouk breathed, "What did you see?"

"Royals. A small contingent. In a forest. Riding horses, not motorcycles. Eating lamb roast over a bonfire, not sushi from Le Petit Japonais. Their lips were dusted with powder that glittered like crystals. They were led by a king and queen dressed in bear pelts. They had an army of enchanted Pretties with them."

"The ancient Royals," Anouk whispered. "King Svatyr and Queen Mid Ruath of the Snowfire Court, just like Jak told us about."

Hunter Black nodded. "They ordered their Pretty slaves to pack away their encampment, while the contingent led by the king and queen rode a mile away to a clearing where enormous stones rose from the ground and smoke covered the earth."

"Stonehenge," Cricket said.

He nodded. "They revered it. I don't think they or their ancestors built it—it seemed ancient even to them. They burned hemlock and whispered a kindred spell that drew smoke into the stones. They camped at the stones and celebrated with honey wine." He paused, uncertain whether to continue, then said, "At midnight, when the others were passed out, Queen Mid Ruath stepped outside of the stones. She sang into the wind. I don't know if it was a spell or a ballad—I didn't understand the words—but they're burned into my brain:

"Baz perrik, baz mare, baz teri,
en utidrava aedenum sa nav."

A chill ran through Anouk. Something scratched at her ankles like the remaining few wisps of smoke had grown fingernails. Hunter Black went moody and quiet.

A block away, Petra rounded the corner and called to them. She jogged over, marveling at the pile of clocks. "Finished! Hey, I think that cuckoo clock over there was one of mine! You should have seen all the clocks that came out of the primary school on Dover Street. Almost no clocks in the government buildings, which is alarming, don't you think? Shouldn't Pretty politicians care about time more than schoolchildren?" She turned back to them and frowned. "Hunter Black, good God, are you feeling okay?"

Anouk spun to him. He was still fidgeting with his buttons, but his moodiness had shifted. His face was now oddly slack.

Cricket asked, "Hunter Black?"

The assassin stood very straight, head tilted up at the illuminated clock face of Big Ben. A tiny curl of smoke—almost imperceptible—snaked out of his ear.

Anouk took a quick step away from him. "Hunter Black!"

Cricket caught sight of the curl of smoke. "Oh, *merde*." She pulled her knives.

Another curl of smoke twisted from his nostrils. His lips parted. An inhuman growl came from his throat. Anouk's eyes dropped to the button at his shirt collar that he kept toying with. It was one of the three buttons that Petra had charmed in the Castle Ides billiard room when she'd made his new clothes.

"Petra, the glass you used to make Hunter Black's buttons—where did you get it?"

"It was a paperweight," she sputtered. "On the floor. Someone must have knocked it over when we carried Rennar in."

Anouk thought back to the lump of glass, how it was raw cut and oddly shaped. At the time, she hadn't thought twice about it. But now she realized how out of place a paperweight would be on the floor of an impeccably tidy billiard room.

"The sand," Anouk whispered. Then: "Cricket, keep your distance from him!" Anouk's throat tightened as she pulled Cricket back.

Petra looked at the buttons blankly. "Sand? What sand? I told you I made them out of glass!"

"Glass *is* made of sand, Petra! Haven't you ever read a book on geology? The Noirceur was able to possess King Kaspar and Mia through the sand from the broken hourglass. But when the Royals used magic against the possession, it must have melted some of the sand into glass, like lightning does in nature. We must have accidentally brought the glass to the billiard room with Rennar, not realizing what it was at the time."

Petra frowned. "So that means the buttons I made . . . *oh*."

All eyes turned to Hunter Black.

"Hunter Black, look at me," Anouk said.

Her voice trembled, but not because she was afraid of him. She was afraid *for* him. She was no maid anymore, no pastry chef useful only for making sweet treats. She was the Gargoyle. Magic hummed in her palms. The Faustine jacket covered her skin like battle armor. Its golden threads had protected her before, and now its pockets held owl feathers, her crux. She didn't want to hurt him, but what if he gave her no choice? He squared himself and faced her. His eyes were threaded with smoke. Ribbons of it poured out of his mouth as he continued to make that awful growling. The sound slowly took the form of the Selentium Vox.

"Previso . . . rivet . . . morfin . . ."

It was the same warnings and curses King Kaspar had whispered.

"Hunter Black, if you're still in there, give us a sign." Anouk eyes darted from him to the pyre of clocks to the knives in Cricket's hands. Cricket wouldn't hesitate to strike whether Hunter Black was in possession of his own body or not. Spells scrolled through Anouk's mind. Containment spells. Defensive spells. Exorcism spells. But the Royals had attempted all of those on King Kaspar and none had worked.

Hunter Black's hand moved to draw his knife from the sheath strapped beneath his shirt. His movements were stilted. Anouk plunged her hand in her jacket, whispered open her oubliette pockets, and pulled out a long white feather. Just as he rushed forward with the knife raised, she pushed the feather down her throat and swallowed.

"Ak ignis bleu!" she whispered. The knife sparked in his hand, burning hot. He dropped it with a hiss.

"Anouk? Cricket? Petra?" From across the park, someone was calling to them.

She dared a glance. It was December, hurtling forward on her enchanted roller skates. In the distance, the orange and purple lights had stopped flashing, though the blue and green ones continued. The Royals and Goblins hadn't finished yet.

Anouk whipped her head back toward Hunter Black, bristling for an attack, but Hunter Black had fled. December skated up and crashed into Anouk. Her eyes went wide when they explained what had happened.

"He could be headed anywhere in the city," Anouk said.

"Um, or he could be right there." December pointed in the direction of the Pickwick and Rue's.

Chapter 43

ANOUK LOOKED JUST IN TIME to see Hunter Black disappear through the department store's revolving glass door. Petra aimed her hands toward him and whispered, *"Dorma, sonora precimo!"* But she wasn't fast enough to put him to sleep before the door stopped spinning. If there was any place where it would be nearly impossible to find someone, it was Pickwick and Rue's.

Cricket and December grabbed Anouk around the waist and helped her to stand.

"Wouldn't the Noirceur compel him to go to Big Ben?" Cricket asked. "Or stop the teams who haven't finished collecting all the clocks?"

Petra adjusted her champagne sunglasses. "There must be something in the store that the Noirceur wants."

Anouk felt her stomach plummet. "Beau."

December gasped, clapping her hands over her mouth. "Wait, why would he go after Beau?"

Anouk raked her nails over her scalp as she put it together. "Because there are still a few teams out in the city gathering clocks. They're using Beau's sight to do it. If they didn't have the sight, they wouldn't be able to finish. Hunter Black doesn't have to stop every one of the Royals—he only has to kill Beau to stop them all."

December gasped again.

Cricket threw back her jacket to have better access to her knives. "What are we waiting for?"

Anouk, Cricket, and Petra ran toward the revolving door. December skated ahead of them and slammed into it first. They crammed into the same partition, a tangle of limbs, and pushed their way in. The door spat them out into the lobby with its beautiful spiral staircases and tables laden with delectable treasures. Anouk's stomach turned at the too-sweet smells. A thick layer of frost covered the perfume cases. The escalators and elevators were frozen too.

"There!" Cricket spotted movement on the stairs to the second floor. Hunter Black moved like a rippling shadow past racks of men's suits. Cricket cast a whisper to topple the racks and block his path, but Hunter Black dodged the first rack, leaped over the second, and disappeared deeper into the store.

"*Merde!*" Cricket cursed.

"We have to divide up," Anouk said in a rush. "Petra, you and I'll go after Hunter Black. I'll take the second and third floors, you take the fourth and fifth. Cricket, you look for Viggo—he doesn't know Hunter Black is possessed, and he's likely to do something stupid because, well, he's Viggo. December . . ." She stopped short, frowning down at the Goblin's skates. "You can't go upstairs with those."

December groaned. "I know! These awful skates! It takes a special word to unlock them. I wrote it down and then lost it somewhere in Piccadilly Circus."

381

Anouk tried a few unlocking spells, but without the code word, they only sparked off the roller skates.

"We're losing time," Cricket warned.

"It's okay," December said. "I'll stay on the ground floor and see if I can't catch him with a few spells from here."

Anouk nodded. "Try not to hurt him. He can't be blamed for his actions when he's possessed."

Cricket looked ready to contradict that but then sighed. "Ugh, fine, you're right. He's family. A shunned cousin or something, but still family." She spun on her heel and disappeared into the department store.

Petra went to the staircase and climbed to the fourth floor. December clambered down to her hands and knees and looked under the closest display table for spiders to swallow as life-essence.

Anouk scanned the different balconies. Everything was as perfectly still here as it was outside. There was no sign of movement. All the mannequins and mirrors only tricked her eyes into seeing things that weren't there.

She took the stairs to the rear of the second floor, the children's department. She pushed past prams and weaved between cribs and poked through piles of stuffed animals, but Hunter Black wasn't hiding in them. She climbed to the third floor, Accessories, and made her way through the handbag department. The only other department store she'd ever been in was Galeries Lafayette back in Paris, and a saleswoman had escorted her the entire time. Now, alone, every shadow made her jump. She caught a flash of movement and spun, raising her hands in a protective gesture, but it was only her own reflection in a mirror. She let out a tight breath, turned, and jumped as her own face again peered at her. Mirrors were everywhere, tracking her sunken eyes and messy hair as she made her way among the handbags.

Each purse reminded her of a version of Mada Vittora's oubliette. Balenciaga wallets, Valentino clutches, Diane von Furstenberg purses. A heavy Gucci suitcase suddenly fell from the highest shelf and she ducked as it crashed into a display of wallets. She caught a flash of movement that wasn't in a mirror. Charcoal hair and a black shirt. Hunter Black! He darted across the handbag department and took cover behind a stack of designer backpacks. Her heart raced. She swallowed a pinch of feather and ran after him, but when she reached the backpacks, he'd vanished. She raced to the end of the shelves and turned the corner just in time to see him disappearing around a display of ties.

She ran past a row of disembodied wooden torsos wearing silk ties to an enormous display of hats. Hats with feathers, hats with faux flowers, hats with lace and ribbons, hats that looked like they'd swallow a person whole. It was unsettling, seeing all these bodiless mannequin heads.

Without warning, one of the racks behind her started swaying. She collapsed to her knees and rolled out of the way a second before it would have crushed her. Shaking, she pushed herself back to her feet.

Another flash of movement came from the New Arrivals section.

"Hunter Black!"

He was moving strangely, his steps lurching. Even after downing a full glass of gin, he'd always been sharp. But now something else was moving his body, and Anouk had to hope that the small lag could give her an edge.

She took a step backward, looking around. A heavy gold bracelet glittered on a mannequin. She tugged it off and threw it across the room. When Hunter Black spun toward the clatter it made, she took advantage of the distraction.

"Lancae!"

She threw out a blast of energy from her palms. Two shelves of designer jeans fell on him. He roared as the metal shelving unit smashed against his skull. Pant legs tangled around him, and he struggled to extract himself from the mess. Anouk stepped closer with a spell on her lips to summon wind. *"Zefyr traga . . ."*

He was clutching his head, but he managed to throw a purse at her before she got the final words out. Its long strap hooked onto her wrist like a lasso, and with a sharp tug, he pulled her over. Before she could scramble back up, he was on top of her. His eyes were threaded with black. Smoke curled from his nostrils. Blood from the cuts on his hands dripped onto her cheek.

He pulled back and aimed a punch at her head. She blocked it with a shield spell, and his hand glided off into air, but he was an assassin trained by Mada Vittora. He'd killed Royals, Goblins, even other witches. If there was one thing he knew how to fight against, it was magic.

He curled his hand in the back of her hair, a blade glimmering in his other palm. He was going to slice her throat—she'd seen him do it before. It was a highly effective move—if it didn't kill a witch outright, it at least kept her from whispering spells.

Pulse racing, she cast out Cricket's stealing spell but used the word referring to objects. *"Ut vol pas rein ut deux!"*

The spell summoned a crystal-studded clutch she'd seen in the handbag department. It materialized in her hand and she threw it in front of his knife; the purse hit it with a shower of sparks, breaking off the blade from the hilt. He gave a hollow grunt as he dived for the broken blade. Anouk pitched forward, pushing herself up to all fours. Her hair was wild in her face; she shoved it back.

She turned to Hunter Black, swallowed a pinch of feathers, and whispered the stealing spell on *him,* using the word that referred to people.

"Ut vol fer rein ut deux!"

Hunter Black vanished. He was simply there one moment and gone the next, disappearing with only the slightest flicker of surprise on his face. Even using the wording variation that Rennar had described, it wasn't as easy to transfer a person as it was a purse. The farthest she could cast him was one floor down—but it was far enough. Anouk rolled back and lay on the floor, breathing hard.

Dieu, had it really worked?

She listened for Hunter Black's heavy footsteps racing back toward her, but there was nothing. She was alone amid the mess of handbags. She took a second to wipe his blood from her cheek. She checked her stash of owl feathers and other life-essences—dwindling, but if she rationed it, it should last.

Someone screamed on the ground floor, followed by a curse, then another scream. She groaned. Just once couldn't she savor a victory?

She shoved herself up and ran through the Accessories department to the balcony.

"Cricket?" she yelled, leaning over the rail.

"Here!"

It had come from the Baked Goods section of the ground floor.

Anouk scanned the tables full of treats until she saw a scuffle by the front doors. She'd expected Cricket to be fighting Hunter Black, but to her shock, Cricket was in hand-to-hand combat with someone else.

A Goblin in roller skates.

Chapter 44

*D*ECEMBER?"

Anouk could scarcely believe her eyes. December was hurling herself at Cricket, casting vicious cutting spells that sliced at Cricket's arms; in return, Cricket threw out a spell to make the Goblin's wheels stop. December slammed to the floor abruptly, but then immediately pushed herself up to her knees and started crawling toward Cricket. She moved so fast, so stiffly. Cricket leaped onto a table to get away, not wanting to hurt someone who, until seconds ago, had been an ally.

Cricket called up to Anouk, "Uh, you said a button possessed Hunter Black, right? A glass button?"

"That's right."

"He came charging through here a moment ago. I thought he was going to try to kill me. But he just thrust a button in December's pocket. She turned into . . . into this demon on wheels." December was snarling out tricks in the Selentium Vox to burn Cricket. "I could use a little help!"

Anouk clutched the railing. Her mind went between the ground floor and the top one. Hunter Black had to have known that she'd rush to Cricket's aid, giving him a clear shot to the fifth floor to kill Beau.

Did she help Cricket or did she save Beau?

She closed her eyes briefly.

"Petra!" she called.

In another moment, the Ash Witch appeared on the fourth floor and leaned over the railing. "What? Make it fast, I'm right on Hunter Black's tail!"

"Forget him!" Anouk pointed to the ground floor. "Help Cricket."

Petra peered down and let out a groan. She swallowed a pinch of her lavender ash and, faster than Anouk could track, leaped over the railing.

"Petra, wait, no!" Anouk squeezed her eyes shut.

Petra was four stories up. No Pretty could jump from that distance and survive. But Petra wasn't a Pretty anymore.

Hesitantly, Anouk opened one eye.

Petra plunged four stories down and landed primly on a table full of chocolate truffles. The truffles were ruined, but Petra was in one piece. She stood up, dusted chocolate off her boots, and stretched her neck.

"Did you just . . . did you *fly?*" Anouk shook her head—after everything she'd seen, sometimes the Haute could still surprise her.

"More like graceful falling." Petra leaped off the truffle table and swallowed more ash.

Anouk looked back up to the fifth floor. "Beau," she whispered.

She raced through the Accessories department until she reached the stairs. Her breath came ragged as she climbed from the third floor to the fourth, then started up to the fifth. A few steps from the top, a dark shape came hurtling through the air in her direction. *Saint!* What was the falcon doing *here?* His eyes were piercingly black. He was aiming straight for her. She barely had time to wonder why the falcon wasn't with Duke Karolinge before it slammed into her.

"Saint, stop!"

She shielded her face from his talons. His wings pummeled the air. He let out a sharp cry as he aimed for her eyes. She stumbled back until her hips hit the railing. She couldn't retreat any farther.

"Saint, no!"

She tried to reach into her pocket for another owl feather, but the falcon's talons sliced at her wrist. Had Duke Karolinge commanded Saint to attack her? Why? Something was rattling around in the falcon's bell — something bigger than a brass ball. She caught a glimpse of something glass.

"Oh no." Hunter Black must have slipped the third of his glass buttons into the bird's bell, possessing him just like he had with December. If she couldn't reach her oubliette pockets, she couldn't swallow life-essence and stop him. His talons kept tearing at her wrists. She pushed away, shielding herself, but the bird came at her harder. He was going to slice her apart. She had to think . . .

On an impulse, she stopped pushing the bird away. Maybe it was crazy, but she grabbed a fistful of his feathers and pulled him *closer*. She hugged the bird so hard against her chest that she pinned his wings and talons. For a second, she was safe. She could think. Her mind raced. Struggling to hold the bird tightly, she leaned over the railing. Below, Cricket and Petra were on opposite sides of December, casting out whispers. Petra was subject to the vitae echo, but Cricket wasn't, so theoretically she could kill the Goblin. But it was clear that, like with Hunter Black, they didn't want to hurt someone who wasn't in possession of her own body.

Footsteps sounded across the atrium and one floor up. The ground suddenly rumbled like an enormous truck had driven by. Shards of frost broke off the ceiling and rained down. Anouk's head whipped around. Hunter Black wasn't the most skilled with magic, but somehow, he'd managed to cast a spell to separate the top of the staircase from the upper floor. A ten-foot-wide chasm now blocked her access to the top level.

If she moved her hands even an inch to get her crux, Saint would get free and claw out her eyes—but without life-essence, how could she span the chasm to stop Hunter Black?

A nauseating idea came to her.

Tenpenny had bitten off his own pet rat's head and drunk the blood to save them from the Marble Ladies. She couldn't bring herself to bite anything's head off, even to save Beau, but maybe she could handle something slightly less grisly.

"I'm sorry, Saint."

She forced herself to grab the bird by the throat. Mada Vittora had been fond of baked-crow cassoulet, so it wasn't the first time Anouk had slaughtered a bird, but it never got easier. She gritted her teeth and twisted the bird's head until she heard a crack. It ripped something in her heart too, but she forced herself to ignore her feelings. Saint, dead, fell heavily to the stairs. Wisps of feathers floated in the air, wrenched out from when she'd twisted his neck. The stairs were slick with her blood, dripping from where his talons had sliced her.

The worse part was, she wasn't done.

The vitae echo kept magic in check because handlers couldn't take an entire life—that much life-essence would double back and kill the handler too. But Anouk wasn't subject to the vitae echo. She grimaced as she crouched on the stairs, working fast. She pulled a knife and a bottle from her oubliette pockets and made quick work of draining Saint's blood.

In a few seconds she'd gagged down half of the bird's still-warm blood. She could feel it spreading through her body, giving her power. She had an idea for how to get around Hunter Black's chasm. Petra hadn't exactly *flown,* but then again, wasn't gravity just another fairy tale?

"Volart kael."

She climbed over the stair railing and, sucking in a breath, jumped. She didn't think. Fear shot through her heart but . . . she didn't fall. She hovered four stories up. She was floating toward the fifth story like a leaf caught in an updraft. Her feet kicked at air. She felt that awful terrifying moment of having nothing beneath her and she knew that she should be plunging down four stories—but she wasn't. She reached out her hands like a trapeze artist and grabbed hold of the fifth-floor balcony.

"Aha!"

The rail was solid beneath her palms. She was so shocked that it worked that she nearly let go, but the spell was fading and gravity was quickly rushing back. She scrambled to climb up and over the railing into the shoe department.

It was a wreck. Shoes were scattered all over the floor, tables were overturned, and shoeboxes were stacked into makeshift barricades. At the end of the department, by the domed window, Beau sat immobile in the armchair.

"Beau!"

When she called his name, he turned his head in her direction. She was flushed with relief. *He's okay!* But he was also alone. Exposed.

"Damn it, Viggo, you promised to watch out for him," she muttered.

Without warning, Viggo leaped out from behind a barricade of shoeboxes, pistol in hand. His face twisted in surprise when he saw her. "Anouk!"

She stopped, pressing a hand to her heart. "Viggo!"

He lowered the gun. "I thought you were Hunter Black! Cricket warned me he was on the loose."

She dropped her hand, scowling. "So you set up Beau as *bait?*"

"It was his idea!"

"Cabbage?" Beau perked up, his sightless eyes searching. She climbed over the mountains of shoeboxes and knelt at his side. She pressed her hand to his cheek.

"Beau, I'm here."

"Is it true about Hunter Black?"

"We'll get him. We'll exorcise the Noirceur before it destroys him."

Beau's head tilted in the direction of the window, as though he were asking a silent question. She glanced at the glowing face of Big Ben beyond the glass. No more colored lights flashed on the horizon. The entire contingent of Royals were gathered at the base by the pyre of clocks. Prince Aleksi, Queen Violante, all of the lesser Royals were there, and all the Goblins, except for December. They were waiting for her to banish the Noirceur into the Heart of Alexandrite.

But first, she had to get past Hunter Black.

She knew he was there even before she heard him. His footsteps were heavy on the marble floors. In a roomful of shoes, only his made any sound.

"Anouk." His voice wasn't his own. Like when the Noirceur had possessed King Kaspar, it was that awful rumble. There was something familiar about the way he said her name, as though the force inside Hunter Black recognized her. The Noirceur wasn't sentient, but that didn't mean it wasn't drawn to its own kind.

The Noirceur to the Dark Thing.

Nature to nature.

Dark to dark.

Chapter 45

BEAU GRIPPED THE EDGES of the chair. His sightless eyes darted toward Hunter Black's voice. His fingers curled. He was going to do something stupid, she knew it. Something brave.

"Be the damsel in distress for once in your life," she whispered to him. "Let me save *you*."

"Cabbage, no." But without sight, he couldn't stop her, and they both knew it.

She turned to Hunter Black. She could hear Cricket and Petra fighting December on the ground floor. Beyond the windows, snow was falling. Clouds were low and dark on the horizon, as though the world itself were angry.

Smoke poured out of Hunter Black's mouth as he whispered phrases in a language even more ancient than the Selentium Vox. Before she could think, he rushed at her.

"*Sokdet!*" She threw up her hands in a sweeping gesture. The spell pulled the rug out from under him and he was flung backward, though at the last moment he torqued his body and landed in a crouch. He sprang up and threw a high kick at her ear. She dodged it and pivoted out of his range, sucking in a quick breath while she could.

Viggo, hiding behind the checkout counter, popped up long

enough to hurl a shoe at him. It bounced off the assassin's back harmlessly, but it did cause him to turn with a growl, giving Anouk a rare opening.

"*Cessa-col!*"

Her spell enchanted Hunter Black's boots and made them stick to the floor. As soon as he tried to take a step, he lost his balance and toppled over into a mountain of shoeboxes. Couture shoes tumbled all over the floor. He kicked out of his boots and stood barefoot. He came toward her with a growl but tripped on a Bergdorf heel, giving Anouk time to cast another spell.

"*Versik, versik sa . . .*"

But she cut off her own spell before speaking the final word. A bleeding spell could kill him. The same with a cutting spell, a burning spell, a transmutation spell. She didn't want to kill Hunter Black. Her mind scrolled through other options, something to merely incapacitate . . .

He took advantage of her moment of hesitation. He spun into a roundhouse turn that brought him close enough to grab her calf. She cried out and jerked back, but his grip was like a vise. He gave a sharp tug and she fell over. He dragged her closer as she screamed and clawed at the floor.

He reached for her throat with bleeding hands. From behind the cash register, Viggo threw a pair of sneakers at him, then a boot, but the shoes only bounced off his shoulders and tumbled to the floor. Anouk swallowed. What choice did she have but to use a fatal spell?

She opened her mouth . . .

Hunter Black drew back a fist and, before she could get out another whisper, slammed it into the side of Anouk's head.

She crashed backward against the floor. Pain radiated through her skull. She clutched her jaw, which felt terrifyingly loose. She coughed and tried to whisper the spell.

"Armur ver . . ."

It didn't work. She edged back, still clutching her jaw. It was broken! With the fractured bones, she couldn't speak in the right tone. For a moment, panic filled her. She'd taken a risky journey to the Cottage, she'd agreed to a dangerous marriage, she'd faced turning back into an animal, she'd faced almost certain death in the Coal Baths, she'd even sacrificed Saint, and now, with one punch, Hunter Black had taken everything from her.

He loomed over her so fast that she barely had time to think. His eyes were devastatingly blank. She knew, in that moment, there was no pleading with a force that couldn't be reasoned with. The Noirceur was going to use her friend to kill her.

She spared a last look at Beau. He was out of the chair and on all fours, trying to feel his way across the floor to help her, but Viggo crawled out from behind the counter and grabbed him, holding him back. Finally Viggo was good for something.

"Anouk!" Beau cried.

She wanted to answer. Tell him she loved him. Tell him that if life was a fairy tale, he was her heart's greatest desire. But only unintelligible words came from her broken jaw.

Just as Hunter Black raised another fist, someone else started whispering.

"Armur ver, armur ex, armur nime."

Anouk whipped her head toward the sound. Petra! The witch

raced across the marble floor with the whisper on her lips, the same spell Anouk had tried and failed to cast. With her shock of red hair and black coat simmering with live embers, she looked every bit the vicious and formidable Ash Witch. Hard to believe it was the same girl they'd found on the side of the road taking out the recycling in ripped jeans.

The sheer force of Petra's spell shoved Hunter Black backward, threw him twenty feet across the floor, and pinned him against the balcony railing. Petra held both hands out, palms directed at Hunter Black, continuing the whisper to hold him there.

"Anouk!"

Cricket was behind Petra, using ropes made of clothing to cross the detached staircase. Rennar was with her. He held a scrap of fabric that looked like December's pocket—he must have helped them break the Goblin's possession. Rennar took one look at the scene and strode to Petra's side to take over the difficult spell. As soon as he had Hunter Black trapped against the railing, Petra fell back, gasping for air.

Cricket fell to her knees by Anouk. "Are you okay?"

Anouk pushed herself up, still holding her jaw.

"December?" she choked out.

Cricket nodded. "She's okay. Rennar finished clearing Westminster and came looking for you. We got the button out of December's pocket. Lucky for us there was a time slip in the gelato department. Rennar unfroze it and we threw in the button before it could possess us. December is groggy, but she's coming back to herself. What happened to your jaw?"

Anouk gestured to Hunter Black. Rennar had him pinned against the balcony railing so hard that black tears were streaking down his cheeks.

Viggo finally let Beau go, and Beau crawled across the marble floor in the direction of their voices. Anouk clambered toward him. She grabbed hold of his shirt and pulled him into a hug. "Cabbage," he whispered. His arms were holding her as though he never wanted to let her go. "Gargoyle. Princess." His hands ran along her back and her arms, as though he were reassuring himself she was still in one piece, but when he reached for her jaw, she pulled back sharply.

His eyebrows came together. "Why aren't you saying anything?"

Cricket explained about Anouk's jaw.

"Well, tell Rennar to heal it!" Beau cried. "He's your husband—he has to be good for something!" But every ounce of Rennar's magic was aimed at keeping Hunter Black pinned to the balcony railing. When Beau heard Rennar's whispers, he cursed. "Petra. Get Petra. She can do it."

Anouk and Cricket turned toward Petra, who was slumped in the leather armchair they'd dragged down for Beau, still trying to catch her breath.

"Can you heal her?" Cricket asked.

Petra leaned forward, nodding amid heaving breaths. "Yes, if we can get more lavender ash, but at the moment we have bigger problems." She pointed to the domed window. Beyond the glass was the familiar city skyline. Anouk's head was doing strange wobbly things from pain and exhaustion, and she let out something like a delirious laugh when she realized what Petra meant.

"What is it?" Beau cried.

For a moment, none of them could bear to answer. Cricket finally said in a dark tone, "It's stopped snowing. Duke Karolinge must have given up. Or . . . he's dead."

Anouk sank back on her heels. She closed her eyes. Her heart was beating too fast, pumping blood so hard that she was afraid she might pass out. Awful images filled her head. The Duke dead on the museum roof. The mummies stirring back to life. The entire city thawing. Storms of toads. Time loops out of control. Pretties screaming.

When she opened her eyes and looked more closely out the window, she started shaking. Just like in her worst fears, the city *was* thawing. In fits and jerks, the world restarted. Tires began to spin. Cars honked endlessly. Sidewalks rumbled and split apart, and people caught in the rift plunged to their demise. Giant waves swelled up from the Thames, swallowing Pretties whole.

Anouk pressed her palm against her mouth. *"Pas possible."*

Big Ben stood tall, the clock hands still moving, the only thing that wasn't caught up in the chaos around it. The Royals and Goblins below desperately hurled spells at the encroaching time slips, but their magic only vanished into the chaos.

"The city's going to fall apart." Cricket spun away from the windows, pacing. "Space and time are literally fracturing. We'll be lucky to have five minutes left before it all ends. Anouk, you have to get down there. Prince Aleksi can heal your jaw. You have to stop the Noirceur."

Anouk felt like a kettle left too long on the stove, burning and boiling and then ruined and empty. Wincing through the pain, she muttered, "If we . . . trap the Noirceur, it'll kill . . . Hunter Black!"

"Not if he isn't possessed anymore," Viggo said quietly.

She'd almost forgotten about Viggo. During the whole fight with Hunter Black and Saint and December, he'd been a distraction at best, an encumbrance at worse, managing only to throw a few shoes as he cowered behind the cash register. But there was an odd look on his face now. His eyes shone like he was drunk, but for once he hadn't had a sip.

His eyes shifted to Hunter Black, still pinned to the railing by Prince Rennar's steady whisper. He took a few quick steps toward the balcony. No one realized what he was thinking until it was too late. He ripped the last glass button off Hunter Black's shirt. An awful hiss emerged from somewhere deep in Hunter Black's throat. Smoke poured out of his mouth. His body began to convulse. His eyes began to clear.

Viggo palmed the button. "Rennar, unfreeze another time slip!"

But Rennar was whispering with all his focus. Petra cried out, "There aren't any up here, you idiot! Only the one downstairs, and you'll never make it in time."

Viggo went pale. His hand curled around the button. Quietly, as though reciting something from a dream, he said, "Where you go, I go, my friend. But where I go, you can't follow. Not this time." In a quick movement, he swallowed it. All the smoke started pouring into him instead, into his eyes, his ears, his throat. Cricket's mouth fell open. The spell froze on Rennar's lips.

Anouk took a halting step forward. "Viggo . . . don't!"

It was too late. Hunter Black, free of the possession, blinked, dazed and disoriented. He cleared his throat. His eyes narrowed, confused. "Viggo?"

Viggo rested a hand on his shoulder. His face had gone completely white. "I'm sorry. It's horrid. But this is the only way."

Hunter Black couldn't stop Viggo in time. None of them could. A second before the possession fully consumed Viggo, when he was still himself enough to think straight, he tipped himself over the balcony railing and plunged five stories down.

Chapter 46

OTHER THAN HUNTER BLACK, Cricket was closest to the balcony. She rushed to the railing and leaned over to grab Viggo, but for once she wasn't fast enough. Her fingers closed over air.

Anouk clamped a palm over her mouth. Her other hand was still extended in warning. Her fingers started to tremble. "Viggo!" The words came out garbled through her broken jaw. She took a halting step toward the railing. Cricket spun around with a face like stone. She jumped in front of Anouk, blocking her from getting any closer.

"Don't," Cricket ordered sharply. "Don't look."

Her voice broke on the final word. For all the death that Cricket had seen, it had never been one of their own. And Viggo, the fool, was *their* fool.

Anouk's mind was hazy and muffled. "Viggo. He . . ."

Cricket clamped her arms around Anouk. Her arms were protective, but they were shaking a little too. "He saved our skin," Cricket hissed fiercely. "That's what he's done. He's saved Hunter Black and he's given us what we need to save this entire city." Cricket pulled back. Her eyes were damp but she didn't cry. She swiped a hand under her nose, then gave Anouk a sharp shove. "Go, Anouk. Time's almost up."

Anouk stumbled toward the broken staircase. Hunter Black was standing between her and the detached stairs. He looked as stunned as she felt. He, too, was staring at the balcony with wide eyes.

Rennar touched Anouk's shoulder, making her jump. "We have to go."

She stepped forward jerkily. Hunter Black didn't flinch as she passed him. She wanted to comfort him, but what could she do? What could she say?

"Hunter Black . . ." Her jaw ached with the effort to speak.

"Go."

It was a sharp bark, and he turned away before tears spilled out of his eyes. Anouk's heart ached. She couldn't seem to get her feet to move until Petra came up behind her and shepherded her toward the broken staircase. The ground began to rumble. Shoes were tumbling off displays to the ground. The chandelier overhead danced wildly. It took her a second to realize the quakes were coming from the city being ripped apart outside. If they didn't hurry, there would be no London anymore.

Wincing at the pain, she managed to order, *"Beau. Stay here."*

"I'm not going anywhere, Princess."

Anouk, Petra, Prince Rennar, and Cricket ran toward the detached stairs. With a whisper, Rennar commanded the stairs to rejoin the fifth floor, and they clambered down the newly intact staircase, flight after flight, until they reached the ground floor, with its tables bursting with flowers and chocolates. December, who'd been recovering on a bench, pushed herself to her feet, wobbling a little on her skates. Her eyes were still glassy but no longer streaked with black.

December said quietly, "I saw Viggo fall. I'll . . . I'll take care of the body. Go."

Anouk gave her a grateful nod. They ran across the marble floor and pushed through the revolving door until it spat them out in the city. Anouk stifled a moan. It was even worse than it had looked from above. The ground was slick with fallen toads, and more rained down, smacking against the pavement with sickening thuds. The time slips were moving unpredictably, catching parts of Pretties, sending a foot or an elbow or half a head into another time. Foam and vomit and blood bubbled up from the mouths of those who still had them. The rest of the Pretties screamed and ran to take cover in doorways, but as the ground shook, pieces of stone and brick broke off and hurtled down, crushing anyone below. Great fissures opened in the street, pouring out smoke that no amount of rock music would ever defeat. Any second, the city would fracture completely and be swallowed by the chaos, and then it would spread beyond London, to other cities and countries throughout the world, to realms that the Pretties didn't even know existed.

Cities falling one by one
White to Red
White to Red . . .

"Anouk! Rennar! Where the *hell* have you been?" Queen Violante's face was uncharacteristically splotched with red. "This city is barely holding itself together!"

Prince Aleksi caught sight of how Anouk was cradling her jaw and, with a few whispers, reset the bones so that she could speak.

The Royals and Goblins formed an uneven circle around the base of Big Ben, struggling to dodge falling debris and yawning cracks in the streets. Their kindred whisper was spoken as loudly as they could, but even so, it was barely audible amid the chaos. Flashes of purple and red and orange crackled within the clock pyre as they isolated and held the Noirceur. The ticking clocks began to explode, flinging out glass and metal. Rennar grabbed Anouk's hand. They clasped hands with the circle of Royals and joined the chant.

Their voices came together in a mesmerizing and strange harmony:

Omni terra das royale oscura
omni figuras das visine etan absconsia
Voc, voc eta commandet suma suspiras
Pozua ek vijik
Congred, congred,
Ut element terik.

Omni terra das royale oscura
omni figuras das visine etan absconsia
Voc, voc eta commandet suma suspiras
Des tempo de novej arca
Resid, resid,
Ut element terik.

Omni terra das royale oscura
omni figuras das visine etan absconsia
Voc, voc eta commandet suma suspiras.

The flashes of color intensified. Anouk felt the sensation of wind rushing past her face, though the air was perfectly still. The colored flashes began to draw in the remaining few wisps of smoke. It swirled into a miniature tornado of ticking clocks.

"Do you have the Heart of Alexandrite?" Prince Aleksi yelled above the roar.

Cricket took it out of her pocket. It was the size of a macaron, glittering in its heart-shaped cut, flashing purple and green and pink depending on the angle. She passed the jewel to Anouk.

"We must finish the entrapment spell!" Violante yelled. "Any moment this will all break apart. Every clock within the city is here. We've done as much as we can."

Rennar faced Anouk. "Lead us in the final verse."

The city rumbled again. The quake grew until entire buildings cracked and shattered, raining debris down into the street, and a tsunami rose up from the Thames and began hurtling toward them.

She drew in a deep breath.

A maid who had become a princess. A princess who had become a witch. A beastie who had promised the world that she was better than the dark purposes she'd been created for.

She closed her eyes.

All around her, the plagues were tearing the city apart. Trapped in their loops, Pretties howled and screeched. The air was filled with the sounds of crashing cars and tearing metal. The clocks in the pyre chimed wildly.

This was the moment.

This was why she'd gone to the Black Forest. Why she'd picked herself up after failure. Why she'd risked everything to try again and, this time, to succeed. She was the Gargoyle. Part beast and part girl, part wings and talons, part monster and part savior, and all of her destined to be a legend.

She opened her eyes and looked at Cricket, who silently nodded.

Anouk stood within the circle of Royals, clutching the jewel in both hands. She drew in a deep breath. Closed her eyes again. Stilled her mind. And whispered:

Omni terra das royale oscura
omni figuras das visine etan absconsia
Voc, voc eta commandet suma suspiras
Capik tu foris
capik tu intur.

The Royals echoed her whisper. She opened her eyes. For a second she saw the city on the brink of annihilation. A swirl of death and destruction swathed with smoke, two moons overhead flickering in and out of reality. And the tornado of clocks and smoke spinning faster and faster.

Then the storm burst apart.

Blinding lights flashed across the sky.

Anouk cried out, shading her eyes. Royals and Goblins around her did the same. The ground beneath their feet rumbled again but not like the devastating quakes from seconds before. This felt more like sliding plates straightening and realigning. When Anouk blinked at the city, it looked as though she was seeing the whole world through the glass of a kaleidoscope; fractured pieces of color and light filling the air around them like the northern lights. She felt the Heart of Alexandrite in her hands burning. The dancing lights sparked and crackled around the gem. She held it out, chanting low under her breath. Felt the energy shift from the jewel to her voice. She smelled her skin burning but she didn't dare let go. The light was so bright that she could no longer see London. Only blisteringly vivid yellows and reds and greens. She kept chanting. The light blinded her, reached into her, painted her words with wild energy that shot straight to her throat and bumped around inside her like a pinball machine all the way to her toes, her head, her fingers, until every word she spoke was a live coal too.

Almost as soon as it started, it stopped.

Anouk felt sun on her face.

Daylight poured over every inch of the city, chasing away shadows, warming the last of the frost and ice. It shone on the heads of the Royals and Goblins, who were all blinking into the sun in a daze. Buildings that had fallen were standing again. The chasms that had opened in the street were closed, and there were no slick bodies of toads smeared on the pavement. The waters of the Thames flowed as calmly as always. Pretties went about their business as though nothing had happened, though some seemed a bit puzzled to find that it was the middle of the day, as though they thought they might have had too much to drink the night before and lost track of time.

A taxi slammed on its brakes and blared its horn.

Anouk stared at it until she realized she was standing in the middle of a busy street with the world's most priceless gemstone outstretched in her hands.

Cricket held open the paper bag from the museum gift shop and cleared her throat.

"It's done?" Cricket said quietly.

Anouk gave her a long, steady look. "It's done."

Anouk dropped the Heart of Alexandrite into the bag and Cricket wrapped it up, stowed it in her pocket. "That's it, *toute le monde!*" she announced. "Time to get this sparkly thing back to its jail cell. It doesn't matter if every creature in the Haute knows that this is where we've placed the Noirceur. We'll have every trick and whisper aimed at protecting it. I wish them luck."

The taxi honked again. Anouk gave the driver what she hoped passed for a smile and, still in a daze, moved onto the sidewalk. The taxi driver yelled something out the window and sped past.

A Pretty in a suit and tie, chatting into his phone, stopped abruptly in front of the three sisters of the Crimson Court. He stopped talking. Slowly lifted his sunglasses.

"Rennar," Queen Violante said, staring in contempt at the Pretty, "they are noticing us."

Several Pretties had stopped in the street and were eyeing the crowd of finely dressed Royals and witches and Goblins, perhaps wondering if some strange and glittering new circus had come to town.

Rennar rolled his eyes and cast his hand over the surrounding area. *"Non avis nos."*

The Pretties who'd been eyeing them turned instead to fix their gazes on pigeons, and if any of them still noticed the magic handlers, they walked by with a huff as though fighting to pass a slow tour group.

Anouk turned to Big Ben. The tower stood as it always had, limestone and iron. She'd trapped the force within it but not destroyed the tower itself. The giant pyre of clocks at the base ticked away steadily. A group of Pretties dodged around a fallen grandfather clock as though — thanks to Rennar's whisper — nothing were amiss in the existence of a small mountain of tens of thousands of clocks.

"Well." Violante beat the remnants of soot from her silk gown. "I don't know about the rest of you, but I need a drink." She lifted the hem of her dress and stomped off on teetering heels (which looked suspiciously like the fireball Louboutins from Pickwick and Rue's) toward the pub on the corner.

Prince Aleksi's shadow loomed over Anouk. The handsome prince nodded solemnly at her before he and the other members of the Lunar Court followed Violante to the pub. Anouk rolled her eyes. For all their bravado, she had the feeling that they'd rarely been tested like that in all their centuries of life. Every bottle of wine would be drained tonight in the penthouse of Castle Ides, she imagined. Would they toast her? Their princess, their savior, their beastie?

Probably not.

The Goblins were dancing in the streets. London was their home city; expelled by the witches, they finally were back. December came roller-skating up to Anouk; she grabbed her arm to wheel herself to a stop. "Anouk! I'm so sorry about trying to kill you. My mistake. Come on, we're throwing a party and the whole city is our club."

Anouk steadied the wobbly Goblin. "Save me some champagne, okay? I'll join you when I can. There are a few things I have to do first."

December skated away to join a group of Goblin revelers.

Anouk turned to Pickwick and Rue's and looked up at the window, hoping to see a figure standing there, tall and handsome with a sandy mop of hair, looking down at her with eyes that could once more see.

Her smile disappeared. No one stood at the window.

"There!" Cricket pointed to the revolving door. It was turning, and in the next partition, Hunter Black appeared with Beau by his side. He was holding Beau by the upper arm, guiding him out. When Beau felt the sunlight on his face, he tilted his chin up.

Anouk ran up to them breathlessly. Beau turned at the sound of her footsteps, but his eyes didn't track her face. She threw her arms around him. "Beau. Oh, Beau. I should have known better than to trust their promises." She spun toward Rennar. "Why can't he see? His vision should have returned."

Rennar held out his hands. "The ways of magic are mysterious. We played with forces using methods we've never used before. No one knew exactly what would happen."

She scowled at him, but then Beau pulled her close. "A small price to pay," he said, "for a lifetime together in a world that's no longer broken."

She pressed her cheek against his. "We'll get your vision back. Someone will have the answer. I'll find it."

"I know you will, Princess." He pressed a kiss to her temple. "Now get me someplace where we can eat and drink and sleep and kiss. And kiss. And kiss."

She smiled and pressed her lips to his.

When she broke away, she caught sight of Hunter Black standing a few paces off, head turned so that his charcoal hair obscured his face.

"Hunter Black . . ."

He turned his head slowly, as though wounded.

Anouk rested a hand on his shoulder. "I'm so sorry, Hunter Black. He did it to save you."

He swiped at his eyes with the back of his hand. "He shouldn't have. Mada Vittora made me to be his protector, not the other way around."

"We aren't bound by anything Mada Vittora made us for. Not anymore. And neither was Viggo. Since she died, he's been free to make his own choices too. You saved his life countless times. It was his choice to save yours."

Hunter Black turned away to hide the dampness pooling in his dark eyes. Cricket uncertainly offered him an Hermès scarf she'd stolen from Pickwick and Rue's. He grumbled at the floral pattern but then took it.

The chimes of Big Ben tolled.

Anouk's heart lurched until she realized the clock was simply tolling the hour. Once more, she was taken by how normal the city was. How delightful it was just to see regular Pretties going about their regular little lives, tourists bent over guidebooks, police chasing after a stray dog, a boy and a girl walking hand in hand.

And coming down the sidewalk was Luc. He was limping slightly, a fever sheen in his eyes, straining just to walk. He should have been fully healed by now, but he looked ten times worse than he had when he'd gone to the museum to check on Duke Karolinge. When he caught sight of Anouk and saw that she was safe, his pained expression eased.

She stared at his weakened state. "Luc, you look—"

He shook his head like it didn't matter. Clammy sweat was slick on his temples. "Duke Karolinge is gone. The snow spell exhausted him. He couldn't continue. As soon as he stopped whispering, the mummies unfroze and found him on the roof before he had the strength to start casting again. It wasn't pretty."

Her stomach felt suddenly hollow. "I was afraid that was the case."

It had taken her a long time to trust a man—a Royal—whose job was to watch so many Pretty girls die. In the end, he'd finally faced his own coals.

Luc faltered. He leaned against a building, wheezing.

Anouk frowned. "Rennar, I need a favor." She eyed the bright midday sun. "I need for you to make it snow one last time."

Chapter 47

ONCE MORE, THE DAY turned dark. Prince Renar stood on Westminster Bridge, casting a whisper and circling his left hand, pulling in clouds over the London skyline. Pretties frowned up at the sky and opened their umbrellas against fresh snow. The fact that the snowstorm spanned only the length of the bridge and that the sun was still shining on both banks didn't seem to vex them.

Anouk stepped onto the bridge. "Will you join me, Luc?"

He limped onto the bridge in halting steps, one hand pressed to his heart. Snow collected on his head and shoulders.

He took her hand and asked softly, "What are you doing, Dust Bunny?"

"Saving you."

She squeezed his hand in hers. If Luc had taught her to believe in anything, it was the power of hope. But she'd also learned that wishes weren't enough. True magic didn't happen by accident. It took blood and bone and bargains with ancient creatures that looked like little boys.

An icy gust of wind blustered at her back, announcing his presence.

"Hello, lovely."

She turned toward Jak. He was perched on the bridge railing beneath a streetlamp, its lantern casting a halo over his head.

"Hello, Jak."

He grinned his sharp-toothed smile. "Have you summoned me so that I can collect my prize?"

Luc's palm was sweating, though from the poison or from nerves, Anouk wasn't sure. Rennar continued his quiet whisper behind them, left hand gesturing in an endless circle, and one by one, the other Snow Children materialized on the lampposts and railings of the bridge, their eyes hungry.

Anouk squeezed Luc's hand. He still smelled like thyme, and it took her back to Mada Vittora's townhouse attic, to the stories Luc made up for her, to games of invisible ink and secret messages. At the end of the bridge, where the snow stopped, Cricket and Petra and Beau waited. Their faces were pinched. They didn't try to interfere.

"Luc," Anouk whispered. "I can reason with Jak. I can take your place. There are ways to give up being a witch."

She expected him to argue. She was even ready for him to try to throw her over the side of the bridge to keep her from making such a deadly promise. But she didn't expect him to laugh. It came out of him in deep rolling bursts that gradually turned to coughs, and he doubled over and hacked into the snow. When he straightened, he wasn't smiling.

"Dust Bunny, I thought you'd have guessed."

Her face pulled tight. "Guessed what?"

He pressed his hand against his heart. "The poison."

She shook her head. "I drew it out of you. I saw it. It poured out of your hand, that awful black mess."

He gave her a sad smile. "It was too late, Dust Bunny. A dose had already gotten to my heart. That's why I agreed to Jak's deal, don't you understand? Either way, I'm going. I might as well go with a kiss."

Anouk blinked, trying to make sense of what she was hearing. She twisted toward Cricket, Petra, and Beau, but they were too far away to have heard Luc's words. Rennar was closer. His whisper wavered when he overheard Luc's confession, but only for a moment. His face was hard. He was used to losing those close to him.

Anouk wasn't.

Angry, she spun on Jak. "Did you know he was dying?"

He blinked lazily at her accusation. "I know a lot of things, and I knew that too."

Anouk felt tears pushing at her eyes. They'd lost Tenpenny. They'd lost Saint. They'd lost Duke Karolinge. They'd lost Viggo. Beau was without sight and they didn't know if he'd get it back. She'd traded her hand in marriage to Rennar in a deal that had pitted the Courts against one another, and they were now on the brink of a Royal war.

She couldn't lose Luc too.

She grabbed his lapels in both hands, made fists out of the fabric, and gave him a good solid shake. "Luc, you idiot."

She'd faced losing him before—where had that gotten her? Alone in Paris, unmoored, like a ship without a captain. It was true that in his absence, she'd learned to stand on her own two feet and do incredible things: ride a motorcycle, kill witches, twist time itself. But she'd never looked to Luc to do any of those things anyway. He'd been her friend. His stories had taken the place of memories she never had; if it weren't for his fairy tales, she wouldn't have known about the Pretty World, about monsters, love, and luck.

"You won't lose him."

She was so focused on Luc that she'd forgotten Jak was there. At his words, she frowned. "What do you mean?"

"A kiss from a Snow Child doesn't kill."

"What about the frozen girls in the Black Forest?" Her voice was hard. If this was another one of his tricks, she'd lost her patience for it.

Jak glanced over his shoulder at one of the other Snow Children. A girl, on her own, by the opposite lamppost. She sat on the railing, kicking her bare feet in the air, one arm wrapped around the lamppost. Her hair was the color of frost, like the others, but there was something oddly familiar in the hunched way she sat.

Anouk's eyes widened. "The girl in the woods. The frozen corpse. It's *her*."

Jak nodded. "A kiss from a Snow Child might end one life, but it starts another. There are so many realms, lovely. Did you think yours was the only one?"

It began to dawn on her that Luc must have known this. Luc was a story master, and he'd shared so many tales with her, even ones about the Snow Children, but he'd never told her the ending.

Before she could stop him, Jak clutched the lamppost, crouched on the railing, and leaned forward. Luc hesitated for a breath before leaning forward too. Their lips met as the snow fell around them. At first it was simply a kiss. Two young men on Westminster Bridge sharing a moment. But then Luc's body stiffened. It shook. Black lines threaded over his mouth and down his neck, and he started to convulse. Jak grabbed his head, not letting him pull away. He softened the kiss and, after a shiver, Luc's body relaxed. The black lines settled deeper into his skin. His face took on a sheen of ice, and when he at last pulled away from Jak, frost laced his breath.

Anouk grabbed his shirt. "Luc!"

"I'm here." His icy breath fogged in the air. His eyes were threaded through with black that bled into the whites. His eyelashes were coated in ice. His lips were tinged with blue. His scalp, where he had a shadow of hair, was like frost at dawn.

She felt a sob in her throat. "You're ice cold."

To her surprise, Luc smiled. "I feel warm." He tilted his head. "For now."

Jak jumped down from the railing, hopping over with nimble limbs. "See, lovely? Your friend is not gone. Dead, yes, but not gone. Every time it snows, you'll have him again."

She looked sadly at Luc. She couldn't help but feel that he was still lost to her. They'd never again pass secret notes to each other, never share the latest Goblin gossip over a bowl of praline cream, never sneak into the townhouse courtyard to watch the midnight roses bloom under a full moon. But the roses and the townhouse were gone anyway. There was no going back for any of them.

Luc cupped her face and pressed their foreheads together. "Anouk, don't give up hope. Do you know how stories come to be? There's magic to stories, but not the kind made with tricks and whispers. Stories begin with one person and one idea. Fairy tales don't need spells to bring them into existence; they only need a dreamer with a good tale about people who fight for what they love and a world that hinges on their actions. Dust Bunny, you don't need any more of my fairy tales, do you understand? All they ever were was words and wishes. I made them up. You're living your own story now. The story of a beastie who became a princess. A maid who saved a city. There's a place for you in this world. Find it. Write your own story. I promise you, it'll be told for ages to come by Pretties gathered around campfires, by Goblins over tea, even by Royals. You're magic, Anouk."

She thought of Cricket stealing the artifacts from Castle Ides and the British Museum, the clues that she thought led to the existence of other beasties. *Haven't you ever wondered what our place in the world is? What it could be?* Cricket had asked. They weren't maids and chauffeurs and gardeners anymore. They didn't answer to witches or Royals. The Haute ran through their veins. They were bound to it and it to them. Ages ago, Prince Rennar had created the beastie spell for a reason.

"Oh, Luc." She threw her arms around him. "I'm going to miss you."

"Whenever you need me," he said in her ear, "summon the snow and I'll be there."

She squeezed him tight. For a moment she wished time could freeze as it had for the Pretties. But every story had to end sometime. At least they had helped the Goblins retake their city. Even now, she could hear the hoots and yelps of Goblins racing through London on motorcycles and bursting into pubs, taking all the liquor, and throwing gold coins at Pretties in exchange. She'd never known what it meant to have a home that she truly called hers, but she could see what it meant for them. Goblins were the oldest of the orders, even older than the Royals, and yet for centuries they'd been treated as errand boys. That changed now. The Court of Isles, based in London, was gone. Without Prince Maxim and Lady Imogen, the city was free.

She let Luc go and nodded to Rennar. He understood her signal and let the snow whisper die on his lips. The snowfall lessened until the last flakes were nearly on the ground. Luc raised a hand. Then he, Jak, and all the rest vanished.

Anouk stared at the place where they'd been. She heard footsteps and felt Beau's presence at her side. He rested one hand on the railing, felt his way along it, and then wrapped a hand around her waist. She leaned her head against his shoulder.

"We're going to get you your sight back," she promised. "And then we're going to help Cricket find what she's looking for."

"And then what, Princess?"

"Then we're going to do whatever we want, Beau. Go to America and drive in that race you want. NASCAR. Eat shrimp and grits and deep-dish pizza and ride horses over mountains and lie out on sunny beaches. And when we're done, we're going to find our place in this world, like Luc said. We're the only ones in the Haute whom the vitae echo doesn't affect. That has to mean something. We can kill, but killing was never our primary purpose. I think we're meant to be guardians of magic, in a sense. Ensuring the balance of magic and technology. Safeguarding the rules. Making sure that no Royals or witches or anyone else treads into territory that could harm others."

"A magic army."

"Maybe more like magic police. There *are* only five of us. A bit small for an army."

She pressed her hands against the sides of his face and guided his lips to hers. Beneath their feet, the Thames gurgled. In the distance, the Eye of London spun in its Ferris-wheel circle, giving Pretty tourists a view of a city that had very nearly been annihilated—not that any of them remembered. Beau's hand traced up to her nape. She tilted her head back, letting her hair fall over her shoulders. If she had dust on her cheek, she didn't care. She kissed Beau deeper. He smelled like cologne from Pickwick and Rue's, winter frost, and magic. She smiled to herself, thinking of Jak, and almost laughed. He was right. There was nothing in the world better than a good kiss.

She pulled back and ran a playful finger down Beau's nose.

When the crash came, she heard it distantly, like something that had happened in a half-forgotten nightmare. Her head turned toward the sound instinctively, and Beau's did too, even though his eyes saw nothing. He didn't see the odd way that the Ferris wheel had stopped. He didn't see the tangle of bodies on the street next to Westminster Bridge. He didn't see the Goblin motorcycles and buses that had crashed together in a horrifying wreck.

He didn't see that standing on top of the Ferris wheel, commanding the wreck like a conductor leading an orchestra, was the man Anouk had stood with under a trellis of roses and married.

Prince Rennar.

Head of the Shadow Royals of Paris, overseer of the Haute.

She'd saved London, and now, for some reason she couldn't possibly fathom, the man she'd bound herself to was tearing it apart all over again.

Chapter 48

❧

"*RENNAR!*"

She ran across Westminster Bridge toward the London Eye Ferris wheel, the city a blur from the wind stinging her eyes. She gritted her teeth and whispered a spell to give her feet greater speed. Her heart pounded. What did Rennar think he was doing? They'd stopped the Noirceur! The battle was over! London was rightfully back in the hands of the Goblins, as they'd always planned.

I'm tired, Anouk, he had said. *For too long, power has been in the wrong hands.*

She leaped over a chain onto the pier that housed the Ferris wheel, startling the Pretties who operated the ride. They shouted at her. She cast a quick whisper that made her invisible to them.

"Rennar!" she called up. "Stop this!"

On the Thames, the Goblins had commandeered a party boat that blasted out rock music. The boat was now rocking wildly back and forth, though the rest of the river was calm. The boat suddenly tipped far too much to one side and started taking on water. The Goblins screamed. The boat continued to take on water until it rolled over and began sinking. Giant air bubbles churned as it sank. Goblins were thrown into the roiling waves.

It had happened in seconds.

Anouk froze at the edge of the pier, watching in horror. Goblins were terrible swimmers. She didn't know how to swim either, but what did that matter to a witch? She had to save them. With enough life-essence, she could drain the entire Thames. But as if sensing her line of thinking, the water began to spin like a funnel, sucking down the Goblins and the boat. She swallowed the last of her owl feathers and cast a spell to stop the water, but it was too late. Every one of the Goblins vanished beneath the surface. As fiercely as she whispered, none resurfaced.

She shook her head as though she hadn't seen right. The Goblins in the water were . . . gone. How many of them? Twenty? Thirty? How many more had died on the buses and motorcycles Rennar had made crash?

Fury stormed in her chest until she felt it was going to erupt out of her. Power ached in her hands and feet. She spun toward the stopped Ferris wheel. He'd doubtlessly try to prevent anyone from climbing it. But she'd *flown* before. She uncorked the bottle that held the rest of Saint's blood and sucked down a few hungry sips.

"Volart kael."

She felt the thrill of her feet leaving solid ground. She held on to the bars of the Ferris wheel as she rose, not exactly flying but certainly climbing with ease, rising higher and higher until the city skyline fanned out on the horizon and then she was at the very top, and she grabbed the metal rim to keep from rising higher.

She was breathing hard. This high, the wind whipped at her, blowing her hair in her face. She pushed it away, steadying herself on the precarious bars of the Ferris wheel, and faced Rennar. He turned to her with a conflicted expression. The spell to capsize the party boat was still fresh on his lips.

The world was so far below them that it made her feel dizzy, and she clutched the bar harder.

"What are you doing?" she cried.

"What we always planned to do, you and I."

She sputtered in surprise. "We agreed to turn over power to the lesser orders, not kill them! Tell me you didn't lie to me, Rennar. Tell me this isn't a trick."

Hesitation wavered in his eyes. His brows knit together. "Anouk, you knew all along what I planned. The Court of Isles is gone. The Coven of Oxford is dead. London is free for the taking. I'm the ruler of the Haute, which extends as far as the sun shines. I'm taking back what belongs to me."

She felt like she was going mad. "No. You said you were tired of ruling. You said that power had been in the wrong hands for too long. That being a Royal meant knowing when to hold on to power and when to give it up."

He took a hesitant step toward her. "I *am* tired. Tired of usurpers like the Coven of Oxford trying to take what is mine." He ran a hand over his face and then held it out pleadingly. "Whose wrong hands did you think I meant, if not theirs?"

"Yours! *You* hold too much power!"

His lips parted. He took another step forward. "Anouk. I thought you understood . . . when I said I had to make difficult decisions about whether to hold on to power or let it go, I meant that *I had to hold on*. At all costs. Power belongs to whoever takes it. That is the way of the Haute. That is the way of the Pretty World. That is the way of *everything*." He licked his dry lips, his hair whipping in the wind. "And it's yours too. You are one of us now, Anouk. Princess. We rule the Haute together. This is why I wanted you at my side, because you would temper my ambitions. Even your misunderstanding came from a good place. We'll take London together, but you can show me how to rule it fairly. Damn the terms of our marriage—you can fall in love with that chauffeur if you must, but it won't last. In the end, we'll be faithful to each other, regardless of who else ends up in our beds."

She gripped the rails of the Ferris wheel with white knuckles. Below, the Thames kept churning. She could still hear the lingering screams as the last Goblins drowned.

"This is never what I agreed to. You're robbing this city from the Goblins."

"The Goblins? They can't be trusted to feed themselves at a reasonable hour! They're barely more than children. It is our mandate to care for them. Show them what is right and wrong. We can do that together."

Bile rose in her throat. "The Goblins survived being thrown out of their city. They built a new life in Paris. They didn't have much, but what they had, they shared. So what if they make a few mistakes? What they do or don't do isn't any of our business, don't you get that? They're entitled to forge their own paths!"

There was longing in the way he looked at her. In a few steps he crossed the perilous framework of the Ferris wheel and crouched beside her. Impulsively, he touched her cheek.

His voice was a whisper. "This is why I need you. To show me the wisest course."

She jerked her head away from his hand. "You're killing Goblins who fought alongside you. You don't need me to tell you that's wrong."

"I've lived centuries, Anouk. Do you know what that feels like? Of course you don't. You've barely lived a single year."

She narrowed her eyes. "And in that year I've learned more about the world than you have." She paused. "Or maybe you knew once, but you've forgotten."

His face turned grave. The wind whipped at their hair, threatening to push them off of the Ferris wheel. "Anouk." His voice had changed. "Let's drop these games once and for all. You are alive because of a spell I wrote, but you've proven yourself to be so much more than I ever envisioned. I don't care what you started life as. I respect you all the more for how far you've come. You were never handed anything. You didn't come from royalty, and yet here you are at the top of the world with me."

He paused and then continued. "I'm no fool, like that bumbling chauffeur of yours. You think I married you because it would bring the other Royals in line? Of course not. I married you because I, too, have dreams late at night, dreams that I do not dare tell another living soul. Dreams of a girl with a broom in her hand who might one day touch me as she touches the ones she cares about, who might smile at me as she does those she loves. A girl who is capable of loving the witch who raised her, even if she was a monster. A girl whom I would fall to my knees for. Whom I would serve, as she has served others. Command me to sweep and I will sweep. Command me to cook and I will cook. How else can I tell you that I am yours, Anouk? Heart, soul, body, mind. All of it has been yours since the moment I saw you on the steps of Mada Vittora's townhouse."

Her palms were sweating. Below, the waves of the Thames rose and fell peacefully. It would be so easy to forget the boat he'd capsized. The bus he'd crashed. The innocent people he'd killed.

She closed her eyes. "It was you, wasn't it? You burned down Mada Vittora's townhouse. It wasn't an accident."

"And what if I did?" He spoke quietly.

She could imagine him standing on Rue des Amants, whispering a spark into the dry bushes in front of the house, blaming it on the Goblins and Viggo. He didn't want her to have a home unless it was with him.

There'd been a time when she'd seen a possible future with him. Beau had still been a dog, would possibly never be human again, and Rennar had been by her side, telling her everything she'd ever wanted to hear. How easy it had been to overlook his ambition.

Below, Beau was standing on the bridge, waiting for her.

She jerked her head to the side. She knew what she had to do, but it didn't make it any easier.

"Anouk." Rennar whispered into her ear. "I've done so much to bring you into my world. To give you what you deserve: luxury, power, wealth." He pulled back to meet her eyes. His were wide open, and for a second she saw the boy that he had been. "I'll do anything you ask of me."

But he wouldn't. She knew it as well as she knew her own heart. He'd twist the truth; he'd find a way to install himself back on top, as he always had.

She squeezed her eyes shut. Drew in a deep breath, let it out, and then opened her eyes and looked up at him.

"I might have loved you, Rennar," she said softly, "but you see, it's wrong, all of it."

Before he could process her words, she swallowed the last of Saint's blood. It churned in her belly with the remains of the owl feathers, spreading power through her entire body. Blood and crux. Suddenly it didn't matter that she was perched high up above the world on a wheel of matchsticks.

"I'm sorry," she blurted out.

He cocked his head, a question on his lips, but he couldn't get it out before she whispered, *"Des forma humana, fiska ek skalla animaeux."*

Chapter 49

FOR THE MIDDLE OF JANUARY, there was warmth in the air. Anouk made her way from the spinning London Eye, full of Pretties laughing in their glass orbs that crested over the city skyline, and ran her hand along the railing of Westminster Bridge. She felt herself swaying slightly—she needed to hold on to something. She'd lost a lot of blood from her fight with Saint. And performing the contra-beastie spell had taken all the remaining strength she had.

She paused to catch her breath. Below, ducks bobbed along on the Thames. The breeze was light. Any trace of clouds that had once hung in the sky was gone now, and it was blue, blue, blue overhead. She closed her eyes and felt the sun on her face.

The warmth vanished for a moment and her eyes snapped open. A shadow flew over the water. It was of a bird with wings that were compact but powerful. It glided on a gust of air, seeming to hover just above her, its shadow a perpetual twin to her own.

She took a deep breath and forced herself to keep walking.

Now, sounds of merriment came from the Ferris wheel, but just moments ago, she'd been perched high above the city, facing a prince who ruled a shadow kingdom that commanded every aspect of the known world. It was almost touching, how deep his sentiment had been. Living with a witch, she'd learned a thing or two about sincerity, and despite how little he'd told the truth in his long life, Rennar hadn't been lying when he'd said he loved her. If she'd given him her hand, they would have ruled the world together, Prince and Princess of the Haute, seated in the glittering capital of Paris.

But that was before he'd murdered every Goblin in sight. Before that, she thought his soul could have been saved. And maybe it could have been, once upon a time, when he was twenty years old, or fifty, or two hundred, when there'd still been a pure heart beating within his chest. But power corrupted so completely.

The shadow of the falcon glided above her. She hadn't expected Rennar to turn into a falcon. Was it because she'd used Saint's blood as part of the spell? Or because there was something piercing and regal about Rennar, like a bird? Or was it just a twist of fate? That was the trick about beastie spells—you never knew what you would get. One would think that a sly person would become a snake and a burly person would become a bear, but that wasn't how it worked. In the end, it was the magic that decided, and when she'd whispered the contra-beastie spell to turn him into an animal, the magic had chosen a falcon. His skin had turned in on itself until radiant gray feathers burst from the seams, and he'd doubled over and twisted entirely around and then there was simply no man anymore. His handsome clothes fell away. There were only wings and talons. At first she thought he might have become an owl. It wouldn't have been altogether surprising—they were similar in so many ways. But then she saw the sharpened beak, the piercing eyes. The falcon had let out a cry and flown high over the city.

She'd thought that might be the last she'd ever see of him, but then on the walk back to Pickwick and Rue's, the shadow had fallen over her.

She crossed Westminster Bridge and, amid the tourists snapping photos of Big Ben and Westminster Abbey, she spotted some familiar faces rushing toward her. Petra, champagne sunglasses glittering like diamonds, dressed in her fabulous black coat. Cricket guiding Beau by the elbow. And Hunter Black behind them, ever the bodyguard.

"The Goblins!" Cricket cried, her eyes filled with the horror of it.

"I know." Anouk's voice broke.

Petra searched the streets, scowling. "I knew Rennar was a monster! Where is he?"

Anouk glanced over her shoulder hesitantly. The shadow wasn't right behind her as it had been on the bridge, but when she scanned the trees, she saw the falcon perched on a branch, black eyes fixed on her.

"Let's . . . say he's on an indefinite vacation. He won't be harming Goblins or anyone else for a while."

Cricket followed her gaze to the falcon and barked a laugh. "Anouk, you didn't! You turned him into an animal! Oh, bravo."

"I had to. He was going to take London from the Goblins."

Beau made a moderately satisfied grunt.

Anouk sighed anxiously. "Yes, but now I'm afraid of what's going to happen with the Royals. The Nochte Pax is over and they're released from their bonds. Rennar was the closest thing standing between us and an all-out war."

Beau ran a hand over her shoulder. "Let them fight. Let them kill one another. We've nothing to do with their wars."

Anouk was silent. Cricket shifted uneasily at his side. Hunter Black's face was an even deeper scowl.

"What?" Beau asked. "Why is no one saying anything? *Merde.* You all want to get involved, don't you?"

"We aren't subject to the vitae echo," Anouk explained. "We can kill. We could kill entire realms if we wanted to and if we learned the right spells. We have to face the fact that there is a rift in this world. We trapped the Noirceur in a new vessel, but technology is still growing. The balance is still tipping. And as magic shrinks, the Haute will continue to fight over whatever remains. It's going to get ugly, Beau. That's where we come in. We can keep the peace. We're the only ones who can."

He let out a long breath, shaking his head like he was about to be drawn into something he knew he didn't want to get involved in.

She took his hand. "I saw strawberries in the market back there. We'll go home. I'll make a cake. Talk of war goes down better when one has pastries in one's belly."

They turned and made their way back through the winding streets toward Castle Ides. She thought of the kitchens there, the library, the enormous bedrooms and bathrooms. A princess could live a comfortable life there. A witch could study magic for centuries in that library. But the beastie in her craved only a cozy bed and a good book, Beau at her side, the smell of herbs and the scent of adventure in the air.

Cricket sighed sadly. "Luc would have turned this into a fairy tale."

"He still might," Beau said. "We just have to wait for the next snow."

Hunter Black walked ahead of them, scanning the street, always protecting his motley family, and behind them was the shadow of the falcon. Anouk had a feeling it would always be hanging just over her shoulder wherever she went.

They made their way through London, passing Pretties going about their Pretty lives, passing the occasional Goblin roaring by on a motorcycle, to Omen House. Hunter Black checked for any signs of ambush, then gave them the all-clear. Cricket rolled her eyes, telling him what a paranoid *salaud* he could be. Anouk led Beau to the door but paused before following him inside.

A strange string of words ruffled through her mind, the ones she'd whispered under her breath while trapping the Noirceur in its new vessel. Cricket seemed to notice and fell in step with Anouk.

Cricket spoke in a low voice. "You're certain that it worked? Our . . . plan?"

Anouk remembered the feeling she'd gotten when the Noirceur had been transferred out of the clocks and into the new vessel—like the world had become a giant kaleidoscope that radiated out its power in a burst of colored light.

"It worked."

"Word will spread. Everyone within the Haute will soon think that the Noirceur is trapped in the Heart of Alexandrite, barricaded within the museum. Let anyone try to steal it. Ha! I'd like to see them get past the spells I put up. Even if they did, imagine their faces when they realized the Noirceur wasn't contained in the jewel at all. Only you and I know the truth."

Anouk nodded. On the rooftop, she'd suggested a crazy plan to Cricket: In order to truly contain the Noirceur, it needed to be trapped in something that could never be stolen. Not an object. Rather, in a concept. The original Royals had been clever to trap it in *time*, but time manifested itself in too many ways. Anouk had a better idea. Trap it in *language*. She'd always been fascinated by spells, and at the Cottage she'd learned powerful words of the Selentium Vox. She realized it was possible to trap the Noirceur in specific words, nothing that might accidentally pop up in a book or conversation and once more awaken the chaos. It wasn't until Hunter Black had shared his vision with her that she'd realized what words to use. He didn't know what Queen Mid Ruath's song to the stones meant, but she did.

Baz perrik, baz mare, baz teri,
en utidrava aedenum sa nav.

Words only she knew, a song unique to her. In that way, she was the guardian of the Noirceur. And meanwhile, if everyone believed it was trapped in the Heart of Alexandrite, no one would bother to look for it elsewhere.

"Thanks for your help," Anouk said.

"That's what thieves are for."

Ahead, Beau stood in the open doorway, head turned toward her but eyes distant. "Are you two coming?"

Behind her, the falcon cawed sharply. She stared at the bird's fathomless dark eyes. He stared back.

"Yes, Beau. I'm coming."

They entered Omen House and joined the other beasties in the elevator. She was the highest-ranking Royal of all the Haute now. Kings and queens would bow at her command. The elevator dinged on the top floor, and they stepped out, leaving London behind and crossing the enchanted threshold back into the penthouse floor. *Paris.* The glittering skyline showed the Eiffel Tower and a sea of rose-colored lights. She couldn't help but feel that even though she was a princess and a witch now, they would still be bowing to a maid. But maybe being a nobody wasn't so bad. What had power ever brought anyone except ruin?

She pressed her hand against the window.

It was a beautiful city. A beautiful world. Maybe there were more beasties out there, living beyond the oversight of the Haute. Maybe they would find them. Maybe they'd figure out what path was theirs to walk. Or maybe, as Beau kept insisting, they would simply pile into the kitchen, he and Anouk and Cricket and Hunter Black, cut fat slices of strawberry cake, summon snow in the dessert pantry, and listen to Luc tell them stories about animals who turned into servants who turned into heroes who forged themselves into a family.

Acknowledgments

A special thanks to Megan Miranda for her keen insight into the heart of this story, to Ashley Lauren Rogers (the original Ash Witch!) for her wisdom, and to my marvelous beastie team: Josh and Tracey Adams, Emilia Rhodes, Tara Sonin, Tara Shanahan, Cat Onder, Veronica Wasserman, and everyone at Houghton Mifflin Harcourt. I'd also to thank the bookstores and libraries that have embraced beasties of all kinds, and to these special supporters with the hope that some magic leaps off these pages and into your lives: Nancy Lane, Corey Daniel, Corey Dingess, Liz Cozart, Christy Bass, Ben and Daisy Crosswell, Courtney Lix, Justin and Anna Laman, Janet Kim, Rebecca Weston, Shelley Waldon, Madeline Jones, Joy Neaves, Rebecca Knoche, Brian "The Man" Woodward, Cathy Goden, Sabra Stewart, Cindy Miskowiec, David and Karen Shepherd, Laurel Jernigan, and Meredith Schonfeld-Hicks.

Merci tout le monde.